NO FORTUNATE SON

Also by Brad Taylor

One Rough Man
All Necessary Force
Enemy of Mine
The Widow's Strike
The Polaris Protocol
Days of Rage

Short Works

The Callsign
Gut Instinct
Black Flag
The Dig

NO FORTUNATE SON

Brad Taylor

A Pike Logan Thriller

DUTTON
— est. 1852 —

DUTTON
— est. 1852 —

Published by the Penguin Group
Penguin Group (USA) LLC
375 Hudson Street
New York, New York 10014

USA I Canada I UK I Ireland I Australia I New Zealand I India I South Africa I China
penguin.com
A Penguin Random House Company

LIBRARY OF CONGRESS CATALOGING-IN-PUBLICATION DATA
Taylor, Brad, 1965–
No fortunate son : a Pike Logan thriller / Brad Taylor.
pages ; cm.—(A Pike Logan thriller)
ISBN 978-0-525-95399-9 (hardcover)
1. Special forces (Military science)—United States—Fiction. 2. Special operations (Military science)—
Fiction. 3. Terrorism—Prevention—Fiction. I. Title.
PS3620.A9353N6 2015
813'.6—dc23
2014036011

Printed in the United States of America
1 3 5 7 9 10 8 6 4 2

Set in Sabon Lt Std
Designed by Leonard Telesca

To my siblings:
Scott, while lying in the mud with flashlights all over,
for showing me that humans see what they want to see.
Something that served me well in some sticky situations
later in life. "You only get arrested if you're caught."

Cindy, for showing me a strength that few possess. You'll never
know how much I leaned on that during some hard times.

Becca, after an ill-advised prank, for showing me I didn't
have to be faster than the man chasing us. I only had
to be faster than you. Sorry about the beating . . .

I've helped to wind up the clock—I might as well hear it strike.

The O'Rahilly, Easter Sunday, Dublin, Ireland, 1916

DAY ONE

The Misfire

1

The woman caught Aiden's eye a second time and he realized she was stalking him. Which he found ironic, given he was in the process of hunting another, although he was fairly sure her idea of success was much different than his. Older than the average female at the bar, she projected an air of quiet desperation, with a sultry smile covering her misery like a cheap coat of paint, the pain clearly evident underneath.

Surrounded on all sides by soldiers barely over drinking age, most having recently returned from a combat deployment with the 82nd Airborne, she longed to get away from the smell of stale beer and testosterone. She was searching for someone to take her from the bravado of arms. Someone who didn't have the stench of combat surrounding his every move. A civilized man who didn't believe that training to kill was a decent way to make a living.

She could be forgiven in her assessment, as Aiden Kelleher was much older than most of the men in the bar. His haircut, clothes, and demeanor did not mark him as a soldier. At least not a US one, with Tapout T-shirts, shaved heads, and skull tattoos. If asked, he certainly considered himself no less a soldier than the rowdy men in the bar. He had taken lives in the name of a cause, and he most certainly knew that killing was a noble way to make a living.

Maybe I'll come back here later. Taste a little American sweetness.

He smiled to himself, knowing that wasn't going to happen. He'd already raised his signature simply by opening his mouth, his accent causing the bartender to comment. He might be remembered, which wasn't good, considering what he had planned.

He felt his phone vibrate and checked the number. He held the cell up in the air, letting his partner see it at a table across from the bar, then exited so he could talk in private.

"I have him in the bar, but I've raised my signature. The police will retrace his steps, and I might be mentioned."

"Can you still get him?"

"I think so, if you want to push it. I would prefer to wait."

"We don't have time. He's set to go on a military exercise tomorrow, and we only have three days. You miss him tonight, and we lose him."

"We still have the others, right?"

"Maybe. All will have the same issues as you, so we might miss more than just this one. Once they connect who we're after, they will lock them all down tight. All six will be protected. It might even take less than three days for that to happen."

"Then tonight it is."

He hung up, texting the numbers 11111 to his partner's phone, letting him know the mission was being forced, then reentered the bar, looking instinctively at the target's table. He was gone, and so was Aiden's partner. He felt his phone vibrate and read the text.

In the cigar bar. Paying his tab.

The establishment their target had chosen was called Itz Entertainment City, a large building with a multitude of different venues, including a standard sports bar with the usual chain of flat-screen televisions, a comedy club, a dance club, and a cigar bar. It was a place frequented by soldiers from the sprawling Fort Bragg in Fayetteville, North Carolina. For the most part, their target had spent his time in the sports bar, drinking sparingly and talking with friends. He'd come alone, and, given his field time tomorrow, Aiden was sure he'd leave alone.

Aiden turned to exit, staging for the follow, and bumped into the woman. He saw she was considerably more intoxicated than he'd thought before, swaying slightly and using the bar for support.

"Hey, I'd thought you'd left." She gave a crooked smile. "Did you come back looking for something?"

"I'm sorry, no. I'm actually leaving now."

Her eyes clouded in confusion, his accent struggling to find a foothold in her soaked brain. He moved past her, hearing, "Hey, are you British?"

The comment drove a needle of anger deep between his eyes, causing him to squeeze them shut harshly. He whirled around and said, "No, you stupid American cow. Irish. *Irish*."

She stumbled back at his ferocity, and he knew he'd made a mistake. Knew he'd let his hatred overcome his discipline for the mission. She would remember him for sure now. He smiled and said, "You going to be here when I get back?"

Caught off guard, the liquor clouding her judgment, she said nothing, a confused grin on her face. She hesitantly nodded. He smiled again and brushed her shoulder, saying, "See you soon."

The touch made her beam, but Aiden didn't notice. Behind her he saw his target leaving the establishment. She said something he didn't catch, and he walked to the exit, waiting a beat to let the target get some distance. He dialed his partner.

"Dermot, it's Aiden. Where are you?"

"Already in the car. I got him in sight. You're clear to leave."

Aiden speed-walked to the driver's side of their rental, sliding behind the wheel. Fiddling with a laptop, Dermot said, "Backup is on station. Waiting on the beacon to lock. What did Seamus say?"

"It's now or never. We miss him tonight, we pull out."

Dermot's computer flashed and he said, "Then let's get him tonight."

"Where's he headed?"

"That road called Skeebo or Skibo or whatever."

Aiden took a right on Legend Avenue, saying, "We keep following until he gives up for the night. Same plan. We take him at the apartment."

They traveled through the heart of Fayetteville, passing malls and hotels, until eventually they were on a road called Morganton, the target seven cars up in the right-hand turn lane.

Aiden said, "Is that Reilly Road?"

"Yes." Dermot's teeth flashed in the dark. "Good omen."

"He's headed home. Get the backup ready."

Dermot began dialing as the light turned green. Aiden crowded the car in front of him, pushing to get into the turn lane. Unconcerned before about maintaining a close distance to the target—in fact preferring to let the beacon do the work—he now needed to be in a position to assault. He heard one horn blare, saw the light go yellow, and blasted through the turn, now two cars back.

Aiden saw a sign for Stewarts Creek Condominiums and felt the excitement of the hunt rise. He said, "Get ready. Get backup ready. Remember, no shooting. No harm."

The target's turn signal began to blink, and Aiden's mind flashed to Belfast and the hunting of men. He felt his lip curl involuntarily, his hands crimping the steering wheel in an effort to release the adrenaline. He had to consciously remind himself that there would be no killing here. A death would be *worse* than counterproductive.

The target pulled into the entrance for the complex and Aiden goosed the pedal to catch up. His headlights splashed the back window, and he saw the brake lights too late. He skidded forward, punching the bumper hard enough to slam Dermot against the dash.

The world stopped for a moment, the only sound the ticking of the engine under the crumpled hood. This was not what Aiden had intended at all.

Dermot said, "Abort."

Aiden saw the door open in front of him and said, "Call the backup. We take him here. Right now, before someone else shows up."

"He's completely alert. What if he comes out shooting?"

"God damn it, all he knows is he was hit from behind. Why would he come out shooting?"

"Because this is America. Everyone has a gun."

Aiden snorted and said, "Bullshit. That's Hollywood." He opened the door and swung out, seeing his target in the glare of a streetlight, standing next to the car with his hands on his hips. He said, "Hey, sorry. My fault."

He took two steps forward, not realizing his mistake. While Aiden was correct in his assessment of the average American civilian, it fell woefully short for his given target. He knew Staff Sergeant Bryan Cransfield had recently returned from Afghanistan but did not realize that the man's hard-fought sense of survival had not yet returned to civilization. This soldier was still living in a world where green-on-blue attacks dominated his psyche. Where he'd seen a friend killed by the very men he was training. And unlike the majority of America, Sergeant Cransfield now traveled armed.

He'd survived a year in Afghanistan, but the experience had killed him without him even knowing. Had he been less aware, less attuned to potential threats, he would have lived to see the sunrise. He would have only been captured. But he couldn't be faulted for that. He couldn't know that the car behind him wasn't armed. Or about the car in front that was.

Sergeant Cransfield said, "Why are you following me?"

Aiden saw the blunt glare of a semiautomatic pistol. He shot his arms in the air, shouting, "Hey, no, wait!"

The soldier raised the weapon and said again, "Why are you fucking following me? I saw you in the bar. What do you want?"

Aiden saw a flurry of movement behind the soldier and knew it was too late. He shouted, "No! Don't!" but the rounds cracked anyway, the backup team removing the threat. Sergeant Cransfield was struck in the shoulder and collapsed into the car. From the seat he ripped off three rounds. Aiden heard the bullets puncture his windshield and dove to the ground. He crawled backward and heard two more sharp cracks, then his name called.

He stood up and ran, reaching the target car and the backup team. Staff Sergeant Cransfield was lying across the seat, eyes open and skull split from the kill shot. Aiden slammed the backup against the doorframe, shouting, "What the fuck are you doing?"

The man bucked forward, shoving Aiden hard enough to cause him to stumble. "He was going to kill you, you fucking tool!"

Aiden leaned back and rubbed his face, thinking. He said, "Shit. Get your team and leg it out of here. Drive his vehicle deep into the woods. We'll deal with this later."

Without another word, Aiden ran back to his car and slid behind the wheel. He said, "That Muppet Smythe killed the target."

He got no reply. He turned to the right and saw a single hole settled just below Dermot's right eye.

"Jesus Christ."

He put the car in gear and backed out, assessing the disaster. Not only had they failed to take their target alive, but they'd lost a man in the process. He hoped the other five targets went better than this.

He turned onto Morganton, running through his mind how he was going to deal with Dermot, cataloging his network of American contacts to make the corpse disappear. It wasn't until he reached Skibo that he realized the target's body would be found, causing a police investigation.

Which meant the killing wasn't done. He turned onto Skibo heading back to the sports bar, and the woman who knew his accent.

DAY TWO

The Prize

2

The car windows began to steam, Kylie feeling the man's hands fumbling inexpertly at her bra, half of her brain begging him to figure it out while the other half focused on his belt. She felt the strap on her back release and had a split second of regret, wondering if she should stop the train of hormones raging in the cloistered confines. Get back to just talking, like she'd promised herself would happen.

She thought of what her Scottish roommate had told her just before she'd left, after she'd emphatically stated yet again that she wasn't seeing anyone. An impish grin on her face, the roommate had said, "I know what you Americans call this. When I did my student exchange to Virginia, it was all about 'what happens on an exchange stays on the exchange.'"

And now she was in the backseat of a car, not with a British aristocrat, but an American soldier. Someone she'd been trying hard not to like, but had been failing. Her mother would lose her mind if she knew she was seeing someone in the military, which is why she'd been so secretive—even in a foreign country.

But maybe that was part of the attraction.

He parted her shirt and leaned forward, using his mouth, causing an involuntary gasp. She forgot about his belt and arched her back, wrapping her hands in his hair with her eyes closed.

She heard metal hammer the window behind her and felt an explosion of glass rain down. Her date jerked upright, shouting something unintelligible, and then it was a tangle of confusion, men all over her, dragging her out of the car.

She heard, "What the fuck is this? He was supposed to be alone."

Irish.

Her date began to fight like a wild thing until he was cuffed in the head with the barrel of a pistol. He shouted and rolled onto the ground, holding his skull. He was hoisted to his knees and shown the gun.

He said, "What do you want? Money? The car? Take it."

The man jammed the barrel into his mouth, the tear on his scalp from the earlier blow leaking blood down his cheek. The man twisted the barrel until the front sight grated against the teeth, saying, "Shut. Up."

The one holding her said, "What do we do now? Kill her?"

She tried to cover her naked breasts, and the man jerked her arms to the rear, saying, "Don't move."

The first man removed the pistol from her date's mouth and walked to her, a slow, measured pace.

Her date said, "Don't fucking touch her. I mean it."

The man smiled and cupped her breast, bouncing it slightly. She felt the tears form and began to tremble. She heard him say, "Why? Is she special?"

Her date remained silent, and the man laughed. He said, "Sterilize the area and leave the Morocco receipt. Don't make it obvious. Make them find it."

The man holding her said, "And the girl?"

"Pack her up. We can't have a body found around here."

Which was a mistake. Had he left her broken corpse on the deserted English road, he might have lived to see another birthday. Unlike her date, she had no value to be traded, no pedigree that could leverage powerful political forces, but she was special to some.

Very special.

I stomped inside, freezing from the run and grouchy that Jennifer had forced me to do it. I hated cold weather, and for some reason Charleston had turned into the arctic the last two winters. As far as I was concerned, jogging in anything below fifty degrees was flat-out stupid and exactly why treadmills were invented, but Jennifer hated running in place. Even when the temperature was close to freezing.

Global warming my ass.

Last night, she'd asked if I wanted to run the Ravenel Bridge, and after secretly checking the weather, I'd said yes. Of course, that damn prediction had been wrong. When I'd stepped out onto our balcony this morning, I'd immediately tried to change her mind. She'd shamed me, and we'd taken off, running up East Bay toward the bridge spanning the Cooper River, the cold making me more pissed off the farther I went. We'd crossed and headed back, the steep uphill climb whipped by a bone-chilling wind coming from the lack of protection and the height. I'd stepped it out at that point, leaving her behind, my pace fueled by my aggravation and absolute desire to get out of the cold.

I kicked the door closed, knowing Jennifer wasn't far behind me and that she'd be peeved about me deserting her. I was pretty sure she could have hung with me, but it would have been hard. And she had no time for mental games anyway.

I moved into the kitchen of our little apartment, the top floor of an antique row house just off East Bay. It was old and sometimes cranky about things like hot water, but the kitchen had been renovated and the location was perfect. All in all, one of the reasons I loved the Holy City.

I put on a pot of coffee and began making Jennifer's favorite healthy goop of berries, granola, and Greek yogurt, moving into the required apology mode. Our cat came out from underneath the table and hissed at me. I was thinking about kicking the shit out of him when the door opened. Jennifer saw me glaring down and said, "Don't you dare!"

Caught in the act, I just stuttered, trying to pretend I had been contemplating something else besides squashing the beast's skeevy head.

Saying he was "our" cat was giving a little too much credit. Jennifer had rescued him from a garbage can outside of our place, and he showed her every bit of love in his vicious little soul in return. He hated me, and believe me, the feeling was mutual.

He was a skinny calico with a potbelly and bald patches from some unknown disease. I couldn't count the number of times he'd jumped on me when I was sound asleep, tearing his claws into my back.

He twitched his tail in disdain and trotted over to her, rubbing up against her legs and purring. She picked him up with one arm, cooing in a faux baby voice directed at me. "Was Pike mean to my little Knuckles? Hmmm?" The cat looked at me, and I swear he was smiling.

One day, you little shit.

The only good thing about him was his name. Jennifer had decided to anoint him with the callsign of my best friend as a little punishment. Knuckles had given her the callsign Koko on a mission—as in the talking gorilla—and it was something she despised but couldn't shake. Everyone on our team perpetuated the name no matter what she did. Calling the rat with claws "Knuckles" was her version of payback, although it fell a little short because the satanic beast treated his human namesake just like he treated Jennifer. Apparently, I was the only one worthy of his ire.

Jennifer dropped him to the floor, and he sauntered away, now supreme in his kingdom with the queen preventing any harm. She looked at me, and I prepared to start my defense, but I saw no anger. Before I could begin my groveling she held up a letter in her hand.

"We got something from Blaisdell Consulting."

Which was really odd. All the transactions for our company ran through Blaisdell for pay purposes—an umbrella cover company for the counterterrorist unit that employed us—but electronic transmissions were the order of the day. Snail mail was some old-school stuff we didn't do.

She said, "Well, you want to open it, or you want me to?"

Feeling a little flow of adrenaline, I sat down, saying, "Go ahead. Must be pretty important." Which meant it must be a mission outside the usual scope. Something even crazier than what we habitually did. A little high adventure that had the potential to be a lot of fun.

She slit it open, and I saw her eyes scrunch up. She looked at me in confusion. I said, "Well? Where do they need the expert services of Grolier Recovery? Bali? Phuket?"

She said, "We've been fired."

3

Since I'd been expecting to hear about a mission-impossible tasking, the words made no sense. I stood up so fast the chair I was in fell over.

She said, "It's a letter saying they no longer need our services."

I took it and saw professional letterhead, wondering what intelligence egghead had created it. I read *Dear sir, While we hold your services in the utmost regard, we won't be requiring your assistance in the foreseeable future. . . .*

The rest was a bunch of legalese BS about settling accounts and turning in any outstanding equipment. It was signed *Kurt Hale, President.*

What the hell?

Jennifer said, "They can't *fire* us. We aren't even in the government."

I said nothing, only staring at the official piece of paper that would destroy my life. I knew I'd gone a little overboard on our last mission, but it had turned out pretty damn good. In fact, better than good. If I hadn't gone off the reservation, tens of thousands of people would have died. Knuckles had warned me of the repercussions, but I never thought it would come to pass. I mean, surely results mattered. *Didn't they?*

She said, "Pike?"

Brought out of my reverie, I said, "I don't know, but Knuckles will."

I knew he was in North Carolina running our unit's Assessment and Selection, so he would be away from the flagpole and able to talk. Although it sort of pissed me off that he hadn't called to warn me in the first place. He was still on active duty and tied into the goings-on of the unit we called the Taskforce.

An unorthodox command so far off the books it didn't even have an official name, it routinely flouted the law to protect civilian lives—and did so successfully. There were many, many souls walking the streets unwitting of how close they had come to seeing the afterlife. Firing me for exceeding the limits of operational risk was like handing out speeding tickets at Daytona. At least that was my opinion.

I pulled up Knuckles on speed dial and it connected on the third ring. "Hey, Pike, what's up?"

"You got a minute?"

"Yeah, just finished the final. Candidate is a bolo. He's headed back to the hole. I think he'll jack it in shortly." Meaning someone had just failed to solve the problem and was being transported back to the "resistance training laboratory" for more interrogation. Knuckles thought the candidate would quit instead of starting over.

I said, "Call me back secure."

He did so, saying, "What's so top secret? You and Koko on the rocks?"

"What's going on with Colonel Hale?"

"Huh? He's got some shit sandwich on his plate. How'd you hear about it?"

That meant nothing. Kurt Hale *always* had a shit sandwich on his plate.

"Tell me you didn't know."

"Pike, I have no idea what you're talking about."

"I got a letter saying Grolier Recovery Services has been fired."

I heard nothing for a moment, then, "You're kidding me. They pulled the trigger?"

"You knew?"

He heard the anger coming through and said, "No, no. I told you what was happening after that last mission. The Oversight Council was skittish at how you'd gone on the warpath. They were kicking around letting you go. You're the one who said Kurt vouched for you. You knew more than *me* six months ago. Last I heard, you were on probation."

The Oversight Council was our approval authority. Since we were outside the traditional military or intelligence architecture, we had our own unique command structure. Composed of about a dozen men in the upper echelons of the government, including the president, it dictated Taskforce actions. I'd ignored their orders on our last mission, and now I was apparently paying the price—even though the refusal had ended up preventing a weapon of mass destruction from slaughtering thousands.

"How did you not know this was coming?"

"Pike, I've been out here for a month, working eighteen-hour days. I don't track what the brass is thinking. If I had known it was coming, I would have called."

I said nothing, the ramifications settling in my stomach like spoiled milk. He had been kept in the dark, which meant the letter was real. They'd known he'd fight it, and so they'd just cut him out. Something that was very easy to do in our cellular, top secret world. The letter wasn't a sick joke, and I was losing the reason I existed. The thing that made me whole.

He said, "You still there?"

"Yeah. . . . Knuckles, what the hell am I going to do?"

Knuckles heard the pain in my voice and understood why. He lived for the missions the same way I did. I'd been his team leader when I was on active duty, and he'd helped pull me through a traumatic event after I'd left. He'd been the first to sign on as our notional "employee" for the experiment of a civilian company of Operators working inside the Taskforce. The first to embrace Jennifer—a female—as an operational member when everyone else in our testosterone-driven organization wanted to give her the boot without even seeing if she was capable. And the first to ask me to kill the men who'd murdered his teammate on our last mission. The actions that had gotten me fired.

He said, "Pike, I won't let them erase the database. I'll keep the documents, leases, contracts, and all that other stuff."

Meaning, I could be fired on paper, but the enormous cover architecture we'd painstakingly built with Grolier Recovery Services would remain on a shelf, ready to be dusted off. If those linkages were deleted, we'd be done forever. He was telling me what I needed to hear: The

Oversight Council could say what it wanted, but the men who mattered most understood and would protect me.

It meant a lot, but in the end, I wasn't sure he had the power. The commander would dictate that.

I said, "I'm calling Kurt. See what's up."

Colonel Kurt Hale and I had been through more than one scrape together, and—if he weren't the commander—I would consider him a friend. Hell, he *was* a friend. But he also had to make judgments in the best interest of the Taskforce—not for any single Operator—and if the Oversight Council had spoken, there was nothing he could do.

Knuckles said, "Don't call him today. Let it sit. He's way too busy right now, and you won't get a chance to make your case."

"Why? What's going on? Why's this shit sandwich any worse than our usual stew?"

"I don't know. I've seen some reports, but I'm not sure what it is beyond the fact that everyone inside the Beltway is starting to spin out of control."

"A threat? Something against the homeland?"

"No, nothing like that. Apparently, somebody's kid or nephew got killed. A military guy that was related to someone on the House Armed Services Committee. Then somebody else's kid came up missing."

"Afghanistan?"

"I don't know. Yeah, I guess . . . the reports don't say. I'm just reading between the lines."

"Why would that have any Taskforce fingerprints? The Armed Services Committee's not even read onto the program."

"He's not, but the vice president is. The kid that's missing is his son."

DAY THREE

The Rollup

4

Navy Lieutenant Kaelyn Clute saw a white Toyota four-door sedan enter the parking lot, causing her to lean forward. The glare broke off the windshield and she saw it wasn't her brother. She sat back, disgusted. She'd been told to wait outside the main exchange on Kadena Air Base and he'd be by to get her at noon. He'd said he was driving a white Toyota, which would have been fine except it seemed *everyone* here on Okinawa drove bland white Toyotas.

Just like a jarhead.

Captain McKinley Clute was her twin brother, and together they came from a long line of distinguished naval aviators. Their grandfather had retired as a four-star admiral, pioneering fleet aviation in the modern era. Their father had decided on a different path, retiring as a captain and going into politics, first as a representative, then as a senator, and was now the chair of the Senate Select Committee on Intelligence.

There had been no question where the Clute twins would end up.

Unfortunately, through a quirk of heredity passed down from their mother, McKinley was genetically red-green color-blind. It wasn't that he couldn't see colors, just that he sometimes mixed those two specifically. They didn't find out until he was tested in high school, and just like that, his dreams of being the next *Top Gun* Maverick went up in smoke. He'd done the next best thing, joining the Marine Corps. Currently a captain in the military police, he'd been stationed at the provost marshal's office on Camp Foster, Okinawa, for the last two years.

Kaelyn had continued in the family tradition and was one of the few females flying the F/A-18F Super Hornet. Assigned to VFA-103, she had been detailed for mission planning and review of OPLAN 5027—the order of battle for the Korean Peninsula. A mundane tasking, it meant she'd spend her days validating such things as targets, refueling responsibilities, logistics trails, and a smorgasbord of other requirements that needed to be planned in advance if they had any hope of winning a fight with North Korea. She wasn't looking forward to working with her joint partners in the Air Force and Army, but there was one bright spot: The meetings were all taking place on Kadena Air Base, just a stone's throw from Camp Foster.

She hadn't seen McKinley for eight months and had wrangled a way to fly in a day early to make that happen. Now if he'd only show up.

She saw another ubiquitous white four-door sedan enter the parking lot and recognized the shock of red hair even with most of it shorn off. An involuntary smile broke out.

McKinley pulled to the curb and leapt out, holding his arms wide, and she jumped off the bench, saying, "Mack!"

She ran into his embrace, ignoring the stares from the people coming and going. She said, "What took so long? Today's the only day I have."

He made an excuse, then got back behind the wheel saying, "The wait will be worth it. I've got a treat for you."

As he drove out of the parking lot she said, "What's that?"

"A place called Kajinho, which apparently means 'Pizza in the Sky.' "

"Pizza? You're shitting me. Why can't we go to a local place? Something Okinawan."

"I see the Navy has done wonders for your vocabulary. Don't worry. It *is* local, and you'll get to see more of the island getting there than eating around here. It's about an hour and a half north, on the tip of the island, and it has the best views around. I'll play tour guide."

He turned onto National Route 58 and they began the tour, Mack pointing out landmarks as they passed. The Army post Torii Station, the Marine Corps' Camp Hansen, Shinto shrines, Okinawan tombs, and anything else he could find, all the while talking like an expert. In between they caught up and compared notes on their two military careers.

About ninety minutes later they were off of 58, winding through the mountainous jungle. Eventually, the road was only a car and a half wide, the switchbacks coming every five hundred feet, concrete tombs peeking out from the tangled jungle growth on the hills.

Kaeyln said, "You sure you know where you're going?"

"Yeah. It's right up here another hundred meters."

They broke through to the top and she saw what looked like an old Okinawan house, with a view 360 degrees around. Her brother had been right; it was gorgeous.

They ordered their pizza and struck up a conversation with a couple of foreign backpackers new to the island. On their way to Australia, they had only a day to spend but had still managed to find the little slice of heaven at the top of Okinawa. They asked for further things to explore and McKinley was more than willing to play tour guide. While paying the bill, he agreed to lead them to the Okinawa Aquarium just fifteen minutes away.

They never made it.

Captain McKinley Clute's car wasn't found for two days, lodged in a ditch on a winding dirt road. The Okinawan police and Camp Butler Provost Marshal questioned everyone in the surrounding area but came up with nothing. The Clute twins had disappeared without a trace. The only lead was a couple of Irishmen who had been seen talking to them at a pizza joint a mile away.

All attempts to locate them for questioning failed.

Governor Rachel Deleon speed-walked to her car to get out of the crisp winter air. The driver, a sergeant in the Texas Department of Public Safety, opened her door. She said, "Bill, take the long way in. I'm expecting a call."

He said, "Yes, ma'am," and closed the door.

As the governor of Texas, she had a mansion within spitting distance of the capitol, but instead of a convenience, the closeness made her feel as if the job never left. In reality, it didn't leave no matter where she went, but she preferred her house on West Lake.

As the most powerful person in one of the largest states, she had defied the odds to achieve the position. Right off the bat, she was a female fighting in a man's world. To make matters worse, she wasn't classically beautiful. In fact, she was downright homely, something that every campaign manager she'd ever known said made her dead on arrival. She had fought a vicious campaign on the usual issues separating the parties and would have lost handily, but she had a couple of assets that nobody else in the running could tear down.

For one, she was Hispanic in heritage, which in Texas could do quite a bit to counterbalance her less than telegenic appearance. But it wasn't enough. She needed the dyed-in-the-wool conservative vote from the people who were scared of that very heritage. People who might believe she had an agenda related to the immigrants swimming across the Rio Grande, which is where her husband came in.

A fifth-generation Texan, he was also a lieutenant colonel in the Texas Army National Guard. A veteran of both Afghanistan and Iraq. Never mind that his military specialty was public affairs, and that he'd not once heard a shot fired in anger. Not once left the perimeter of Balad and Bagram Air Bases. The fact that his job was no more dangerous than a publicist at a corporation was irrelevant. He was a war hero. A veteran. And that title had proved decisive.

Currently, he was on temporary duty with the Texas Adjutant General at NATO Headquarters in Brussels, helping craft some deployment schedule or other thing. He'd promised to call at lunch, and given the seven-hour time difference, that meant she could take it on her way to work.

They turned onto Guadalupe Street, the dome of the capitol coming into view, and she began to wonder if she was going to miss the call. Paralleling the University of Texas, she started to tell her driver to turn onto MLK Boulevard and circle the school when her phone rang.

She said, "Finally! I thought I was going to miss you. Headed into work?"

"Yeah. Unfortunately, the general bumped up a meeting, so I've only got a second. How's life in the music capital?"

"Still ticking. Usual fights. That asshole Reese is talking about investigating our stock purchase into Dell again. Nothing I can't handle."

She heard him say, "What the hell," then, "Hang on, honey, there's some sort of accident. These cops are death on cells while driving."

The phone went silent, then she heard her husband's voice as if spoken from a distance. The other party was muffled and inaudible.

—"Officer, you speak English?"

—"Huh. Sorry about that. No insult intended. I never expected to hear that accent. Can I get through here?"

Her husband's voice grew strident, the cell signal strong enough for Rachel to sense the fear.

—"Hey, what the hell are you doing? Don't . . . no, wait!"

She heard him scream and she began shouting into the phone, causing her driver to whip his head toward the backseat.

Her husband didn't respond. The only sound coming over the line was a car door slamming.

Airman First Class Curtis Oglethorpe bounced his beat-up jeep down the road, pushing it faster than was safe. Well, safe for the jeep, that is. As for Curtis, he needed to get off the lonely highway leading from Soto Cano Air Base to Tegucigalpa, the nearest city to his miserable station.

An air traffic controller for Joint Task Force–Bravo, he'd paid his roommate to take his shift, which wasn't exactly kosher as far as the chain of command went. But then again, Curtis never found the rules worth following. Far from it, he was what was known in military parlance as a shitbag. The guy who could always be depended on to disappear whenever extra duty came around. Which gave his father no small amount of fits.

The son of the current secretary of defense, Curtis had been given everything—the proverbial silver spoon jammed up his ass from birth—and had done everything in his power to reject it. Not out of any pride in making his way on his own, but simply out of laziness. When he'd failed out of Dartmouth—a school that had been no mean feat to get him into in the first place—his father had had enough. He'd told Curtis in no uncertain terms he was joining the military or getting cut off.

Being a little bit of a coward at heart, Curtis had agreed, searching out the least "military" occupational specialty he could find, eventually settling for air traffic controller in the Air Force. The recruiter had told him it was all gravy, with nothing but stateside assignments and nine-to-five work, then he'd been shipped off to JTF–Bravo in the stinking jungles of Honduras, controlling flights targeted against the drug trade, along with a multitude of other taskings.

Not his idea of the cush life promised by the recruiter.

The work was grinding, and the base grew tiresome within a month. He'd spent every waking moment he could haunting the bars in Tegucigalpa, searching for some companionship. In that, he'd failed, with the women seeming to smell the broken promises in his DNA. He'd started hunting Honduran women in Internet chat rooms and had found one who had taken a liking to him. So much so she'd agreed to meet him in Tegucigalpa at a place called the Bull Bar. The catch was he had to come tonight. Which meant he had to get out of his shift. Which also meant he had to get off the two-lane highway that led to the city.

JTF–Bravo was a small place, and if he passed anyone coming back from Tegucigalpa, they'd recognize his jeep. Then realize he was supposed to be on duty right now. And that wouldn't be a good thing.

The old jeep groaned down the road, the suspension complaining at every pothole, the rusted holes in the body whistling with the wind. Curtis fought the vehicle, straining to keep the four wheels on the rutted blacktop at a speed that caused the jeep to become nearly unstable. He began to pass houses, then side streets, then entered the city itself, breathing a sigh of relief.

He wound through the small town to his rendezvous at the Bull Bar, the fear of getting caught now replaced with the hormones of getting laid. He parked out front and took a quick look in the mirror, smoothing back his longer-than-regulation hair, then sauntered inside.

It was fairly early, the sun still in the sky, and the bar looked old and worn without the cloak of darkness. But Curtis cared little about ambiance. His head on a swivel, he looked from the bar to the tables, finally settling his eyes on the mechanical bull in the corner. He saw nothing but a couple of males at the bar sipping whiskey out of highball glasses.

He approached and took a seat on a stool, seeing the men were inebriated. He turned back to the door, and one leaned over to him, saying, "Where you from, bud?"

He heard the accent but couldn't place it. He said, "America. You?"

"America! Land of the free! Home of the brave! We just came from there. We're from Dublin, on the great Emerald Isle."

"Emerald Isle?"

"Ireland, friend, Ireland. The land of the leprechauns. Let me buy you a drink."

Curtis took another glance around the bar, still not seeing what he wanted. He said, "Sure. Whatever you're having."

"Irish whiskey. What else? Although the bog down here isn't exactly pedigreed."

The bartender poured and his new friend picked it up, turning a complete circle to hand it to him, staggering as he did so. Curtis took a sip and nodded. "Good stuff."

The Irishman clinked his glass and said, "Who are you here to meet?"

"Supposed to hook up with a girl here."

"A horny little lass? Some hot Honduran gee?" He gave a drunken wink, and Curtis took another sip, wondering how he was going to break contact from the sots when his date showed up.

Curtis said, "Well, I just met her online . . ." He stopped, unable to continue his train of thought, his head beginning to swim. *What the hell? I only had two sips.*

He focused on the Irishman and saw double, the room starting to swim. The Irishman said, "What's the girl's name? Is it Esmeralda?"

His head was spinning, and he was fighting the bar stool as if he was riding the mechanical bull in the corner. The only thing that penetrated was the name.

Woozily, he said, "You know her?"

"Yes. I do." The Irishman smiled, not looking nearly as drunk as he had a moment ago. "Sorry, bud. She's not coming."

Curtis started to slide off the stool and felt someone grab both of his arms. Then he felt nothing.

DAY FOUR

The Panic

5

Colonel Kurt Hale could barely make out the words through the sobbing in the phone, the hitches of his sister's voice making her incoherent.

"Kathy, calm down. Take a deep breath. I can't understand what you're saying."

He heard sniffling and looked at his watch. *Running out of time.*

"Kathy, listen, I have a meeting I have to be at in thirty minutes and it's all the way across town. I'll give you a call back when I'm done."

The hitches stopped and he felt the heat through the phone. "Meeting? I'm talking about your *niece*. She could be lying in a ditch or dead. Jesus Christ, she loves you better than her own father, and you're not even giving her the time of day."

"Okay, okay, calm down. What's he doing about it? Did you call him?"

He knew the answer before she even spoke. Kathy's ex-husband, a Wall Street bond trader, was a philandering, narcissistic jerk. Kurt had always wanted to punch the smirk off his face, but it had taken Kathy five years to figure out his true stripes. Kathy now used him only to provide for her daughter, like paying for Kylie's student exchange to England.

"That asshole just offered money. He can't do anything anyway."

"Kathy, neither can I."

"Bullshit! You work for the CIA or something. You can find her. You're the only person I know. Nobody else cares. Maybe you don't either."

He rolled his eyes up in frustration. He loved his sister dearly, but her views on how the world worked were distinctly different from his. She was a pacifist, to the point that it had taken seven long years before she'd even speak to him again after he'd joined the Army. When he started working in classified assignments, she naturally defaulted to thinking he was some Black Ops assassin and—even when he told her he was in a Special Forces unit—she believed it to be the CIA. She believed *everything* was the CIA. For twenty years he'd listened to her conspiracy theories, and, ironically, if he told her what he was doing now, all her fears would be realized.

He deflected the line of discussion, saying, "Kathy, look, it's only been twenty-four hours. There's probably a simple explanation. Maybe she's just out partying. Shit, she's grown up now. A college kid. You remember what that was like."

"Kurt, that line of BS would work when we were her age, but not now. She's got a cell phone, Instagram, Skype, Twitter, Facebook, Snapchat, and Lord knows how many other means of communication. All of them have been stagnant. Her cell phone goes straight to voice mail, and she's not posted a thing when she usually does that four or five times a day."

Which were the first words his sister had said that made Kurt pause. The first clear signal that this wasn't a college drunken blackout.

Kathy spoke again, the rage gone, replaced by fear. "Kurt, I don't know anyone else to call. She's not important enough for anyone to care. She's just another lost American. And she's in trouble. I know it as a mother. You've got to help me. I have no one else."

He said nothing for a moment, then: "Okay, Kathy. Send me an email with all of her information. Don't forget all that social media stuff. Let me get this meeting over with and I'll see what I can do."

Driving across the Key Bridge, George Wolffe finally broke the silence. "Hey, you going to let me in on what's going through that head? You thinking about those missing soldiers, or are you finally accepting what happened to Pike? Still time to change your mind on this brief."

Interrupted from his trance, Kurt faked a grin and said, "No, nothing like that. Just some personal stuff."

"Personal? Last I saw you had no life outside of this organization. You seeing someone? After my forty-two attempts at a setup? Marge is going to be pissed."

This time Kurt grinned for real. Wolffe was the deputy commander of the Taskforce—Kurt Hale's number two. Like Kurt, he'd basically torpedoed his career to create and help command Project Prometheus, the thrill of the mission much more attractive than the potential future rank. Unlike Kurt, he had a family to come home to, complete with a wife who took pity on the vaunted Taskforce Commander, trying to set him up with every middle-aged divorcée she could find.

Kurt said, "It's not like that. It's some trouble with my sister. Nothing like the trouble Pike is in."

George continued in silence for a moment, weaving through the downtown DC traffic, then said, "You know, falling on your sword is so 1990s. The nobility of sticking to your convictions doesn't fly anymore."

Kurt said, "Tough shit. It flies in our organization. It's what makes our organization what it is."

"Kurt, I get the military code, but you don't know this place like I do. That code is fine on the battlefield, when bullets are flying. This battlefield is all about *what have you done for me lately*."

Unlike Kurt—who'd grown up in special-mission units in the Department of Defense—George was CIA. As such, he had lived through quite a few purges and witch hunts, all looking to hang good men for a petty political edge.

George turned from the wheel and caught Kurt's eye. "This isn't going anywhere. All you'll do is cause a lack of trust in your judgment. You defend Pike and they're going to think you agree with what he did. Agree that ignoring their orders is okay. Which will cause them to question you on everything you bring forward. Think about that."

Kurt reflected a moment, then said, "Trust is the cornerstone of our organization. Faith is how we operate. Faith that the Operator will do the right thing. Pike was the man on the ground. We were a thousand miles away. He ignored Oversight Council orders and made a call. It ended up being correct. He saved tens of thousands of lives at great risk to himself. I will not destroy him because a bunch of political animals now find it expedient."

"Kurt, he went on the warpath over Decoy's death. He *lucked* into the thread of the WMD by hunting the Russians. He wanted to kill those men, and he did. You have to see that. He cannot be controlled. Even you couldn't control him."

"He didn't luck into shit."

"What's that mean?"

Kurt looked at his trusted friend and said what he thought would never be uttered. "I let him off the chain."

"What? Are you saying you gave him permission?"

Kurt sagged in the seat and said, "No. Not in so many words. But I knew what he would do, and I didn't stop him. He would have listened to me. I let him go. Hell, I gave him assets to do so."

"Jesus. Kurt, you can't say that. That is *not* a defense. That will *destroy* the Taskforce."

Kurt smiled. "Calm down. I never thought I'd say those words out loud, and I'm certainly not going to tell the Council. I'm not even sure Pike realizes how I felt. Look, the Oversight Council is a necessary thing to keep us in check, but he's what's right in our organization. And I'll defend what's right."

6

They rolled into the security checkpoint for the West Wing of the White House, the granite monolith of the Old Executive Office Building off to the left. Alexander Palmer, the president's national security advisor—one of about a dozen read onto the Taskforce—had been promising for years to get the Oversight Council a permanent home, but so far the Council members still trekked inside the same building like a multitude of other government employees. It made Kurt skittish, because sooner or later someone was going to ask what the hell the top secret meetings were about. All it would take was one NSC staffer to speculate, and *The Washington Post* would go into a frenzy.

Trudging up the stairs, Kurt began to rehearse what he was going to say. George had said Kurt was naïve to the ways inside the Beltway, but that wasn't the case. He understood completely what he was facing, including who was an ally and who was an enemy. He needed to massage both.

They reached the conference room and Kurt saw no Secret Service. Which meant no President Warren, the biggest gun who could help. George stopped, his hand on the door. "Last chance. I have that offer to open a yogurt shop. You want in?"

Kurt grimaced and said, "Sharks aren't out yet. Let me chum the waters before I give you an answer."

George swung the door open, and Kurt saw bedlam.

Everyone in the room was waving their arms or talking over one another. Usually, the Council was sitting still when he entered, like Supreme Court justices about to hear an argument before them. Hand-picked by the president of the United States, they were all members of the executive branch or private citizens. By design, none were in the legislative branch, in order to allow a calm, unbiased analysis of the potential fallout of Taskforce actions, free from competing political pressures. And usually they *were* calm, but what Kurt saw looked like a couple of cliques at a junior high yelling at each other.

He moved to the podium unnoticed, laying his computer on the desk next to it. He plugged it into the Proxima projector and looked for Alexander Palmer, the man who chaired the meetings in the absence of the president. He saw a heated argument between Mark Oglethorpe, the secretary of defense, and Kerry Bostwick, the director of the CIA, but no Palmer.

The conference room door opened and Palmer entered, followed by another man, a youngish-looking bureaucrat who appeared as scared as a rabbit cornered by a pack of wolves. The man moved to the front of the room, unplugged Kurt's laptop, and plugged in his own. Palmer walked to Kurt.

"Hey, plans have changed. We aren't going to hear about Pike's status today. He's inactive indefinitely."

"What's going on?"

"You heard about the missing military folks, right? This NSC staffer has the latest information."

"How is that Taskforce business? Who gives a shit? I'm not going to let Pike rot because of some political crap."

Palmer scowled at Kurt's nonchalant attitude and said, "*Everyone* gives a shit. Pike's done for now. Take a seat."

Surprised at the ferocity of the reproach, Kurt nodded and joined George at the back of the room. The staffer turned on the projector and the room became silent. He waited a bit until the bulb settled and the computer had a signal, then cleared his throat, studiously avoiding the secretary of defense's eyes. Palmer said, "Get it going. Give them the damage."

The man cleared his throat again and said, "Gentlemen, it appears that our initial fears have been realized. This is not a coincidence or a random act. An organization has targeted military relatives of key members of the United States government. Currently, we know this."

He clicked a slide, and Kurt grew cold at the two headings.

KIA:
- Staff Sergeant Bryan Cransfield, Fort Bragg, North Carolina, nephew of Representative Duncan Cransfield, ranking member of the House Armed Services Committee

MIA:
- Lieutenant Colonel Travis Deleon, Brussels, Belgium, husband of Rachel Deleon, Governor of Texas
- Captain McKinley Clute and Lieutenant Kaelyn Clute, Okinawa, Japan, son and daughter of Easton Beau Clute, Chair of the Senate Select Committee on Intelligence
- Airman First Class Curtis Oglethorpe, Soto Cano Air Base, Honduras, son of Mark Oglethorpe, Secretary of Defense

Next to each bullet was a picture of the missing person. Kurt saw the last name and picture, a smiling man in Air Force camouflage, and understood why the SECDEF had been so agitated when he'd entered. He caught George's eye but said nothing.

Jonathan Billings, the secretary of state, said, "So the vice president's son is okay? That was bad intelligence?"

Palmer said, "Unfortunately, no. That information is close-hold, so much so that nothing is being put on hard copy or electrons. Nick was an analyst at the NATO Intelligence Fusion Centre at RAF Molesworth, England." He paused for a moment, going eye to eye with the men in the room, then said, "He's missing as well, and if that leaks, I swear I'm going to cut someone's nuts off."

The D/CIA brushed aside the threat and said, "The NIFC? What did he do there?" He pronounced it *Nif-See*.

Billings said, "What's the NIFC?"

"It's the intelligence hub for NATO. They're responsible for all operational targeting, both possible and actual."

Palmer said, "He's an Air Force weatherman. He provided predictive analysis for operations."

"Shit. So he was read onto ongoing and planned missions?"

"Yes. I guess."

"Well then, his being the vice president's son may not be the worst of this. He's like the guy in the mail room who knows everything going on in the corporation. He's potentially got information in his head that could damage current operations worldwide, from Afghanistan to the Ukraine." He leaned back into his chair and said, "What's in that man's head may be more important than who his father is."

7

A low murmur went through the room, then grew into a buzz. The young staffer remained silent. Alexander Palmer said, "Quiet. Let him continue. Give them what we think."

The bureaucrat clicked a slide and Kurt read:

We value the sanctity of human life above all else, but the fact remains that if a person takes up arms against our nation, he becomes a threat to our way of life and will be dealt with, whether he's a United States citizen or not. Rest assured, though, every operation is thoroughly reviewed and every person targeted is given the same due diligence whether he's a foreign national or an American.

Beneath that quote was another.

I beg to differ. Not every life is the same. You kill people all over the world without any thought to the collateral damage. Farmers in Yemen, civilians in Pakistan, goat herders in Somalia, it's all the same to you. What would it take to alter your behavior? Whose life is more valuable than the ones you target? It's an interesting question, isn't it? Perhaps we will see.

The staffer said, "Eight months ago the administration hosted a virtual town hall on the website Reddit. The last question asked dealt with our armed UAV program. The top quote is from the administration, given eight months ago. The bottom rejoinder appeared yesterday."

The D/CIA said, "So you think this is connected?"

Palmer said, "We're assuming so, and before you ask, the NSA is doing everything it can to identify the location of the message. They've come up with nothing. Or more precisely, with about a hundred different possibilities. The sender covered his tracks well."

"So, given the topic of the Reddit thread, we're assuming an Islamic group?"

"Yes, for now."

The D/CIA leaned back and said, "I don't see it. This scope is too big. Too much ground to cover. Too much overt work that had to be done. There's no Islamic group out there with the capability to conduct synchronized operations that span the globe. For one, they stick out too much. How are a bunch of Arabs going to do operational work on Okinawa? They would have been compromised. For another, they're too fractured, especially with all of the internal fighting going on. We would have heard something."

The SECDEF spoke up. "Well, there are two facts right now: One, they're missing. Two, we *didn't* hear anything. So what are we doing?"

His statement was calm and measured. Considering what was at stake for him personally, Kurt was impressed with the control.

"We've locked down anyone remotely believed to be a target, including redeploying two from the war zone in Afghanistan."

Oglethorpe's control fractured a smidgen. "Well, that's great proactive work, but I meant, what the hell are we doing about the ones missing?"

Understanding the pressure, Palmer let the jibe go. "The president has made this priority number one for every single federal agency that might be of use. And that includes the Taskforce."

Kurt popped his head up at the comment. Palmer saw the movement and said, "What?"

"Sir, that's not what we do. We're not a law enforcement investigative organization and we aren't focused on hostage rescue. Our operations take months—sometimes years. This is going to be time sensitive, and forcing the issue will get us compromised. I understand the wish to do something, but you're trying to use a flat-head screwdriver on a Phillips screw. It may do more harm than good."

Palmer tapped his chin, then said, "What is your primary mission?"

"Counterterrorism. Preemptive activities against designated substate groups with an end state of preventing harm to the homeland through long-term analysis and disruption."

"Don't give me that official doctrinal crap. You know what I mean. What do you *do*?"

Kurt pursed his lips, seeing where his question was leading. "Manhunting."

"Exactly."

"Sir, you know we're tracking two separate threats coming out of Syria." Kurt looked at the SECDEF. "I understand completely the feelings here, but if I divert to this mission, it may mean we lose the thread. It may mean we miss the ability to stop an attack. We're putting five people's lives ahead of possibly many, many more."

Palmer rubbed his eyes, saying nothing. The SECDEF said, "Don't make a decision about the Taskforce because of me. I'm recusing myself from the vote on this."

Palmer said, "There is no voting this time around. This briefing is for information only. The Taskforce is going to dedicate all assets to recovering the five hostages. That's from the president of the United States. Anyone has an issue with it, take it up with him."

Kurt heard the words and felt a little disquieted by them. He believed President Warren to be a good and trusted man, but in one fell swoop he had just castrated the very council that was designed to keep the Taskforce in check. Designed for oversight, as the name implied.

Palmer focused directly on Kurt. "You'll brief just like any other operation, letting the Oversight Council know what's going on and gaining concurrence for operational activity, but you're doing the mission."

Kurt nodded, and after a little more discussion about the absence of any leads, the meeting broke up, the various members returning to their day jobs. Kurt held his tongue until he and George were back in the car and outside the gate. With the White House in the rearview mirror, he said, "What the hell just happened?"

George said, "I'd say the president is a little fired up about assholes taking our people."

"Yeah, I get that, but we're proving the terrorist on Reddit to be right. We just put five lives ahead of everything else. Shit, they fired Pike for ignoring the Council, and now the president is ignoring the Council. It's not good."

"You've got his ear. You can talk to him."

"No. Not yet. I'm not the neophyte you think I am in this world. He sent Palmer on purpose. He didn't want to see me."

George looked at him and smiled. "Very good, meat-eater. Perhaps there's hope for you yet."

Kurt felt his phone vibrate with a text. *Call me. Please.*

It was from Kathy, and his niece popped back in his mind, causing his stomach to sour. On the drive over he'd toyed with the idea of diverting Taskforce assets or maybe even a couple of Operators to England to see what they could find, but that was out of the question now.

George said, "Too bad we don't have Pike in the lineup for this. He's got a habit of stumbling into the heart of every bad thing."

Kurt heard the words and dialed the phone.

"Who're you calling?"

"Pike. I need someone to stumble onto some bad things."

8

Kylie Hale felt shame wash through her as her bladder released, leaking through her jeans and staining the concrete floor. She tried to prevent it, but she had been tied up for so long, and she was afraid to shout out. Afraid of drawing attention to herself. She could see nothing in the darkness and probably couldn't even if there was light because of the cloth bag on her head. She began to weep, small hitches that she willed herself to contain. She failed. Lost in the fear of what had occurred, wondering where her date had been taken, she lay and shook, the urine dribbling on the floor.

Twenty-four hours ago she'd been worried about college finals. Now she feared for her very life. She could barely comprehend the turnabout. On the dirt road the men had flex-tied and hooded both of them, showing little compassion before shoving them both in the trunk of a car. They'd been told not to say a word, then tapped in the head with the barrel of a pistol to seal the threat. Driven for roughly an hour, they'd stopped, and she'd spent the night in the trunk, the claustrophobic hood preventing her from seeing anything. When the engine had fired up hours later, it had snapped her eyes open, the panic returning. She heard a multitude of other engines, then felt the vehicle drive up a ramp. She heard a bellowing foghorn and knew they were on a boat. Which meant they'd left England.

Eventually, they'd begun moving again, the engine lulling her and the exhaustion taking over. By the time they'd stopped again, she'd lost track of how long they'd been driving. She'd been ripped out of the trunk, hearing her date shouting behind her. She was thrown into a dank basement smelling of loam and mold, the cold seeping through her clothes. For the longest time, she'd lain completely still, afraid to move. She remembered what the men had said when they'd originally captured her and knew she was in serious jeopardy. The only thing unknown was the time.

She rolled over onto her back, worming her way out of the urine puddle. She sagged into a ball and began weeping again, then heard a shuffle in the darkness. She froze, the sound shooting fear through her body. A groan, then scraping. She remained mute. She heard a whisper.

"Kylie? Kylie, are you in here?"

It took a moment for the words to penetrate, then the relief flowed through her. "Yes. Yes, I'm here. Are you hurt?"

"Only my pride. I'm okay."

Before she'd been crammed in the trunk, she'd heard him fighting, and heard the punishment delivered. She was fairly sure he was downplaying how hard they'd treated him.

She said, "What do they want? Why did they take us?"

"It's me. I won't let them hurt you. I promise."

"You? Why? What did you do?"

"Nothing. But it's me."

She heard a squeak, and then footfalls on wooden steps, each one ratcheting up her anxiety. They reached the concrete and stopped next to her. She strained her eyes through the bag, seeing a dim shadow.

"You pissed on my floor? Jesus, Mother Mary, and Joseph."

The Irish accent was pronounced, so much so she had trouble following it. She was jerked upright into a sitting position, causing her to tremble. She felt hands on her skull and she began to scuttle backward. The voice said, "Calm down. I'm removing your hood."

It slid off her head and she saw two men, one over her and one over her date, both with rough clothes. The man above her was tall and thin, with an ascetic, hatchet face, the veins on his neck standing out like a marble sculpture. Behind his left ear was a tattoo of a harp. The man over her date was younger, with a thick beard, like a lumberjack.

The man with the tattoo squatted down to her level. "Why would you piss on my floor?"

The view of him was disconcerting. Scary. "I . . . I didn't want to."

He studied her. He said, "You may call me Seamus. I am a soldier and work with a soldier's creed. I do not kill civilians if I can prevent it, but you've presented me with a problem."

Her date said, "Leave her alone. You have me. That's enough."

Seamus stood up and walked to him. He removed the hood and said, "Nicholas Hannister. Yes, we do have you, and unlike the lady, you are not a civilian. And don't think your name will protect you."

Nick said, "Look, everyone will know soon enough that you have me. Letting her go won't matter. You can take her back where you found us and just let her walk away."

"No, everyone will *not* know. The last thing the United States wants is this to become a circus in the press. And there will be enormous pressure from your government to find you. I cannot risk that your floozie has some clue in her head."

The back-and-forth between them confused Kylie, making her wonder who Nick really was. She knew his last name as Seacrest, not Hannister, and he hadn't told her anything to indicate his family was rich or well connected. If that were the case, why was he enlisted in the US Air Force?

Seamus walked back to Kylie and said, "What is your name? I know his, but not yours."

"Kylie. Kylie Hale."

"Well, Kylie, do you have any reason I should keep you alive? Are you valuable to anyone?"

She began to weep, saying nothing, the tears running down her face.

His eyes stayed on her for a beat, then he stood and nodded at the bearded man. He came over and untied her feet, then raised her up. Nick started thrashing, getting nowhere with his feet tied at the ankles and his hands behind his back.

He shouted, "Don't do it! Leave her alone. I'm warning you. Don't."

Seamus slammed a boot into his stomach and said, "Shut the fuck up. If you'd told someone you were going out with her, we would have waited. Blame yourself."

Kylie was halfway up the stairs, her legs barely moving, the bearded man dragging her steadily upward. Seamus turned to go and Nick shouted, "She's my fiancée! She flew in to surprise me. I didn't know she was coming. Don't kill her because of that."

Seamus turned back. "Your fiancée?"

He nodded furiously. "Yes. My mother and father love her like me. Even more than me. She was staying with them last week and set up this surprise."

"Then why were you fucking her in the backseat of a car?"

Nick paused, then said, "Girls aren't allowed in the barracks."

"You never heard of a hotel?"

"Look, I don't know. We were just . . . overcome, I guess."

Seamus shouted up the stairs. "Hold it."

Kylie sagged to a step, still weeping. Seamus marched up to her, cupped her chin, and raised her head. "Is this true?"

Lost in her own despair, Kylie hadn't heard the conversation. She said nothing, almost catatonic. He squeezed her chin and repeated, "Is it true?"

"What? Is what true?"

"Are you his fiancée?"

She looked down the stairs and saw Nick staring at her intently. He faintly nodded his head. She hesitatingly said, "Yes."

Her mind struggled to keep up. To comprehend what Nick was doing. She saw Seamus considering her answer and prayed he didn't ask any questions about Nick's family. Nick had been extremely evasive whenever anything like that came up. Even secretive. She'd never pressed.

He leaned back and said, "We researched Nicholas for over six months, and you never surfaced. Why is that?"

From the floor, Nick said, "The Secret Service insisted we keep it quiet. She can't be officially protected, and they saw her as a potential leverage point."

Kylie thought, *Secret Service?*

Seamus smiled. "Well, they were right." He nodded at the man holding her. "Take her back. We'll see how the honorable Phillip Hannister deals with two missing he holds dear."

As the man jerked her back down the stairs, the name swam around her head, seeking purchase. He kicked the back of her knee and forced her to the ground, flex-tying her feet again. As the darkness descended from the hood, her memory clicked, and she knew why they wanted Nick.

Phillip Hannister, the vice president of the United States.

DAY FIVE

The Hunt

9

Going through the metal detectors of the Smithsonian Air and Space Museum, I was a little disappointed in Kurt's choice of meeting location. I always preferred hitting up a small pub—of which there were plenty in DC—but for some reason, Kurt had decided that the McDonald's attached to the museum was the way to go. Considering it was ten in the morning, I guessed that was okay.

On the civilian side, Kurt was ostensibly the president of Blaisdell Consulting. On the military side he was a PowerPoint Ranger staff officer working at the Special Operations Division of the Joint Staff in the Pentagon. The multiple personalities would have given me schizophrenia. For security reasons, because of the myriad different cutouts and cover companies tangentially associated with the front known as Blaisdell Consulting, Jennifer and I never went to the physical building next to Arlington Cemetery in Clarendon. Any time we needed a face-to-face with our command, we did it off-site. And this situation was definitely one for a face-to-face, especially given the strange instructions Kurt had relayed on the phone call yesterday.

Based on Knuckles's recommendation, I'd patiently let the letter sit on my desk for the better part of two long days. Well, *patiently* was a polite way of putting it. I'd paced around and read it so many times that Jennifer had asked if I'd worn out the words. I'd finally figured that a day and a half was long enough and picked up the phone to call Kurt. Jennifer had stopped me, saying I'd promised her to let it sit for two full days. I'd started to argue, then my cell had rung. Strangely enough, it was Kurt.

Stranger still, he didn't want to talk on the phone. He'd told me to pack clothes for a week and to fly to DC. To which I'd responded, "Is the Taskforce going to reimburse me for the airfare? If not, you can fly your ass down here."

He'd said, "I'll pay you back. Both you and Jennifer."

Not *the Taskforce will pay you back* or *Blaisdell Consulting will reimburse you*, but *I'll pay you back*. And he wanted Jennifer to come as well, with enough clothes for a week. Strange indeed.

We wound our way through the displays, moving around the simulated moon landing outside of the interior entrance to the food court. Through the glass I saw Kurt in the corner, sipping a cup of coffee. Dressed like a businessman, he glanced my way and nodded. Jennifer broke to the counter to get her own cup and I went straight to him. He stood up and shook my hand, saying, "I know you have questions. Let me talk first."

I nodded and sat down. He said, "Did you get a hotel?"

"Yeah. Just dropped our luggage off. Embassy Suites in Old Town."

"Good. Well, first things first: It's true Grolier Recovery Services has been 'laid off.' I'm working to rectify that, but my briefing to the Council on your behalf was preempted by other things."

"What does that mean?"

"I'll get to that in a minute. For you, the primary problem is that prick Billings. He's steadily grown convinced that you are a threat, and Brazil was the last straw. As secretary of state he convinced enough Council members to vote you out."

"Brazil? I stopped a nuclear weapon!"

"I know, I know. But you also went on the warpath, eliminating Russian members of the FSB. When we originally sent you to Bulgaria, Billings was the dissenting vote. When you ignored the Council's orders, he went into 'I told you so' mode."

"They attacked *us*, sir. They killed Turbo, Radcliffe, and Decoy. Came damn close to killing Jennifer and me. And it was the Israelis who did most of the killing."

He held up his hands, "Pike, you don't have to convince me. I have no problem with what you did. Well, except when you basically told me to fuck off."

I felt my face grow red in embarrassment. He was right about that.

He said, "Look, I've ordered the Taskforce to keep all linkages. We aren't shredding the cover mechanisms and you'll be kept on Blaisdell Consulting's books like everyone else. But I'm going to need some time before I can get in front of the Council again."

"Why? Knuckles said something about a soldier dying and that the VP's son was missing. Is that what's got the Beltway's panties in a knot?"

And he told me about the whole hostage mess, which was pretty damaging. I could see why everyone was spinning out of control. If we didn't find them, the administration would be held hostage by both the press *and* the terrorists. Everything that occurred would be under the prism of the captured Americans, with half saying any military action the United States executed was unjustified and conducted solely to prove we don't listen to terrorists, and the other half saying we were cowering down and *not* doing military action because of the terrorist demands. It wouldn't matter what crisis we were dealing with—the hostages would taint our response.

He then topped off the debacle with a nice little cherry that the VP's son was apparently an analyst with potentially catastrophic intelligence in his little weenie head.

"Who do they think it is?"

"The consensus is an Islamic group, but I tend to agree with the D/CIA. It's much too complex for them. I guess we'll know soon enough, because we've been given the mission to find out."

"The Taskforce? How the hell are they going to do that? It's not like they can liaison with a foreign police force as an official US government entity. Whose bright idea was that?"

"The president's. The entire Taskforce is now dedicated to this. I've got teams headed to Okinawa, Brussels, and Honduras. Knuckles is going to England."

The conversation was starting to confuse me. Why tell me what the teams were doing when I had no need to know?

Jennifer sat down, sliding over a cup of coffee. Kurt said, "Good to see you, Koko."

She took his hand, smiled, and said, "Good to see you as well, but please don't call me Koko unless I'm on a radio."

Kurt looked at me and I said, "Yeah, she's not into the whole callsign thing. Aggravates her. Anyway, are you telling me that you want Jennifer and me to help with this mission? Even after letting us go from the Taskforce?"

"No. Unfortunately, I'm not. Remember my niece? Kylie?"

"Well, yeah, of course, what about her?"

When I was still in the Army, on active duty, Kylie had been a fixture at any unit function. The truth was we all took a liking to her to the point where she became sort of a unit mascot. She was always hanging around at our get-togethers, grabbing us beers and wanting to hear stories from the teammates. My wife actually took her under her wing for a little bit, letting her babysit our daughter and taking her out for "girl talk" occasionally. But that had been years ago. When I had a wife and daughter.

"She's on a student exchange from the University of Virginia to Cambridge University in England. My sister called right when this other crap was brewing. Kylie hasn't called home, and I'm worried about her."

Kurt was a permanent bachelor, but he treated Kylie like a daughter, much to her mother's regret. In turn, Kylie adored him as if he were her real father. Like the father she'd never had. When Kurt's sister had divorced, Kylie had taken her mother's maiden name, and I was fairly sure it was because of Kurt and not her mother.

The mother, on the other hand, was a piece of work. Kurt seemed to tolerate her, but she was a peacenik with her head in the dirt. Always going on and on about how evil the CIA was and how the United States used the military to ensure the flow of oil or whatever else was current at the time. If she'd called Kurt for help, she was desperate.

Still not understanding the significance, I said, "Worried how? She's a college kid. They do that shit all the time. What do you mean?"

"Not like this. She's been gone for forty-eight hours, Pike. Just gone. She's dropped off the face of the earth, and I think she's in real trouble."

The fear on his face was a little bit of a punch, reminding me of my own daughter. Reminding me of what I'd lost. He saw my face and immediately knew the wound he was cutting open. Jennifer saw it too. She clasped my hand and they both closed in, leaning forward as if they were now discussing a terminal disease with a patient, which aggravated me. I could take the pain. I'd been through it already.

I said, "What do you want me to do? Why'd you tell me about the missing men? The Taskforce mission?"

"No reason, except we bought a new Rock Star bird. A Gulfstream 650. It has longer range, faster flight, and more storage than the G-Four you blew up. Knuckles is taking it to England on its maiden voyage. I want you to go with him."

The Rock Star bird was a nickname we had for a Taskforce Gulfstream IV that was specially modified to infiltrate Taskforce equipment into a country. It was outfitted with everything from suppressed weapons to technical surveillance kit, all hidden in special compartments in the walls of the aircraft to defeat host nation immigration procedures. I'd used it on the last mission to detonate a nuclear bomb over the ocean—which hadn't gone over too well, considering its cost.

He continued, "I want you to find my niece. Make sure she's okay. I'll pay for your flight up here today and pay for your per diem in country. Just tell me she's okay."

I saw the pain on his face and felt my own memories start to bubble. The loss. And the chance to prevent another one.

I said, "As a Taskforce member, doing secret shit?"

"No. As a friend of the family. Knuckles will be doing the secret stuff under a cellular telephone contract. You land and walk away. I've already talked to Knuckles, which is why I'm sending him to England. He can keep a secret. You can't mention that I allowed you to use Taskforce assets. You get there, you can talk to anyone you want. Give them my number, my sister's number, whatever. The only thing you'll be doing with Knuckles is flying over with him."

I was running the implications through my head, and he misinterpreted it as hesitation or aggravation at having to hide what I was doing. He said, "Pike, I'm sorry about the Oversight Council. I didn't want that to happen, and you're getting a raw deal, but I need you on this. I need you to do what you do best. Find her for me. Please. As a friend."

Jennifer said, "Kurt, of course we'll go."

He leaned back and exhaled.

I said, "Sir, there was never a question about that. And don't worry about the pay."

He said, "I'm really scared. I'm afraid of what you'll find."

I grinned. "Focus on the circus going on back here. Kylie's probably teaching the limeys to play beer pong. It'll be a walk in the park."

"And if she's not?"

Jennifer said, "She is. Don't think that way."

Kurt kept his eyes on me, an unspoken question on his face, the pain just behind the eyes. He and I knew of a different world that could have touched Kylie. A place of evil that rarely knocked on the door of the average civilian. A place that was causing him nightmares. A place that had found me already. And he knew it.

I said, "Jennifer's right. Don't worry about it. I'll go get her. I understand no backup. No official help. Doesn't matter. If she's in real trouble, they made a mistake in the target. Whoever took her will wish they'd taken the VP's son instead."

He squeezed my arm, glancing at Jennifer. "Pike, I know I have no right to ask you, but I don't want just questions answered like the police have already given. I don't want to hear 'no clues.' I cannot live with 'we've done all we can.'"

He looked out the window and said, "She's in a world of shit. I can feel it, and I can't do anything about it with the crap going on around here. I can't leave." He returned to me, I swear with a touch of shame. "Will you do what's necessary? Can you? After what happened with the Council? I need to know."

I understood what he was asking, and I was a little surprised that he thought he had to. I knew he'd given me permission to go after the Russians, even if it wasn't articulated, but this was on a whole different level. This wasn't about national security. This was personal. Which in my internal code was much, much higher.

I locked eyes with him, feeling my daughter. Feeling a chance at redemption. I gave him the answer he wanted. "I'll get her back. Trust me, there is no measure of the pain I will inflict to do so."

10

Kylie waited for thirty minutes before speaking. When she was sure none of the kidnappers were still in the basement, she blew air, getting a gap in the hood, and said, "Nick? You still here?"

She heard nothing. She said again, a little louder, "Nick?"

She heard a shuffle, then, "Yeah, I'm here. Sorry. My head's a little woozy. I think I have a concussion. I keep going in and out."

The words scared her. He was her only anchor.

"Nick . . . I don't know what to do. They're going to come back, and they're going to find out the truth. I don't know what to say."

She heard a scuffling, then his voice much closer. "Kylie, they won't. Just pretend like I said. The Secret Service prevented you from getting too involved. You don't know how anything works, because you were kept away. I'm sorry I ever did this to you. I've never gotten involved with anyone for this very reason. I just . . . just couldn't help myself with you. I'm sorry."

She heard the words and felt a warmth, despite the circumstances. "I appreciate what you did. You didn't have to."

She heard nothing for a moment, then, "No. I did. And not because I feel responsible. Strange to have it come out here, I suppose, but I'd have liked to have a few more dates with you."

She smiled in her hood, the conversation taking her away from the situation. "Maybe we could do that. Why are you going by the name of Seacrest?"

"It's my mother's maiden name. Secret Service thought it would help protect me. Guess that was a crock of shit."

They sat in silence for a moment, then he said, "You know, I *do* blame you. Who else in this whole damn country drinks rum and Coke? Nobody. That's what caught me. My favorite drink."

She turned her head in the hood, focusing on his voice, wanting the connection. The only thing she had. "I got that from a friend of my uncle. That's all he drinks."

Then she remembered who the friend was. "Hey, my uncle is a pretty important guy. And his friend is a holy terror. When I come up missing, they'll start to hunt for me."

Nick chuckled and said, "Kylie, I'm the vice president's son. You can't get any more important."

"No, you don't understand. My uncle is in the military. He does something all classified. He isn't important in a political way. He's . . . he's . . . just . . . I don't know what he is. But he's someone these guys don't want to meet."

She heard the condescension in his voice. "Well, maybe he'll do something. Can't hurt."

Kylie focused on the face of her uncle, drawing strength from it, knowing what he would do. She reached her hand to her neck and rubbed a gold pendant on a simple chain. Shaped in a circle, it looked like a thick golden washer. Stenciled around the rim was a Bible verse. Romans 3:8. It was a gift from her uncle, and just having it made her feel secure, as if he were watching over her right this minute.

She remembered his friend she'd met at picnics and unit parties, full of volcanic heat and restrained violence. Remembering how she'd been scared by him and drawn to him at the same time. Unlike the men a floor above, he was a predator. And he would come. She was sure of it. She lay down, feeling the first sense of calm since the ordeal had started.

More to herself than Nick, she touched the pendant and said, "He'll come. And these fuckers are going to pay."

She heard the door open above, and her nascent confidence wilted like a flower in the desert. She heard footsteps, but not of someone walking clean. They were dragging a body down.

She perked her head up, straining to see anything through the hood. She heard something large slap the concrete, then a wail. "I work for NATO! I don't know anything about Ireland. I haven't done anything."

She heard something like a sack of dirt being kicked, then coughing.

"Shut the fuck up. I'm sick of your whining. Keep it up, and you'll be the first we kill."

The steps retreated, and they were in silence again. Eventually, Nick brought up the courage to break it. "Hello? Who was just brought down?"

She heard nothing. Nick tried again. "Hello?"

A voice tentatively said, "Who are you?"

"Nicholas Seacrest. American. You?"

"Travis Deleon. American as well."

Nick said, "Who are you related to?"

"What's that mean?"

"Why did they take you? Who do you know?"

Kylie heard nothing for a moment, then, "I don't know anyone. Why would you ask that?"

He thinks we're trying to trick him.

She said, "Travis, I'm Kylie and we're just trying to figure out why we've been taken."

"Kylie who?"

"Kylie Hale. I'm sitting here with a hood on my head as well."

He didn't respond. She heard scraping and worming, then heard Nick say, "You're in ACUs. You're Army."

"How would you know that? If you're hooded?"

"I just got my hood off. Listen, I'm an Air Force weatherman stationed at RAF Molesworth in England. I see your rank. You're a lieutenant colonel in the Army. Something's going on, and I want to know if it's because of what's in our heads, or something else. What do you do?"

"Quit talking. They'll hear us. They'll come down here."

"Maybe so, but they took us alive for a reason. They aren't going to kill us because we piss them off. No matter what threats they throw out. I thought originally it was for intelligence, but you shouted you work for NATO, just like I do, and these guys are Irish, so that makes no sense. It must be because of who we are. So, who are you?"

Kylie heard the door open and curled up, praying Nick was right. She heard footsteps, then a struggle with the slapping of flesh. A man said, "Keep your fucking hoods on." She heard a kick, then coughing. "All of you shut the hell up, or I'll cave your faces in."

The footsteps retreated, the door slammed, and there was silence. She heard someone spit something thick, then Nick said, "Well, which is it? Do you work in a capacity that they'd want what's in your head, or is it you?"

Travis hissed, "Be quiet. They'll come beat us."

Nick said, "They just did. And I can take it. The scare's over. They'll only kill who can't help them, and you can. Why?"

Kylie whispered, "Nick. Maybe he's right. Maybe we should just wait to see what's going to happen."

"Bullshit. I'm not waiting. Nobody is coming for us. If we want to get out, we'll do it ourselves. We need to start thinking about escape. Get ready for an opportunity."

His voice strident, Travis said, "No. No, no, no! We will do nothing. *Nothing*, do you hear? Let the US government sort this out."

Kylie heard Nick exhale, then say, "The US government won't come for us in time. These fucks intend to use us to *leverage* our government. To alter some policy. They will use our lives to harm the United States. We have to plan an escape. You're in the Army, for Christ's sakes."

The steel in his voice was new. Something different from the soft man who had talked her out of her shirt. Something like her uncle's friend. She debated whether he was putting them in jeopardy, and whose side she would take. Her uncle's friend came to her mind's eye, all hard edges and predatory skill. She decided.

Better to fight.

She said, "Travis, he's right. We need to plan for a way out. Sitting here waiting on the police isn't going to work."

Travis said, "I am a lieutenant colonel in the US Army. I am the senior officer here. I'm giving you an order to not do anything. *Nothing.* Do you understand?"

Kylie had no idea what any of that meant, but got a clue from Nick's response.

"Jesus Christ. They put a pussy in here with us."

11

Standing behind a man working a laptop, Seamus McKee saw Colin return. He said, "What were they talking about?"

"Nothing. Trying to figure out why they have bags on their heads."

"They'll know that soon enough."

He returned to the man on the computer. "Christ, Kevin, you said this Reddit thread would catch their attention. They still haven't responded. Are they that stupid?"

"The ragheads don't send riddles. This isn't Belfast. They aren't used to your signature."

"Well, maybe we'll have to acquaint them."

Colin said, "We don't have a drone strike yet, and even if we do, I still don't think this will work."

Seamus smiled. "A little late for that."

"They won't deal. And there will be no end to the search."

"As long as the press is in the dark, they'll deal. Remember the US Iran-Contra scandal? When President Reagan tried to exchange arms for hostages? After all of his tough talk about smashing terrorists? Just like Whitehall when they handed out those secret immunity deals to the Irish traitors in '98. Doesn't matter which government. They're always willing to deal."

Seamus McKee was a dying breed. A leader of a splinter group of the fading Irish Republican Army, he was one of the last who still believed Irish unity could be achieved through violence. In his eyes, Northern Ireland was an affront to every person of Celtic blood, and he was determined to see the final six counties under it returned to Irish control. Or at least punish those who disagreed.

Calling themselves the Real IRA, they'd been fighting since the Provisional IRA had called a cease-fire in 1998. When the cowards in the PIRA put down their arms, preferring to grovel for a half-step political solution, the RIRA split off and continued the campaign of violence. Car bombs, land mines, mortar attacks, and assassinations were all in its repertoire. Its goal: a unified Ireland—just like Michael Collins had envisioned so many years ago. Others could quit under the strain, but Seamus McKee never would.

The fight had been going on for decades—centuries, really—but Seamus and his brother Braden had been at it just under ten years. In that time Seamus had carved out a leadership niche and had proven his dedication to the cause. There was no shortage of will to attack, but operations cost money, and the cash flow had become harder and harder to maintain. Gone were the days of passing the hat in the pub, with even Americans of Irish descent supporting the cause.

For the most part, the younger generation didn't really think about Northern Ireland, and the older generation had grown complacent, satisfied with a country of twenty-six counties instead of the total island of thirty-two. Because of it, the RIRA's primary source of income was from crime. Gaining small-scale payoffs from extorting drug dealers and businesses, they spent more effort trying to collect operational funds than on the operations themselves.

In order to increase the flow of money, Seamus had had some of his men migrate to the continent, working with a team of Serbian jewel thieves who were experts in their chosen field. Called the Pink Panthers by Interpol, they'd pulled off some spectacular heists. While their nickname implied buffoonery, the operations were anything but. In less than a decade they'd netted over five hundred million dollars in places as far flung as Dubai and Tokyo, conducting hits that looked more fit for a Hollywood movie than real life.

Even with that, the Serbs were the undisputed leaders of the team. They used Seamus's men for their specific skills but took most of the profits, leaving him little to show for the risk. But through it he'd learned that there was money to be made if one found something valuable enough to steal. He'd decided to graduate from material things. After all, at the root, what was more valuable than life?

While his men thought the entire operation was about money, for him it was personal. Make no mistake, he intended to earn enough funds to keep them in operations for decades, but he also had some lessons for the special relationship between Britain and the United States. Lessons only his brother Braden knew about.

Kevin turned from the computer, a Reuters press report on the screen. "Looks like they just conducted a strike in Yemen. Hit a wedding party by mistake. Talk about perfect timing."

Seamus smiled. "You see, you can always count on the Yanks. They don't take any shit. Unless something valuable is at stake." He turned to Colin and said, "Execute the plan. Get the package in the air. Time to show we're serious." To Kevin, "Go ahead and send the message."

Kevin pulled up the Whitehouse.gov contact page and filled out the return information using the name of one Abu Mustafa. He typed a message, then turned around and looked at Seamus, waiting on permission.

Dialing his phone, a concerned look on his face, Colin said, "You sure that can't be traced? The government owns that website and the United States will bring everything they have to bear. The NSA is no joke."

Kevin said, "I'd try to explain it to you, but it would be wasted effort. Just consider it magic, and me Gandalf. It can't be traced. Unlike me, the NSA isn't a magician."

Seamus said, "Send it."

With Colin talking in the background, Kevin posted the message. Seamus waited until Colin was done and asked, "Any issues?"

"No. They're ready to leave Honduras. They'd already made the tape. Now it's just a matter of cutting the limbs. The issue is whether we've gone too far too soon. This is going to cause the US to explode."

Seamus bristled, saying, "What is your fucking problem? Are you afraid of them? Afraid of the fight? They are no more powerful than

England. No more powerful than the intelligence agencies we've been fighting for years. They know nothing of us. They're babies in our fight. They'll never figure it out. The secret is the power *we* hold. They will be looking for the wrong people, and in the meantime someone will pay for them. One way or the other."

"What about later? When the hostages say it wasn't a bunch of rag-heads who held them? How long can we hold up under that pressure? Christ, all they have to say is we had Irish accents."

"The hostages will never talk. It'll work out. Worst case, we blame the Serbs. We're paying them enough."

Colin said, "One more weak link. Those bastards will sell their own mothers. They have no cause."

"You're wrong. They have the omertà. They will never utter a word. I'm more worried about you."

Colin said nothing under Seamus's withering gaze. He eventually nodded, wanting to break the contact.

Seamus held his glare one moment longer, then said, "Call Braden. Tell him to deliver the package as soon as it arrives."

Colin began dialing and Seamus said, "Let the games begin."

Twenty-eight hours later a nondescript two-door Fiat pulled over on rue Royale, a large expanse of park separating the driver from the US embassy in Brussels, Belgium. A man exited carrying a small Styrofoam ice chest, just large enough for a six-pack of soda. The Belgium weather was blustery, and he didn't look out of place wearing a hat and scarf, his cheekbones the only thing visible just below the sunglasses on his face.

He entered the park and walked through until he reached rue Du-cale, the rear of the US embassy just in front of him, local national guards surveying everyone who exited. He circled the block, coming south down boulevard du Régent. He passed the Russian embassy and saw the black chain-link fence and the Belgian guards protecting the front entrance to the US embassy. He continued to approach, nodding to the guards and proceeding around the fence, just one more pedestrian walking the boulevard.

When he reached the front of the embassy, still outside the fence, he bent over and placed the ice chest on the ground, in full view of the guards and the cameras, then walked rapidly away. Before the guards could react, he was gone.

A suspicious package alert was called, requiring a response from the Brussels police force bomb squad. They used their robots and other technical kit, setting back Seamus's plan by another four hours and aggravating the hell out of the drivers on boulevard du Régent, now closed in the name of safety. Finally, after enough exploration, a man in a full-on blast suit stiffly advanced, looking like a character from a Saturday morning cartoon. He bent over the container, searching all around for hidden triggers. When he saw none, he removed the lid. Then he fell back.

At first, the men in his squad thought he'd tripped but when they saw him crawling away they became agitated. One zoomed a camera in on the Plexiglas shield of his helmet.

It was covered in vomit.

12

As Kurt raced as fast as he could through the DC traffic, George Wolffe said, "They didn't give you any indication of what this is about?"

"No. But it's serious. I haven't seen this much activity since Khalid Sheikh Mohammed. Everyone's spinning. And it's going to leak. Only a matter of time."

"Who are the players?"

"The chair of the Senate Intelligence Committee is going bonkers. He's a powerful guy, and his twins are gone. The SECDEF wants to start bombing Pakistan. And that fucking governor of Texas is raising holy hell."

"What about the vice president?"

"Surprisingly, I haven't heard much from him. They're really hoping to keep that under wraps. Can't see how that'll happen, though."

"This meeting is Oversight Council only, right?"

"Yeah. Something's broken free."

As they pulled into the lane for White House security, George considered his words, then said, "I hate to be a CIA stickler about sources and methods, but we're starting to blend Taskforce activities with the traditional intelligence architecture. The pressure to share is going to be enormous, and we're going to be compromised."

Kurt showed his identification to the uniformed Secret Service manning the gate at the West Wing, waited until he was checked off a list, then pulled through. He said, "Maybe. Maybe not. We can use the director of Central Intelligence. Thank God he's a Council member. We can feed all of our intelligence into the CIA, and they can sanitize it for the FBI. Hopefully they'll do the same in return."

"That's not going to be timely. And what happens if we find one of them? Are we going to conduct an assault? Or call for someone else?"

"I don't know. I haven't thought that far ahead."

"We need to start. If we conduct a rescue, successfully or not, we're going to end up splashed on the world stage. We might be able to hide who did it from the public, but we won't from all of the other elements involved. And some of those elements will forget the gratitude in one news cycle, especially if the press continues to push. After all of the other crap that's happened in the intelligence world, they'll throw us to the wolves to save their elective ass."

Kurt parked and said, "Yeah, I know. I'm worried about having to make a call like that. As bad as it sounds, it might be better to let them go. I'm not sure their lives will be worth all the lives that will be lost if our counterterrorist capability is eviscerated."

"Maybe you should bring this up to the president. He knows the stakes."

"Maybe. But not just yet. We aren't at that stage, and odds are we won't be. Police work is what will solve this, and we can't do direct interface. Waiting on the CIA to feed us what the FBI learns from a host-country liaison is way too slow. Someone will beat us to the punch. Or it'll just all go bad without our ability to help."

George climbed the cracked granite stairs in the Old Executive Office Building, replying, "I hate to say it, but we'd better hope so."

Kurt rounded the corner, seeing the Secret Service flanking the conference room doors, knowing that meant President Peyton Warren was attending this meeting. Knowing that couldn't be good news.

They showed their badges and passed into the room. Unlike the bedlam last time, there was stone quiet, all eyes on them as they entered. A discomfiting feeling, given that Kurt had no idea why he'd been summoned.

He looked at the president and said, "Sir, I . . . uh . . . is the Council expecting a briefing on something? Because I don't think I got the memo."

"No. We're expecting some biometric results, then an update. You can give us yours while we wait."

Kurt nodded at George to take his seat, then said, "Well, I don't have a lot. I've got four teams in the air, each headed to a disappearance location. Honduras, England, Okinawa, and Belgium."

"What's taking so long? We gave the order to launch over two days ago."

That came from Secretary of State Jonathan Billings, the same prick who had pulled Pike Logan from his operational capacity. Worried about Pike's habit of pushing the envelope, he now wanted it both ways. Wanted the envelope pushed to the point of compromise. Or maybe he just didn't get it.

Kurt said, "Sir, I don't have a division of commandos sitting around waiting to launch. I had to redirect teams that were on operational missions. Two on Alpha, one on Omega, and one running Assessment and Selection."

The Taskforce called every stage of an operation a different Greek letter, each representing an escalation of potential actions. Before a mission moved to a different stage, the Oversight Council had to sanction the elevation.

Alpha meant the introduction of forces to explore a potential target. Basically, poke around a little bit and develop whether he or she was actually out to harm the United States. Omega, the last letter in the alphabet, meant that the target was an imminent threat and the Oversight Council had granted permission for hostile action, either to capture or kill the target.

In this case, nobody seemed concerned about the potential threat or the Omega authority given. It didn't matter that a team that had been granted permission to remove an impending danger to national security was now being redirected to hunt for hostages. Something that wasn't even in their mission profile. Instead, Billings was pressing the time lag.

Kurt looked around the room for the secretary of defense, knowing he understood the intricacies involved with moving forces on the chessboard of global operations. For the first time, he noticed the man was absent.

Focusing back on Billings, Kurt said, "Sir, it takes time to get them redirected. It's not like they can just jump on a plane. It takes time to close out cover contracts and get deployment assets on station. Time to assess whether the redirect will spike host-nation intelligence services. Time to establish a new cover mechanism in the redirect country. Time to ensure the new cover status they'll be operating under will withstand scrutiny. It's what I talked about before. This isn't our forte. We're not an alert force that can turn on a dime."

Billings started to grumble when the door opened. Alexander Palmer entered with the same NSC staff weenie from before. He still looked as if he were a rabbit in the wolves' den.

Kurt waited on President Warren to dismiss him, noticing the man was haggard from sleepless nights. Warren said, "Good enough, Kurt. Have a seat for the update."

Kurt nodded, understanding without words that the president already knew what was about to be briefed and that it wasn't going to be good. He thought about expanding on his statements to Billings, conveying the danger the mission was placing on the Taskforce to the only man in the room who really mattered, then thought better of it. He took his seat at the rear of the room.

The staffer booted up his laptop and without any preamble said, "We got this through the White House website contact page. The email address is bogus and the ISP terminates in Guam. We've already explored the ISP with in-country assets and got nowhere. It's clearly a redirect."

On the screen, Kurt read:

Dear Mr. President. You never answered the question we posed on Reddit, so we have to assume you thought it rhetorical. It wasn't. You just conducted a strike against a harmless wedding party in Yemen, and because of it, you have forced our hand. We ask once again, are all lives equal? Will you continue such actions when the end result involves something you hold dear? There are seven innocent families weeping over the loss of loved ones in the Sada'a Province. Who will weep in your inner circle from this attack? Nobody. But someone will weep. We promise.

Kurt had read about the strike in his daily intel update. The al Qaida propaganda machine was saying it was a wedding party, which had been picked up in the press, but the intel track had shown a terrorist convoy. It was hard to determine what the convoy actually was, but regardless, inside that convoy had been three definite terrorists, now dead. The chatter afterward had confirmed that. Along with the loss of four civilians with an indeterminate heritage.

The staffer said, "Given the enormous number of comments that are directed at the White House contact page each day, it took over twenty hours for the Reddit thread connection to reach someone who understood the significance. By the time we had begun tracing the digital trail, a package had been delivered to the front gate of the US embassy in Brussels. Inside was a DVD recording and the hands and feet of a human being."

A low murmur went through the room, and Kurt had a horrible intuition about why the secretary of defense—a principal in the Oversight Council—wasn't attending.

The screen flipped to an MP4 movie, and the lights went dim. Kurt saw a person hunched in the center, a hood on his head, surrounded by men wearing kaffiyehs that covered their faces, each brandishing an AK-47. There was no sound. The hood was removed, and he saw the secretary of defense's son. The boy began to cry in silence, and the man to his right held up a section of poster board displaying the words EXPERIENCE THE PAIN.

The man began to flip the poster boards like a high school YouTube video, each one with a different sentence about the casualties of United States policy. The last placard read, AND NOW IT IS YOUR TURN. REAP WHAT YOU SOW.

The man behind the captive raised his barrel, placing it on the back of the boy's head. There was a second pause, and then he pulled the trigger. The frontal lobe of the skull exploded outward, taking the eye orbit with it in a shower of gore. The secretary of defense's son fell forward, his mouth open, his jaw the only thing remaining as a human face.

13

Startled gasps filled the room, followed by murmurs. President Warren held up his hand and everyone grew quiet, subdued by the intimacy of the death. Something they ordered often in their duties but now were forced to see in hyperreal detail. It left them dumbstruck.

As if he were talking about the national orange crop, the staffer said, "DNA and fingerprint testing has proven that the body parts delivered in Brussels match Curtis Oglethorpe, Mark Oglethorpe's son. We believe the video is genuine, as is the Reddit thread and White House comment. Furthermore, we believe that all of the missing have been taken as leverage against our policy of armed counterterrorist drone strikes."

He finished and looked to Alexander Palmer for guidance on what else to say.

For his part, Palmer looked to the president of the United States.

President Warren said, "Gentlemen, the entire fabric of our country is now under attack. The barbaric method is new and unique, but the outcome is the same. An attack against our ability to defend the nation. And it's effective. I've already given orders for all strikes against terrorist targets to halt immediately. What I want to know is how we're going to get them back. And barring that, what we're going to do about it."

Kurt heard the words, and the enormity of the stakes came home. There would be no evenhanded discussion of how best to use the Taskforce. The administration was going to destroy anything tangentially associated with the video. And after seeing it, Kurt was more than willing to light the fuse.

Ignoring the emotion, Kerry Bostwick, the director of the CIA, said, "So we're still feeling that it's an Islamic group?"

Palmer snorted at the question.

Billings said, "Well, what the hell else could it be? The name on the contact is Abu Mustafa, the target of the action is our drone strikes, and the men in the video are clearly Arabic. Yes, it is an Islamic group. We need to focus on transits to Yemen, Pakistan, or Somalia. Places where they feel secure. That's where the hostages are going. That's where Curtis was killed."

Ignoring the outburst, Kurt said, "What do you mean, Kerry?"

"Well, it still doesn't ring true to me. I just can't see them able to conduct such a wide-ranging operation."

President Warren said, "And neither could your organization on September tenth. We've always discounted the threat. I don't intend to do so again."

Kerry bristled, and Kurt backed him up, saying, "There's more to it than Kerry's gut feeling. I agree with the CIA on assessments of the operation. Besides just being able to coordinate it, they'd have to execute, and we'd have some indication of Arabic men doing the job. We don't. Which means they might have help from a non-Arabic group, like what used to happen in the '70s and '80s. Maybe there's an Islamic organization behind it, but we shouldn't discount help from someone else. Someone who could penetrate, like the Japanese Red Army at the Lod Airport."

Billings said, "What the hell are you talking about?"

Kurt rolled his eyes, disgusted at the lack of knowledge on basic terrorism. "The Popular Front for the Liberation of Palestine . . ." He paused and said, "You know who they are, right?"

Billings grew red and nodded. Kurt continued. "The PFLP couldn't penetrate Israeli airport security because of their nationality. They hired terrorists from the Japanese Red Army to attack for them. In 1972, the Japanese terrorists came into Israel as tourists, then began flinging hand grenades and shooting up the place. I'm saying it could be the same here."

Billings said, "But that was when the radical ideology was similar.

When all the groups had a Marxist bent. This Islamic thing is different. They'd never accept help like that."

Kerry said, "There's something more. In Islamic videos, they almost always cut the head off of the victim on camera. Like Daniel Pearl. Like those Islamic State barbarians in Iraq." He saw everyone react to his flat words and said, "Look, let's deal with this clinically. Get over the death on-screen. It's horrific, but getting emotional won't solve any problems." He turned to the president. "Sir, I've never seen one where they simply shoot the victim, especially since the Islamic State came around. It's crucifixions and beheadings all the time. Shooting happens in tit-for-tat reprisals on the battlefield, but not in a staged video designed to maximize propaganda value. Designed to elicit maximum fear. And there's no talking. No shouting *Allahu Akbar* along with something we have to translate. This was done on cards, like they didn't want us to hear them speak."

Kurt said, "And that final card is interesting. 'Reap what you sow' is a Christian thing from the Bible."

President Warren said, "Is it? Only Christian, I mean?"

Kerry said, "No. It's in the Quran as well, but only in concept. You'll find plenty of references about doing good to gather good or doing evil to gather evil, but you won't find the words *reap* and *sow* like you do in the Bible. Maybe they're poking us in the eye by using it, but it's another data point."

President Warren considered the words, then said, "At this point, it's irrelevant. We go with what we know. We have no indication of any other groups and every indication it's from some Islamic terrorist organization. They've mentioned Yemen twice, and that matters. We've never had an indication that Islamic groups were connecting to organizations they would consider infidels, but we *do* have a ton of connections *between* Islamic groups. That I could believe. Right now, we focus on the Islamic ones."

Kurt said, "Sir, you know if they get them to the FATA tribal lands in Pakistan, or the Sada'a Province of Yemen, we're out of luck. Shit, even if they get them to Mali or some of the outlaw lands of Libya that have been created since Qaddafi fell, we'll never find them."

The president looked at Kurt and said, "That's where you come in. We'll provide all the intelligence we have, but nobody has the agility across the globe like you do. Everything we do as a government is compartmented by region or even nation. I can do a fine job of crime-scene work in Okinawa, or counterterrorism in Somalia, but when that shifts to another theater, we're fucked. The guy who finds the lead in Okinawa can't follow up in Mali. He has no global experience, and he'll just pass his information into the network. Unlike you. You can work across bureaucratic boundaries. And you have."

Kurt looked at George and saw a slight nod. He said, "Sir, we need to talk about that. I'm with you on the threat, but I want to make sure you understand what you're asking. I do this, and there's a good chance the Taskforce will be exposed. A very good chance."

He saw Billings draw back, not liking the words. Understanding what exposure could cause and not liking having his skin in the game. Billings said, "What do you mean by that?"

"You heard me talking about cover before, but it's more than that. Sooner or later, this is going to break in the press, and it's going to be ferocious. If I resolve the problem, there will be no way to keep it secret. It's not like causing a terrorist to disappear who nobody knew about in the first place."

Billings said, "I thought you could do this without any fingerprints. That's what you always brag about."

"I can, right up until we have a bunch of rescued hostages in the press. We won't be able to keep it secret, and like bin Laden, everyone will want to know how it was done."

"So unlike bin Laden, we don't blab about who it was."

"That might work for the public. You might be able to keep us secret from them, but you won't from the insiders. Shit, the chair of the Senate Select Committee on Intelligence has missing kids. He's going to want to know what happened, and he's going to find out. I just want to make sure we all understand the repercussions."

Billings sat back for a moment, then said, "Maybe Kurt's right. Maybe we should use traditional assets on this. Even if they aren't as good."

President Warren's face showed disgust. He said, "Have you talked to the vice president?"

Billings shook his head.

President Warren said, "I have. And I'm also the one who told Mark about his son. The one who had to deliver the news on how he died." President Warren's face was stone, the anger leaking out of his voice like acid. "I promise that Mark could give a shit about any exposure. He'd gladly spend the rest of his life in disgrace or prison if it meant vengeance for his son. Vice President Hannister has seen the Curtis tape. I guarantee he'll do anything in his power to prevent his son from ending up on a tape of his own. Think about what you would do if it were your son or daughter."

When Billings said nothing, preferring to sit back and hide his eyes from the president's gaze, Warren turned to Kurt. "You understand my orders?"

"Yes, sir. I think you've been plain."

"Well, let me make it absolutely clear: If you've got the means to resolve this situation, and the end result is compromise, you *will* compromise. Do you understand?"

Kurt nodded. "Yes, sir. Perfectly."

President Warren's eyes bored into him. He pointed at the screen, the still of Curtis Oglethorpe's body on the ground. "No mercy. Burn it to the ground. Whether we get them back or not."

14

Lieutenant Kaelyn Clute slowly came to consciousness, the world a hazy kaleidoscope of light. She felt a ravenous thirst, but also queasy, as if she'd just been on a roller coaster, her inner ears in turmoil from repeated spinning. She strained her eyes, trying to penetrate the gloom, but still couldn't see anything concrete. Only vague light and shadow. She realized it was because of a rough burlap sack on her head. In a panic, she attempted to sit up only to find she was tied at the ankles, knees, wrists, and elbows.

And it all came back.

The Irishmen's car pulling over to the side of the road, flashing its lights. Mack cursing his luck, saying he wished he'd hadn't agreed to show them to the aquarium. Her calming him down as they pulled alongside the disabled car, one Irishman already out and under the hood. Her exiting the vehicle, then seeing the pistols. Mack shouting and fighting. The needle being injected into her neck. Her vision blurring as she watched Mack being beaten.

The memories slammed home, making her tremble, sweat popping out on her neck. She rolled onto her back, the nausea returning, her body feeling as if it were rocking left and right even as she lay still. She felt damp, rough-hewn lumber under her and heard a steady mechanical noise. A pump. She smelled diesel and realized it wasn't the drugs affecting her equilibrium. She was on a boat. Or more precisely, in the bowels of a boat, next to the bilge pump. But where was Mack?

Afraid to speak, afraid of alerting anyone that she was awake, she slowly lowered her head down to the wood and scraped, feeling the sack move an inch. She continued until she had a sliver of light at the base of her neck, enough so that she could see her chest. She lay still, waiting to see if the motion had caused anyone to notice. Wondering if someone was watching her right this minute. Nothing happened. She repeated the maneuver until she had a good five inches of vision at the base of her chin. She rolled her head to the left and saw the dim interior of a ship's engine room, but no Mack. She turned right and saw a pair of legs, tied.

McKinley.

She wormed her way forward until she made contact with him, then did the best she could to wake him, rolling her body on top of his and patting his chest with her restrained hands. He did nothing, sending fear through her that he was dead.

She slid off him and squeezed her eyes shut, fighting the panic. She chastised herself, reverting to the discipline it took to achieve her position in naval aviation. Remembering her survival and resistance training, she began thinking through the problem just as she would if she'd had a catastrophic failure in her aircraft, putting aside the fact that she had absolutely no control over anything.

Then McKinley's legs moved.

She sensed it more than anything else. She cocked her head back to see, remaining still as a stone. A moment passed, and she saw them move again. She sagged to the hull, letting out pent-up relief in one ragged breath. She waited, knowing Mack was working through the aftereffects of the drugs just as she had. He slowly showed more animation, and she could stand it no longer.

She wormed toward his head and whispered, "Mack . . . Mack, are you awake?"

He groaned, a noise that overshadowed the bilge pump. She hissed, "Mack, quiet. Whisper to me."

She craned her head again until she could see the burlap over his face. It turned toward her. She said, "Mack, can you hear me?"

"Kaelyn?"

"Yes."

"Are you all right?"

She snorted quietly and said, "Well, I'm alive. I don't think this qualifies as 'okay.' "

"Where are we?"

"On a boat. Somewhere in the ocean, but it's got to be near the island chain. This thing isn't big enough to cross the Pacific. I have no idea how long we've been out. Could be hours. Could be days."

She saw his head sag back. He said, "What the hell is going on?"

Before she could answer, she heard a hatch slam onto the deck and saw a spike of light near the engine. Footsteps resonated from someone coming down, and she lay still.

Through the gap in her hood she watched the legs approach, stopping between Mack and her, just next to her chest. She studied the leather boots, waiting.

The man said, "Looks like that needle worked as advertised. I was beginning to wonder if you two was in a coma, but it cleared out just like they said."

The accent was heavy, and Slavic. *Not Irish. Eastern European.*

Mack fought to sit up, shouting, "What do you want from us?"

She saw the boot rise, then push McKinley back to the hull, not harshly, but with enough force to show he meant business.

"I want nothing from you. I'm but a delivery boy. We will be stopping soon. When that happens, I'm going to untie your legs and remove your hood. You have some walking to do. If you try to escape, I'll kill you."

She felt the boat shift, the engine slowing down. He said, "I want both of you to roll onto your belly. Now."

She did so and felt the rope around her knees and ankles fall away. She remained still. The hood was removed and she was told to stand. She complied and found she was a half a head taller than her captor, a short, wiry man wearing a wool sweater, with close-cropped black hair and eyes as dull and lifeless as a chunk of burnt wood. He reminded her of a KGB agent from a cartoon. All he was missing was a pencil-thin mustache. In one calloused hand he held a fillet knife, undermining any notion that the man was a comic book buffoon.

He pointed to the ladder and said, "Go onto the deck. Sit down and wait."

She hesitated, looking at Mack still tied up, and he said, "Do as I say. I'm not going to harm him. I just don't want two of you loose down here at the same time."

She climbed the ladder carefully, afraid of tumbling back down below without the use of her hands. She reached the top and was hoisted out by another man, then forced into a sitting position. He showed her a pistol and shook his head. She understood.

She found the boat much larger than the engine room indicated. A fishing trawler with great nets attached to booms on either side. The ladder came up just outside the wheelhouse, where she saw another man steering and cursing. To the left, a third man was lowering a rubber dinghy with an outboard motor, working the cable winch and answering the curses with foul language of his own.

She heard scuffling, and Mack appeared, his hands still tied behind him, the small man from below keeping him from falling backward. He turned to face her, and she was shocked at the damage. His left eye was swollen shut, his lip split, dried blood looking like ketchup stains from a greasy burger underneath his nose and on his chin. He smiled to give her confidence, but it came out hideous, like a caricature from a horror movie makeup room. It did little to ease her fear.

They were ordered to the stern of the boat, where the edge was closest to the water. The dinghy was brought around, and they were passed into it one by one, dropping unceremoniously onto the rigid deck. The original man, now armed with a pistol and wearing a rucksack, climbed in behind them and said, "Just sit still."

And off they went.

Five hundred meters away, she could see an island. It grew until she could pick out the shore and the jungle beyond. No houses or other signs of civilization. They beached on a short, rocky stretch of sand. They were made to exit, then began walking up a steep footpath, slipping and falling among the roots of windswept brush. They reached the top away from the shore, breaking out onto a road facing a large open area with concrete pads stretching off into the distance.

Mack said, "Holy shit. I know this place. It's Tinian Island. We're at North Field."

The man pushed them forward, saying "Quiet."

They walked for another hundred meters, getting close to an outbuilding of crumbling concrete and indeterminate usage. When they reached it, he pointed with the pistol and said, "Sit."

They did so, and he walked fifty meters away, withdrawing a radio from his rucksack.

Seeing he was out of earshot, Kaelyn whispered to Mack, "Where are we? And how do you know?"

Mack said, "Northern Mariana Islands. It's an American protectorate. Way south of Japan. East of the Philippines. It's the base where the *Enola Gay* took off from when it dropped the bomb."

She said, "*Enola Gay*? How on earth can you tell that from looking at a bunch of concrete?"

"Remember a year ago when I finally got to leave Oki? Go on an exercise instead of working provost marshal stuff? Well, it was to this godforsaken lump of rock. Exercise Forager Fury. The whole point was to establish a forward landing strip for the Marine Expeditionary Force. That was the exercise. I pretended to pull security with a platoon of MPs while they rebuilt the old World War II infrastructure. It culminated with C-130s landing, proving we could project force in an austere environment." He leaned back and said, "I spent twenty-eight days on this piece of shit, patrolling the perimeter over and over. I'd recognize it in my sleep."

She took in what he said and instinctively knew the implications: It was an abandoned airfield with new, serviceable runways. They were waiting on an aircraft.

No sooner had the thought entered her head than the man returned, saying, "Get up."

They did so, and she scanned the sky. To the west she saw a speck, which grew into an aircraft. It hit the ground, and she recognized a Viking de Havilland Twin Otter, a twin-engine plane designed for short takeoff and landing. Used the world over for harsh environments, it was loved by bush pilots for its ability to get into tight, rough spaces. But it wasn't known for its endurance.

He pushed them forward, and she began to see the plan fall apart.

To see their death. She said, "Listen, we're going to be lucky to get to another piece of land on that thing. I don't know what the pilot told you, but I'm surprised it made it out here on one tank. Getting back is suicide. You're going to kill us in the ocean."

The man said, "Perhaps we should let you fly it, hmm?"

The words caused an involuntary spike of fear, belying his earlier words about being just a "delivery boy." He knew exactly who she was.

The plane taxied to their location and stopped, the engines still turning. Two men exited, moved to the concrete building, and pushed out a large cylinder on wheels, with a gas nozzle attached. They began refueling, and Kaelyn finally realized how much effort had been put into their capture. How much coordination and preparation.

Which meant the men had something very valuable in mind in return.

15

I stepped out of the train station behind Jennifer, dragging our two carry-ons behind me. She pointed to the street and said, "Guess I was right about the rental car."

In front of me was a sea of bicycles, all chained and stacked haphazardly as if the Tour de France had decided to stop for a train ride. Well, that is if the Tour de France was run with rusted beachcombers and ancient ten-speeds. It looked like a bicycle graveyard. Which did nothing to help my mood.

My entire plan of attack had started to disintegrate over the Atlantic Ocean, ten minutes out from the British Isles. Knuckles had gotten a redirect. Apparently, the vice president's son's car had been found out in the English countryside, and it had been clean with the exception of one clue: a ferry receipt for Tangier, Morocco. It had necked down the potential kidnappers significantly, pointing to three or four different Islamic groups. As hunting terrorists was more of the Taskforce forte, he was given a mission change to explore the connection, leaving the English criminal investigation with the FBI, which meant we were dumped as soon as possible at Heathrow in London, nowhere near Cambridge.

Poking out of the hatch of the Gulfstream, he'd said, "Sorry to do this to you, but orders are orders." Then he'd smiled and waved before closing the door and leaving us on the tarmac holding our bags. I knew he thought it was incredibly funny, and I felt like a hitchhiker that had been tricked and taken to the wrong destination.

I'd wanted to get a rental car and drive to Cambridge, but Jennifer said that taking a train would be much easier. I'd argued that we needed the flexibility, and she'd stated that she'd done the research on Cambridge University and the surrounding town and that having a car would be more of a hindrance than a help. I'd acquiesced, mainly because I'm the one who had tasked her with the research, so I had to live with the results. But I was sure I'd prove her wrong when we arrived.

That certainty faded in view of the bicycle graveyard, sending a little stab of aggravation through me. Jennifer said, "Want to rent some bikes? The hotel I booked is right around the corner."

I said, "And what? Strap these bags to the seat like a Vietcong on the Ho Chi Minh Trail?"

I saw a tiny grin slip out and realized she was screwing with me. Knowing that I had been all set on a big ol' *I told you so*, she was returning the favor.

I shook my head, unable to stop my own smile. I tried to maintain my annoyance, but it was impossible with her. I said, "Can we get a cab instead?"

Three minutes later and we were headed to our hotel in downtown Cambridge. It turned out that the university didn't have a single campus but instead spanned the entire town. Composed of over thirty colleges, each with its own separate green, the school was impossible to separate from the town. And the town was old. I mean, really old, having been founded in 1209. Charleston, South Carolina, prided itself on its history, but it had nothing on this village, something that Jennifer loved.

Getting the history lesson on the cab drive over, I began to regret giving her the research task. Right up until she corrected the cabdriver on his knowledge of the town, which was funny as hell.

We dumped our bags at the hotel and asked directions to Queens' College, the campus where Kylie was conducting her exchange. A third-year student studying English literature, she should have been finishing up her first semester here. Instead, she'd disappeared, and I dearly hoped to find out it was just a college prank.

Kurt had already smoothed the way with the administration, and they were expecting us, so I didn't think we'd have any trouble with the school. Her roommate might be a different story.

I tried to get a cab, but Jennifer insisted on renting some bikes from the hotel, and we set out, pedaling through history, the stone buildings and alleys projecting a stoic reticence at our very presence. Allowing us to view them, but knowing we would never appreciate the history they embodied. Well, that's what I thought, anyway. For her part, Jennifer kept exclaiming one thing after another from her research, making me wish we could explore and let her run around like a puppy in a field. Making me wish we had some time before we began to dig into what had happened to Kylie. Something I was dreading.

After a short ride, we chained the bikes outside of Queens' College and entered through the arch to the administration building, stepping back in time in more ways than one. The first person who met us was an ancient dragon lady with a dour expression soaking through her wrinkles. Apparently, one of the first to graduate from Queens' College in the fifteenth century, she was convinced we were a couple of slimy Yank tourists out to deface her beloved grounds. We spent about twenty minutes trying to break through her prejudice, with me growing more and more aggravated.

Jennifer saw me getting pissed and knew my nascent social skills were at the breaking point. I was on the verge of simply walking into the courtyard, ignoring the old prune's protests. Jennifer glared at me, giving me her disappointed-teacher stare, and I hissed, "Well, you take over then. Before I crack that bitch in the head."

I saw her face flush at my cursing, her expression looking like she was trying to contain a volcanic eruption. I immediately regretted my choice of words. She clenched her teeth and bored into me with her eyes. I did what every man on earth had done since leaving the cave. I cowered.

She said, "Don't utter another word," then turned to the battle-axe, all sweetness and sunshine. After a bit of back and forth, the biddy was on the phone, calling down Kylie's roommate and giving me the stink-eye. Reminding me yet again how much fun Knuckles must be having chasing bloodthirsty terrorists.

Five minutes later a slight girl with long black hair, glasses, and bushy eyebrows entered the office. She had a piercing next to her right eye, and my first thought was *English lit major*, but I knew better than to allow that to escape out of my mouth. Jennifer would probably punch me. I decided to let the females handle the introductions.

She shook our hands, then, speaking with a Scottish accent, said, "I'm Blair, Kylie's roommate, and I'll help you any way I can. I'm worried about her."

Which popped any ideas I had about a bender in London and ramped up my concern. I said, "So you haven't heard from her? At all?"

"No. I haven't heard from her since she went out the other night. She never came home, and that's not like her."

Jennifer said, "Can we see her room? Her stuff?"

Blair looked at the battle-axe, who nodded, squinting at me as she did so. I almost said, "I won't shit on the floor, I promise," but bit my tongue. We left the dragon lady behind, walking to the dorm.

16

Strolling across the courtyard, Blair said, "She was seeing someone, and I figured she'd gone dancing at Cindies, but when she texted to tell me where she'd left my bike, it wasn't anywhere near there. That was the last thing I heard from her."

I said, "Wait a minute. One step at a time. What makes you think she was seeing someone?"

"She just was. She was very secretive about it, but I could tell. She spent too much time getting ready. Too much time trying to look nice. It was for a man."

"So she never told you who it was?"

"No. Like I said, she kept it a big secret. I mean, she wouldn't even admit to going out with someone. I think she was afraid of being labeled a slut or something."

Jennifer said, "What's Cindies?"

"It's a local dance club. It's actually changed names from Cinderella to Ballare, but everyone still calls it Cindies. But she didn't go there. Well, at least that wasn't the last place she went."

We turned the corner, walking through an arch in a building older than our entire nation. A wooden bridge spanned a canal, and Jennifer said, "Oh my God, is that the Mathematical Bridge?"

Blair nodded and started to say something about it when I interjected, "Can we stay on point here?"

Jennifer glared at me, and Blair went back and forth between us. I stepped onto the bridge and said, "How do you know where she stopped last?"

"I don't know exactly where, but she sent me a text telling me where to get my bike—she'd broken the chain on hers and I'd loaned her mine. I needed it later in the night . . . I mean, I was going out as well . . . and she texted where she'd left it locked up. It was nowhere near Cindies, so that's not where she went."

We reached the dorm, which wasn't nearly as old as the original school buildings. It was modern, maybe built in the eighteenth century as opposed to the fifteenth. She led the way up the stairs to the second floor, and I wondered how many people had trodden the same path. I found it a little creepy, with everything built in dark wood and shadowed in a gloomy light.

She unlocked the door to their small apartment and said, "Here's home. Her stuff is through the kitchen on the left. All of it is still there; her computer is on the desk."

I said, "Is there Internet in here, or are you guys supposed to learn like the forefathers?"

Blair laughed and said, "Yeah, there's Wi-Fi. She should already be hooked up, but I can't help you if she has any passwords on her stuff."

I pulled a slip of paper out of my pocket and said, "I got that. Jennifer, see what else Blair knows. I'm going to hit the room."

I left them in the kitchen, walking to the doorway of Kylie's dorm. It was small, with a simple wood desk and a double-size bed, and had a faint musty smell, reminding me of old drapes left hanging way past their service life. It was clean and tidy, with only a single pair of socks on the floor. A MacBook Pro was on the desk, an open notebook next to it, as if Kylie were coming home any minute. For some reason the scene brought about a melancholy feeling, a sad reminder of how fragile life can be.

I shook those thoughts from my head. There was no indication that something bad had happened to Kylie. Not yet anyway.

I went through the desk first, hoping to find a journal or calendar. From the third drawer I pulled out another notebook. Inside was nothing more than a school assignments list, with most of the notebook pages blank. I pulled out a syllabus from a pocket and a small piece of folded paper fluttered to the ground. I opened it and found a visitor's pass made out to Kylie Hale for RAF Molesworth. The escort name was TSgt Nicholas Seacrest of the NATO Intelligence Fusion Centre, with the destination being some pizza joint on the post.

What on earth would she be doing at a British air base? How good could that pizza be?

I put the pass away and turned on the Mac, logging in and going straight to her social media. There were a ton of new posts to her Facebook page, but no comments or posts by her since she'd disappeared. I opened her private messages, feeling a little slimy. I went through them as fast as possible, not wanting to pry, scanning the initial sentences and moving on. I found nothing of interest. The same for her Twitter feed. Just innocuous posts about college life.

I moved on to Instagram and found nothing on her public profile. I went to direct messages and finally got a hit. A picture of a man's hand pointing to a brochure for some place called the Eagle, with a time and date written in blue ink on the border. The date was the day she disappeared. The caption said, *Shhh . . . loose lips sink ships.* I clicked on the profile that had sent it, someone called StNick762, but it went to a dead link. I hollered out of the room, "Blair, could you come here?"

Jennifer entered first, saying, "What did you find?"

I showed her the visitor's pass, then the Instagram picture, saying, "The profile is deleted."

Blair came in and I showed her the pass, asking, "Is this close by?"

"Well, the town of Molesworth is about twenty minutes away. I don't know anything about the military bases, though."

"Why would Kylie go there?"

"I have no idea. She certainly couldn't have ridden her bike there, and we don't have a car."

I looked at Jennifer, frustrated at the lack of answers.

She pointed at the screen and the Instagram picture, saying, "How about this? Do you know where it is?"

Blair took one look and smiled. "Oh yeah, it's a historical landmark. And it's right near where she left my bike."

17

Kylie felt a cold draft sink from the window, breaking through her small bit of warmth and causing her to glare at it in frustration. Their cellar prison was constantly frigid, with only sparse woolen blankets provided to keep them from going into hypothermia. When nighttime came, the cold of their subterranean cell increased, the dampness seeping into her bones and preventing sleep. Her only moment of warmth came when she was allowed out to use the bathroom. Just breaking the door at the top of the stairs provided a welcome blast of heat, and using the toilet allowed her to sit in relative luxury for a scant few minutes, but now the small window was robbing her of her only pleasure.

It was tiny, really a slat more than a viewing pane, maybe ten inches high and two feet wide, and looked as if it was shut tight, but the outside air was leaking through. She stood on the toilet, awkwardly pulling herself up with her tied hands until she was level with the bottom of the pane. She saw that it cranked outward, opened by a small lever—and it was cracked just a smidgen. She rotated the handle, cinching the wood tightly into the frame and sealing out the draft. She stood for a moment and looked through the pane at the freedom beyond. She saw a bed of gravel just below the sill and a concrete wall eight feet away. The window was only six inches above the ground.

Her guard threw a fist against the door, scaring the life out of her. She collapsed back into a sitting position on the toilet, her pants still fastened, saying, "I'm almost done. Please. Another few seconds."

The man grunted something but didn't open the door. She sat for a moment longer, then flushed. The noise brought the guard in, the man clamping down on her flex-tied wrists and leading her back into the hallway. She glanced back at the window, an impossible, lunatic thought flitting through her head.

Back in the cellar darkness, she waited for her eyes to adjust to the small glow escaping from the door at the top of the stairs. They no longer had to wear the hoods at all times, but the basement was still as black as pitch, the edges of the door providing no more illumination than a slice of the moon in a forest.

She whispered, "Nick?"

"Yeah, I'm here. You okay?"

"Yes. I'm fine. I see it didn't warm up while I was gone."

Nick chuckled and said, "But you got the heat of the toilet, right?"

The comment brought a smidgen of shame, as she was the only one allowed the luxury of a toilet. The men were forced to use a bucket in the corner, which would have been bad enough, but she'd told Nick about the warmth. About the brief respite from the dungeon they were in.

He sensed the pause and said, "Kylie, I was kidding. Don't feel bad about what you get in relation to us. Use it."

She said, "That's what I want to talk to you about. I think I can get out of the window in the bathroom. It's so small they don't bother locking it because no man could get through it, but I think I can fit."

"You mean escape?"

"Yes. If you think it's best for me to try."

Lieutenant Colonel Travis Deleon cut in, his voice floating out of the darkness. "*No*. No way. You heard the instructions. Someone even *tries* to escape, and one of us will die. This is a typical hostage situation, and we treat it as such. Let negotiations take their time."

Kylie said, "I don't think they'll harm us while we still have value. We can do whatever we want right now, but they *will* eventually kill us. It's only a matter of time. They have no intention of letting us go."

"Young lady, you don't understand how this works. I cannot allow you to attempt that. You'll put us all in jeopardy."

Nick said, "Sir, what the hell are you talking about? How would you know how this works? Trust me, I've seen what happens to people in this situation, and it isn't pretty. Kylie's right. Our one weapon is our value. There's something these guys hope to get from it, and the minute they do, our value drops to nothing. Until then, they won't hurt us no matter what we do."

Kylie heard the words and thought, *Seen what happens to hostages? Where? In the Air Force? He told me he was a weatherman.* She wondered what else the vice president's son had hidden from her.

LTC Deleon replied, his voice strained in a harsh half whisper, "Nobody is doing anything beyond what they tell us. *Nobody.* Do you two hear me? I'm not getting killed because of idiocy."

Kylie said, "I'm telling you, we're dead anyway. Have you not wondered why nobody bothers to cover their face? Why they don't care how much information we can glean by simple contact? They're even giving us their names. They have no intention of letting us go."

Travis said, "You don't know that. The names could be fake. One thing is for sure: You try to escape, and someone's going to die. Probably me. I'll take my chances on the negotiations. On the rescue."

Nick said, "You fucking sicken me. Nobody is going to find us in time. These men know what they have and know how much pressure will be brought to bear. They've put a lot of thought into this, and they're going to be a step ahead of our government. We need to plan for our own escape."

"So you want to put your girlfriend in the line of fire? And you call *me* a coward."

Nick said nothing for a moment, then, "No. That's not what I want."

She said, "Nobody's putting me anywhere. It's *my* choice. I think I could get out, and Nick's right. These guys are smart. Anybody that's looking for us is on the wrong trail, or they'd have been here already. If I can get out, I can fix that even if they move you guys later."

Travis said, "Move us later? Seriously? Both of you are delusional. Even if you could escape, we'll disappear. You'll be no help. Nobody will find us."

Kylie thought about her uncle, then about her uncle's friend. About the stories she'd heard hovering among the groups of men during her uncle's unit parties. She'd been much younger then, and impressionable, but she was sure the stories were real.

Just above a whisper she said, "That's not true. My uncle is looking, and he has some scary friends. If I could escape, I could get to them. They would rescue everyone."

Travis snorted and said, "Your fantasy isn't worth my life. I'm telling you both again, as the senior officer, nobody is to do anything against the orders of our captors. It's too risky."

The door slammed open and the bearded man came stomping down, shouting, "Shut the fuck up or the hoods go back on."

Caught in the light, Travis tried to get out of the man's path, wrapping his arms over his head. Nick rocked back but kept a defiant look on his face. The man slapped Travis in the head, then saw Nick staring at him. He slammed a boot into Nick's stomach, causing him to grunt and roll onto the ground. The man said, "You want to be taken down a peg and I'm more than willing to do it. We only need you breathing."

Nick squeezed his hands against his gut but maintained his insolent expression.

The man advanced on Kylie, pulling her head up by the hair. He said, "You still want a pissing contest?"

The terror flooded through her, her eyes rolling in a fear that was reflected on Nick's face.

Nick said, "Okay, okay. Stop. I won't talk. Please."

The man stared at him in silence for a moment, then threw Kylie to the ground. He walked away to the stairs without looking back, slamming the door and plunging the room back into darkness. Kylie began to weep.

She lay in the cold, stricken by their utter helplessness, her earlier bravery vanishing as quickly as the light from the door.

Nick wormed over to her and whispered, "It's okay. He's gone. I won't do that again. I promise."

She thought about the window. She sniffled and said, "I don't know if I can do what I said. I don't have the courage."

"I don't want you to do it. I don't think they'll kill us if you get away, but I'm sure they'll kill you if you don't."

She started sobbing again, a low, desperate sound. "We're going to die."

He awkwardly brushed her shoulder with his bound hands. "Shh. Don't think about that. Focus on anything else. Something to draw strength."

She closed her eyes and rubbed her necklace. She pictured her uncle's friend. An executioner who would eradicate every single one of their despicable, cowardly captors. A hunter she dared hope was searching for her right this minute.

18

As if I were slow, the airman manning the gate handed me my pass and repeated, "You can go in, but the lady and the taxi cab must remain out here."

I said, "What sense does that make? If I'm cleared, then I'll vouch for them."

He said, "I can give you a pass based on your ID, but you can't sponsor her since you don't work here and you're not active duty. And his cab company isn't on an approved list to enter."

"So what am I supposed to do? I need to get to the NATO Fusion Centre."

"Sergeant Major, you'll have to walk."

"Walk from here? Seriously?"

I knew fighting the idiotic rules of the US Department of Defense would get me nowhere. Actually, I was surprised to see the front gate of Molesworth being manned by US Air Force in the first place. I figured it would be manned by British soldiers. They'd let me in because of my retired military ID card but wouldn't let in anyone else, which, once again, aggravated the hell out of me for not getting a rental car.

According to the dumbass rules of DoD, if I had a rental, I could drive it in—albeit leaving Jennifer at the gate—but since we'd taken a cab, I was out of luck.

Jennifer and I had argued the point, and I'd eventually backed down when I couldn't find the air base on Google Maps. She'd said a British cabdriver from Cambridge had a hell of a lot better chance of locating the base than we did driving around the English countryside and asking questions at every intersection. I'd relented, then we'd paid the damn cabbie to drive around and ask questions. I guess we paid for the accent. Eventually, we'd passed through the old, World War II outer barbwire gates and driven up to the security checkpoint, only to find that they wouldn't let us in. Which was becoming par for the course on this little adventure. We were getting nowhere.

After finishing in Kylie's dorm room, Blair had taken us to the Eagle, which had turned out to be one of the coolest places I'd ever seen—a pure English pub with a history that made it hallowed ground in my mind. According to the sign outside, over a pint two scientists had solved the riddle of DNA, but what meant much more to me were the names on the ceiling put there by the smoke of a cigarette lighter. All were from American or British bomber crews from World War II, left in between missions over the Continent. I couldn't help but wonder how many had drunk a pint, left their name, then never returned.

One day, I'd be back under better circumstances.

We'd talked to a manager, but as could be expected, he had no idea about Kylie or anyone else on the night in question. To make matters worse, when I asked about waiters or waitresses to interview, I'd been told that all orders were placed at the bar, and the food was sent out by table number. They had no system where a waiter or waitress would remember anyone for any length of time.

I'd walked about the interior, seeing the various little pillbox rooms and the outdoor patio, and knew I was out of luck. Without knowing exactly where she'd had dinner, there was no way I could find someone who would remember Kylie. The place was just too big and chopped up, with nooks and crannies all over. But she'd been here, of that I was sure.

Standing on the patio, staring at the gate to the Corpus Christi campus and trying to find a thread, I was about to throw my hands up when Jennifer had said, "Pike, look above the gate."

I did, and saw a CCTV camera. I then went through the area again, looking for surveillance. They had a camera in almost every room. The entire place was wired. I went back to the manager, pointing at the camera over the bar.

"How long do you keep a recording of this place?"

He said, "I have no idea, but it's irrelevant. I can't show them to you."

"Why not? I'm not looking to get you in trouble for anything. I'm just trying to find a girl."

He held his hands up. "I know. It's a privacy thing. The owner won't show them without a court order. I've seen it in the past. I don't even know how to if I wanted. We don't keep tapes here. It's all contracted out."

"You mean like it's downloaded somewhere else?"

"Well, yeah. Like the cloud. The surveillance company maintains the cameras and keeps the footage. It's all done over the Internet. We don't have it here. It gives the owner a firewall when folks like you come asking."

Which was very good news. It was a firewall, all right, but one I could penetrate with the Taskforce, saving me from cracking this guy in the head and stealing old-school VHS tapes.

"What's the name of the company?"

"Sentinel Security. Out of London."

We left at that point, knowing we wouldn't get anything else, and drove to Molesworth to explore the mysterious visitor's pass, only now I was going to have to hoof it to figure *that* out. Proving yet again how little sway a retired commando had.

The gate guard saw my expression and repeated, "Sergeant Major, if you want to go inside the post, you'll need to park the taxi in the visitor area and walk."

I shook my head in frustration and said, "Okay, damn it. Where is the Fusion Cell?"

"You see that golden dragon? Just walk around to the right . . ."

He continued blathering on and I continued to get aggravated. Eventually, I just waved the cab forward, told Jennifer I'd be right back, and started walking at a pace that I hoped would let off the anger.

The post ended up being very, very small. Originally full of ICBM silos, it had been dedicated entirely to nuclear counterforce strikes during the Cold War, but now it was a collection of intelligence fusion cells for NATO and the newly minted Africa Command, or AFRICOM.

There were no barracks or commissaries. Just a select few buildings that did top secret intelligence activities. It didn't take long to find the NATO cell. All I had to look for were the flags of all the member countries flying in the breeze.

A squat, four-story building with few windows, painted a dull yellow—or maybe white that had faded—it had a fence surrounding its compound with a turnstile not unlike ones you see at amusement parks or New York City subways. A seven-foot thing with multiple rotating bars to prevent entry. Next to it was a phone. Being unannounced, and knowing I was on camera, I picked it up.

"Can I help you?"

"Yes. I'm looking for Tech Sergeant Nicholas Seacrest."

"And you are?"

"Nephilim Logan. Retired sergeant major, US Army."

"Purpose of your visit?"

"I have some questions for him regarding a missing female."

With the enormous scandals going on with sexual assaults in the Department of Defense, I hoped mentioning the word *female* would cause the gates to open. Everyone was so afraid of being accused of not cracking down on anything smacking of sexual harassment, I figured I'd get in just so they could see my face. Instead, I heard, "Do you know the office?"

"No. He's a weatherman in the US Air Force. I need to talk to him."

"Stand by."

I waited for a good ten minutes, then saw an entourage headed my way, which made me wonder if they'd had a few sexual assault problems with this Nicholas Seacrest in the past. There were four people, two Air Force and two Army. As they got closer, I saw the lowest rank was a major.

What the hell?

They reached the gate and a bird colonel named Fairchild did the talking.

"Who are you?"

"I told the desk, I'm Sergeant Major Nephilim Logan. I'm here to see a Nicholas Seacrest."

"Why do you want to see him?"

"He was the last known person with a female who's come up missing. I'm trying to locate her."

"Well, he can't talk. Sorry. He had nothing to do with any female."

"How would you know? You haven't even asked her name. Do you know all of the comings and goings of the men here?"

"Sergeant Major, he had *nothing* to do with any female. Period. He's on a classified assignment."

"Come on, sir. I'm not a *New York Times* reporter. I've got top secret clearance. Stop the bullshit. I just want to talk to him. I'll find him here or at his barracks."

"You won't find him at all. He's on leave. He went back to the United States for thirty days."

"I thought he was on a classified assignment?"

I got a blank stare.

I asked, "When did he fly?"

"That's classified."

The answer tripped a trigger he didn't want to see. I slapped the bars, causing them to jump back. I shouted, "Are you shitting me? Open this fucking gate. Right now."

Colonel Fairchild's face went from amazement to anger at the outburst. He said, "Sergeant Major, I don't know where you've worked in the past, but I will not tolerate such behavior. You will leave here right now, or I will call base security. Tech Sergeant Seacrest is on leave. Period."

I stared at him for a moment, wanting to rip his throat out. I looked at the men to his left and right, then turned away without another word.

By the time I reached the cab I was in a fine mood. I told the driver to hang on a minute, then pulled out my phone, moving out of earshot of the cabbie. Jennifer exited the car and asked what had happened. I said, "Nothing. Absolutely nothing."

She said, "What's that mean?"

I dialed and said, "It means we need some help."

I waited for the connection, fuming, and Jennifer said nothing more, knowing she'd get the answer from my call. After a few seconds, I got Kurt on the phone, his voice sounding tinny from the encryption.

"Tell me you found her."

"No, sir, I haven't. But I will with a couple of requests."

"What? What do you have?"

"First, I need all surveillance video from a place called the Eagle here in Cambridge. It's held on a server for a company called Sentinel in London."

I heard nothing, then, "You want me to hack it?"

I knew what was going through his head. I was telling him to use US assets to penetrate a foreign company for personal business. He wasn't asking because he was unsure of my request. He was running the ramifications through his head. Deciding how far he would go to save his niece. Deciding where his boundaries lay. As the commander of the Taskforce, he had the capability. Now it was only a question of whether he would use it.

I said, "Yes, sir. That's exactly what I'm asking. The Eagle is her last known location. I need the footage to see who she was with."

He said, "You mean she was on a date with someone? That's why you want it?"

"Yeah. And that brings up the second thing. I think I know who she was with, but I'm getting the runaround by the military here."

"Military? What do you mean?"

"I think she went on a date to the Eagle with a Tech Sergeant Seacrest from Molesworth, but they're telling me he's on leave. And they're doing it in a weird way. I got a full-court press from a bunch of Chairborne Rangers when I asked about him. All top brass."

I heard nothing but breathing. I said, "Sir? You there?"

"What was the name?"

"Technical Sergeant Nicholas Seacrest. He's apparently a weatherman here. I need to talk to him. I need you to put some pressure on the NIFC."

I heard an explosion of air, then, "Jesus Christ. Kylie's been taken by terrorists."

I said, "What the hell are you talking about?"

"Nick Seacrest is the vice president's son."

19

Kurt hung up the phone, thinking through the ramifications. He heard his name called and saw George Wolffe at the entrance to the West Wing of the White House, where he'd left him when his cell had rung.

"We're going to be late. I thought you wanted to slip in unnoticed to this meeting. You keep stalling, and you're going to end up interrupting the briefing with all eyes on you."

Kurt waved him over, out of earshot of the security at the entrance. He handed George the simple manila folder in his hand. "I'm thinking of skipping this one and sending you in alone."

"Whoa. Not a good idea. The president called it. You're not briefing or anything." He held up the folder. "All you have to do is hand this to Palmer."

Exactly as George had predicted, the meetings had escalated outside of the small circle that knew about the Taskforce. The president had grown tired with the stovepipe and separate meetings and had scheduled an update briefing in the White House Situation Room. In attendance would be every big shot in the US government, from Homeland Security to the "Gang of Eight" from the House and Senate Intelligence Committees. The majority were not read onto the existence of the Taskforce—much less its activities—so Kurt had been tasked with providing a hard-copy situation report to be hand-carried to Alexander Palmer, the national security advisor. After that, he was supposed to be nothing more than a fly on the wall at the back of the room.

The report itself summarized current Taskforce operations for the missing hostages, which was to say it was a single sheet of paper delineating very little. The only clear lead they had was a ferry receipt from Morocco, but so far Knuckles had turned up zero.

Kurt said, "That call was from Pike. He's found something out about Kylie. He has a thread."

"That's great. Let him work it, and let's get our asses into the briefing room before it fills up and someone wants to question who we are."

As the national security advisor, Palmer had given them cover as members of the NSC watch team, a thirty-man cell that maintained 24/7 operations inside the Situation Room, but that cover would work only if they were at the back, in the cheap seats. Not if they interrupted the briefing as it was in progress, like a couple of prima donnas.

Kurt said, "George, the thread runs through the vice president's son."

George's mouth opened and nothing came out. Kurt didn't wait for him to speak, giving him what little he knew.

George took in the information, then said, "We have to tell Palmer."

Kurt shook his head in frustration. "How? I can't brief in that room, and the information isn't on this hard copy. I'm not even sure it's real. On top of that, it's fucking *Pike*. How am I going to brief the Oversight Council that the one lead we have is from a man they expressly forbade me from using on Taskforce operations? They'll fire me on the spot."

George smiled. "No they won't. Not if it pans out. Nobody argues with success."

"That's just it. That ass-hat Billings will blow a gasket and demand something stupid, like recalling Pike and throwing other assets at the problem. They'll screw up the one lead we have. They'll get Kylie killed. There won't be any success."

George heard the words, now seeing what was really weighing on Kurt's mind. He said, "Okay, look, we let Pike explore. Get the surveillance tapes, see if it's real. If it is, we redirect someone else. Maybe Knuckles. Let them start the chase and then brief the council. Control the mission and preempt any shenanigans. Either way, if it's real, we have to brief."

Kurt started walking toward the entrance to the West Wing, saying, "What a mess."

George fell into step behind him and said, "Well, I have to hand it to you. Sending Pike was a stroke of genius. That guy is a magnet for finding bad things."

They signed in at the entrance, received their badges, and wound their way through the lobby, skirting by the groups starting to form outside the Situation Room, Kurt recognizing several faces as guests from Sunday news shows. Men and women he'd never met in real life. George took a seat at the back while Kurt walked up to Palmer, interrupting his discussion with the director of the CIA.

Palmer took the folder and said, "Anything good?"

"No, sir. Nothing much at all."

He simply nodded, dismissing Kurt to sit with George. Kurt walked away, a feeling of deceit flowing through him, causing conflicting emotions. On the one hand, he wanted any lead on Kylie to pan out. On the other, a part of him hoped it didn't involve the vice president's son.

Lost in his thoughts, he failed to register President Warren entering the room. George elbowed him, and they stood, along with everyone else. To Kurt's surprise, the vice president followed behind. The sight of him brought another twinge of regret for keeping silent.

President Warren said, "Have a seat. Let's get this going."

This time, it was Alexander Palmer himself giving the briefing. He started by stating where they stood on the search, which was basically nowhere. All the investigative effort had come up with very little. The murder of the secretary of defense's son was a bust, with the command in Honduras stating he was supposed to be on duty, and since he'd basically gone AWOL, they had no thread at all. The information on the twins was no better. They had simply disappeared without a trace, and there wasn't the faintest clue as to whether they were still on Okinawa or not. Still alive or not. The only lead was the Morocco ferry receipt from England related to the VP's son, but that, too, had produced little.

Palmer finished the section and the president said, "That's all we've got? The most powerful government on earth and we come up with nothing?"

Kurt had to physically stop himself from rising up at that point.

Palmer saved him. "No, sir. All it will take is one break, and this thing could crack open completely. And we might have that break."

He flipped a slide and said, "We received more communication from the terrorists, which is good. Every time they talk to us, they open themselves up to being found."

The president said, "So we got something from this communication? A possible location? The name of the group?"

"Well, no. Not exactly. They once again masked their ISP." Palmer tilted his head at the side and said, "We don't know where it came from, but here it is:"

We could keep these men forever, much like you have at Guantánamo Bay and your secret prisons, but we are not like you. Lives matter. Even these lives. In the words of the prophet, ". . . if any one slew a person— unless it be for murder or for spreading mischief in the land—it would be as if he slew the whole people: and if any one saved a life, it would be as if he saved the life of the whole people." You are the ones spreading mischief in our lands, but these men are mere puppets of your blasphemous regime. How much are they worth to you? How much are you willing to pay?

President Warren said, "So here we go. Let me guess, get all US persons out of the Middle East?"

"Actually, no. In this case, they're talking about real money."

Kerry Bostwick, the D/CIA, said, "What the hell? They want to ransom them? That makes no sense whatsoever."

The SECDEF said, "What's the price?"

"One hundred thousand Bitcoins."

Secretary Billings said, "What the hell is a Bitcoin?"

20

Alexander Palmer looked to a woman on his right. She rose and said, "Sir, I'm Nancy Phelps of the FBI's financial crimes division. To answer your question, Bitcoin is a form of digital currency that is fairly anonymous. It has no physical, tangible properties, like a dollar bill, but it is worth money and can be exchanged for cash. It's a way for the terrorists to get something of value without us being able to catch them. They want to prevent us from setting up any traps by avoiding hard currency. No wire transfers, no banks, no suitcases full of cash to pass off. Basically, they give us a digital address and we transfer the 'coins,' all done over the Internet."

President Warren said, "Can we track it?"

She said, "Not if they set up certain protocols. It's not like wiring money, with all the regulations involved. The Bitcoins will simply go to an address on the Internet. If their current expertise is any indication, we won't know where that is. But when they exchange it for real money, we might be able to track that. Every Bitcoin transaction is maintained in a log, so when those coins resurface, we'll know they're the ones we paid, and we can then possibly get a real address to work back from. Sooner or later, if they want to use them on anything besides novelty sites on the Web, they have to have a bank account that takes real money. And that account will be tied to a name."

"So if we give them the coins, they can't ever use them? Surely they know that."

"Well, there are ways around the problem. There are mixing sites that will take your coins and intermingle them with others."

"Speak English, please."

She paused for a moment, gathering her thoughts, then said, "Say you marked a bunch of quarters, then gave them to me. Every time I spent one of the marked quarters, someone would know. Now say I want to guarantee my anonymity. I get together with fifty or a hundred other folks with quarters, and we put them all in a bag and shake it up. When I'm done, I simply count out the number of coins I put in the bag. What I end up with is washed quarters. The mixing sites work the same way, only digitally. When they're done, our Bitcoins will be spread out all over the place. We could track them to the mixing site, but little else."

President Warren said, "Why on earth would such a site exist?"

"Because criminals use Bitcoins. Just like these terrorists."

Billings said, "Well, why don't we just make up a bunch of Bitcoins? It's all digits, right? Hell, give 'em a million of them."

Nancy smiled and said, "It doesn't work that way. It *is* digital, but it has a real architecture and backbone behind it. We can't counterfeit Bitcoins. One other thing, the actual dollar amount fluctuates wildly. Currently, one Bitcoin is worth about five hundred US dollars, so he's basically asking for about fifty million. Tomorrow, that could be a hundred million or one million, depending on price fluctuations."

President Warren said, "Can we get a hundred thousand of them? Without spiking what we're doing and causing questions?"

"It will be hard and involve setting up multiple different accounts that purchase small amounts from different exchanges, but we could do it. It will require time."

Kerry Bostwick said, "Wait, wait, before we even go down that road, how do we know this is for real? I cannot believe that an Islamic group would ransom such valuable hostages back to us. It makes no sense. I mean, look at the chain of events: First they talk about stopping our drone attacks, then they kill one of the hostages to prove they're serious, then they tell us they believe in the sanctity of life and we can pay to get them back? How do we know this message is from the group that's got our people?"

Palmer said, "Good question. They also gave us an account and password for an application called Snapchat. They stated they would tell us when to log in."

President Warren looked at the ceiling and said, "Do I need to bring my daughter in here for this? What the hell is Snapchat?"

"It's a picture-sharing application. Basically, you can send an image or video that has a finite time before it deletes itself. You take a picture, send it to a friend, and it disappears seconds later." He coughed and said, "Apparently, it's primarily used to send naughty photos between young people. We think they're going to use it as proof of life."

"So once again, we can't do anything with it? Only get a couple of seconds to analyze it for clues before it self-destructs like a *Mission: Impossible* movie?"

"No. They may have outsmarted themselves this time. We can intercept the picture and do a lot with it, depending on how it was taken and transmitted. It's a mobile application, so it'll be coming from a cell phone, which opens up a host of possibilities."

"Good. About time we get a break. Okay, here's what I want. Continue the full-court press with the units in the field. Something may break." He looked at Nancy. "In the meantime, start buying Bitcoins anonymously. Get up to what they want."

Kerry started to protest, and President Warren held up his hand. "I'm just covering all bases. Finally, get whatever experts we have on standby to receive this Snapchat. I want everything associated with that picture analyzed when it comes in."

Kerry said, "I'm assuming we've already bled the Bitcoin account for any information?"

Palmer nodded. "Yeah. We talked to the company."

Now jotting in a notebook, President Warren snapped his head up at the comment.

Palmer said, "Don't worry, there aren't any fingerprints. We went through the FBI on a routine check. Anyway, it didn't do any good. The account was created from an ISP in Shanghai, which is to say it was spoofed. No help."

President Warren said, "Listen up, everyone. Palmer's last comment reminded me of something. The circle of trust on this thing is getting bigger and bigger, which means a leak is just around the corner. That cannot happen. This isn't about politics, and it isn't about egos." He looked at the vice president, then Easton Clute, the chair of the Senate Select Committee on Intelligence. "There are lives at stake here, and if word gets out to the press, our options will be severely limited." He paused, looking from person to person around the room. "Does everyone understand?"

Kurt saw the powerful first tier sitting around the conference table nod their heads, the various staffers in the back row with him doing the same, and wondered how many times a sitting president had said similar words only to read about something the next day in the newspaper.

One man raised his hand. Kurt recognized the secretary of Homeland Security.

President Warren said, "What is it, Gerald?"

"Sir, I was going to bring this up later, but now's as good a time as any. What are we supposed to say for press inquiries? The reason I ask is that Grant Breedlove contacted me today. He wants to talk. He didn't say what it was about, only that he was working on a story. But he seemed pretty sure he had something explosive and gave the usual threats about posting the story without my input."

Kurt heard the name and inwardly groaned. Grant Breedlove was an investigative reporter for *The Washington Post* and was very, very good at his job. He was Kurt's greatest fear regarding Taskforce exposure. Somehow the man managed to find sources in the deepest, darkest places of the national security architecture—and those people always talked.

Kerry Bostwick said, "Put a bullet in his head."

The table gave a polite chuckle, and President Warren cut it short. "We already have reporters circling? Jesus Christ, if I find out who's talking, I'm going to put a bullet in *their* head."

Palmer said, "Nobody's talking. He's just got his ear to the ground. He's heard about all of these meetings. He's sniffed a story but doesn't know what it is. He won't publish without comment. Why he went to DHS is a mystery."

Kerry said, "Because the leak is in Homeland. That's why. Someone's talked. That's what always happens. They get a whiff of blood and then start swimming for the carcass floating in the water. He's smelled the blood downstream and is now trying to find the body."

Gerald bristled. "Nobody in my office talked. I'm the only one read onto this."

"Bullshit. Someone in your office—a contact of his—has pieced together something and fed it to him. It might be solely based on your schedule, but make no mistake, Grant is good. And honestly, half the time he listens. Maybe we bring him into the fold. He won't want to get anyone killed."

Vice President Hannister spoke up for the first time. "No way. We let him get his nose in the tent, and we're screwed. It'll be just like you say. He might keep his word, but his cubicle mates will then start sniffing. It'll blow, and my son will die."

Easton Clute nodded his head vigorously. "I agree. He can't find out. My son and daughter are worth more than someone's scoop."

President Warren sat back and rubbed his eyes, saying, "The wonders of a free and open press." He pulled his hand away and said, "Meet him. See what it's about but don't look too eager. You agree immediately, and he'll think he's near the body. Drag him out with mundane stuff, then finally agree, as if it's a huge favor. Then find out what he's talking about. Hopefully it's just some stupid noncontroversy. Drones on the border or some other bullshit. If it is, let him run with it. Keep him focused on another story. Hell, it might work in our favor. He breaks a story I don't care about, and the slavering twenty-four-hour news cycle will pick it up and go crazy, letting us work the real problem."

Palmer said, "And if it isn't?"

"Then we deal with it. But let me make this perfectly clear: Nobody in this room had better be keeping secrets from me. You hear anything, and that includes from the press, I want to know."

He looked around the room, catching Kurt's eye. Kurt nodded, once again feeling adrift. Torn between his desire to save his niece and his loyalty to the administration. But the president was only one man. As much as Kurt trusted him, he knew Warren would defer to the "expertise" in the room, and Kylie would die.

Kurt glanced at the secretary of defense, the man's grief radiating out like heat in a sauna. He focused on the vice president and recognized the same visceral fear that was eating at his own soul.

Come on, Pike. Work your magic. I need it now more than ever.

21

Kevin Fegan pulled a sheet of paper out of the printer and handed it to Seamus. "This is a paper wallet. It doesn't look like much, but it'll hold all of the Bitcoins."

Seamus looked at the printout. In the center was an orange rectangle with a QR code. Sticking out of the end of the rectangle was a smaller tail with another QR code. He said, "I'm supposed to trust this thing?"

"Better than online. Someone could hack your account, or we could be tracked. This way, you can move the money anywhere you want, between different accounts, and it's air-gapped."

"How does it work?"

"Once we get the Bitcoins in our online wallet, we scan that big QR code and simply send the coins to that address. To remove them, we set up a new online wallet and scan the smaller code."

"Why's it shaped like this?"

"That's just the Web design. You're supposed to cut it out and fold it up like some stupid origami thing. Turn it into a 'real' wallet. All that really matters are the QR codes. You could cut just those out if you wanted, but make no mistake—if you lose those codes, it's the same as losing a real wallet. Your Bitcoins are gone forever."

Seamus said, "This is the weirdest crap I've ever seen. You sure Bitcoins are real and untraceable?"

"Oh, they're real all right, and after I send them through the Bitcoin Fog website, they'll be clean. The only hang-up is that we'll have to do small amounts each time. Like no more than ten thousand dollars' worth."

"That's not a problem. How long will it take the Americans to come up with the Bitcoins?"

"They'll want to keep it secret, so they'll be buying them in small lots. To not spike, I'd say a few days. A week at the most."

Peering over Kevin's shoulder, Colin said, "All of that sounds good, but this'll only work if we stay alive to spend it. Tricking the Americans into thinking a Muslim group took the hostages will only last as long as they never talk. You said before that wouldn't happen, but killing them won't stop the hunt for us. It's a very dangerous game."

"I never said *I* was going to kill them."

Colin crossed his arms. He said, "I think it's high time you let us in on your secret plan."

Seamus looked at Kevin. He nodded in agreement. Seamus considered, then said, "Okay. I suppose you deserve to know the whole scope of what we're about to do. Remember our contacts in Croatia? The ones who got us the weapons a few years ago?"

"Yeah. Muslims. I didn't trust them at all."

"Right. Well, trust or not, they've connected me to some Somali expats on the continent who are willing to make a trade. A group called Al-Shabaab. They're going to end up with the hostages, which I assume they'll use to actually stop the American drone strikes in Somalia. I don't really care. What's critical is that a real Islamic group is going to end up with them, so, like the Bitcoins Kevin was just talking about, we'll be washed."

Colin tugged on his beard, thinking. He said, "How are you going to get the Americans to pay? I mean, without giving them the hostages?"

"Oh, they'll pay. We have all the leverage. They might not give it all to us, but we'll get enough to fund the coming fight."

Kevin said, "You talked about a trade. Are the Somalis paying as well?"

"Yes. But not in money."

Here Seamus paused, knowing his next words might not be well received, given Colin's apprehension about being hunted.

Kevin said, "What then?"

Seamus said, "Tell me, why did our ancestors take up arms against the British?"

Colin's face soured. "Spare me the history quiz."

"Just answer."

Kevin said, "Because of the famine. Because of the way they treated us, letting us starve to death. Because they put a boot to our head for centuries. Because we wanted to be free."

"Exactly. And that's the problem with freeing the final six counties. The British have learned. They give in with a dribble of political theater and we lap it up like kittens. We need the boot to return to kindle the fire of the population."

Colin said, "What does that mean?"

"The Somalis will conduct an attack that will rival the '93 Bishopsgate bombing. We'll take credit for it. Because we won't have any direct fingerprints, there will be no way to find us, but the RIRA will declare it our work."

Kevin said, "And? That's it?"

"No. What do you think the Brits will do? I'll tell you what: They'll bring back the Black and Tans. Belfast will turn into a police state. They'll start kicking in doors, conducting extrajudicial killings, torture, you name it. Just like they used to. And the people will see the truth."

Colin raised his voice, saying, "Just because of a single attack? How could you keep this secret from us? It'll make us hunted men. We won't do anything but spend our time running."

"The attack will be very spectacular, but no. It alone will not suffice. It is just the fuse. We are the bomb. We are the vanguard. I have no intention of running. We'll take our money from the hostages and start a new front. The final one. We will end up in the history books alongside the gallant men of the Easter Rebellion. And yes, some of us will die."

Colin's face grew dark, his hands clenched. Bigger and stronger than Seamus, he leaned forward. "Why didn't you tell us this before, when we were laying the groundwork? When we were building the infrastructure to capture the hostages? Or are Kevin and I the last to know?"

What Seamus lacked in physical prowess, he more than made up in intensity. He matched Colin's glare and said, "I'm telling you now. You want out, feel free to drive back to Cork. Go get drunk in the pubs until you puke. I'm giving you a chance to unite the land. To *do* something with your life."

Seamus knew he was at a crossroads. He would either become the undisputed leader of the new war, or his cell of men would splinter. He waited, the tension thick in the room. It was broken by a cell phone ringing, one of several on the windowsill. Kevin picked it up, saw the number, and said, "It's our contact at Molesworth."

Seamus took the phone without looking, maintaining his staring contest with Colin. The bearded man broke first, turning away as if the conversation didn't matter. Seamus smiled and brought the phone to his ear. "What's up?"

"You told me to call if something strange happened."

"Yeah? So what happened?"

The contact was a janitor who worked inside the NATO fusion cell. He'd been the man who'd provided most of the tactical information about Nick Seacrest's pattern of life.

"We had a man here asking about Seacrest."

"You've had a platoon of men doing that. We expected Scotland Yard and the FBI to be all over the command."

"No, no. This guy wanted to *talk* to Seacrest. He had no idea he was missing. On top of that, he wasn't cleared. He was a walk-in."

The words alarmed Seamus. Strange was right. "Has the disappearance leaked? Was he press?"

"No. He's retired military. Even with the investigation, the command's managed to keep the disappearance secret."

"What did he want to talk to Seacrest about?"

"I don't know. The man wasn't ever let in. Whatever he told them, he did it at the gate. They turned him away. I got a copy of his visitor's pass, though. If you want to follow up. It has his name and where he's staying."

"Yeah. Yeah, I want it. Send it to me."

He hung up, wondering if it was a complete coincidence. Even if it was, he'd put too much time and effort into this project not to be sure. He picked up a different phone and manipulated it, dialing his brother in Brussels using the Internet instead of the cell network.

"Braden, it's Seamus."

He heard a laugh. "That damn VOIP app comes up with a different number every time you call. I always expect it to be a telemarketer."

"How goes the planning?"

"Good. These Serbs are no joke, and the lasses they're using for the recce are pure blades. I don't know how they find them, but they turn heads."

"And the diversion?"

"I took the explosives and pre-positioned them. They're ready to be primed. The packages are tucked away with Clooney and Smythe. They're just sitting around waiting on me to return."

"That's what they get for botching the North Carolina capture. They get to play backup again. The Serbs okay with the plan?"

"Yeah. If this diversion goes off like we promised, they're more than okay. The target is pretty prominent, and they're going to need all the help they can get diverting the French police."

"How soon do they want to go?"

"They're in no rush. Why all the questions?"

"I need their help."

He explained what he'd been told minutes earlier.

"You want them to break some legs? They won't be too keen on that."

"Tell them the man is about to screw up their heist. Tell them it will affect the diversion, and anyway, all I want to do is confirm what this guy is up to. No contact. Just follow and report."

Seamus heard nothing for a moment, then, "Okay. I'll give it a go."

"Get them on a train to the UK. They need to move fast. The only handle I have is the DoubleTree hotel in Cambridge, and I don't know how long he'll stay. Tonight for sure, but that's all I've got."

Braden agreed and Seamus broached something he didn't want to. He said, "You did that right, didn't you? Was there anything you left? Any clue?"

"Fuck no, Seamus. Your damn information proved incorrect. He was supposed to be alone. Instead he met that girl. I was forced to take them both."

Seamus said, "Okay, okay. I had to ask. There's too much at stake."

"I did it right. Left the ferry clue and cleansed the site. It isn't me."

"I believe you. Remember why we're doing this. Get the Serbs moving."

His brother said good-bye the same way he always did. "For Brian."

Seamus replied, "For Brian. Let's make these fuckers pay."

22

Captain McKinley Clute heard the footsteps coming across the floor and he sat up, trying to see through a small hole in his hood. He managed to cock it just right, flipping his head to keep it in place, but caused a string of drool to fly up from the cloth gag in his mouth.

He stared at the door, hearing the footsteps approach, wondering if it would be his or Kaelyn's that was opened.

It was his.

He heard the boots clomp across the floor and tensed his stomach, curling into a ball. In the past, they'd kicked him just because they could, and he'd taken to protecting himself whenever they approached.

His hood was ripped off, the command "Rise" echoing in his ears. He blinked his eyes, getting used to the light, and stood. This could be either good or bad.

Sometimes he met Kaelyn in the central den to eat—the only time he saw her—both being forced to their knees, hands tied behind their backs, a rabid bit of punching and shouting to keep him off-balance. He'd begun to believe it was just harassment, designed to ensure he didn't entertain the notion of fleeing, but the pain was real all the same.

He shuffled through the door, hands behind his back and head bowed. He reached the den of the apartment and saw his sister on her knees, looking up at him in concern, her mouth gagged like his. The sight brought a sense of relief, for one because he knew he wasn't getting a beating, and two, because he could see she was okay, even with the cloth cinched tight into her mouth.

A hand was placed on his shoulder and he was made to kneel like

Kaelyn. The flex ties were switched, with their ankles bound together and their hands released, then the gags removed. A bowl was placed in front of each of them, some sort of oatmeal-like gruel with the color and consistency of wet concrete.

The man who'd led out McKinley said, "Eat. Fifteen minutes."

The man turned away and sat on a rusted metal chair, the only furniture in the room. He pushed the chair onto its hind legs, the back leaning into the wall precariously. He crossed his arms, staring at both of them. The other man stood inside Kaelyn's doorframe behind them, out of sight, making McKinley want to protect his kidneys from an unseen kick.

McKinley dipped the spoon into the paste and took a bite, wincing at the acrid smell but knowing it would be the only sustenance he was given. He brushed Kaelyn's arm on the way down, receiving no punishment, even though he knew they'd seen it.

It confirmed something in his mind. He'd put some serious thought into their captivity, not having anything else to occupy his time, and while it was alternately brutal and barely tolerable, he was sure it was all scripted. There was a reason they were separated for twenty-three hours a day. It was to instill a sense of hopelessness and prevent any collusion, the same reason they spent their days in the dark with a hood on their head. His beatings appeared random but were designed solely to convince him that his captors were on the ragged edge and prone to snapping at the slightest provocation. To prevent him from even thinking about escape. But they never touched Kaelyn.

The gags were the final proof in his theory. They'd never had them crammed in their mouths for the entire trip, through hours on boats, planes, and cars, sometimes drugged, but most of the time not. They'd been subjected to the indignity only when they were first tied up in the apartment, the drool running freely from the cloth to the floor. Which meant one thing: The captors were afraid of the damage the noise would do if they started screaming. That, along with the beatings to keep him cowed, told him they were very, very close to other people who had no idea what was going on. Perhaps in the apartment next door.

He didn't know where they were, not even the country, having woken up in the trunk of a car and been brought into the building in the dark, but he was sure it wasn't some murky safe house full of thugs. He'd been forced to walk up four floors, and he now believed he was surrounded by innocent civilians. People he might be able to contact, if only to get them to investigate. To call the police.

He surveyed the room again, focusing on the locks of the front door. He saw the bolt lock was worked by a key and felt his hopes dim. He couldn't break through that, and they always kept it bolted. He surreptitiously glanced around, eating his cement, and realized something was missing.

The explosives were gone.

The first time he'd eaten in the room, he'd seen packages of RDX stacked against the wall, the white crystal spilling out of one waxed paper container, the chemical name CYCLOTRIMETHYLENETRINITRAMINE clearly stenciled on the outside, something he'd seen in predeployment training for IEDs in Afghanistan. A powerful explosive, it had been invented in World War II and was the weapon of choice for terrorists.

Next to the packages had been an assortment of equipment that would have made his Marine Corps IED instructors shiver: cell phones, electronic wiring, detonation cord, and containers designed to camouflage and increase the fragmentation of the blast. Things that had made him wonder if he was the bait for an ambush. The goat tied to the tree, waiting for the tiger to enter so it could be killed.

The fact that he'd been allowed to see it at all meant that they had no intention of him or Kaelyn being a witness, able to report what they'd experienced. No intention of them surviving whatever was planned. The goat never survived, whether the tiger escaped or not.

Now the explosives were all gone. And they were waiting to be chained to a tree.

23

Lost in thought, running through my conversation with Kurt, I had stopped counting the stops in the London Underground. Jennifer brought me back to the present, saying, "This is us."

I saw the sign for Sloane Square and stood up, following her out the door along with a flow of other people. We exited to street level, and I got my bearings, saying, "It's over this way."

We started walking down Sloane Street in silence, Jennifer recognizing my mood and letting me think. We reached Royal Hospital Road, and I could see the Royal Hospital Chelsea in the distance. Home to the Chelsea Pensioners—retired veterans of the British military—it was not unlike our own VA system in the States, although it was much, much older. And also my last clue.

Before I'd gone to sleep the night before, Kurt had managed to hack into the servers of Sentinel Security and retrieve the footage from the Eagle. He'd sent it to me, along with a detailed report that basically said there was no evidence of Nick Seacrest. Kylie was there with a man, but the camera wasn't positioned in such a way to get positive ID. All they could see was the back of his head. The tone of the email made it seem as if he was somewhat relieved, but he'd sent it to me anyway.

With Jennifer, I'd stayed up for hours reviewing the footage, and he was right. Along with the video package he'd sent the official military photo of Nick Seacrest, and I couldn't match the face with the person sitting with Kylie. She'd been with someone, but it was impossible to positively ID the man. I'd stopped trying and taken a look at the footage from a different perspective—surveying for anyone who appeared inter-ested in the couple. And had found something.

Kylie had sat outside, on the patio, and was clearly close to the man she was with, touching his hand and laughing at what he said, which I know must have broken Kurt's heart to watch. Her date returned the gestures, whispering in her ear and laughing at her comments, silent on the tape. Jennifer had turned away at that point, knowing how the night ended. For me, it brought a feeling of impotence. I wanted to reach through the camera and tell her to leave. To go back to campus. To prevent what was going to happen.

I'd refocused, studying the patrons around her. Most were clearly there solely for the pub, the tables full of college kids and tourists. One small table, though, caught my eye. It sat right behind her, in full view of the camera, and held a single man. He was drinking coffee and doing nothing but smoking a cigarette. Twenty-three minutes into the tape, he was met by another man. A rough-looking guy in a black leather jacket and with a three-day beard. They sat together, not talking, just looking. Both smoking cigarettes.

Eventually, the date took Kylie's hand and led her off camera. The two men waited for about thirty seconds and left as well. An indicator.

I went through the footage until I located the outside cameras, trying to identify when the second man had arrived. Eventually, I'd found it. He'd driven up on a beat-down Honda motorcycle, missing fenders and rolling on threadbare tires. But its license plate was in view of the cam-era.

When the two men left, they walked right by the bike. As if it wouldn't be useful for what was about to happen. At least that's what I thought.

I'd called Kurt with another request, the night now growing into morning. With the time difference, it was 8:00 P.M. in the United States, and the Taskforce was going to bed. I'd told him what I had and de-manded that he run the plate.

He'd said, "How? This isn't *The Rockford Files*. I don't have a con-tact in the British police to do that."

"Hack it. Get into their system and give me who owns it. You want to find Kylie or not?"

He exploded. "Don't accuse me of that, damn it! Of course I do." The phone went quiet, then, "You really think this is something? Because I'm about to go deep into the red. I hack UK government systems, and we're treading on dangerous ground."

I said, "I have no idea if it's anything at all. None. But it's all I've got. Those guys were sketchy, and maybe this has nothing to do with the VP, but my gut tells me those two assholes had everything to do with Kylie."

I could almost hear the smoke grinding off the gears in his head. I was asking him to step one foot deeper into the chasm. In the end, he did so, and I got an email about two hours later. It said, *Here you go. Don't do this again. I want Kylie back more than life itself, but I can't use national assets on a whim. If this comes to light, there will be no explanation.* I was all set to ask Kurt for some support, maybe redirecting Knuckles, but that was cut short by the information he'd sent. The bike was registered to a retired British noncommissioned officer. A guy in his eighties now living at the Royal Chelsea Hospital and retirement home. I could see why Kurt was aggravated. It wasn't exactly a smoking gun, but it was all I had. I didn't have the courage to call Kurt back. In truth, I felt a little like an ass.

We entered the grounds of the hospital, the security guard telling us we could visit freely and pointing to an ancient cemetery as a highlight. Jennifer thanked him and we moved down an old stone walkway to the newer infirmary.

The lady at the front desk said, "Are you here for a visitation?"

Unsure of how this worked, I jumped right in, saying, "Yes, I'm here to see Dylan McKee. I understand he's staying here."

She tapped on a computer and said, "Yes. Is he expecting you?"

"No. Not really. It's a surprise."

She smiled as if that were the best thing in the world. She said, "He'll love that."

"You know him?"

"No. Not personally, but they all like surprise visits. Take a seat in the coffee shop. I'll send someone to fetch him."

24

We did so, seeing old warriors talking to family and visitors touring the grounds. Uncomfortable, I asked Jennifer what the hell I was going to say. I mean, I couldn't accuse an eighty-year-old man of kidnapping a US citizen. I was beginning to regret coming here. The only reason I had done so was because of the risk Kurt had taken to get the information. There was no way it would lead anywhere.

She smiled and placed her hand over mine. "This guy is you in forty years. Your blood. Just talk to him. If there's something here, he'll let you know. If not, then make an old veteran happy. Tell war stories."

Her words were exactly what I needed to hear. I relaxed. I wasn't the best at social stuff, as Jennifer would attest, but I had no trouble talking to soldiers.

Eventually an administrative assistant entered the coffee shop, followed by a man who stood ramrod straight. At least six feet tall, he was gaunt, as if eaten by an unknown disease, but his eyes were alive. Blue and full of mischief.

She pointed to us, and he walked over. I stood. "Mr. McKee, I'm Nephilim Logan. From the US."

He said, "Well, I didn't think you were a relative." He shook my hand, then took Jennifer's and actually kissed it.

He sat down and said, "To what do I owe the pleasure of this visit? You Yanks just pick a name out of the reception book?"

Wanting a connection before I accused him of stealing my boss's niece, I said, "Where did you serve? Malaysia? Borneo? Yemen?"

He looked at me with a new light and said, "You're in the American Army."

"Not anymore. But I was."

"You'll find few civilians here who even remember those places. It's all about the blitz in World War II or Iraq and Afghanistan. The fights in between are forgotten."

Jennifer said, "I'm a history buff, but the only thing I can get Pike interested in is a fight. It's the one area he knows more than me."

The old man said, "I was in Malaysia. Back when it was the Wild West, as you Yanks say. We were going to lose it to a bunch of Chinese. I'll tell you, we're fighting the same thing now in Afghanistan. We already quit in Iraq. Nobody listens to the history of the past. . . ."

From there I let him go, and we spent an hour telling war stories. He was a strong man with strong opinions, not unlike any old soldier from the United States. I learned he was from Belfast, Northern Ireland, and that he'd been torn during the troubles there. Being in the British Army had put him on the horns of a dilemma, with many treating him like a traitor. Because of it, he'd spent as much time as he could deployed, moving his family away from their ancestral homeland. The conflict was too close, and the wounds too deep. When his daughter had married, she had returned, but he never did.

I told him about my life in the Army, tours in Iraq and Afghanistan and other places, leaving out the top secret shit I'd done. He told me about his grandson, a man named Brian McKee who had served as well and had been killed in an IED attack in Basra, Iraq, in 2006. Eventually, the stories wound down, and he said, "I appreciate the visit, but you didn't come here to talk about British success in Malaysia."

I said, "No, sir, I didn't." And I laid it out for him, camouflaging the true problem by talking about a stolen rental car. Making up a story about how I had misunderstood the insurance requirements and now was trying to find the car instead of being forced to pay for it. I told him about the video tape, then asked why a motorcycle registered in his name would be in Cambridge.

He said, "I have no idea why. My daughter sometimes uses my name for things. Maybe she did something with a motorcycle, but she's got nothing to do with Cambridge."

Which was no help. I said, "Would she have loaned it out to someone? Given her bike to a friend?"

He thought a moment, then said, "No, but I could see Seamus pulling some crap like this."

"Who is he?"

"My other grandson. Brian's brother, and a waste of good flesh. He's done nothing with his life. Brian joined the military, proud to serve. Seamus refused, going on about our Irish heritage and hating the British military. When Brian was killed in 2006, he went off the deep end, spouting his hatred of the United States for pulling us into Iraq, then talking about joining the Irish Republican Army and fighting the very country I served. I had nothing more to do with him."

The conversation was a curveball but held enough to keep my interest. Enough to see where it went.

I said, "Is he—are you—Catholic?"

The old soldier laughed. "No. That's what's so stupid about Seamus. We're Protestant, but he's convinced he's been shit on by Whitehall. He's just crazy."

I pulled a surveillance photo from the Eagle out of my bag, saying, "Is this Seamus?"

He looked at it and said, "Christ. No. That's Braden. My other grandson. Seamus's got his arse in the mix now?"

I heard the words and felt a spark. Rationally, I knew it was nothing. All I'd done was prove that the bike registration was correct, and the guy riding it was connected to the old soldier, but my sixth sense was telling me I had found a vein to mine. And my sixth sense was rarely wrong.

I said, "I don't know. This is from where the car was taken. It's all I have. Is Braden like Seamus? I mean, would he steal a car?"

"No. Not the Braden I know. But he always looked up to Seamus. Looked up to Seamus *and* Brian. He was a follower."

I said, "I'm sorry. I didn't mean to open up wounds for your family, but I'd like to talk to Braden. Do you know where I might find him?"

"No. My daughter would, but she's out of the country for the winter. She won't be back until the spring, and even then, I don't know how much she's kept in touch with them. After Brian died, everything changed. Braden used to visit, but I haven't seen him in years."

"What about Seamus?"

He scoffed. "I disowned that bloke years ago. He's a bad seed, and always was." He stood and stretched his legs. "I have an old address for Braden. It's from two or three years ago, but maybe it'll help."

"You don't mind giving it to us?"

"Hell no. I've got more in common with you than I do with them. Promise me one thing, though."

"What?"

"You find out they took your car, break them down and teach them a lesson. Something I failed to do."

I nodded. "Sir, if they have the car I'm thinking about, I promise they'll regret taking it."

25

Kylie felt the cold through the window, someone in the house having cracked it yet again. She held in her urine, wanting to drag out the time. The gust interrupted her warmth as before, but this time it beckoned. Told her the men held no fear of her escaping. She stared at the window, hoping an answer would present itself, hoping some sign would tell her to gather the courage to make the attempt.

She was the only one who could. The only one who had the ability to get free. To contact someone on the outside. She remembered a story about a man who'd held three women for years, conducting unspeakable acts while the neighbors had no idea. It wasn't until one escaped, running a mere fifty yards out of the house, that they were rescued.

She should have the courage to do the same. She stood on the toilet and cranked the window open, wincing with the noise and glancing reflexively at the door. No knock came. She got it fully open, now worrying that the influx of cold air would alert her captor.

She hoisted herself up, sticking her head through, her hands scratching the gravel six inches below. One pull, one kick, and she would be out, running down the concrete alley.

Do it. Get out. Do it now.

Her arms refused to move. She couldn't commit. She pulled herself back in and sagged against the toilet, silently crying.

The guard banged on the door, sending a primeval fear through her. *He'll see the window.*

Hoping she sounded strong, but hearing terror in her voice, she said, "Almost done."

She hoisted herself back up and closed the window, then flushed the toilet, hating herself. Hating her cowardice.

The bearded guard opened the door and said, "Come on. Back down to the cellar."

She entered the hallway and heard the man Seamus on a phone, shouting.

—"He went where?"

—"Who did he see?"

—"What? You're shitting me."

—"Yes, it matters. That's my damn grandfather."

—"Take him out. I don't know how he's gotten that far, but it's too close."

—"Don't give me that shit. I don't work for you. I'm *helping* your operation. You want the diversion, you need to get rid of him. If I have to do it, I'm pulling my men to execute. You got that?"

She heard him hang up as they reached the door to the basement. To someone she couldn't see, Seamus said, "Pack them up. We're getting out of here."

The other man said, "You sure? We don't have enough drugs for two movements. This was supposed to be base."

The bearded man opened the door, the darkness splitting open before her, and she heard, "Pack them up. I'll get more drugs."

She was led down and forced to sit. She waited until the light disappeared, then hissed, "Nick?"

She could tell he recognized the urgency in her voice by the tone of his response, vibrating in concern. "Yes?" She heard him shuffle toward her. He said, "Yeah, I'm here. What's up? What's wrong?"

"They're moving us. We're going somewhere else."

"Why?"

"I don't know. Someone did something that's made them afraid."

Unconsciously, she brought her bound hands up and rubbed her necklace, a talisman.

Travis said, "This is good. If we're bringing pressure on them, our negotiations only get stronger."

She ignored him, talking in the dark to Nick. "If we leave here, I lose the chance at escape. We don't know where we're going. This might be it."

Travis hissed, "No, damn it. No way. Let this play out."

She said, "Nick? What should I do?"

Nick was silent. Travis said, "I can't let you do this. You're putting our lives in jeopardy."

She repeated, "Nick?"

He said, "Kylie, I can't ask that of you. I . . . I just can't."

The door above opened, spilling light in the room. Kylie recognized the problem. Saw the wall separating Nick from a decision. She said, "Is it because you feel responsible for me?"

She heard no response and said, "Nick. Please. Tell me what to do."

Nick said, "Kylie, maybe if—"

The man on the landing shouted, "Shut the fuck up."

The boots clomped down the stairs, the window of decision shrinking with each step. She sat back and made her choice.

The bearded man ordered them to rise, stating they were leaving. Hands still bound, they marched to the stairs. They reached the top and Kylie said, "Please, can I use the bathroom one more time?"

"What the fuck? You just did."

"Yes, but I have a small bladder. If we're leaving, I'd like to go again. I don't want to pee myself in a trunk. Please?"

He grunted, and said, "You two stay right here. No movement. I can see you from the bathroom door."

She caught Nick's eyes and saw fear. She nodded slightly and followed the bearded man.

Inside, she closed the door and put down the seat of the toilet loud enough for him to hear. She made cloth-on-cloth noise, as if she was lowering her pants, then stood still, listening. Hearing only the shuffling of feet.

She glanced at the window and swallowed. She took a deep breath and climbed onto the toilet. She cranked open the window as fast as she could. When it squeaked, she stopped, adrenaline racing through her.

She looked back at the door, but it remained closed. She continued, working the lever much slower, as she had before, getting it as wide as possible. She paused one more time, hearing footsteps outside the door, as if the man was moving away, back down the corridor.

Nick. He was making a diversion. She was sure of it.

She crammed her body into the window, her bound hands outside and clawing for a grip in the gravel. Her breasts caught, preventing further movement. In desperation, she jammed her elbow against the windowsill and pulled, feeling her back getting ground as if a cheese grater was running over it. In a brief moment of panic, she realized she was stuck. Absolute fear took over, her response like that of a person caught in a tangle of rope underwater.

She thrashed about, desperately trying to get her upper body through the small aperture. She rolled right, then left, clawing the dirt and pulling. She felt the blood on her back, the pain shooting through her. She came close to crying out, but clamped her jaw shut and continued pulling.

She popped through.

She dragged her legs out, stood up, and began running down the alley, looking for a way out. The house was on the right, a concrete wall topped with razor wire on her left, another house rising behind it. She rounded a corner and saw a street to her front. Freedom. She sprinted as fast as she could, trying to reach a car or a neighbor.

She raised her bound hands, preparing to shout and flag down any vehicle that appeared. Seamus stepped around the corner, the sight sending fear bolting through her. He was so close she couldn't avoid a collision and tried to duck underneath him. He snagged her collar and she felt her necklace snap from her forward momentum, the gold circle flying out of her peripheral vision. She twisted under his arm, trying to break his hold, and he punched her straight in the face.

Her head exploded in stars and she collapsed onto the ground, barely hanging on to consciousness. He grabbed her hair and began to drag her backward. She saw her necklace in the dirt, her last connection to her uncle. She scraped the ground, touched the chain, then felt it slip from her fingers. He jerked her to her feet and slapped her hard, causing the blood running from her nose to spray out against the wall. Dazed, she was shoved through a small access hatch on the side of the house. She fell two feet to the flooring below, slamming her shoulder into the ground.

In a haze, she saw Nick's unconscious body on the floor next to her, his face bloodied anew. Standing above him, without any damage, was Travis, looking appalled at what had occurred. Looking guilty.

Before she lost consciousness, the truth sank through the pain. *That bastard betrayed us.*

26

Walking up the steps to the flat, Jennifer wasn't too keen on the plan Pike had in mind, but she let him go with it. The mailbox for apartment 4A was registered to a J. B. McFadden, so there probably wouldn't be any drama anyway. Her concern was what Pike would do if this lead panned out and Braden showed his face.

The address from Dylan McKee led to the famed Piccadilly Circus, an area of London with a less than stellar reputation, which fit what Dylan had told them about his grandson Braden. They'd exited the tube at the Piccadilly stop, getting topside and seeing performance artists and giant LED billboards, not unlike Times Square in New York City.

They'd fought through the crowds of tourists, passing a man dressed like Yoda, painted entirely in gold and magically suspended in the air, only his cane touching the ground. Jennifer had done a double take and run into a seven-foot Darth Vader. He poked her with his fake light-saber, making her jump.

Pike had laughed and kept moving, parting the people in front of him and ignoring the fact that he was interrupting their attempts at taking pictures. They went deeper into the neighborhood, past the tourist traps like the Ripley's Believe It or Not! museum, and the area got decidedly seedier. Strip clubs and worn-out watering holes began to dot the landscape. They passed a gay cabaret, with an Asian massage parlor on the second floor, the neon blinking in the daylight.

Jennifer said, "Great area."

Ignoring the scenery, Pike said, "Better than some other shit holes I've been to."

Jennifer said, "What are we going to do when we get to the address? How long do you want to conduct surveillance?"

Looking at the street name on the brick building to his front, Pike turned down an alley and said, "No surveillance. I'm just going to knock on the door."

Jennifer glanced at the grime on the windows and said, "You sure that's smart? What if it spooks him?"

"If he's here, he's living in the open. He'll answer the door. If he doesn't, I'll pick the lock and enter anyway."

"And if he does?"

"If the guy on the surveillance video opens that door, he's answering questions. Whether he wants to or not."

Pike stopped and looked at a number on a dilapidated brownstone, now chopped up into a number of different flats. He said, "This is it."

They'd entered a foyer and checked the mailboxes, seeing the name of J. B. McFadden on the flat in question. Pike had grunted and walked up the stairs to the first floor, Jennifer trailing behind. He reached the flat's door, the hallway extending another thirty feet before terminating in a right-hand corridor. Jennifer automatically moved beyond him, checking for threats. She reached the end, peeked around the corner, and saw two more doors, one labeled maintenance, the other with an apartment number. At the end was a stairwell. She returned just as Pike knocked, looking at her with a grin.

"What?"

"I didn't have to tell you anything. You're learning, young Jedi."

She smiled back and said, "You're no Yoda. For one, you can't levitate like that guy in the square."

"Maybe I should paint myself gold and put on a mask."

"I don't think the Taskforce would appreciate the cover problems that would cause. It would be hard to blend in anywhere besides Piccadilly Circus."

"I was talking about in the bedroom."

She saw her reaction reflected in Pike's grin and started to retort when they heard footsteps behind the door. She grew serious. "Pike, don't hurt this guy. I don't want to spend the night in jail explaining why you broke his thumbs."

He said, "That's entirely up to him."

The door opened and Jennifer let out a small sigh of relief. It wasn't the man from the surveillance photo. This guy was short, fat, and slovenly. He resembled Danny DeVito, if the actor had fallen on hard times and completely ignored personal hygiene. Wearing a stained white T-shirt, jeans, and no shoes, he looked like a hobo in a movie from the '20s. His bodily odor wafted out, coating the hallway and forcing Pike to take a step back.

Breathing through his mouth, Pike said, "Mr. McFadden?"

"Who wants to know?"

"Me."

Pike said nothing else, letting the unspoken command settle. From behind, Jennifer couldn't see Pike's expression but knew what he projected. She'd been on the receiving end, back when they'd first met, and she had no doubt the man would talk first. After one second of silence, he did.

"Yeah, I'm McFadden. What do you want? If you're selling, I'm not buying."

Pike said, "Mind if we come in?"

McFadden scowled and said, "Yeah, I mind."

Pike pushed open the door and said, "That was just a formality. Like saying 'I mean no disrespect,' then calling you a jackass."

He said, "Hey! What are you doing? I'll call the police."

Pike flicked his head at Jennifer, and she sidestepped, moving into the flat. She walked through the den and entered the bedroom, hearing Pike say, "Call whoever the fuck you want."

McFadden said, "Hey, she's got no right—" She heard a thump, and knew Pike had just stepped over the threshold, letting the man know that rights were held only by those who had the monopoly on violence. She had no illusions about who that was.

Six months before, she would have regretted her participation. Maybe even tried to intervene. Actually, most certainly would have intervened, if only to prevent Pike from causing permanent damage to an innocent man. Today, those feelings never surfaced. She expected remorse, but all she felt was the press of time and the loss of Kylie. The fact surprised her. She pulled up short, hearing the man protest again, then Pike begin his questions. She heard a slap and started to go back to make sure Pike didn't do anything she would regret.

Kylie's picture floated in her head, and she stopped. *Finding her is the priority.* She'd seen the pain on both Kurt's and Pike's faces, and the little turd in the other room meant nothing. They needed answers, and he might have them. Her thoughts surprised her again, making her wonder what she'd become.

She took a quick glance in the bedroom, seeing no threats—and nothing to indicate anyone was being held here. Well, anyone that wasn't a science experiment for contact diseases. She picked her way through the dirty underwear and smashed beer cans, getting to a closet at the back of the room. She opened it and found a sunlamp and a few marijuana plants growing, making her smile.

She went to the bathroom, cringing at the moldy shower curtain and grimy tile. There was nothing else of interest. She caught her reflection in a mirror and paused, looking to see if she was different. If she was now like Pike, devoid of empathy. Devoid of the natural human desire to stop someone like him from extracting what he wanted from a weaker being. The person who looked back was a cheerful woman, hair in a ponytail and dancing gray eyes. No remorse. No thousand-yard stare.

And she had an epiphany. *Pike is right. Sometimes you need to be a little bad to ensure the good.*

Monsters were holding Kylie, and no amount of goodness was going to stop them from harming her. There was no "natural" human desire to prevent atrocities. She'd seen enough brutality to shatter any notion about innate human virtue. If they wanted Kylie back, they would have to take her by force, carving a path through men like the one in the next room. If that meant violence, then so be it. It was his choice.

The conviction was something new. And a little unsettling.

At Jennifer's core, she knew she wasn't evil. Knew she didn't yearn to harm others, so it was something else that kept her former tendencies at bay. And she found it in the mirror. In the woman looking back.

She saw Kylie in her own reflection. Saw herself four years ago in a drug lord's house in Guatemala, begging to be saved. Begging for anyone to come and destroy the men who'd held her, to rescue her before they physically took from her everything she had. That day, handcuffed half naked and nearly catatonic, about to be forced into unspeakable acts, she'd prayed for a miracle. What had shown up was Pike.

And he had exacted every bit of punishment she had fervently wished for.

What Pike was doing now might not be legal, but it was just. And she would do what she could to help. She looked back into the mirror, remembering the terror. Understanding what Kylie was experiencing.

We're coming. We'll find you.

She reentered the den to find McFadden sitting on a dingy stool, his face swelling and fear oozing from him like pus from a blister. Pike sat across from him, in a chair turned backward, his arms on the backrest. He said, "Get me the address, and we'll be gone."

Pike saw her and said, "Anything?"

"No. Other than the fact that he's trying to re-create the Black Plague."

McFadden started scribbling on a napkin, and Pike stood. McFadden handed him the address and looked at her with apprehension.

She said, "Don't worry. We don't care about your indoor gardening."

Relief flitted across his face. Pike said, "What are you talking about?"

"Nothing. You ready to go? Or you want to pound the crap out of him?"

McFadden cringed, realizing she wasn't an ally. Pike scowled, saying, "What's that supposed to mean?"

She smiled, disarming his aggravation. "Just teasing. We have everything we're going to get?"

McFadden breathed a sigh of relief and said, "You've got all I'm going to give."

Jennifer's smile faded. "There's more?"

McFadden shook his head rapidly, saying, "No, no. That's not what I meant."

She walked over to him and said, "This is no game. I was joking before, but this man will tear you apart for no other reason than he likes it."

Pike stood up, towering over the smaller man, and Jennifer let him, not saying a word.

McFadden raised his hands and said, "I don't know anything about the guy. He was here a year or two ago. Jesus. Call him off."

Jennifer looked at Pike. He held up the napkin, flicked his head to the door, and said, "Let's get out of here."

27

They hit the street and Jennifer asked, "So what did you get? What's on the napkin?"

"The landlord. He said this guy might have a forwarding address. I doubt it because McFadden's been there for over a year. And he wasn't the only tenant. There's been a revolving door in there since Braden stayed. But it's worth a shot."

They retraced their steps, walking back into the light of the tourist area. She asked, "Where is the landlord?"

"Believe it or not, pretty close. Down someplace in a Chinatown section about a half mile from here. He gave me a restaurant to look for, and an alley next to it. I guess the landlord is some foreign expat. He didn't know if he was Vietnamese, Chinese, or something else. Only that he was Asian. The whole thing is shady."

They walked back to the center of Piccadilly Circus, passing Ripley's again, and Pike said, "Why'd you say that about beating the crap out of him? Asking as if I would like it? You still don't trust me, do you?"

She looked up at him to see if he was just pressing her buttons and realized he was serious. She said, "Yes, I do. Completely."

"You say that, but you still question. It's like you only want part of me. The good part. But the world doesn't work that way. I've come a long way from when we first met, but I'm not going to ask politely to get Kylie back."

"I know. I'm okay with the necessary violence. I really am."

"But you think what I do is unnecessary?"

She walked a little bit, thinking of the mirror, then said, "I used to.

But not now. I'm not sure what I believe anymore. You say you've come a long way, but maybe it's the opposite, and I'm the one changing. Does it matter?"

He said, "It does to me." He walked in silence for a minute, then said, "Heather never saw me in operations. She only saw the good. She had no idea what I've done in the name of national security. I sometimes wonder what she would have thought if she had. I used to lie in bed at night, hearing her talk about how proud she was of me, and I felt a little dirty. She thought the world was split neatly into black and white, but it's not."

Jennifer stopped walking, getting his attention. He turned to her and she said, "I never want to hear that again. She loved you for what you were. What you are. *You.* Nothing more. And certainly nothing less. She saw the man. Warts and all. I've seen the same. And I feel the same way."

He held her eyes, trying to determine if it was just talk. He felt the honesty behind her words and said, "Getting Kylie home is going to be violent. It won't be clean. You good with that? Because I can't have you holding back based on some sense of morality for a world that doesn't exist."

She thought about the mirror again and said, "I know. I've been to that world. I'm good with it. I mean *really* good."

He looked at her a moment longer, then started walking. "Okay. Let's go find Kylie."

She smiled, and in a stilted Yoda voice said, "Finding her good would be."

He laughed. "You've got a few miles left before I make you a Jedi."

They walked down Wardour Street and entered a section full of Asian restaurants. He pulled out the napkin and said, "Okay, we're in the right area. Now keep an eye out for Little Wu Chinese Restaurant. It should be close."

She pointed to the left and said, "That's it right there."

He said, "Holy shit. That was easy."

He walked to an alley right next to the restaurant. A sign with Chinese lettering underneath indicated it was called Dansey Place. "This is it. Should be straight back."

She peered down the alley, cloyingly small, full of trash cans and other refuse. She said, "Wow. That doesn't look safe."

"Well, it is what it is."

He entered the alley without another word, walking past the backs of restaurants, Asian men sitting on steps and smoking, glaring at the intrusion away from the tourist area.

He counted doors and then pointed at one, right next to a man in a white apron sitting on a stoop. "That's it."

The man said, "Who you look for?"

"A Mr. Ling. A landlord."

The man said, "He no here. Go away."

Pike said, "I'll be the judge of that."

The man stood, and Pike said nothing, letting the implied consequences flow out by his gaze alone. The man sat back down, saying, "He no here."

They mounted the stairs and the man said, "He no buy girls like her." He cackled and said, "But I know who will."

Pike turned around, bristling with venom. Jennifer put a hand on his arm and said, "Kylie. Nothing more. Let it go."

Pike did, entering a small hallway. He read his napkin again and said, "Last door on the left." They walked to the end of the hall, seeing nobody. The door had frosted glass with SHINTO LLC stenciled on it. Pike knocked but got no response. He knocked again and waited. When nobody appeared, he pulled out a lockpick kit and said, "Take security."

Without a word, Jennifer went back the way they'd come, pausing between the last two hallway doors, with an eye on the entrance. She felt the adrenaline rise and considered how she'd stop anyone from entering. Prevent them from seeing Pike. The tension mounted until it was almost unbearable, making her want to shout down the hallway and ask if Pike was building the lock from the ground up.

She heard a whistle from him and raced back down the hallway. She said, "What the hell were you doing? Filing a key from an imprint?"

He opened the door and said, "I'm rusty. Sorry."

They found a room with a utilitarian metal desk and at least a dozen file cabinets. Clearly, Mr. Ling did more than just landlord. Pike said, "Jesus. We don't have the time for this."

Jennifer said, "It's got to be in some order. Ignore anything that doesn't have the address on it."

Pike pulled open the first cabinet and the door flew open.

Jennifer whirled at the noise and saw two men, both with a black three-day growth of beard. One had a receding hairline and a tangle of long hair in a ponytail; the other had buckteeth that made him look as if he were wearing novelty dentures. Overbite pulled out a pistol, and she saw the suppressor on the barrel.

Not local thugs.

28

Overbite trained the weapon on Pike and said, "Hands up. No movement."

The accent was hard to place, but it wasn't from the UK. Somewhere from Eastern Europe.

Pike did as he asked, moving slow and deliberate. Behind the two men, the Asian from outside entered with a smirk on his face.

Pike said, "Hey, wait. This isn't what it looks like. We aren't stealing anything. We're just trying to locate a lost friend."

Overbite said, "I don't give a shit what you're doing. I'm just happy you broke in here. Makes my job of killing you that much easier for the police investigation."

Jennifer said, "Wait, wait. We haven't done anything. This is just a misunderstanding."

The Asian said, "Kill him. Sell her. I split the profits with you."

Pike closed the distance to them, getting in range of the pistol. He said, "You don't want to do this. You're making a mistake."

Overbite said, "You have one chance to live. One question. And one answer. You answer correctly, and you get to walk out of here. You don't, and you're dead."

Hands raised, Pike said, "What is it? I've got nothing to hide."

"Besides you, who knows about Bulgari in Paris?"

Jennifer heard the words and thought she was in a bad TV movie. *What in the world is he talking about?*

The man continued, "You tell me the leak, and you can walk. Otherwise, you'll die. And I don't mean quietly."

Pike's eyes watered, his voice pathetic, his hands trembling. "Please, please, don't harm us. I can't kill both of you. Without help, I'm no threat."

The man with the pistol looked confused by his words, but Jennifer knew exactly what Pike meant. She floated forward, closing the distance to Ponytail, ignoring the Asian, waiting on the move.

Overbite said, "Get on your knees." He motioned to the other man and said, "Get her under control."

Pike lowered himself down, not looking at Jennifer at all. Giving no indication of his intentions, yet she had no doubt that there was about to be a cyclone of violence. And she had a part.

Ponytail approached, and she knelt down as well, watching Pike. Waiting on the explosion. The man sidled next to her, pulled out a pistol of his own, also with a suppressor. He watched Overbite, the leader. Ignoring her, he used the weapon alone as the threat for compliance.

Pike began pleading, his voice sounding pitiful, amazing Jennifer. "Please. Don't hurt us. I don't know what you're talking about. I have no idea. I'm here looking for a friend. Please, dear God, don't kill us."

Overbite advanced and placed the barrel directly on Pike's forehead, the suppressor embedded into the skin. Death inches away. Close enough to negate the very reason pistols were invented.

He said, "You're a long way from your friend. Trust me, I know. Last chance. You don't answer, and I'll rape the girl in front of you, then kill you both."

Looking him dead in the eyes, the barrel still buried in his forehead, Pike snarled, "I doubt that."

He jerked his head down and to the right and the weapon went off, the soft *pfft* of the bullet embedding harmlessly into the wall over his shoulder. Pike slapped his hands forward, trapping the pistol before it had even cycled another round. He twisted it upward, locking Overbite's wrists against the frame and causing the man to scream. Controlling the weapon with one hand, Pike hammered a rabbit punch into the man's kidneys, then twisted the barrel until it was aimed at Overbite's chest.

The action occurred so quickly that even Jennifer was surprised.

Before Ponytail could register what had happened, she sprang to her feet and drove a palm strike into his face, splitting his nose. She wrapped her arm over his gun hand as he fell back shouting, trying to get her off him. He pulled the trigger and the round shattered the window in the door.

He kneed her in the groin, bringing her to the floor with a starburst of pain. She lost control of the weapon. He swung it around, and she slapped the barrel a second time, the bullet snapping by her head like a wasp. She punched him in the gut as hard as she could, causing an explosion of air. She grabbed the pistol again, fighting for control. He began squeezing the trigger, the rounds cycling by her head and stitching the roof.

Pike heard Jennifer shout and knew he needed to end the fight *now*. Still wrestling Overbite for the pistol, he torqued it harshly backward, feeling the man's fingers snap. He jammed his left thumb into the trigger guard of the pistol and forced the man's index finger to break the trigger to the rear. The weapon cycled upside down, the round punching through the man's chest. His eyes flared open and he fell to the floor, releasing the pistol.

Realizing the threat, Ponytail went wild trying to get control of his own gun. He whirled to the left, lifting Jennifer off the ground and slamming her into a wall. She fell and began scrambling backward. He leapt toward Pike, training the barrel for a kill shot. Pike was quicker. A small cough, and the man's head exploded, the pistol falling to the floor, useless.

Breathing heavy, the pump from the fight racing through her, Jennifer checked to make sure he was truly down. She looked up at Pike and nodded.

Pike went over to the other man, hearing the labored breathing from his chest. Knowing he was near the afterlife. He said, "Who are you? Where is my friend?"

The man said, "Fuck you."

And died.

Jennifer surveyed the carnage, shaking from the stench of death. The closeness of her mortality. She saw the Asian break from the corner and try to dart from the room. She sprang forward, beating him to the door.

He raised a fist and screamed. She parried with her left and ducked under it, driving an uppercut with her whole weight behind the punch, lifting his slight frame off the ground. He collapsed in a daze.

She took a knee on the floor, shaking her hand from the blow and looking at Pike. He checked the chamber of his pistol. Satisfied, he let the slide close.

He walked to the Asian and said, "You still want to sell her, asshole?"

The man recoiled, pulling himself along the floor, getting away from the specter floating above him. To Jennifer, Pike said, "Search the bodies."

She started going through Ponytail's clothing, and Pike bent over the Asian, digging through his pockets. He pulled out a satchel, flipped it open, and glanced at the contents. He closed it and tapped the Asian in the head with the barrel of his newfound weapon. "You talk to anyone about what happened here, you'll end up just like those two, understand?"

The man nodded, and Pike held up the satchel. "I know who you are. I won't kill you. That would be too easy. I'll sell *your* ass to friends of mine, and you'll beg for the pain to end."

The Asian cowered. Pike raised the weapon, saying, "Then again . . ."

His expression was so visceral Jennifer was sure the man was dead. *Don't do it.*

Her earlier conviction faltered. Violence for Kylie's sake was one thing, but killing innocents—even asshole innocents—was crossing a deadly line. A step into the abyss. A fall into blackness that no rescue would absolve.

In a voice just loud enough to be heard, she said, "Pike?"

He glanced at her, the rage boiling out like a white-hot furnace. The Asian scuttled through the door, then began running for his life. Pike settled back and let out a breath.

She said, "You okay?"

He smiled, the violence having drained away as rapidly as the man fleeing the room. He said, "Me? I'm the one who should be asking that question."

"I'm fine. I thought for sure you were going to kill that guy."

"Perfect. I wanted him to feel the same way."

She squinted at him, continuing her search of Overbite's body. She found a thick keycard for someplace called B-Aparthotel, pocketed it, then held up a cell phone.

Pike saw the phone and understood the implications. He moved to the other body and said, "Good. Really good."

Confused by the Jekyll and Hyde, she asked, "That was an act? What you just did with that guy?"

Pike started going through Ponytail's clothes and said, "Yep. Sometimes you've got to act like a badass. Other times like a pussy."

With conviction, or maybe confusion, she said, "You never do that. *Never.*"

He grinned, real humor showing through. "Not as far as you know, huh?"

Her mouth dropped open; she didn't know what to say. Pike was meat and potatoes. Shoot or no-shoot. Kill or be killed. There was no nuance. If he wanted to break you apart, he did so. If he didn't, you got to walk away, but she had never, ever seen any capacity for subterfuge, and now he'd just shown it twice.

He saw the realization sinking in and said, "You really thought I was losing it, huh?"

On new ground, she almost said no, not wanting to admit to her narrow, fallacious view of his psyche, but it would have done no good. He didn't wait for an answer.

He winked and said, "Makes you think, doesn't it? Women aren't the only ones controlling *that* terrain."

He tucked the weapon in his pants, hiding it with his shirttail. He nodded, satisfied with himself. "Yeah. I should get an Oscar if it fooled you. Trust me, I'm better than okay."

He pointed at Overbite. "That asshole said we were a long way from our friend. He confirmed we're on to something. I don't know what, but Kylie's at the end of it."

29

"Turn off the recorder. This isn't for attribution. I told you that already."

Grant Breedlove clicked a button, and the red light faded. He said, "But you've already said you have no idea what I'm talking about. Why would you care if you were recorded?"

The waiter came by, dropped off a crystal glass full of expensive bourbon, then stood there expectantly. Located just blocks from the White House, Old Ebbitt Grill was an institution of political horse trading in Washington, DC, dating back more than a century. Crowded even during off-hours, it was jam-packed at 6:00 P.M., the tourists easily distinguishable from the power brokers by the cameras around their necks. Because of it, the waiter had no patience for someone who was going to take a booth and not order food.

Gerald Walker, the secretary of Homeland Security, picked up the glass of bourbon and gave the waiter a look that reminded him of his station. "Give us a minute, please."

Gerald fiddled with his glass until the man was out of earshot, then said, "I've been here twenty minutes and you haven't asked me a damn thing about my department. I'm not even sure why I agreed to show up."

Grant leaned back. "That's bullshit and you know it. Something's afoot. I can smell it. I'm not asking for you to leak. I have that already. I'm asking for some administration perspective. Whether you give that is up to you."

Gerald rolled his eyes and said, "Yeah, whatever. Maybe if you gave me a question I could answer, we'd get somewhere."

Grant said nothing for a moment, then, "Okay. Here's what I think. You tell me if I'm close: We're pulling out of Afghanistan, wanting to leave as rapidly as possible, no combat forces left, and someone's come up missing. Someone important, which is going to cause all kinds of hell about withdrawal. The Taliban have him, and, after the last POW, are demanding some type of exchange. A big one."

"What the hell has any of this got to do with DHS? How would I know?"

Grant held up his hand. "Hear me out. So, we have one American who was held for five years—a possible deserter—and we release five Taliban. Now, they have another. Someone who's the son or daughter of someone important—but from the last firestorm there's no way the administration can deal for him. At least not in public. They want to keep it quiet. Conduct the negotiations in secret. Get the guy back without any fanfare, since the last one was an abortion. How am I doing?"

Gerald rattled his glass and said, "As a fantasy, pretty good. Honestly, I don't know where you guys come up with this stuff."

"Mr. Secretary, I'm currently going through every single soldier and civilian in a war zone who's even tangentially related to a political elite. The records are open information. From there, I'm going to start sending emails. When one doesn't come back, your side of the story is going to be decidedly less rosy. More like a Watergate cover-up."

Gerald drained the last of his bourbon and said, "Once again, I have no idea about any of this. Department of Homeland Security wouldn't have a say in this even if it were real."

He stood, and Grant grabbed his arm, saying, "Then why are you going to all of those off-the-books meetings?"

Gerald shook his hand free and said, "Let me guess: You're talking to Rivers. Because I'm canning his ass for fraud."

Gerald saw a flicker and knew he'd hit pay dirt. "Grant, you should really vet your sources a little more. He's being fired for travel fraud, taking trips on the government dime for personal business. Which I guess explains why your last story had DHS filling American skies with killer drones armed with Hellfire missiles. Your sources are shit."

Grant watched him walk away, then shouted above the noise in the restaurant, "I'm still going through the names."

Gerald waved a hand without looking back, fighting through the crowd to the front door. Grant watched him go, then signaled the waiter for the check. He threw a twenty down, enough to cover the glass of water for him and the bourbon for Gerald, then stood, scribbling in a notebook.

He reached the door and stopped, surveying the room one final time, a reflex to see if there was anyone of interest he could annoy or groom for a source. Lost in his own world, searching for the power elite—or those scrambling to achieve that lofty position—he ignored anyone who worked the room as beneath his interest.

Others focused on the same story did not possess his snobbery. Because of it, Grant failed to notice his waiter curiously working underneath his vacated booth.

Acting dejected, the waiter told the woman who was assigned Grant's section that the booth had left without dinner.

The waitress laughed, saying, "You still owe me twenty for giving you the table."

He passed the money, then wiped sweat from his brow. She said, "You okay? You look a little sick."

He said, "Yeah. Just a little pissed at the lack of a tip. Tell Carver that I'm going for a smoke break."

She said, "You still got tables . . ."

Pulling off his apron, he said, "Cover for me. I'll be back in twenty."

He exited on Fifteenth Street and went north, turning onto G Street. He walked about a block and entered a parking garage, hugging the wall to let cars pass. He went straight up the ramp, winding around and moving directly through where cars were trying to pass.

He reached the second level and went left, to the end of the garage. He saw the white Ford and felt his heart rate increase. He waved his hand, hoping the man behind the wheel would see it in the rearview, not wanting to surprise him. From their earlier meeting, he had an instinctive feeling the end result wouldn't be good. Like waking a sleeping Doberman.

He paused, waving again, staring at the silhouette in the driver's seat for a reaction. The car's lights flashed against the wall and he started forward blindly, without looking. He leapt out of the way as another vehicle came around the turn much too fast for the space. A horn honked, and the idiot was gone.

Jesus. Never again. I'm never doing this again.

He darted across the space and opened the passenger door, taking a seat and pulling out the digital recorder he'd been given four hours before.

He said, "They came, and I managed to get their table, but they didn't eat."

"Did they talk at all?"

"Yes. I don't know what about, but they did talk."

"How long?"

"Maybe twenty minutes. The older guy seemed pissed. He left early."

The man grunted and said, "Okay." Nothing more.

The waiter screwed up his courage and said, "You're still going to pay me, right? I mean, it's not my fault they left. I took a huge risk."

The man looked at him, and he felt the same fear he had when he'd agreed to this stupid idea. Like his bladder wanted to release right there in the car. He said, "Never mind. You keep the money. We're even."

The man tossed a bundle of bills in a rubber band into the waiter's lap and said, "Go."

When he was halfway out the door, wanting desperately to get back to the safety of his job, his new employer touched his arm. A light caress that brought him up short. The man said, "You understand what will happen if anyone hears about this, correct?"

He looked into the black eyes, devoid of any emotion, and understood the man never made a threat. Only a commitment. In abject fear, he felt his bowels want to release. He said, "Yes, yes. Of course. Believe me, I want nothing to do with this."

The man nodded and he fled the parking garage before Black Eyes could change his mind. He emerged back onto G Street and felt more secure, the people swirling around him. He speed-walked back to Ebbitt Grill, questioning why he'd ever agreed to do the eavesdropping.

It was the damn accent. All jovial and safe.

He wondered what the entire affair had been about, but not enough to investigate. No way would he investigate. The waiter would work at Old Ebbitt Grill for another five years, never knowing his part in the greatest manhunt since Osama bin Laden. Every March 17, when the patrons wore green and the bar descended into chaos, he would be reminded of the man with black eyes.

And he would fear the man's return.

30

Seamus McKee looked at the rotten wood doors covering the hole in the ground and felt a twinge of remorse. This place was decidedly less comfortable than the last, but there was nothing he could do about it. The connection made to his grandfather was too big to ignore, and he needed a clean break. Collecting favors from ancient men who still considered the fight a virtue, moving to the old country was the answer. Which meant a broken-down, abandoned farmhouse in the Irish countryside, complete with a root cellar.

A very nasty root cellar.

He leaned over and pulled up the door, a split-wood affair lying on the ground, vines creeping over to reclaim the land it housed. He splashed the light of a torch onto the stairwell leading down and heard a scraping. He walked halfway down and shone the torch into the cellar, the beam hitting the woman. She flinched from the blade of light, still groggy from the drugs used to get her here. There was a smear of crusted blood on the outside of the hood where he'd struck her, the rough cloth stuck to the skin. He watched to make sure the sack puffed out from breath. His eyes tracked to her partner, his hood also stained, but the spot much larger. He saw breathing, but it looked labored, which scared him. Nick was the prize. If he died, the whole enterprise might fall apart.

He went to the third captive, the only one not drugged or hooded, and was sickened at the cowardice. Like a roach looking for food, the man started crawling toward him, his bound legs and hands scraping the dirt. Reminding Seamus of the groveling men who'd sold out their progress in the peace talks. Reminding him of those he hated.

In a hoarse voice, the man said, "You promised me I'd get treated better. I told you what was planned, just like you asked. I'm trying to help this negotiation."

Seamus said, "Have you checked on your mates yet? Made sure they're okay?"

The man paused, clearly unsure how to respond. He said, "I thought I'd be punished for that."

Seamus said, "You disgust me. Make no mistake, if either of them die, I *will* punish you."

He tossed down four liter-size bottles of water and a satchel full of medical supplies. He said, "I come here again, they'd better look improved."

He walked back up the stairs and returned the cellar to darkness. He closed his eyes, breathing the clean farm air, smelling the dew and hearing the birds chirp. Reminding him of what he was fighting for.

He heard a vehicle approach and looked past the farmhouse, across a field bounded by a large creek, seeing a lorry bouncing down the tiny lane a hundred meters away, the ribbon of asphalt paralleling the far side of the water.

The house was as dilapidated as the root cellar door, slowly falling into chaos as the forest began to reclaim what it had lost decades ago. It had no running water or electricity, but with a little help from a generator, it provided enough protection from the elements. More important, the farm was deep inside Ireland, just outside the small village of Macroom and thirty minutes away from Cork City. The nearest structure was an old water mill a half mile upstream, now defunct. With the creek at their back, and the only access a gravel road to their front two hundred meters away, across an open field, a vehicle couldn't approach without early warning. The house was a clean break from anything his grandfather would know and the perfect place to run the endgame.

Nobody would find them here.

He pushed through the brush from the cellar to the side of the house, stamping down harder than necessary to break a path. Squeaking open the faded wood door, the hinges threatening to fail, he found Colin eating a microwave dinner on a dilapidated table. Next to him, using a desk made of scrounged lumber, Kevin worked to establish an Internet connection using an Inmarsat BGAN satellite system. Overhead, a single lightbulb dangled from an extension cord.

Speaking over the rumble of a generator in the next room, Seamus said, "How're we looking?"

Colin said, "Got the space heaters hooked up. If you still want to run one to the cellar, we'll need a longer extension cord."

"I'll get one. That place is frigid."

"How long we going to stay here?"

"Till we're done. This is it. Kevin, what's up with the Internet? Are we going to need to go to Cork to do this?"

"No. I'm up. Just don't have the bandwidth I want, but I will."

Colin interrupted. "Hey, you sure this place is secure? I mean, you got it from the drug dealer."

Annoyed, Seamus said, "The church owns the land. Not Clynne. And yeah, he deals drugs, but he's with the cause. He doesn't know why we want it and simply thinks we need a place to cool out for a while. That's all. He won't talk."

"You got the knockout drugs from him, didn't you?"

"So what?"

"So he's not stupid. He doesn't think you're out here sedating cattle."

Seamus started to retort, then reconsidered, thinking about the risk Clynne represented. He said, "Okay, Colin, I hear you. I still need to get the replacement drugs for the hand-off. I'll have a word with him. Feel him out."

He grabbed the keys for the Range Rover off a nail and said, "I'll be back in an hour or so. I'll buy an extension cord while I'm out. Check on the hostages in the meantime. Especially that coward—"

One of the four phones on the windowsill began vibrating, echoing against the concrete ledge. Seamus said, "Christ. What now?" He snatched it off the sill, looking at the number.

Kevin saw his expression and said, "Who is it?"

Seamus held up a finger, bringing the phone to his ear. "Aiden. How's Washington treating you?"

"Better than that crap town of Fayetteville. At least until yesterday."

"What's up?"

"Your instinct was right. I've kept my ear to the ground like you asked, and found a bogger from *The Washington Post* that's onto our game."

Seamus listened as Aiden recounted what he knew, the implications growing worse with each passing sentence. When he was done, Seamus asked, "So he doesn't have the full story?"

"No. But he's going to get it. He's checking everyone with any connection. Eventually, he'll get to our five, and the story will break."

Seamus began pacing.

Colin said, "What is it?"

Seamus ignored him, thinking. He heard Aiden say, "What do you want to do?"

"How much time do we have?"

"Not enough. Two days. Maybe less."

"Shit. They'll never pay if it breaks. It'll put their backs against the wall."

Colin stood up, and Seamus waved him back down. He took a deep breath and said, "Take him out."

This time Aiden said nothing.

Seamus repeated, "Take him out, understand? Make it look like a robbery, car wreck, I don't care, but cut him down."

Aiden said, "You want me to kill an American reporter working for one of the premier newspapers in the United States?"

"Yes. Kill him. We're too close."

After a pause, Aiden said, "Okay. But you might be opening up a hornets' nest."

Seamus said, "We opened that up when you killed the man in Fayetteville."

31

Colonel Kurt Hale ordered a straight black coffee and took a seat, ignoring the look of incredulity from the patrons in the line behind him, all amazed that he didn't ask for a grande decaf mocha choco caffe latte.

He checked his watch and saw his sister was running late, as usual. Ordinarily, he would have been aggravated at the lack of courtesy, but given what they were going to discuss, he was glad for the reprieve. Kathy expected a miracle from him, and the update wasn't going to satisfy her. Not that his last meeting with Alexander Palmer and the president had been any more enjoyable.

After Pike's situation report, he'd had no choice but to let the National Command Authority know he was freelancing Taskforce assets because of a personal loss. Well, not *officially* freelancing, since by the Oversight Council's own order, Pike was no longer a Taskforce asset, but because what he'd turned up crossed over into current operations, Kurt had known it wouldn't be construed that way. And it wasn't.

He'd provided a sanitized three-page update to Alexander Palmer at the latest update briefing, including the bare bones of the search for Kylie, and as expected, he'd been asked to kindly accompany the national security advisor to the Oval Office. Because the president would "like a word."

This was after the update itself had turned into a feeding frenzy.

After each section and department completed the status of current activities, Gerald, the secretary of Homeland Security, had briefed that Grant Breedlove was on the trail like a bloodhound and getting close.

Hearing the news, the table of men had broken into a heated discussion, all centered on who the leaker could be. Gerald began to state his theory when President Warren stopped the verbal dance with a raised hand. He'd said, "Okay, we can discuss how he got the initial lead all day long, but the facts are what they are. The leaker is secondary. Breedlove going to press is a bigger threat than the hostage-takers right now. What do we do?"

Kerry, the D/CIA, had said, "Bring pressure to bear. Pull him in. One on one."

Billings, the secretary of state, said, "That'll only confirm he's on the right trail. It won't stop the story. We've seen what they do with this sort of thing. They play games of 'wanting to get both sides,' but only want the information."

Kerry said, "He's going to get the information. We can't stop that. Unless you want to start faking email traffic."

President Warren said, "What about that? Can we do it?"

Palmer said, "Sir, in short, yes we can. But that's a slippery slope. We're talking Nixon-type stuff here now. We'll never be able to keep it contained. Sooner or later, someone is going to know."

Warren said, "Honestly, if we get them home alive, I don't really care."

"Sir, I understand the sentiment, but if we do that, and word gets out, we'll be asking for similar hostage events in the future. It's the whole reason we have a 'don't negotiate with terrorists' stance. You can't say it and then be proved a hypocrite. You'll be setting up future administrations for failure."

President Warren slammed his fist into the table and said, "I don't give a damn about what *might* occur in the future. I care about the here and now. And that damn reporter is going to severely restrict our ability to operate. Both on our side and on the terrorists' side. Right now, they're communicating directly with us. They've made no overt propaganda statements, which means they don't want the publicity any more than we do."

Nobody said a word, letting the president's outburst settle. Kerry broke the silence, saying, "Will no one rid me of this meddlesome priest?"

His words hung in the room, some men looking confused but others understanding exactly what he meant.

Kurt leaned over to George Wolffe and whispered, "What the hell is he talking about?"

George said, "Don't remember your high school world history? In the twelfth century, King Henry II's authority was challenged by the priest Thomas Becket. Henry said those words, apparently just venting. The men present took it as a command and assassinated Becket."

President Warren drew back and said, "Do not misconstrue my words. I am not giving orders." He looked from man to man, making eye contact with each, then said, "Nobody is to interfere in anything that reporter does. Understand?"

He finished the table glare with his eyes on Kerry, the director of the CIA. Kerry simply nodded, and Kurt wondered how far out they had gone.

Billings said, "So what are we going to do?"

"Nothing. Let it ride. We continue with what we're doing and pray to God we beat him. Period."

The rest of the meeting was more mundane discussion, and after it broke up, Kurt had waited, knowing Palmer would read his report. He'd watched Palmer's eyes squint, then glance his way. He'd seen him lean over to the president and whisper. Then waited for the inevitable.

The people had cleared the room, leaving only Palmer, George, and Kurt. Palmer had said, "Kurt, interesting report."

"I thought it would get your attention."

"The president would like a word."

Kurt had followed Palmer the short distance to the Oval Office, continuing what would prove to be one of the most difficult days of his life.

He entered, seeing President Warren behind the Resolute desk in the Oval Office. Looking as if he had no patience for more bad news.

Palmer took a seat on the couch parallel to the desk, appearing weary and rubbing his eyes. Kurt remained standing.

President Warren said, "Well, are you going to explain yourself or wait for me to call the Justice Department to arrest your ass for breaking about a hundred laws and disobeying *my* orders?"

Kurt took a breath and said, "It's exactly like I reported. My niece disappeared in England. Pike was cut free and couldn't help with the current issue—a mistake, I might add. Anyway, I paid for his trip to

England to find her. As it turns out, she was on a date with Nicholas Seacrest. The vice president's son."

"You expect me to believe that? Pike stumbled on Nick's trail by following your niece?"

"Sir, *I'm* not sure what to believe. All I can tell you is where the trail is going. Pike isn't making this up. Shit, I didn't even read him onto the problem. He didn't know where Nick worked or where he was taken. He figured all of that out on his own."

President Warren threw the report on his desk and said, "Pike Logan. Bane of my existence. That man could find trouble in a Girl Scout cookie sale."

Kurt said, "Well, this time he found the right trouble."

Palmer said, "Why didn't you report this earlier?"

"I had no reason to. It was all conjecture. My niece really *is* missing. Pike is really trying to find her. We still don't have confirmation about the VP connection, but it was growing too hot to ignore. I felt it prudent to report."

Warren said, "You mean because that lunatic killed two Serbian thugs? So you could give him sanction? Report it to me, and now he's working for us? After we specifically cut him free?"

Kurt scowled. "Hell no. Not at all. Because I believe he's onto something. Something real for the problem set here. If it was just Kylie, I'd let him continue on his own. But it's not just Kylie. He's onto the vice president's son."

Palmer said, "How do you know?"

Kurt let out a sigh and said, "I don't. All I know is Pike Logan's instinct. And that guy is never wrong."

"So what do you want to do?"

"Redirect assets. Give him help. Get Knuckles's team out of Morocco and into Ireland."

"Ireland? Pike's in London."

"Uh . . . no, he's not. We found a cell phone on the Serb. He was talking to a guy in Dublin. I geolocated the grid and Pike's on his way to investigate. He has this crazy idea that an Irishman is behind this whole thing."

32

Braden McKee stepped off the Métro at the Château Rouge stop, the people swirling around him all of African descent. He walked up the stairs toward rue Doudeauville and was swarmed by several young men surreptitiously flashing smartphones for sale from the palms of their hands. Samsung Galaxies, iPhones, HTC Droids, each man vied for his attention with a different flavor.

He ignored them, not wanting to do business in view of anyone entering the Métro. He walked a block and turned in to an open-air market, the only Caucasian to be found. Shouting in French, two of the men followed him, as he knew they would.

Their persistence would earn his business this day.

Getting to the center of the market, surrounded on all sides by people hawking goods, he turned and waved them forward. They sprinted to him, both fighting for his attention. And his money. He said, "You speak English?"

The smaller one, holding a Galaxy, said, "Yes. Good phone. Unlocked."

The thief manipulated the touch screen, showing a multitude of apps and that they functioned.

Braden said, "Does it have a SIM card?"

"Yes! It work right now!"

The taller one, with an iPhone 5s, blurted, "My phone real. His is junk. Fake." He began the showmanship dance, flipping through apps left and right. Braden ignored the iPhone, focusing on the Galaxy thief. "Dial someone. Right now."

The boy began to do so, and the iPhone thief became agitated, pushing the Galaxy away and saying, "My phone real! Unlocked. You hook to your service."

Braden needed both but only the Wi-Fi capability of the iPhone. He cared not at all that it wasn't hooked to a cellular service. He said, "How much?"

The iPhone thief said, "Two hundred euro."

Braden didn't even bother to haggle, not concerned about the cost. "Okay. I'll take it."

The Galaxy thief became irate, believing he'd lost the sale in the time he was dialing. He shouted, "His won't work. Listen! Listen!"

He held the phone up to Braden's ear, a ringtone coming through. A man answered in French, and Braden hung up, saying, "I'll take yours as well."

He pocketed both phones, letting the little thieves scamper off with a smile. He left the market, walking east, deeper into the neighborhood of Goutte d'Or, a lone Caucasian in a sea of Africans. He passed two gendarmes, both looking at him curiously, and he understood why.

Unlike England, which worked to prevent localized concentrations of indigenous populations and attempted to force immigrants to integrate, France had specific pockets that—if it weren't for the distinctive French architecture—could be mistaken for a different country. Goutte d'Or was one such area.

Since the Algerian War, it was known as the place for African immigrants. Originally full of Algerian expats who fled the troubles of their home country in the '50s and '60s, it had spread to include people from all over Africa. Somalia, Eritrea, Kenya, and others, they all came here— illegally or otherwise.

As a Caucasian, Braden had raised the gendarmes' interest, because he was either lost or clearly looking for something shady. He opted to appear lost, knowing that if they had any idea what he was truly planning, they would have done much more than stare at him.

His brother Seamus had called him in Brussels the night before, agitated and asking if the Serbs were ready to execute their jewelry heist. Originally having told Braden he'd have a five-day preparatory window,

Seamus now wanted the operation conducted immediately. He'd asked if it could be done.

Braden had said, "Maybe. But it'll be something like two days. One, I need to establish the trap. Two, the Serbs are going to want at least a day for a final look-see."

"I thought you said the explosives were ready?"

"They're staged but not primed. That's the easy part. The Serbs are harder. Ratko Illic is no joke. You know his two men haven't contacted him in twenty-four hours? He's asking why, and I have no fucking idea what to tell him. He's liable to go off."

Seamus told him what had transpired, ending with "I have no idea about his men either, but that's just another reason we need to move."

Braden was shocked at the revelations. Shocked and scared. He said, "Seamus, suppose he needs those two men? Ratko may kill me if I demand this. He'll blame me."

"He *needs you*. Aren't you the getaway? The break from the Serbs? I thought they were worried about getting caught with the jewels. Interpol is all over their ass. Didn't they expect to get pulled in as a matter of course after the robbery?"

"Yeah, that's true, but I'm not sure if that'll be enough. He might just put a bullet in my head for the trouble and call the whole thing off. These guys are clannish. You've never worked with them, but they're scary."

Seamus said, "That won't happen. They've put too much time into this. How long have they worked it?"

"Two months. Two that I've been involved with, anyway."

"That's nothing compared to what we've done. They've given us six months of work, with aircraft, boats, reconnaissance, and everything else. They won't throw that away. They want the diamonds."

Braden said nothing, running the ramifications of what Seamus was asking.

Seamus said, "You still there?"

"Yeah. I'm here. Okay, Seamus, I'll give it a try."

Braden had gone to the extended-stay hotel the Serbs were occupying in Brussels, the living room full of corkboards, each one with a selection of pictures of their target in Paris, the note cards above the photos delineating a specific activity. Response times for police, traffic patterns throughout the day, tourist pedestrian flows, the rotations of the guards manning each door. *Everything* involving the assault. Even the glare of the sun on the surveillance cameras.

The Pink Panthers conducted operations timed to the nanosecond, utilizing intelligence that would make any Special Forces team proud. The surveillance video later would look random, with the Panthers overwhelming the security by brute force, but the preparation belied the technique. It was why they'd been so successful.

Braden heard Ratko on the phone.

—"So it's there? Inside?"

—"Doesn't matter where they put that fucker at night. It'll be on display during the day. We're good."

Ratko hung up the phone and saw Braden. He said, "Looks like the necklace is in place. But the gendarmes have increased their patrols in the area because of it. A week's worth of extra vigilance like we expected. You know what that means, right?"

"Yeah."

"Your diversion had better be good. It had better consume them."

"Ratko, we need to talk."

The man rose up from the couch, a brute standing over six feet, covered in coarse black hair. "Yes. We do. I still cannot contact the men I sent on your fool's errand."

Braden felt more than heard the two other men in the room stand. Closing in on him.

He said, "I don't know about your men, but I had a call from Seamus. You need to execute as soon as possible. We have to do the diversion now, or we lose the leverage of it."

Ratko moved to the board, studying the different cards. He said, "You know why I helped you? You understand how much this necklace is worth?"

"No. I mean, yes, I know why you helped, but I have no idea about the necklace. I don't want to know about the necklace. My payment is your help. You've done that, and I'll take the necklace to you as you asked. After the operation."

Ratko turned to him and smiled. A grin like a ferret, all teeth and no joy. "I don't like being played. I have put a great deal of effort into this operation, including securing your hostages." He tapped the map of the target with a knife, saying, "This will be our biggest success ever, but I won't take the risk if I have a weak link." He pointed the knife at Braden. "My men have worked for me a long time. Some since the Bosnian War, fighting with the Arkan's Tigers. I trust them. You, not so much."

Braden knew well the name of the paramilitary group that fought in Bosnia. Their cruelty was legendary. He was unsure if the mention was designed to instill fear or even if it was true. Ratko looked too young to have fought in Bosnia, but age could be deceptive.

Braden said, "I understand a soldier's code just like your men. I am not a weak link. I don't know what happened to the two you sent, but the fact remains that they found a penetration. Someone is tracking our other operation, which puts yours in jeopardy. The diversion has to go now. If you want the Paris gendarmes looking somewhere else, then you need to do the robbery soon."

Braden sensed the other two men in the room taking positions to his left and right and knew he was within a breath of Serb punishment.

Ratko said, "You take but never give. I have provided more for you than you have ever offered in return. And I'm done with that."

Braden sidled to the left, putting his back to a wall. Knowing that any sign of weakness would end in punishment, he steeled himself and said, "Ratko, all of that was predicated on this robbery. Your payoff was my help in transporting the necklace across the border and getting rid of the police presence. You need us. You need the police to look somewhere else. We're set. We just need to execute sooner than we thought."

Ratko stared at him, his marble eyes reminding Braden of the pigs from the farm of his youth. Braden remained steady, holding but not challenging Ratko's gaze in return. Showing strength but not arrogance.

Ratko hissed, spun the blade in his hand, and stabbed it into a picture of the target. He said, "We will execute. But you had better fulfill your end."

Braden nodded, not letting the relief show.

Ratko flicked his head at the men beside Braden, and they moved away. He said, "You know the price of failure?"

Braden nodded again.

Ratko smiled his ferret grin. "No. You don't. You think you do, but you don't. I promise, if you cross me, you will."

Braden had left the room in a rush, clomping down the stairs of the hotel, followed by the two men, both as stoic as if they'd been made of granite.

Twenty-four hours later and a country away, the memory still made him tremble. He would be glad when his relationship with Ratko and the other Serbs was done.

33

Alexander Palmer heard Kurt's words and exploded. "Have you lost your fucking mind? Ireland? Who gave you authority to start operating in Ireland? You *cannot* execute operations without the expressed consent of the Oversight Council. What the hell are you doing?"

Kurt went instinctively to military attention, back ramrod straight and hands to his sides. He said, "Pike was not on a Taskforce mission. He was working for me, as a friend. You guys cut him free. He was helping me find my niece. Someone I consider my daughter. And yes, I gave him some help." He turned his head and glared at Palmer. "You want to fire me for that, then do it. But you'd better be ready to bury the vice president's son."

Palmer stood up, the anger on his face spilling out. He said, "You sanctimonious son of a bitch, nobody gives a shit about your niece. We have bigger issues here than your personal problems. Nicholas Seacrest could be divulging secrets right this minute."

Kurt broke his stance, advancing on Palmer with his fists balled, the violence barely contained. In a low hiss he said, "Fuck you and your bigger issues. This isn't about intelligence, and my niece means more to me than the vice president's son. More than all of those people."

Palmer stood his ground, his legs shaking, the fear evident on his face. Kurt reached him and President Warren said, "Stop!"

Kurt held up, glaring at Palmer. Wanting to rip his throat out.

President Warren said, "This is getting us nowhere. Quit the childish dick contest."

Kurt glanced at him, and the president repeated, "Quit it. Right now."

Kurt backed down, turning away and muttering under his breath.

Palmer breathed out, then said, "Kurt, hey, those words were poorly chosen. I'm sorry. Sorry about your niece, and sorry I said what I did. But you can't freelance like this. You know that."

Accepting the apology in the spirit it was given, Kurt said, "Then don't make me freelance anymore. Let's bring it to the Council. Pike's onto something here. Get him Taskforce assets. Get Knuckles there."

President Warren flipped to the second page of the report and said, "But you reported that Knuckles had found a connection. The ferry trip ticket was tied to some Somalis who came from Paris. And your Taskforce penetration of French immigration says they've returned there."

Kurt sighed and said, "Yes. That's what we know, but we can't find a couple of Somalis in the city of Paris. We've got nothing. Pike has a lead."

"You mean Pike has a lead to your niece."

"Well, yeah, but she's tied to the VP. I don't understand this Somalia connection, but Pike's onto something real. It's in Ireland, and it's not about torturing these guys for information."

Palmer said, "Maybe. Maybe not. We know an Islamic group has the hostages. Knuckles has now confirmed it's Somali. Al-Shabaab. We don't know where they are, but we now know who they are. Might be Paris, might be Mali, but they sure as shit aren't in Ireland. That would be the last place they'd go."

Kurt said, "Sir, I don't buy that Islamic crap. You think a bunch of Somalis straight out of the Stone Age could do this? Shit, there's no way they could even track someone on Okinawa, much less kidnap them. There's something else going on here."

President Warren said, "Because you want it to be that way? For your niece? Or because you have some evidence?"

Kurt balled his fists up again, this time in frustration, and said, "It's the same damn thing."

President Warren had looked at him with sympathy and said, "Kurt, I understand where you're coming from, but I have to play the intelligence as I see it. I'll let you freelance Pike. No word to the Council. But Knuckles is going to follow the trail where it goes."

Now, sitting with his cup of black coffee surrounded by twentysome-things whose greatest problem was figuring out which blend to buy, he was about to go through the same pain again. With his sister.

He glanced at his watch one more time, wondering if she was even going to show. He pulled out his cell phone to call and saw her walking at a fast pace up to the door. She entered, and he waved. She ignored the line and marched right up to his table, sitting across from him.

In the harsh fluorescent light, she looked aged. As if someone had taken a picture of her two days ago, then put it through software ma-nipulation to show how she would appear in twenty years. She looked lost.

She said, "So you have something? Tell me you have something. The police over there are still giving me the stone wall."

He steeled himself and said, "Kathy, I have a thin lead, and I'm ex-ploring it, but you have to understand that it might go nowhere."

"Exploring it? What does that mean? You sound like you're looking for oil."

He told her what he'd found, leaving out all aspects of the vice pres-ident's son and the Serbian connection, washing it all into a date with a ghost who he was trying to find. When he was done, she sagged into her chair and began to cry.

He reached across and rubbed her arm, saying, "Hey, it doesn't sound like much, but it's something. We're going forward."

She snapped back and said, "Bullshit! You're doing nothing. I knew you would do nothing from that first phone call. You're sitting here on your ass while she gets gang-raped or sold into slavery." She broke down again and began sobbing into her hands, the patrons around them look-ing on in concern.

Kurt let the barbs fall and said, "Kathy, that's not true. Yes, I'm here, but it's only because I've sent someone better than me. I have a man over there. He's looking right now."

A bitter look on her face, she spat out, "*Better* than you. Sure. I get it."

He nodded, a soothing gesture. "Yes. Better than me."

He saw a glimmer of hope, quickly dissolved by the pain of her fear.

She said, "Kylie always talked about you being some great hunter of terrorists. I knew that was bullshit, but she thought you were saving the world. I guess she was wrong."

"No. She wasn't wrong. She just misconstrued how I hunt. I *will* find her."

The hope returned to her eyes, as much as she tried to prevent it. She said, "Who? Who do you have looking?"

He clasped her hand in both of his and said, "I can't give you his name, but he's the best man I have."

She sniffled and said, "Is he good enough? Will he bring her home?"

Kurt smiled, intending to show warmth. What came out was the grin of a shark. "Trust me, he's a predator. His target is the man who took her. And he has never failed me."

34

I failed to see the exit from the roundabout in time and swerved, trying to make it. I reached the lane and caused a flurry of honking horns. Apparently, it wasn't a one-way road, and I was driving head-on into traffic.

Jennifer barked, "Pike!" and threw her hands onto the dash. I swerved back into the roundabout and said, "What the hell? The road's painted with white stripes."

The GPS said, "Recalculating" in a female Irish voice, and I expected it to follow up with a "dumbass."

I circled around again and said, "Look, it's Big Ben . . ."

Jennifer, not getting my movie reference, said, "Are you crazy?"

Now knowing how Chevy Chase felt, I said, "This driving on the wrong side of the road is killing me."

She turned to the window and said, "Some world traveler. Maybe when Knuckles gets here we can survive the roads."

I whipped into the correct exit and said, "He's not coming."

"What? I thought you'd told Kurt what we'd found?"

"I did. But Knuckles has apparently found a connection with the ferry ticket. We're still on our own. Which, honestly, I don't care about. Easier to do what I want without some command from eight thousand miles away telling me what my left and right limits are."

Jennifer said, "Until we need the backup."

I turned down a lane, watching the GPS track, and said, "Yeah, there is that. I called someone else for help, but it'll be a while before he can get here."

Jennifer said, "What? You're turning into the Man of Mystery. Who did you call?"

"Nung. Remember him?"

"The guy from Thailand? How on earth did you have his number?"

"He gave it to me after we rescued Knuckles. I've kept it for a special occasion, and this is it."

Nung was the son of an old Air America pilot in Bangkok. Half Thai and half American, he had helped us get Knuckles out of a little prison predicament that hadn't been exactly smooth. He was as calm a person as I've ever seen in a scrape. To be honest, I thought he might be a little crazy, but he was definitely good at mayhem, and that's something we might need now that Knuckles was off the table.

"Do you even know his name?"

"Well, yeah. It's Nung."

"His *real* name. *Nung* is the number one in Thai. Did you call for Song as well?"

Song meant the number two in the Thai language and was the name of another guy who had helped us. I said, "No, I don't know his name. If he wants to tell us, he can. And it's just him, no Song."

"Why'd he agree to come? What did you promise?"

"I told him I'd pay him for his services after we found Kylie."

She leaned her head back into the rest and closed her eyes, rubbing her forehead as though she had a migraine. We traveled through the small roads, leaving the city center of Dublin behind and heading to the west. Eventually, she said, "How are you going to do that? We don't have that much cash in the till from Grolier, and the damn plane ticket alone will be enormous."

Sheepishly, I said, "I haven't figured that out yet. Maybe I'll bill Kurt."

She looked at me like I had truly gone off the deep end. She said, "Maybe we should go back to the hotel and get on the VPN. See what Kurt wants. What he's willing to do before we start building a makeshift team. Before we start wrecking things."

I knew what she was asking. She understood that we were hanging out in the wind here. We'd been lucky with the Serbs, but if we found Kylie, it would more than likely be along with a bunch of armed men.

Even given our conversation before, she knew someone was going to get killed, and it wasn't a foregone conclusion that it would be the bad guys, even with Nung on the team.

I'd been running that very scenario through my head for the short flight over from London. Wondering how far I wanted to go. I'd decided to go as far as it took. Kylie free, or me dead. But that probably wasn't fair to ask of Jennifer.

I said, "Hey, I know Kurt. He wants his niece back. And so do I. By giving us the geolocation of the Serb phone call, he's provided his intent. If I call him now, questioning what I can do, he'll tell me to back off. He won't order me to do what's right. He can't."

I pulled over next to one of the ubiquitous pubs that dotted the city, letting the car idle. I looked at her and said, "I'm going to get her back, but I understand if you want out. It *is* risky without a team."

Jennifer studied my face, then said, "Is this about her, or you?"

"What's that mean?"

"Is this about your daughter?"

The question touched a nerve that deserved to be left alone. I said, "What the fuck are you talking about?" I began to wind up for a fine verbal joust, sick of the unfair accusations, but she just stared at me. Burrowing past the scar tissue with her gaze alone. I sagged into the seat and said, "Maybe. Maybe it is. But that doesn't make it wrong."

She said, "I know. Remember Guatemala?"

Surprised, I turned to face her, wondering where this was going. "Yes. Of course."

"I wanted you to come. I didn't think you would, but I prayed."

"And?"

"And if she's praying for you like I did, she's in good company. I just want to know where you stand. What you're about to do. What *we're* about to do."

I felt a grin break on my face. "You don't have to come. I can get her back with Nung."

She said, "Are you kidding me? You can't even drive over here."

I put the car in park and said, "Then why don't you try your hand at driving, since I suck so much?"

She smiled and said, "Fine by me."

We switched seats and drove in silence, the only sound the idiotic voice from the GPS.

Finally, I said, "I won't turn into the monster you knew before. That won't happen."

She looked at me, judging my face. She said, "I don't believe that."

Stung, I said, "I *won't*. I'm not like that anymore."

She said, "You miss my meaning. I understand the monster, and sometimes it's good to let it run free."

I couldn't believe the words had come out of her mouth. I wondered if it was a trick.

Turning down a small side road, she said, "These people are evil. *They* are the monsters."

35

Braden McKee passed the gendarme patrol and continued southeast on rue Saint-Luc, walking at an unhurried pace. He saw the church known as Saint-Bernard de la Chapelle, the landmark for their safe house. He began counting alleys and turned down the fourth one. He found himself in a courtyard of brick, the small area full of broken wine bottles and newspapers, a rusty bicycle chained to a fence, its seat long gone. After a quick glance around, he entered a repugnant apartment complex through an unlocked gate made of black iron.

Walking by a rack of mailboxes, most with the hatch open or missing, he left the sunlight of the courtyard, the only illumination available. He entered a stairwell and turned on a flashlight to fight the gloom. He carefully walked to the fourth floor, stepping around the debris his torch revealed and breathing through his mouth to avoid the smell of urine. He used a key on the second door to the left, entering a small flat. Inside, there was no furniture. Just cracked linoleum and stained walls. He went to the bedroom and found a neat stack of boxes on the floor. Packages of RDX, rolls of detonation cord, and boxes of nails.

He went to work, first covering the windows on the eastern wall with sackcloth to block out any snooping eyes, then set about building the trap, working with no more excitement than a man hanging drywall.

Ringing the room in small packets of explosives, he worked to ensure the detonation was contained within this flat and that nobody in the flats to the left or right would be harmed. The only targets would be those who entered.

Once he was finished daisy-chaining the explosives to the detonation cord, he began mating them with the nails. He paid special attention to the entry door. It was here that the greatest chance of escape lay, either because of a bottleneck at entry, or because they'd figured out the trap and were rushing to exit.

He'd positioned four explosive charges, two low and two high, and now aimed the nail packages so they would crisscross two feet in front of the door, like four shower heads spraying out. They would eviscerate anyone unlucky enough to be standing in the cone of fire.

Finished, he surveyed the room, ensuring that at detonation no corner would be free from the hail of metal or flame. His last act was to set the Samsung phone on the windowsill, running its charger to an outlet just below. He checked to make sure the det cord and initiation device would reach the tail hanging from the mini USB plug of the phone.

Satisfied, he stood, hands on his hips. Proud of his work. The pain of the men receiving his creation never crossed his mind. The same way the United States hadn't thought about his brother when he was ripped in half by an IED in Iraq.

Reap what you sow.

36

The GPS burped, and Jennifer pulled over to the side of the road. "This is it."

I looked out and saw a row of town houses, split by alleys every fifty meters or so. I pulled out my smartphone, looking at the geolocation that Colonel Hale had sent. It was centered right over a house a hundred meters down the road, but that technology wasn't perfectly accurate. I said, "Shit. That grid isn't going to be good enough. We could be a house over. I was hoping for a stand-alone."

Jennifer said, "You want to watch awhile? See what we can find?"

I thought about it, then said, "Yeah. Let's see what comes out."

Four hours later, after watching the comings and goings of various families from the town houses to the left and right of our target, but nothing from the house itself, I said, "The grid's correct. The other houses all have kids, so I doubt there's someone chained in the bathroom. I think our target is deserted. Let's do what we did before. Go bang on the door. Let's stir things up."

"And if Braden answers?"

I pulled out the weapon from the Serbs, a Glock 19 complete with suppressor, and said, "He gets to meet the monster."

She nodded, then said, "Okay, but the monster only comes out if necessary. Right?"

I chuckled. "Yeah, okay. I won't shoot someone just to do it, but odds are this is a dead end."

We went to the front stoop and I peered into the glass on the door, unable to see anything because of the drapes. I surveyed the area, seeing a small front yard that was overgrown and trash-ridden, a beat-up grill rusting on the side. The house to the left, across a cinderblock wall, had an immaculate lawn, complete with birdbath. The one on the opposite side of the street had the same manicured landscape with children's toys littered about. To the right was a narrow alley, made of concrete and gravel and lined with trash cans.

This house is unoccupied.

I looked at Jennifer and raised my hand to knock. She took a knee against the brick wall, her weapon held low. I banged on the door, my own pistol held at the ready. Nobody answered. I waited and knocked again. Nothing. The lead had turned into a bust.

We could find the landlord, see who had rented the place, but it was looking as if there had been some spoofing with the phone. Hell, maybe the damn thing hadn't even connected in Ireland. I was beginning to feel foolish for contacting Kurt. I said, "This is a dry hole."

Jennifer said, "Let's check around back. See if we can find something that way."

She pointed to the alley, and I agreed, if only to keep the pain of failure at bay. We stashed our weapons and walked around the corner, then down the alley. One side was the edge of the town house, the other a concrete wall that was taller than me and topped with razor wire, making me wonder what the hell kind of neighborhood had birdbaths out front and slicing metal in the rear.

We turned the corner, walking down the back of the town house until we reached a large rolling metal gate. Jennifer started snooping. I held back, checking our six. Waiting on someone to ask what we were doing.

She prodded a window just above ground level, saying, "This is open."

I said, "So?"

"So let's check out the inside."

Surprised at her willingness to break the law, I mentally measured and said, "I can't fit."

"I can."

I cocked an eyebrow. "You sure?"

For an answer, she pried it open and began squirming through. I took a knee and pulled security, feeling a little like a loser. Me pulling security while she did the work.

She slipped in and I waited, hearing nothing, but prepared to run around to the front and kick in the door if I did. Eventually, she reappeared.

She wriggled out, struggling to escape the small window. Kneeling, she said, "Someone was held here."

"What? How do you know?"

"The place is empty, but inside the basement is a bucket, and it's full of excrement. Someone was forced to use it."

I took that in, and she continued, "Also, I think there's blood on the floor. Near a side door."

I said, "Blood? How do you know?"

"I don't, but there are two smears that look like blood."

"Where? What side door?" I hadn't seen one when we had come down the alley.

She started walking back, pacing the distance. She stopped and pointed at a hatch, barely four feet tall. A piece of plywood, but sure enough, it had hinges and a handle. It looked like access to an HVAC, not an entrance. She said, "That's it. The floor is another two feet below."

I tugged on the handle, and she said, "It's padlocked from the inside."

I studied the plywood hatch, seeing what looked like a spray of old ketchup on it. I immediately pulled my eyes away, not wanting to dwell on the repercussions of what that might be. I knelt down and studied the gravel at the base. I saw what looked like drag marks. Like someone had towed a large bag of trash out of the door. I followed the marks out with my eyes, searching the ground. And saw something.

A glint of metal. I bent down, picked it up, and found Kylie Hale.

I said, "She was here. You were right."

Jennifer said, "What is it?"

I held up a pendant. A small circle of gold, shaped like a Flintstones tire. Inside the rim of the gold were the words ROMANS 3:8.

It referred to the Bible verse that said, "Let us do evil that good may come," and was an unofficial Taskforce motto. Something we placed on ball caps and coffee mugs. The only people who would get the meaning were Taskforce members, but it pretty much summarized exactly what we did, and there was no way this was a coincidence. Kurt must have given it to Kylie.

I thought of the blood and said, "It's hers. Damn it, it's hers. We're too late."

37

Kylie saw the light come in through the hood, then heard the footsteps coming down.

Feeding time.

She no longer had the energy to cower, and simply waited for the bearded man to arrive. She coughed, a phlegm-ridden rattle, and realized she was feeling worse. She had a low-grade ache behind her eyes that had nothing to do with the bruises inflicted by Seamus. She was sick and growing weaker.

She heard the man shuffling to the other two captives first, then felt him next to her. He removed her hood, then set a bowl of microwave chicken nuggets in front of her, next to a bottle of water. The same food she'd had for days, but she understood why. It didn't require any utensils. So no potential weapons.

Since her escape attempt their captivity had grown more strict. The hoods stayed on at all times, and they were forbidden from talking. Feeding time was a mixed blessing, as she got to see around her, but she was required to drop her blanket from her shoulders to eat. Losing the precious heat the thin covering provided.

Their captors had run two space heaters into the cellar, but both only managed to raise the temperature a few notches. Even with them on, it was a constant fifty-five degrees. Cold, damp, and rotten.

Usually, the bearded man waited until they were through. Waited and watched. This time, he did not. He said, "I'll be back in thirty minutes. No talking," and tromped back up the stairs. He closed the hatch, plunging the room into darkness, and she heard the padlock click shut.

She sat for a minute, allowing her eyes to adjust to the soft red glow put out by the heaters. She saw Nick watching her intently, his face a battered mess. Off to the side, by himself, Travis ate without looking up. The sight of him caused a spasm of anger. She gave an involuntary cough and spit out a glob of phlegm. Nick flinched, then sidled over to her, bringing his meager portion.

He whispered, "Hey, take my food. You need the strength."

She said, "You weigh much more than me. I'm not stealing your food. Anyway, I'm not hungry."

"You need to eat. And to increase your fluid intake. Take my water bottle as well."

She tried to smile and said, "What, are you a doctor now?"

"No. Not really. But I've had some training in this sort of thing. You have to keep your strength up. And collectively, we have to help you do it."

She gave a small chuckle. "You've been trained to be chained in a cellar after getting beaten? Was that right after you learned what a cumulus cloud was?"

She saw he was serious. He said, "I did something else before I was a weatherman. For that job I had to go through SERE. Survival, evasion, resistance, and escape training. And one of the key things the POWs from Vietnam stressed was that disease was the killer. Looking at you, they were right. Eat."

She did so, nibbling on a nugget. She said, "What did you do before?"

"Not worth talking about. Bottom line, I had the misfortune of running across an IED."

"You were blown up? What happened? You don't look handicapped."

He held out the water bottle. "Drink up. You need it."

She took it in her bound hands, and he said, "I'm not hurt anymore. It was a bullshit political move. Because of my father. I was told I'd be medically retired, but I fought to stay in and change my specialty to something a little softer. They were petrified I was going to get killed, and they couldn't have that in the press. They faked the medical stuff, but I raised such a stink that they agreed I could stay in if I changed jobs."

She downed a few large gulps and handed the bottle back to him. "I can't take all of it. You need some."

He said, "Naw, I'm good. I don't want to have to piss anyway."

She saw the small grin and realized this time he was kidding. She pointed at the bucket and said, "You think I like using that? With beard guy staring at me?"

They heard Travis cough, and she realized he'd come closer as well. She saw Nick's face and said, "Ignore him."

He said, "I will, because we might need to steal his food sooner or later, but I swear I'm going to kick his ass when we get out of here."

He saw her face fall and said, "What?"

"I don't think we're getting out."

"Whoa. I don't want to hear that. Hope is the one thing we have. You lose that, and you lose the will to live. We're getting out. What about your friend? The predator?"

She reached for the pendant she no longer had and her eyes watered. She said, "I don't think he's coming. He would have been here by now if he could."

"Then we make another escape attempt."

"Have you looked around? This is like *The Texas Chainsaw Massacre*. We get out of here, and we're probably going to be running for help right into some clan of people that are with these guys."

Travis spoke for the first time. "She's right. I saw it on the way in. You guys were drugged and carried down. They let me walk. We're out in the middle of nowhere."

Nick snarled, "If I want your opinion, I'll squeeze it out of your head like a pimple." To Kylie, "Don't listen to him. We're getting out."

Travis said, "I didn't mean we weren't getting out. I meant running out of here isn't the right way to go about it. Look, I'm sorry about what happened. I didn't think they'd beat her, but she was putting lives at risk."

Nick said, "If what you say is true, and even if we manage to get out of this hole, we still have a run through the woods, then *you* put our lives at risk. She could have made it. Jackass."

"There are more than just us. They captured others, and if we were to escape, it would force an endgame on them. They'd probably be dead. What I did was hard but the right thing to do. You can't see it, but it was."

"How the hell would you know that?"

"I heard them talking while we got gas. While I was still in the trunk."

"So you heard this *after* her escape attempt. How is that the right thing? All you were worried about was getting a beating, you little shit."

"It still makes my decision right. It's why I'm an officer. Because I can intuit the big picture."

"Funny, I was thinking the exact opposite, as in *How on earth did this coward become a lieutenant?*"

Kylie interrupted, saying, "How many others? Where are they?"

"I don't know. I just heard that guy Seamus on the phone. They captured others besides us. They could be in a cellar a hundred feet over for all I know."

Nick said, "No way. It's much easier to keep us together. If they're real, they aren't anywhere near here."

Almost to herself, Kylie said, "You're right. It makes much more sense to keep us together . . ."

Nick said, "And?"

The fear returned to her face. She said, "And if they're somewhere else, there's a reason. They have something special planned."

38

Kaelyn Clute heard her door open and curled up out of reflex. Boots clomped to her head and she felt hands on her body. A pair on her wrists and a pair on her ankles. She started to writhe, and a voice said, "Stop. We're cutting you free."

She felt her restraints fall away, and she became afraid. Her hood was removed, and the man above her said, "Stand. Follow me."

She stood on wobbly legs, her gag still in place, and followed the man into the central den. The other walked behind her, making her glance over her shoulder out of reflex.

She saw Mack on his knees, also cut free. He winked at her, drawing a slap on the head. He scowled at the blow but remained still.

The man who struck him said, "We are going for a ride. Because of that, you will not be tied or gagged. I want to stress: Do not attempt to escape."

He held up a cell phone, saying, "We will be going in separate cars five minutes apart. These phones act as walkie-talkies. Instant communication. If either of you attempts anything, you will cause the other to die. Am I understood?"

She saw Mack nod and followed his lead. The man said, "McKinley, you're first. Remove the gag."

He did so, then said, "Where are we going? I want to stay with my sister."

"Tough shit. No harm will come to either of you, and you'll meet at the end. It's just a precaution."

McKinley looked at Kaelyn, torn, and she nodded at him. He said, "You'd better be telling the truth."

"Whatever, tough guy. Start moving."

Kaelyn watched him disappear, one man in front, one in the rear, then sat waiting with the final man. After a short time, his cell squawked with the command to follow. He motioned to her and said, "You first. Take a left and head toward the stairs. Don't stop at the elevators."

They went down the stairwell and ended up in the ubiquitous Parisian courtyard. The man pointed to a nondescript Renault parked against the curb and said, "You get in the passenger side." He held up the phone. "Remember what Braden said."

If he seemed concerned about using a name, he didn't show it. Causing her more fear. She closed the door, and he said, "Buckle up," in his lyrical accent. "Wouldn't want you to get hurt."

They drove north in the congested traffic, him weaving like a maniac and her trying to determine where they were. She caught plenty of *rues* but couldn't decipher names until she was beyond them. Eventually, they crossed the Seine, and she recognized the Arc de Triomphe. An anchor.

They drove away from it and headed northeast, and the neighborhoods began to become run-down. Eventually, they were traveling down small roads teeming with African immigrants. She saw a sign for an Islamic studies institute and committed the name to memory. Two turns later, and they were driving by an ornate Orthodox church.

Another anchor.

He put the building in the rearview mirror, then turned into a courtyard, honking at two men loitering in front of a wrought-iron gate. They shouted at him in French but moved out of the way. Parking behind another sedan, he exited and walked around to her side and pointed to an archway leading inside a dilapidated apartment complex.

He opened the door, saying, "Inside there. Take it slow. No sudden movements. Show me you want to obey. Don't make me guess."

She walked through an arch. Stung by the smell, she hovered in the shadows, waiting on a command. He turned on a flashlight and pointed to a graffiti-stained stairwell. "Fourth floor."

She walked forward, gingerly picking her way, the small cone of light dancing behind her. They reached the fourth floor and he said, "Right."

She started moving, wondering if she was walking to her death. Wondering if it wouldn't be better to run now. She passed one door and reached a second, having the thought taken from her by a command.

"Stop."

He knocked on the door, and the man called Braden opened it. He said, "Come in."

She hesitated.

Louder, he said, "McKinley, tell her to come in."

She heard, "Kaelyn, I'm here."

The relief was so great she thought she would collapse. She stumbled through the door and walked inside, embracing Mack. Braden broke them apart, saying, "Look. All we're doing is providing proof of life. Your people want you back, and we want to give you to them, provided they pay a price."

She saw Mack steel himself and wanted to stop him from talking. Wanted to acquiesce to whatever they asked. Then felt ashamed, as a Navy officer, that she would.

Mack said, "What price? I won't participate in this as some propaganda stunt. I don't know what you are trying to do, but it won't be with my help."

He looked at her with a sense of regret, and she nodded, saying, "Neither will I."

Braden sighed. "Look, all we're doing is extorting money. I need proof of life from you. I'd like to make it dramatic, but I can do it however you want. Your participation is a foregone conclusion."

Mack said, "Bullshit. What's all of the RDX for? The det cord running around the room? We're dead anyway."

For the first time, Kaelyn saw a myriad of small packages on the walls, all staggered symmetrically. A deathtrap she didn't comprehend, but she understood her brother's words. She went pale.

Braden pulled a pistol and aimed it at Kaelyn's head. He said, "Do it your way, then. Tie him the fuck up."

The two men descended, and Kaelyn sprang toward Mack. Braden grabbed her wrist and jammed the barrel into her head. "Don't. You aren't dying today unless you fight."

She watched, helpless, as her brother was beaten into submission, the two men punching like machines. No joy or anger. Just work. Eventually, he was flex-tied hand and foot.

Braden said, "Now your turn. Would you like to fight?"

Internally, she knew she should. Knew it was required, if only to preserve her own image of what was heroic. She did not. She told herself it was because she needed her strength to escape, if the opportunity presented itself. Needed to prevent any damage that would harm that chance. It was the truth, but it did nothing to salve her feeling of cowardice.

She went to the floor and in short order was tied just like her brother. Braden said, "Put on the hoods."

She lay in the darkness for a moment, hearing scuffling around.

Braden's voice: "Okay, get them parallel. You need to be off camera when you pull the hoods. Do not get in the way of the lens. Don't worry about talking. There is no audio."

She touched her brother in the back, a stroke to let him know she was there. A shadow appeared above her head. Braden said, "Get them on their knees."

A hoist, and she was up.

"Okay, on the count of three. One . . . two . . . three."

The hood was ripped away, and she saw Braden with an iPhone, taking video. She glared at him and realized she'd given him exactly what he wanted when he said, "Perfect."

The hoods returned, and she heard Braden say, "Put them in the bedroom. Cinch them tight. This is home for a while."

She heard the words and realized the man had told the truth. They wouldn't be killed today. But tomorrow was a short twenty-four hours away.

39

Braden exited into the courtyard, dialing Seamus through the VOIP application, and Seamus answered with a flustered tone.

"Hey, it's Braden. You sound like you're in the gym working out."

"I'm on the M7 fighting through the Muppet tourists. Frog called today. Our black friend is in town and wants to meet."

"Now? It's a week early."

"Yeah, I know. This shit has been one short circuit after another. Nothing I can do about it. I'm on my way to Dublin. What's up with you?"

"Got the Snapchat. They're tucked in tight. It'll look good."

"You sure you got the geolocation feature on?"

"Yeah, yeah. It's there. I tested it on Google Maps before I took the video. It spotted me right where I was supposed to be."

"And it's on Wi-Fi? Not the cell network?"

Braden let a little aggravation come through. "Yes, just like you told me. How about a little trust?"

"Sorry. We have to give them just a taste. Make them work for it. Make them feel smart. We can't be obvious."

"Well, I did what Kevin said to do. I can't tell you how smart it is."

"It'll be good enough. Where are the captures?"

"In the apartment."

"They under control?"

"Yeah, but that Marine recognized the explosives. He knows this won't end well."

"Is that going to be a problem?"

"No. Not as long as I keep people there. We had to smack him around a bit, but they'll do what's necessary to survive."

"Do they know what's planned?"

"Of course not. But they suspect. Even a chicken suspects when you show it the axe."

"Keep them under control. We're close. The diversion goes, the Serbs get their jewels, the Americans spin around in confusion trying to figure out how we set a trap, we kill a hostage, and then the money will flow. I promise, the money will flow."

"When do I send the Snapchat? I have to let Ratko know. He has to be ready."

"I don't know just yet. Let me figure out what the fucking Somali has in mind. Probably tomorrow. Are the Serbs in town yet?"

"No, damn it. I told them I would give them a warning. They aren't here and won't execute tomorrow."

"Okay, fine. Calm down. Give them two days."

"I will, but you'd better be ready to execute. They're not of a mind to give us favors."

Seamus hung up the phone and threw it into the car seat next to him. He crossed the M50 and headed into downtown Dublin on Long Mile Road. He wove about, getting closer to the River Liffey. Wanting to ensure he was on his own, and clean from any surveillance, he wound around St Stephen's Green until he found a parking spot on the south side. He sat in the vehicle for a moment, checking the ebb and flow of traffic, looking for a correlation of someone parking because he had. He saw nothing, feeling a growing satisfaction for what he was about to accomplish.

Better men than him had defended this sacred ground in the 1916 Easter Uprising, and he would make them proud. They had sacrificed themselves in a futile attempt at rebellion against the English crown, and their deaths had been the catalyst for the freedom of the first twenty-six counties of Ireland. He would be the catalyst for the final six.

He exited quickly, entering the park through a central gate, getting lost among the tourists. He moved purposely through it, taking the winding paths seemingly at random to prevent anyone from anticipating and jumping ahead of him.

He circled around, reaching a central bridge spanning a neck of water connecting two lakes. A choke point. He crossed it, then sat on a park bench on the other side, surveying his back trail. Nothing appeared out of the ordinary.

He exited the green at the northwest corner, walking through a large stone archway and into a shopping district full of tourists, the lane jammed with stores of all types.

He continued north, hoping the Africans weren't drawing too much attention.

When Frog, his Croatian arms contact, had initially set up the introductions, they were supposed to meet in London, a much more hospitable area for Somalis to blend into the population. But that was also supposed to be next week.

Frog had told him the Somalis had arrived in London and were anxious to conduct business. Seamus had said there was no way he could break free to go to London, and the next thing he knew, Frog had coordinated for one to travel here. To Dublin.

It was the last scenario Seamus wanted. He had no desire to be connected to the Somali in his own land. The risks were too great for someone remembering, and so he'd been forced to think about where to meet. To find a place where they could at least reasonably blend in and also limit the risk of running into someone he knew. He'd decided to send him to a pub. Not just any pub, but the biggest tourist trap pub in Dublin. The Temple Bar.

The streets surrounding the Temple Bar area were once the quarter for locals to go to drink the night away—as the signs proclaimed, the "cultural center of Dublin"—but as happens in every city of note, tourists began going for the "local" atmosphere. Soon enough, the locals went elsewhere, leaving the tourists the victor.

At six in the evening, the bar would be packed with people from all over the world, and with any luck, the Somali would—if not blend in— at least not be noticed because the tourists wouldn't understand how strange it was. The only ones looking would be the waitstaff, and they'd seen plenty of strange events at the Temple Bar. Most involving vomit.

He threaded his way through the alleys, eventually reaching Temple Lane South. He walked toward the Liffey, passing pub after pub, all proclaiming authentic Irish something or other. Irish stew and music, or T-shirts full of leprechauns, and the tourists of the world over ate it up.

The original Temple Bar after which the area was named owned a corner and, like most Irish pubs, was chopped up into a multitude of different rooms. He'd instructed Frog to tell the Somali to head to the beer garden in back, away from the live music, both so they could hear each other and to get away from the drunks he knew would be slobbering to sing along with the Irish verses.

He entered and was immediately accosted by the noise. Even in the dead of winter, the place was packed, so much so it reminded him of a railroad car full of cattle, the people jammed in so tight there was no room to move. On a small stage, a man sang a ditty, and the bar responded with the chorus.

Not exactly the place the authorities would expect for planning a revolution, but then again, England missed all the same connections in 1916.

40

Seamus waded into the crowd, fighting his way to the bar. He reached it and waited. A barkeep came his way, and he said, "Guinness. Also, I'm looking for Dermot."

The bartender nodded and began his pour, shouting over his shoulder.

Dermot was the man who'd done the legwork to find their original safe house in Dublin. A man not unused to helping out the cause, even if he professed not to know what was being done. Seamus had leased the town house with his grandfather's name and had thought that would be the end of the relationship with Dermot. After Frog's call, Seamus had contacted him for another favor.

The beer arrived at the same time as Dermot. Seamus waited until the barkeep was gone, then said, "Well? Seen anything out of place?"

Wiping down a pint glass, Dermot smiled and said, "Yeah. Your two friends are in the garden. Looking like they'd rather be dead."

"Two? There's two of them?"

"Yep. Tall and lanky. Dressed like a couple of vagabonds and sticking out like burnt wood."

Seamus thanked him, then picked up his beer and began fighting the crowd, pushing and twisting to get beyond the bottleneck of live music. He entered the door to the beer garden, really just another room, and the music faded to the back. He glanced around and immediately spotted the Somalis. Both huddled over a small table, drinking what appeared to be tea, they were exactly as advertised. Tall and lanky. Even their skulls were long, almost as if someone had taken them as a child and drawn them out until their features were distorted, the mass of their muscles lost in the stretching.

He threaded his way through the tables until he was next to theirs. Not wanting to alarm them, he stood until they looked up. He said, "Ali Hassan?"

They glanced at each other, then back at him. One had a small hare-lip, his teeth white against the cleft. He said, "I am Ali Hassan. And you are?"

"You may call me Clover. I'd prefer not to give you my name, but Frog is the one who introduced us."

Ali squinted and said, "So you know my name, but I cannot learn yours."

Seamus said, "May I sit?"

Ali nodded.

He did so and said, "Look, I mean no offense, but what you are proposing is pretty significant. I don't want to be tied to a failure, but I'll be more than willing to claim success. I never wanted to meet you here, in Ireland. Too many people know me. I'm sure you understand."

Ali looked at the other Somali, saying nothing.

Seamus said, "Who is your friend?"

Teeth bared, the friend said, "You may call me Ismail. Nothing more."

Seamus nodded and said, "I understand. We're on the same page. I wish Frog had not given me Ali's name, but he did. A necessary risk of doing business. So, you are prepared to conduct the strike? And it will be significant?"

Ali said, "Yes, it will be greater than anything seen on this continent, but we won't do it unless you can deliver. We understood from Frog that you have someone of importance. Someone who will cause the United States to cease their activities in Somalia. I need to know if that's true."

Seamus pulled out his smartphone and flipped to the camera roll. He pulled up one picture and said, "See this? It's the vice president's son. Next to him is his fiancée. The guy in the back is the husband of a governor of the United States. Yes. They're important. I pass them to you, and you get a coup of unimaginable proportions."

Ali took the phone and said, "How do I know this is true? How do I know you didn't manipulate it with Adobe Photoshop?"

A little taken aback, expecting the goat-herder facade to extend to the man's mentality, Seamus said, "You see the faces? See the bruises? You won't find any pictures like this on Facebook. Go ahead and search. I have them, trust me."

"For how long?"

"For as long as it takes. You want them, you need to pay."

Ali looked at Ismail again, and Seamus wondered who was really in charge.

Ismail nodded and Ali said, "We are ready. Right now. Frog said you would provide the explosive material."

"Yes. I can do that, but I need some assurances you can penetrate the target. The RDX is traceable. It was stolen, and if it's found before detonation, it could lead back to my organization. Afterward, I don't care."

Ismail said, "Don't worry about that. We have two people who are working as a cleaning crew at the target. They've been there for two years. We can penetrate. Can you deliver the necessary amount of RDX? It isn't small."

Seamus ignored the question, saying, "A janitor isn't going to get you inside. Tell me you haven't planned everything on that. The security at that place is very high."

Ali said, "No. We are fishermen. We live in the water. We'll swim to it. There is little protection from that side. All we need is someone to unlock a door once we are up."

Seamus considered his words, then said, "Okay. Yes, I can get you the explosives. Are you looking to separate one car or what?"

Ali smiled. "No. The entire thing. I told you it was significant."

Seamus smelled a bluff. He leaned back and said, "Bullshit. No way can you do that. I don't even know if you can rig the explosives, but you sure as shit can't do it in a manner to cause catastrophic failure. I'm not trading for a puff of smoke and thirty minutes on the news. If I'm going to claim the attack, I need thirty *days* of news."

Ali pointed at Ismail and said, "He is a structural engineer. Trained in Egypt. He has studied everything available on the target. He says he can do it. If you give us the proper explosives."

Seamus went from one to the other, then said, "Okay. It's a trade, then. You get the crown jewels of the United States, and I get your attack. You do understand, though, that if you fail, if you get captured, you're on your own."

"Of course. But we won't fail. I promise you that."

41

Grant Breedlove stared at his computer, the thoughts coalescing in his head but not reaching his fingertips. His editor had given him a leash, but it was running out, and he still didn't have a story. Although he knew one was here. A big one.

He'd worked his way through a multitude of emails and had received responses from most but had nothing for a glaring few. Unfortunately, he had no way of knowing if the service members had simply ignored the email. Given military members' normal hatred of the press, he couldn't dismiss the possibility that their lack of response meant they were telling him to stuff it. And there was no way he could print a story on an absence of email contact alone.

But there was something here. He had contacts all over DC, in the highest echelons of government, and whenever he probed on this story he got two responses: One, a blank stare as if he were crazy. Or two, like the secretary of Homeland Security, a spooked expression and a complete retreat.

He needed time. A bit of news to get his editor on board, no matter how small. A nugget to continue the hunt.

He felt the presence of someone and turned to find Kincaid Butler staring over his shoulder. He blanked the laptop and said, "What do you want?"

"Nothing. Just checking out what you're working on. Word on the street is you're onto a Lewinsky/Watergate type thing."

Disgusted, Grant said, "Get out of my cubicle. Find your own damn story."

Kincaid said, "Hey, even Woodward needed a Bernstein. I'm just offering to help."

"I don't need the help. And I don't have a story. If I do, maybe I'll ask."

Kincaid repulsed him. A young up-and-comer, he'd achieved the appropriate check marks—degree from Georgetown, internship at the White House, a battlefield press tour in Afghanistan—but he'd never once done anything on his own. Always snatching the last bit of fabric from the coattail ahead of him.

His report on the crisis of Afghan interpreters—men who'd given all to help the US effort and were now abandoned to the Taliban—had garnered worldwide attention, but Grant knew the truth. The person who'd written it had been killed by a suicide bomber in a Kabul restaurant before it was published, and Kincaid, as the "man on the ground," had snaked it as his own. Ostensibly as a tribute to the fallen reporter.

Having braved hostile fire in Libya for a story, Grant had little time for an asshole who sat in the rear collating reports and then received the accolades over another's dead body.

Kincaid said, "Hey, everyone knows you're working on something. And that Brittle is done with letting you run amok. No time for that in the Internet day. You let me help, and we could cut your leads in half. Get somewhere."

Grant said, "Get the hell out of here. I have nothing, and if I needed help, it wouldn't be from some remora."

Stung, Kincaid wandered away. Grant rubbed his eyes, thinking of what else he could do to drag out the timeline. He stood, pulling his sport coat off the chair. One cubicle over, he heard his friend Dwight say, "Fuck that guy. And screw Brittle too. I'm sick of this instant news shit. You got a story, you follow it."

Dwight was old-school. A man who believed in the fifth estate, with all the due diligence that entailed. Saddened to see it crushed by bloggers and the Internet, he was Grant's biggest cheerleader. He wanted the world to return to normal, but that time had passed long ago.

Grant said, "I hear you, man. But this story is about to—"

His phone rang. He looked at his watch, seeing it was nine at night. He snatched it up.

"Grant Breedlove."

"The reporter?"

Grant heard an accent but couldn't place it. "Yes."

"I have the information you're looking for."

Irish. Why on earth would an Irishman be calling him?

Feeling circumspect, Grant said, "Okay. What, exactly, do you have? What story do you think I'm working?"

The next words slammed into him like a freight train. The break he'd been waiting for.

"Nicholas Seacrest. Aka Hannister. The vice president's son. Now missing, although nobody knows it. I know what's happened to him. And I've said enough on your recording devices. Good-bye."

"Wait, wait, we don't record things here. That's the NSA."

"Bullshit. Give me a cell number, or always wonder."

Rattled, Grant gave him his personal cell, then said, "When will I hear from you?"

"When I'm ready."

The line went dead, and Grant looked at Dwight.

He said, "A break?"

"Yeah. I think so. Hard to tell."

He rushed out of the office, Kincaid following his every move with his eyes.

Grant reached his car before the cell rang. There was no preamble. "You know the C-and-O Canal run?"

"Yes. I've been on it."

"Meet me at Fletcher's Cove in twenty minutes. Park your car and wait. I'll find you."

"How?"

"I know what you drive."

The phone went dead, Grant staring at it as if it could give him a secret he dearly wanted. He entered his car and began to drive.

Winding through the DC streets, he tried to collate the various questions he should ask. The story was the vice president's son in the hands of terrorists or someone else, but the devil was in the details. A true story wasn't just the meat. It was fleshed out all around with sinew and bone. He needed to know the why, when, and how, and he began rehearsing his questions. Trembling at the anticipation of his success.

He eventually reached Georgetown, the streets filled with college kids debating the worth of the world over a beer. He saw the women, bundled up in coats, yoga pants underneath, showing their wares to the leering college boys, and wondered if he'd ever been so vain. He knew he had been, of course, but he'd grown beyond that. At least that's what he told himself.

The truth was he would like to shout at them, tell them what he was doing. Eradicate his college memories of debate with males only and join the fraternity of men who courted such women. It would never happen, and he would have to be content with his life now. Superior in what he was doing, a cut different from the men walking arm in arm with women above their worth. Even if they didn't know it.

He exited on Canal Road, the traffic much sparser, a two-lane affair that led to Fletcher's Cove. He passed two cars, continuing the rest of the drive in the dark, his headlights spearing the night. He slowed, now peering out the windshield for the turnoff. It sprang up before he was ready, and he whipped the wheel, swerving into the lane that led down to the canal. He entered the parking lot, seeing two cars but little else. He pulled to the far side and parked, turning off the lights.

He sat for ten minutes, waiting, for the first time realizing that he was out here on his own and dealing with dangerous forces. He considered going back and forcing the man to call him again, but the story was too great. He couldn't afford to lose this lead.

He waited another five minutes and then considered leaving out of boredom. He reached for the keys in the ignition and heard a knock on his window. The interruption was so stark he literally jumped. He stared for a minute, seeing a shadowy figure in a Washington Nationals hoodie. He cracked the window.

"Open the passenger door."

He did so, and the man circled the car, taking a seat.

He waited. The man said, "You're working on a story, but you don't know the true implications."

The Irish accent came out again, a lyrical hymn that gave comfort to what was being said.

Wanting to build trust, Grant said, "I am, and I'm here. I can promise you complete anonymity. Nobody will know what you tell me."

The man chuckled and said, "Trust me, I understand that."

The words were sinister, but Grant had heard worse. He said, "What do you have?"

"You are on the right trail. There are people missing, but it's much more than you think."

Grant said, "How many more? What do you mean?"

The hood turned toward him. "First, who else knows about this? Who else is in the hunt for the story?"

Seeing competition, worried about losing the source to someone else, Grant said, "Nobody. If you mean you want credit, it's just me. Nobody believes this story for a minute. They all think I'm crazy."

And his words sealed his fate.

The man raised a pistol, the suppressor looking as large as a drainage pipe. He said, "Then I guess they'll all wonder why you're dead."

Grant raised his hands and got out a single scream, cut short by the bullet splitting his head open.

42

Jennifer sat on the bed, toweling her wet hair, and said, "I hate this part. The waiting. All I ever do is start thinking of what can go wrong."

"That's a good thing. As long as it doesn't start to paralyze you."

"You think Dunkin's information is correct? We're basing a lot on it."

"Well, not that much. *We* did the recce, and it matched his information."

It was closing in on midnight, and I'd just kicked out Clifford Delmonty, aka Dunkin, the one bit of Taskforce help Kurt managed to break free to help us.

A five-foot-eight-inch computer geek, at his hiring board for the Taskforce he'd made an impossible claim that he could dunk a basketball. He thought we were looking for some superhuman physical specimen and figured nobody would test him on his claim. Since we were looking for a guy who could work miracles with electronic devices, not play point guard, we hired him. Then made him put his money where his mouth was.

He'd failed miserably and figured he was fired on his first day. We kept him, but he now wore the callsign Dunkin as a reminder that it doesn't pay to exaggerate. The Taskforce needed the ground truth. No spin. Like Robert Rogers's famous dictum from the original Ranger unit in the French and Indian War, "You can lie all you please when you tell other folks about the Rangers, but don't never lie to a Ranger."

I'd expected a whole team to meet me in Brussels after finding the pendant, but the only thing that had shown up was Dunkin, with a RFID reader and other electronic gadgets. We'd done a Google search on the keycards Jennifer had taken off the Serb bodies in London, and they were for an extended-stay hotel in Brussels. Since that's where one of the hostages had been taken, and where the body parts of the SEC-DEF's son had been delivered, I'd called Kurt, convinced it would lead to Knuckles and a team meeting up with us. I was sorely mistaken. Knuckles had apparently turned up something hot and was headed to Paris, leaving me on my own.

It had been a heated conversation, and I felt bad for putting the pressure on Kurt, but I *knew* Kylie was with the vice president's son, and I had proof positive that I had not only found where they'd been kept, but also a follow-on lead. He'd told me it wasn't his call, and that the Oversight Council was frothing at the mouth for Knuckles to get to France. That's when I'd dropped the pendant and the blood smear on him. Which, given how his hands were tied, I now wished I hadn't. I knew he was imagining the worst about Kylie, and it hadn't done any good to tell him. He couldn't break a team free to help me, not with the scrutiny, which I should have recognized before I started dropping Freddy Krueger nightmares about blood splatter and stained floors.

In the end, nobody but him believed I was onto something, and he did only because of Kylie. Like a parent agonizing over a picture on a milk carton, he was willing to believe anything I told him, sucking in the leads as if any movement of mine was forward progress and not just motion.

The only good news was that the president was now read onto what I was doing. He knew I was freelancing, and while he wasn't throwing his weight behind my efforts, it gave Kurt a little bit of cover to help out where he could.

Kurt had an entire support package on the ground in Paris, ostensibly to facilitate Knuckles's operations, but he managed to break Dunkin free for the short train ride to Brussels.

Jennifer said, "You think we can do this clean?"

"I suppose that'll be up to you."

"Great. Just what I wanted to hear."

She was lying on the bed, pillows propped up behind her. I lay down beside her, our hips touching. We both looked at the TV, the sound off because we couldn't understand the language. I said, "You don't want to do it, and we won't. I'll find another way in."

Each dead Serb had two keycards to a hotel near the Grote Markt— or Grand Place—in the heart of Brussels. All four were embedded with an RFID chip, which meant they'd been programmed and held information. Sometimes that information was extreme, including the name, credit card information, dates of stay, and home addresses. Sometimes, it was just the room number. It all depended on the hotel, but that was where Dunkin and his electronic magic came in.

In this case, we got the name, duration of stay, and room number from each key. Two were for separate rooms. Two were for the penthouse on the top floor. I dearly wanted to see inside all of them.

Earlier in the day, Jennifer and I had gone to the hotel, called the B-Aparthotel Grand Place, to check it out. I figured the easiest thing would be to use the cards to enter each room as a patron, as if we were staying there. That plan was cut short by the hotel.

It was a luxury establishment, fulfilling a niche for rich folks looking to stay for a month or more. Situated on the back of the Brussels Grand Place, in a maze of indoor/outdoor restaurants and cafés, it had no fewer than three cameras at the entrance, and Dunkin had told us that any individual card would unlock only a keypad, where we'd have to type in a number code. Something we did not know.

On top of that, just inside the glass front door was the reception desk, which, if it were an Embassy Suites, would have been no problem, but this hotel was a boutique. The reception area was a total of about thirty feet across, and anyone penetrating the front door would have to walk by the desk.

The hotel had only six rooms to a floor, with just two on the top— both penthouses—so, with four floors, we were looking at a total of twenty patrons, and they'd all signed on for a long-term stay. That was the hotel specialty. To top it off, the "reception desk" wasn't there to help the guests check in. It was to protect them. A beefy guy who did nothing but stare at anyone coming or going manned it, and his sole purpose was problem solving of the physical sort. He wasn't there to get you tickets to the opera, and I knew he would recognize on sight anyone staying at the hotel.

So using the keycard as though we owned the place was out of the question. Which meant a little high adventure if we wanted to see the inside of the rooms.

Dunkin had cracked into the floor plan of the hotel on a Belgium government server. He'd failed to get into the hotel servers themselves because of an incredibly high amount of encryption, but the Belgium server had at least identified the location of each of the rooms in question. Two were on the first floor—the second floor in American standards— one facing the promenade of the covered shopping district, and one facing the street known as rue de l'Écuyer. The penthouse was on the top and out of reach of anything.

We'd taken his information and gone to dinner earlier, ostensibly just a couple of American visitors, and had wandered the lanes and alleys around the hotel, seeing the problem up close. The entire area was a tourist mecca, with Grand Place only a couple of blocks away and the surrounding terrain chock-full of small eateries and stores. The only good thing was the weather. A bunch of storm clouds had settled over- head, threatening to burst open with a torrential downpour. The tourists didn't care, but they would when the buckets of water started coming down, especially given that it was about forty degrees.

We'd circled the block on foot, getting to rue de l'Écuyer and passing right in front of the hotel entrance. Walking down the street, we'd con- ducted a full reconnaissance, finding a parking garage underneath the hotel with about twelve spaces, along with a laundry room for the cleaning crew and what I thought was an interior stairwell, but it was locked up tight.

Throughout the garage were the ubiquitous surveillance cameras. There had been no monitor at the reception desk, so it wasn't real-time, but I had no idea if we were now on tape. I'd done my best to stay out of their view. We'd returned to the street and I'd pulled out a neat little Taskforce gizmo we called God's Eye.

It had been invented by a startup called Panono and originally the size of a basketball. We'd stolen the idea and miniaturized it. About the size of a softball, and surrounded with small embedded cameras, it allowed you to toss it into the air and get a panorama snapshot of the area around you. The higher you tossed it, the greater the panorama. The best part about it was that once it took the picture, a software program allowed you to take a point of view from anywhere on the image.

You could analyze everything, from any angle, like the eye of God. Or Google. Or maybe they were the same thing.

We'd started strolling like a couple seeing the sights, and the clouds had opened up, scattering the tourists. I suppose I should have shouted with joy, but we were getting soaked, which aggravated the hell out of me.

I'd waited on a break in traffic, not wanting anyone to see me toss the ball. I cowered under an awning, saw it was clear, then threw the thing in the air. After I'd caught it, we'd walked a little bit more, then repeated the procedure, trying to get a look inside the room next to the street.

We darted from awning to awning, Jennifer holding a newspaper over her head and acting just like a woman on a date. She'd actually taken her leather jacket off and balled it under an arm, saying it would get ruined. On the last awning, I said, "Some commando you are."

She looked at me, hair dripping water and trembling from the cold. She said, "Was that you I just heard cursing? As you tried to throw the Eye from under the awning? What did that get you?"

My last toss had actually caught the edge of the canvas and ricocheted into the street, forcing me to chase it in the rain to keep it from getting run over. I held it out to her and said, "Do better?"

She snatched it out of my hand, gave me her jacket, then stood in the rain and tossed it up, waiting defiantly for it to come down. She caught it, darted back under the awning, and said, "Satisfied?"

I said, "Yeah. I was just trying to get that shirt soaked."

She looked down, saw the damage, and punched me in the arm, now really pissed. She started to stalk off, and I tugged her sleeve, getting her to stop. I pulled off my own jacket, a Gore-Tex one designed for operations in inclement weather. I held it out. She looked at me, and I knew she was going to tell me to stuff it. Arms crossed over her chest, shirt soaked, she was going to let her anger get the better of her.

I said, "So you can keep your leather one dry."

She glared at me, then took it. She slipped it on, then shoved her leather jacket underneath. Still piqued, she said, "We done yet?"

Knowing I was ahead, I said, "Yeah. Let's head back through the indoor mall. Remember how to get there?"

She took off at a brisk walk, hood over her head and not looking back. I trotted to keep up, the rain pelting my face like ice cubes.

43

It took about forty-five minutes for Dunkin to download the data from God's Eye, then massage it with his software programs. When he was finished, he'd given us the damage. Using the pictures and his own internal mapping from the Brussels server, there was no way to get to any of the rooms from the outside without being seen by security, with the exception of one. There was a single break between the various camera angles and the corner room on the first floor. The one that butted up to rue de l'Écuyer, the only road next to the hotel that allowed cars.

The good news was that right next to the window of the target room was one of the hotel security cameras, posted at an angle to see the street. Dunkin had studied it and said we could slave from the cable coming out. We couldn't stop it from recording, but he could see everything that was tied to the surveillance array and give us early warning about anything that happened inside the building.

Looking thoughtful, Jennifer had analyzed the problem and said, "I suppose we could pretend to be a maintenance crew. Get a painting ladder or something and go to work right there. Slave the camera, then work on the window. I could get inside and Pike could give me cover. Can we get some government maintenance uniforms? Can the Taskforce do that on short notice?"

I thought the whole scene was cute. Her brow scrunched up, dissecting the problem, trying to find a solution. Too bad she was way, way off.

She saw my grin and said, "What? Why is that stupid?"

"It's not. But that's way too much work when we have a monkey."

She heard the words and said, "Whoa. Wait. It's raining cats and dogs outside. I can't climb in this weather."

Jennifer was a former Cirque du Soleil performer and about the best climber I had ever seen. She could scale a marble wall and had used that skill on a number of occasions to pull my ass out of the fire.

I said, "Rain is in our favor. Nobody will see. We try to fake a maintenance crew and we're only good until someone asks me a question, regardless of our uniforms. And we don't have the time to prep for that. It would take a couple of days."

She looked at Dunkin, who stared at his shoes, not wanting to be drawn into the conversation. Disgusted, she said, "You're really going to put all this on my shoulders?"

"No. You get in, then get to the laundry room in the garage. Unlock the door. Then we'll both be in. Behind the security."

She looked at the ceiling, breathing through her nose, containing her aggravation. She said, "What do I do if I'm caught on the side of the building?"

"Show them your wet blouse."

Her head snapped to me, the glare like white-hot lava, and I held up my hands, laughing. "I'll be there. I'll handle anything from the ground. You won't have to worry about that."

We'd spent the next ten minutes synchronizing the encryption for the slave device with Dunkin's kit and got a quick class on using it, then I'd sent Dunkin on his way. Now we had about five hours before we executed.

Jennifer flipped the channel, getting another news station we couldn't understand. She said, "You sure this risk is worth it? I don't mean because I'm worried about doing the climb. I mean, it's a hell of a big risk for something that may not pay off at all."

I said, "It's all we've got. Those Serbs in London were tied to both Braden and Kylie. I know I can't prove it, but they were. All we need to find is a connection to Braden. Maybe he's staying in one of the rooms. We find that, then crack some skulls."

She exhaled. "Maybe we should wait for Nung. Get more than just you and me. Let this sit."

"He can't get here for another day, and that's a day more for Kylie. I can't wait, and neither can she. We find an edge, and we can use Nung for the endgame." I squeezed her hand and said, "I'll climb that wall if you don't want to. You don't feel comfortable, I'll do it myself. You can pull security. But . . ." I lapsed off, not wanting to admit something.

She said, "But what?"

I looked at her, then forced it out. "But you're better at this than me. You can do it in half the time. I can't get up to that window like you can."

Her eyes widened a smidgen, then she smiled, "Boy, I'll bet that was hard to get out."

I muttered, "You'll never know."

She said, "What?"

"Nothing. We should get some sleep. We're going to need it."

44

After seeing the text, Braden's first thought was, *We missed the business day*. He called Seamus, making sure it wasn't a mistake.

"You want me to launch the Snapchat now? At this time of night?"

"Yeah. Get them moving across the pond. I'm sure they've got forces in place over here, but they'll need to be redirected to Paris."

"Seamus, even given the time change it's dark over there. Nobody's working. I'm afraid it'll be missed. Best case, this'll sit until morning."

He heard his brother chuckle. "Braden, they've probably got twelve people staring at a computer screen waiting on our contact. Trust me, they'll get it. You have the Bitcoin address?"

"Yeah. I got that."

"Read it back to me. I need to know it's correct."

"You know they're not going to pay up front, right? Who in their right mind would pay just because of a video? I mean, you've put me in a serious problem with the Serbs, and we're not getting anything out of it. Tell me you've got this wired. Seamus, tell me you know what you're doing."

"Braden, calm down. I know what I'm doing. I've met Ali. He's set to go. I've given him the cache location for the explosive, and he's now fire and forget. The hostages are secure, and the plan is working fine."

Braden soaked up the confidence coming from the handset. Something he needed. Something that allowed him to continue. He said, "Okay, Seamus, okay. I'm ready to go here." He read out the Bitcoin address and asked, "You want me to send that at the same time as the Snapchat? Or wait?"

"Same time. You send the Snapchat, then send the message on the White House page. You need to tell me when you do it. Send me a text. As soon as that's done, I'm giving them an address for direct chat that Kevin's created. A way for real-time communication that's autonomous."

"So you think they'll pay? Just because they see the video?"

"No. You're right about that. No way will they pay at first. They'll try to drag it out, try to get clues to our location so they can send in a rescue force. Which is where your diversion comes in. They'll be talking to me but hunting you. We set off that trap, and then I hit them with the chat. They'll be in a panic over the deaths. Stricken by our ability to be one step ahead. Then they'll pay. We keep the prize, and they'll pay."

"How long will that take? I mean, how long until they get here?"

"I don't know. Could be hours. Could be a day, but I'm betting it's more like hours. That's why you've got three people. Work it in shifts. Can you leave the hostages alone?"

"Yeah, yeah. We've taken to roping them up like the goats on a farm. We can leave them for the duration of the operation. Days if necessary." He gave a brittle laugh. "I mean, it's not like we want to be in the room with them anyway."

"Good. But don't let them suffer. That's not our way. We get nothing by dragging out the suffering. Make them as comfortable as you can."

Braden quickly said, "That isn't what I meant. We still let them go to the bathroom and feed them on a schedule. I remember what you told me. I'm doing what's right."

"I know you are. It's why I picked you for this mission."

Braden let the praise wash over him, buoying his psyche. He said, "Keep me in the loop. I'll be working the diversion, so I'll be busy."

"The Serbs ready to go?"

Braden barked a laugh and said, "Yeah, that wasn't pretty. I swear, I thought they were going to gut me."

"But they're on board? Ready to execute?"

"Most of them are here. They left a couple of guys in Brussels, but they brought the hit team with them, including the females. They are *really* not comfortable with me controlling the timeline. Not comfortable at all. I made them leave on the spur of the moment, and now they're sitting around wondering why. I'm not sure they trust me anymore."

"Did you clean out your signature in Brussels?"

"Yeah. I no longer have a room there."

"Then we're good."

Braden said, "We're not good. Only you are. Do you know why he left those guys in Brussels? He was going to use them on the operation, but he didn't. You know why he's not?"

"Why?"

"Me. He thinks we're pulling something shady, and he's left them there to find me after it's done. He wanted some insurance in case things go bad."

"It won't go bad. Remember why we're doing this. Keep the faith."

Braden said, "For Brian."

"For Brian."

45

Four hours later, in a deep fog, I felt something jabbing me. I rolled over and looked at the clock. Three twenty-nine in the morning. *What the hell?*

I turned over and saw Jennifer completely dressed. She said, "It's time."

Irritated, I said, "No, it's not. Jesus."

My watch alarm went off exactly when I'd set it: three thirty. I slammed it to silence. I looked back at her, aggravated at the early-bird bullshit. I saw wide eyes. Someone who needed strength, not my whining about being awakened a minute early. Although I would have liked that damn minute.

I rubbed my face and swung my legs off the bed. "You ready?"

"Yeah. I think so. It's still raining. That's going to make it hard."

I smiled. "And fucking cold."

She said, "Thanks. That's a lot of help. I wish I'd known I'd be climbing. I would have packed different clothes."

She was wearing jeans and a black, long-sleeved tourist T-shirt we'd bought at a bar, with sensible leather shoes on her feet. She had her hair in a tight ponytail and had forgone any makeup. She oozed nothing but business, and it brought a smile to my face.

She said, "What's so funny?"

"Nothing." I pulled on my jeans and said, "You just look so serious."

"Well, we'll see how that works in about thirty minutes." She started pacing while I finished dressing.

I said, "You okay?" She looked at me, and I said, "Hey, this is a walk in the park. Remember Singapore? This is nothing like that. A one-story climb, with a huge window."

She calmed down, saying, "Yeah, but it's a driving rainstorm. And we don't know the reaction time for anyone. We don't even know about alarms. We don't know anything."

"We'll have the cameras once you slave. Is Dunkin ready?"

"Yeah. I called him ten minutes ago to make sure he was set."

Boy, I bet that early wake-up pissed him off.

Finished dressing, I said, "Okay then, let's get it done."

We took the back stairs to avoid the reception desk seeing us leave, exiting on rue Charles Buls and walking straight to the Grand Place. Now dead, the area was spooky. A large expanse of stone surrounded by gothic buildings made of granite, it was full of tourists and markets in the day. Cheerful and airy. Something people the world over came to see. At night, it became sinister.

As we slipped along in the darkness, it seemed the towering stone buildings were looking down on us with disapproval. We scurried through, sticking to the shadows, making a half-assed attempt at looking like tourists out for a stroll at four in the morning but knowing we looked skeevy slinking around.

We passed down the alleys of deserted restaurants, the chairs all on the tables, the rain dripping down. We saw not a soul. We skirted by the hotel's alley entrance and reached rue de l'Écuyer. We paused, waiting for a car to pass. The rain had let up some, turning into a miserable drizzle.

I said, "You sure you can do this? The stone's going to be wet as shit."

She was a bundle of energy, her entire body vibrating in anticipation. No fear. No hesitation. Everything that had been said in the room was gone. I realized my question was stupid.

She pulled me into the wall, out of the rain and into the darkness. She said, "I get caught, you get me out, right?"

I said, "Of course."

She nodded and clicked her earpiece, not even waiting on me, taking over the operation. "Dunkin, Dunkin, this is Koko, you on?"

"I got you Lima Charlie. Ready to slave."

I heard the words from my own earpiece and started to say something, but she put a finger to my lips. "I get to say it this time."

She pulled her shoes off and handed them to me. Standing barefoot, she took a deep breath, looked me in the eyes, and said, "Showtime," then slipped around the edge of the wall.

I watched her leave and felt my emotions go into turmoil. Part of me wanted to stop her, a feeling of impotence flowing through me because I was putting her in harm's way without a means of helping her. If she were hurt, it would be my fault. And I wasn't sure if I could live with that.

I lost sight of her and began the long wait to hear she was inside, the rain dripping down from the awning I was cowering under. I heard a noise and saw a rat, scuttling about the adjacent outdoor café, looking for scraps. I waited a minute more, then leaned out into the street. I saw her thirty feet in the air, clinging to an outcropping of granite, her feet swinging about, searching for purchase. I knew she was in trouble, but, outside of standing below to catch her, I could do nothing. I watched for what felt like hours, but was probably five seconds, and saw her feet connect with a stone, her toes curling into the veins.

She paused, and I clicked in. "Koko, you okay?"

She came on, breathing heavy. "Yeah. I'm okay. This granite is slick as goose shit. You owe me big time."

I smiled. "I'm always owing somebody."

I saw her start climbing again and heard, "But this time I'm making you pay up."

She reached the window, and I saw her lean over and place the slave device on the cable coming out of the camera, working the claws past the insulation with one hand alone. I heard, "Dunkin, slave in place. You got feed?"

"Stand by."

A second later, he said, "Got it. All feeds. Nine cameras. You're good. Everything is empty except for the front desk. Security is in place and bored."

She started cutting the window. From the keycard, we knew this guy had rented the room for three weeks. Since he was dead, we didn't have a whole lot of fear of anyone finding the break-in.

She started to open the window, and I saw headlights on the road. I said, "Car. Hug the wall."

She froze, and I waited. She was outside of the cone of the headlights, and the rain would make it hard for anyone driving by to see her, but movement would be a killer.

The vehicle passed, and she went back to work. Shortly, I saw her disappear, a black blob that simply ceased to exist.

I heard, "Inside. Room is empty. Some clothes, but nothing else."

"Nothing interesting? No documents or anything else?"

"No. But we know this guy was in Dublin. He probably packed out to go there, leaving the bare minimum here."

I said, "Okay, get to the garage. Get me in."

46

I left the alley and rounded the corner, walking to the indoor garage. I reached the entrance and said, "Dunkin, you got the view in the garage?"

"Yep."

"Is it clear?"

"Yeah. Nothing."

"Tell me if you see me on camera." I retraced my steps earlier and said, "I'm set."

"Saw nothing."

Which made me feel a little bit better about our earlier reconnaissance. I said, "Koko, you coming?"

"Yeah. Thirty seconds."

I waited, and then heard a knock on the door. I knocked back, and it opened, Jennifer looking like a bedraggled cat that had been thrown in a bathtub full of water. Except for her eyes. There was no misery in them.

She said, "Stairwell's pretty secure. It's not one used by the guests, but there's a camera on the first floor. We're going to be on tape."

I pulled off my knapsack, handed her the Serb pistol she'd earned in London, then gave her shoes to her and said, "Not bad for a female."

She put them on, saying, "Really? Funny, I didn't see you scaling the wall."

I said, "Touché. Let's go."

We retraced her steps up the stairwell, hugging the sheetrock to avoid the single camera on the first-floor landing. I tossed her my knap-sack and said, "Get out the radar scope."

I peeked out the door and saw it was clear. The floor was small, with two rooms to the left—including the one Jennifer had entered—and two to the right, separated by about fifty feet of hallway. I made a beeline for the target room on the right, then held up, Jennifer bumping into my back like a Three Stooges act. I flashed her the keycard and nodded, a silent command. She placed what looked like a small brick against the door, reading a digital screen.

The radar scope was invented to give assault teams a little advantage when breaching a room, as it could see through walls and identify if anything living was beyond. It worked much better than thermals in that it would identify motion instead of just heat, letting us know if a human was inside, meaning we wouldn't get amped up over a hot light-bulb. It didn't matter if the person was sitting still. A heartbeat alone was enough movement.

She held it up against the door for a moment, then whispered, "Clear."

I swiped the card. And got nothing.

Shit.

Jennifer tugged my arm and pointed at the room across the tiny hall. I nodded, and she repeated the procedure. She gave me the go-ahead, and I swiped again. The light went green.

We both stood there, surprised at the success. The light flicked out and I swiped again, then entered, my own Glock drawn. The room was empty and, after a quick search, gave us as little information as the room she'd entered from the street. I said, "On to the penthouse."

We skulked back to the stairwell and went to the top floor. This one had cameras, I knew. I called Dunkin. "About to break the penthouse floor. Am I clear?"

I heard nothing.

I said, "Dunkin, Dunkin, you copy?"

I heard a snort, then, "Yeah, I'm here."

I said, "Are you fucking sleeping? You little shit, I'm going to break your neck when I get back."

Jennifer, hearing the calls through her own earpiece, grabbed my arm and shook her head, giving me her disapproving-teacher stare. I gritted my teeth and said, "Dunkin, are you monitoring?"

He came back quickly. "I'm here. Floor is clear. The room to the right has a tray of food outside from a delivery service, but your suite is clear."

I shook my head, not believing I was inside a target with my backup asleep at the wheel. I said, "We're going to break the plane of the door. You fall asleep again, and I'll rip you apart. You copy?"

I heard, "Yes, sir."

We exited and went to the penthouse, a DO NOT DISTURB sign hanging on the door handle. Jennifer applied the radar scope and signaled we were good. I swiped the next keycard and the light went green again. We entered, feeling a large space in the darkness. The door closed, and I saw some sort of bulletin board in the center of the room, but I had no time to check it out just yet. I pointed to the room to the left, and Jennifer stalked toward it. I took the room to the right.

I swept the space, moving to the bathroom, and heard, "Left side clear."

I finished clearing my room and met her in the den. I flicked on the lights and saw something out of a Taskforce operations briefing.

There was a sand table on the floor, with little buildings and roads, and a bulletin board full of pictures, with notes above them in Cyrillic writing. Definitely not from a family planning a fun vacation.

Jennifer said, "What the hell is all of this?"

I leaned in to the bulletin board, reading the few English words on it. I said, "Bulgari. That picture says *Bulgari* underneath it. That's what that asshole asked about before we killed him."

Jennifer said, "What in the world is going on? What does this have to do with Kylie?"

"I don't know. Get out your camera. Take pictures of all of this. We'll send it to the Taskforce for translation. I'm going to search the rooms and see if I can find a connection to Braden."

I left her to do the work and entered the bedroom I'd already cleared, now looking for clues instead of threats. Larger than most hotel bedrooms, it was utilitarian, with a desk full of different international electrical outlets and a dresser sporting a forty-inch plasma screen. The bed was made, and there were no indications that anyone had used it.

Unlike the room outside, the desk and everything else were pristine, and I realized what we'd entered: the place was a TOC. A Tactical Operations Center for planning an operation. Nobody was sleeping in here. They'd rented the penthouse only because of the size. They could get the entire team in here for briefings to plan whatever they had going on. I had done the same thing more times than I could count, in more countries than *The Amazing Race* had stamps in its passport, which made me wonder who we were chasing.

I started to leave and heard Dunkin in my earpiece. "Man approaching. Man approaching. I don't know where he came from, but he's at your door."

47

I felt the shock flood my body and said, "Weapon? Any weapon?"
"Not that I can see. He's out of sight now but walking your way."
"Koko, on me, *now*."

She came flying through the door, not speaking a word but saying enough with her expression. A mixture of fear and violence. She held her Glock up and I shook my head. I grabbed her arm and flicked my eyes to the sliding closet.

We entered and I slid the door as quietly as I could. I heard the front lock snick open, and the man began moving around, making small noises. Then I heard the sound of paper ripping and understood what was happening. He was tearing the place down. He shuffled a bit, further scratches of sound reaching us, then called someone on a phone. I could clearly hear what he said, but it did no good, as he was speaking a language I didn't understand.

His voice became loud, shouting, then grew obsequious. I heard him disconnect and thought he was done and we were safe. I was wrong.

The light in our room flared on, the glow stabbing through the crack in our closet. Jennifer stiffened, and I pulled her close, telling her with my body to let it go. To wait until there was a reason to explode. I felt her trembling and raised my Glock. She saw the death in her peripheral vision and raised her own. I leaned in and whispered, "My shot. You do nothing."

She lowered her gun, but I could still feel the tension in her body. Fearing she'd cause a compromise, I leaned in again and said, in a voice that could barely be heard, "You're a ghost. Nobody knows you're here. Let him go about his business."

I felt the trembling stop but kept my weapon at the ready. The man left the room.

We heard more shuffling from the other bedroom, then heard the outside door close. Jennifer sagged against me and said, "Man alive. I don't want to do anything like that again."

I said, "Let's get out of here."

I called Dunkin and got the all clear from the camera. Jennifer used the scope just to be sure, seeing the hallway was empty. We exited, moving straight to the laundry room stairwell. I jerked the handle, and it moved freely up and down but didn't open the door. I tried again, getting the same result. The door was locked.

Feeling like a fool, I said, "Please don't tell me you disabled the lock on the first-floor stairwell before you came down."

"No. Why?"

"Because this fucker is locked."

She tried the handle, saying, "Mine was open. I didn't do anything."

For whatever reason, her doorway had been left unlocked. Which was absolutely no excuse for me not checking this one before I let it close.

Jesus Christ. I should have left a wedge. Idiot.

Jennifer said, "Pick it?"

"Take too long, and I don't want to be on tape doing so. Right now, we're just guests to anyone who reviews the footage."

From Dunkin's floor plan I knew that the hotel guests' stairwell flowed out right past the reception desk, but we could still use it to get out. I said, "Guest stairwell. We'll exit on the first floor, then retrace your steps to the garage."

We speed-walked to the other end of the hall, entering the stairwell and taking the steps two at a time. We reached the second floor, and Dunkin called again. "The man just went to Koko's entry room on the first floor."

Shit. He was sterilizing every room. He'd find the window breach.

I held up and Jennifer said, "We *are* going to get out of here clean, right?"

I said, "Of course," but I was honestly starting to wonder. I started back down, moving much slower, thinking through options. I skipped the door to the first floor and continued to the lobby. Jennifer said, "How are we going to exit? The desk will see us."

I said, "Yeah, that's a threat, but I'd rather the hotel staff see us than the man on the first floor. He has two rooms to sterilize, and it would be just our luck he'd pop into the hallway the same time we do. He takes one look at you and your wet clothes, and he won't have to guess at who was climbing through the window. We'd be forced to take him out, and any lead we've found will be gone. They'll think they're compromised and abort whatever they've got planned."

We reached the lobby, and I had Jennifer lead. Walking into the small atrium, we went past the beefy dude at the front desk.

Moment of truth.

He nodded at us, then did a double take. He said something in French, which I didn't understand.

Here we go.

I tensed up and Jennifer answered in French. Calming the man. I hid a smile and kept walking. The guard said something else, walking around the desk. Jennifer hissed, "He doesn't buy my story. He's asking why I'm all wet."

Still walking, I said, "What did you tell him?"

I saw the door to our front, and she said, "That we were visiting a friend. He asked who."

We were parallel to his desk, the door thirty feet away. I considered just sprinting when he darted in front of us, blocking the exit. He moved surprisingly fast for such a big guy. Over six feet tall, he leaned forward, using his size to intimidate. He said something I couldn't understand, and I decided I'd had enough.

I held my hands up and said, "Speak English?" He shook his head, and I said, "How about ass kicking? You speak that?" My hands already shoulder-high, I balled my fists and popped him in the face with two quick jabs from my left. His head bounced like a paddle ball on a string, and I gave him a right roundhouse punch with all of my weight behind it, snapping my hip into the blow. It connected perfectly with a sharp crack, and he dropped straight down, as if I'd magically touched him with a wand.

Jennifer knelt next to his head and checked to make sure he was breathing. She looked up at me and said, "I guess he got a crash course in that language."

I pulled her to her feet without a word, moving to the front door. We burst out of it, the rain stinging my face. I turned left, dodging through the deserted cafés, Jennifer right behind me.

With any luck, the event would be chalked up as an attempted break-in and not connected with the Serbian TOC operations. Nothing had been stolen, and no other guests had been disturbed, so it was a good bet. After tonight's shenanigans, I figured we were due some good luck. For Kylie's sake.

We sprinted back to the Grand Place square, putting distance between us and the damage we'd left behind.

48

Kurt heard his phone beep but knew switching to the other line would send his sister over the edge. He glanced at the display and saw it was George Wolffe, his deputy. The man in the passenger seat shouted, "Whoa!" and Kurt realized he was about to sail through a red light. He slammed on the brakes, causing the car behind him to blare his horn.

He said, "Sorry, Creed," then brought the phone back up. George Wolffe was gone, and his sister was shouting, "Kurt, Kurt, you still there?"

He said, "Kathy, I'm about to get in a wreck in DC traffic. Look, I've given you all I have. We're following up leads as fast as we can, and hopefully something will break free today. If it does, you'll be the first to know."

He saw his passenger, Bartholomew Creedwater, answer his own phone, and the traffic light went green. He pulled through the intersection and heard Kathy say, "If they found the pendant in Ireland, why are they now in Brussels? You're not making any sense."

Creed held out the phone and mouthed, *George. Important.*

A magician with anything digital, Bartholomew Creedwater worked inside the Taskforce Computer Network Operations cell—which is to say he was a hacker. Late the previous night, the proof-of-life Snapchat had arrived from the terrorists, and after the NSA had managed to capture the video before it self-destructed, he'd been given a crack at it for clues.

The Snapchat had been sent from a Wi-Fi signal, without touching the cell network, preventing the NSA from gleaning any geolocation data from the telephone architecture. Eggheads in the FBI spent the remainder of the night going through the video image itself, looking for clues. Creed had gone deeper, looking specifically at the digital ones and zeros. And had found something.

The cell used was an iPhone, which had a multitude of applications that accessed location services based on GPS. Keeping his fingers crossed, Creed had dissected the digital image, praying the terrorists had not disabled the feature that geotagged anything taken with the camera. They hadn't. The video had a geolocation embedded within it. While the NSA furiously tried to track the MAC address of the Wi-Fi signal and the FBI attempted to derive a clue from the picture, Creed had found something better: the actual location where the video had been taken.

Just after midnight, Kurt had launched Knuckles to link up with an FBI HRT team on the ground in Paris, and the administration had mobilized the very seat of the French government. It had taken hours of work, but now an assault was imminent, and Kurt was taking Creed to the Situation Room as an advisor for any stupid questions that might arise from his computer magic. George first calling Kurt's number, then Creed's, could mean only bad news.

He put Creed's phone to his ear. "Hey, Wolffe. What's up?"

Without preamble, he said, "Grant Breedlove is dead. They found him murdered in his car out on the canal."

"You're shitting me?"

"No. Last contact was someone claiming to have information on a story, about the same time we were getting the Snapchat. He left, and nobody heard from him again. They found him this morning. Bullet hole in the head, contact burns. Up close and personal."

"And? Not to be callous, but why do I care?"

"The president's going batshit. He wants to know if we did it."

"Seriously?"

"Well, not just us, but anybody in the intelligence community."

"He knows better than that. He's been president for over six years. Nobody would assassinate a journalist over a story."

"I'm not so sure."

"Come on. If that were the case, WikiLeaks would have been bloody years ago."

"Stakes are different now. It's not an amorphous threat to national security. It's personal. How far would you go if a journalist was going to jeopardize Kylie?"

"Not that far."

George said nothing.

Kurt let the silence hang, then said, "So he's looking at anyone with skin in the game?"

"I don't know, but it's threatening to derail Paris operations until he gets answers."

Just great.

"Is Knuckles set?"

"Yeah. He's linked up with the hostage rescue guys. They think he's SOCOM. All the French know is he's FBI HRT."

"We got comms with him?"

"Yeah. He'll report to Taskforce, but your comms in the Situation Room will be coming straight from the FBI."

"GIGN has the ball?"

"They're on site. According to Knuckles's last SITREP, the majority of the Parisian gendarmerie is working the problem."

"Then the president may not have a say anymore. The French will go with their own protocols."

Knuckles softly approached the pack of men huddled around a video screen, wanting to get some information on where they stood. Watching the French conduct their precombat checks, he was growing a little more comfortable with merely being an observer.

As a Navy SEAL, he'd never cross-trained with the Groupe d'Intervention de la Gendarmerie Nationale—the vaunted counterterrorist unit known as GIGN—but they had one of the best reputations of any such element, and watching them plan, he could see why.

No panic. No wasted effort. The warehouse they were in was bustling with activity but without the usual shouting of orders you heard from a line unit. The men moved about with a calm detachment, each one preparing for his special role.

On the surface, it appeared that the GIGN had more than fifty soldiers crammed in the warehouse, but Knuckles's practiced eye could pick out the regular gendarmerie from the counterterrorist commandos.

All were dressed in blue-black fatigues, and all had Kevlar helmets with Plexiglas face shields, but the similarities stopped there. The gendarmerie were armed with the standard FAMAS bullpup rifle, while the GIGN men sported SIG SAUER SG 553 carbines equipped with the latest optics and lasers. Both groups of men wore the same black body armor, but the gendarmerie's was slick, with nothing but the plates front and back. The GIGN armor was bristling with equipment, from squad radios to flash-bangs, all cinched down tight, every piece in a specific location.

"What's up with the six-guns?"

Knuckles turned and saw Brett Thorpe, the second in command of his team and the man he'd chosen to accompany him on the raid. Knuckles looked at one of the GIGN commandos, and sure enough, his sidearm of choice was a revolver. "I don't know. Not something I'd take on an assault, but there's got to be a reason. The regular police all have Glocks, so it's not a lack of equipment."

Brett said, "Well, other than that strange choice, they seem to know what they're doing."

"Yeah. I hate being in the back with American lives at stake, but maybe these guys will work out."

Their FBI counterpart, a man who introduced himself only as Brock, overheard his comment and said, "Hey, no heroics. We're here to observe and collect evidence."

Dressed much like the GIGN, only with olive drab fatigues and subdued FBI patches, Brock held up an MP5/10A3 submachine gun. "We don't use these unless things go to absolute shit. Understand?"

Knuckles said, "You mean this one chambered in ten mil? Seriously?" He looked at his loaned 10A3 and said, "Trust me, I won't be pulling the trigger unless my life depends on it, because once I'm dry, I'm done.

Our magazines are probably the only ten mil on the European continent. You guys ever heard of NATO standards?"

Brock scowled, and Knuckles drove home the knife. "What type of battery does the radio take? Something made on the moon?"

Brock started to say something, and Knuckles held up his hands in surrender, saying, "I got it. No joining the fight. Don't worry about us. I'm not looking for a gunfight."

Brock spit tobacco on the ground and said, "I'm not even sure why you SOCOM boys showed up. No reason."

Having had enough fun, Knuckles backed off, not wanting to genuinely aggravate Brock. He'd worked with the FBI hostage rescue team and had a lot of respect for their skills. He knew how Brock felt, because he'd be just as pissed if two strangers showed up and told him he'd been ordered to take them on an assault.

"Hey, just following orders. We work for you. We appreciate the uniforms and kit."

Mildly satisfied, Brock said, "Just remember, that patch doesn't make you FBI. Okay?"

Knuckles nodded.

Brock said, "Good. We're last in. Me and Boyd will take the lead. You follow. I'll leave Lewis out front with the command vehicle. The hit goes down, you guys just look pretty. We'll start the evidence sweep on whatever we find. Remember, this is a GIGN show."

Knuckles pointed to the men around the video screen. "Did they lock the phone? Do we even have a floor, or are we taking down the entire building?"

"They're still working it."

While the Snapchat had given them a geographic location, it didn't work in three dimensions. On a map, the grid from the video location appeared on top of a run-down housing complex, but, since there were four floors, it wasn't enough information. The GIGN was trying to neck down a location using a little spoofing.

From the Wi-Fi signal used to send the Snapchat, the NSA had determined the name of the specific network the phone had used and had

230 / BRAD TAYLOR

passed that to the French, but the node had ended up being a free service from a coffee shop four blocks away. Not a lot of help.

Because the terrorists had made the mistake of failing to turn off location services, the GIGN was hoping they also hadn't told the phone to ask before synching with a known Wi-Fi network the phone had used in the past. They'd loaded a router spoofed with the coffee shop Wi-Fi signal onto a rotary-wing UAV—a little thing with four helicopter blades and a camera—and had launched it to the building. As there was no Wi-Fi in the run-down apartment complex, the phone should pick up the signal and automatically join, not knowing it was a dead link. From there, they hoped to trace the signal back to the phone.

The entire effort, from the US to the French, was reminiscent of Apollo 13, with one expert after another coming up with solutions for locating the hostages. Knuckles was proud that his organization had been the first to start down the chain.

Lucky for us, these guys aren't the evil geniuses they think they are.

He felt his phone vibrate and saw it was Pike. Probably calling to yell at him for once again leaving him hanging. He looked at Brett and said, "I should probably take this. Keep an eye on the team. Flag me if something's coming up."

49

By the fourth ring I was convinced Knuckles was going to blow me off, making me wonder if his team was really onto something. That would be extremely odd, since I was sure Jennifer and I were tearing up the true thread, which had come through Ireland, not Morocco. There was no way some Somali ferry receipt was going to lead to the hostages.

He answered, saying, "Still on your own, huh?"

I laughed and said, "No. I've replaced your sorry ass. I pulled in Nung."

"Nung? From Thailand? Seriously?"

"Yeah. I met him here in Paris last night. I needed someone to help out, and Kurt seems to believe you simpletons know more about this situation than I do. Which we both know is a mistake."

"Not this time, Pike." He gave me the lowdown on the Snapchat video, and for the first time I began to wonder if I was chasing phantoms. But I couldn't be. I had the pendant. And the pendant had been found because of the Serbs.

He continued, "The housing complex is in some area known for African immigrants. A bad-guy land even on good days. The French have had a lot of riots and protests there. It fits perfectly with what we know about the Somalis' travel history. They're here, and so are the hostages."

"You sure that video is real?"

"I am. You sure that pendant is real?"

"Okay, okay. You just keep your head down. Let GIGN do the work. Something's not right about this whole thing. Hopefully it's me, but it might be you."

"No worries. These guys are pretty switched on. What the hell are you and Koko doing, anyway? You got Nung robbing a jewelry store or something? Kurt said you had the Taskforce translate some goofy shit."

The cards from our penthouse photos had ended up being in Serbo-Croatian, and they'd detailed a jewelry heist. Apparently, the Serbs belonged to some ring called the Pink Panthers, and they were planning a hit in Paris. I'd spent the train ride from Brussels doing a little research, and it turned out they were some seriously badass jewel thieves.

Mostly ex-military from the bad-old days in Bosnia, they'd cut their teeth smuggling arms during the Serbian embargo, then had moved on to bigger and better things. I'd stumbled upon a YouTube video of a hit in Dubai where they'd literally driven two Audis into an indoor mall, straight through the glass wall of a high-end jewelry store. They'd cleaned the place out, then simply driven out of the mall, never to be seen again.

Their target in Paris was the Bulgari jewelry store just off the famed strip of Parisian shopping known as the Champs-Élysées. I didn't really care about the robbery, though.

I said, "Yeah, we're conducting a stakeout, waiting on the police to snap these assholes up. The getaway driver is an Irishman named Braden. He was on the surveillance tape I got in Cambridge, and apparently, he's going to transport whatever they take, letting the Serbs cross the border afterward without any issues. My role ends when he gets snagged."

I heard nothing for a minute, then, "Uh . . . You talked to Kurt lately?"

"Last night, before we came down. I gave him a complete dump. Why?"

"Before the Snapchat came in?"

"I guess so. Why do I get the feeling you know more than me? What's up?"

"You're not getting any police. They're not going to show."

"Why? Kurt told me he'd get a cutout from the FBI to link up with the gendarmerie. They're supposed to be all over this place. The Pink Panthers are a big deal, and a successful robbery here would be pretty embarrassing. They won't miss it."

"Well, that would be true. If we told them. We didn't."

"What the hell are you talking about?"

"The hostages take priority. The president made the call not to tell them about your lead. He didn't want to split efforts. He couldn't care less about a jewel heist, and he was afraid the GIGN would get tasked with both targets. The police capability would be diluted. He didn't want that. He wants them completely focused on the hostages. On me."

What the hell? I felt the anger rise and saw Jennifer give me a question with her eyes. "And he wasn't going to tell me that? He was going to let me sit out here and watch it go down? Christ. I don't even have any weapons with me."

"Pike, things have been a little hectic here. They spent all night getting the ball rolling on my operation. Kurt's got to put national security ahead of his niece. Don't blame him. He might be calling any minute."

I said, "I gotta go."

"Pike, don't do something you'll regret."

"I'm not the one who's going to regret that decision."

Kurt introduced Creed, then took a seat in the back of the Situation Room, wondering how he was going to get grilled about Breedlove with all the people floating around the table who were uncleared for Taskforce operations. As far as they knew, he worked in the NSC with Creed. His cell vibrated, and he saw it was Pike, immediately realizing he hadn't told him the new reality of no French help. Alexander Palmer started talking, and he shunted the call to voice mail. *He'll figure it out. I'll call him later.*

Palmer said, "Creed, you sure about the location you found?"

"Yes, sir. No doubt."

"The GIGN is trying to get the Wi-Fi on the phone to link up with a false router. They called it spoofing. Can they do that? Will that work to locate the phone?"

"Sir, in theory—"

President Warren held up his hand. "I need everyone to leave the room but the director of the CIA and Kurt Hale."

The director of the FBI looked startled. He said, "Sir, they may start the operation at any time."

"Fine. The feed in here is coming from the communications room, right?"

"Yes, sir."

"Then monitor it there. I need a word."

The men about the table looked at one another, then began filing out. The door closed, the only sound an occasional burp from the speaker on the desk, background static from the FBI HRT team in Paris. President Warren shut it off.

Kerry Bostwick waited patiently. Warren waved Kurt forward to the table. When he was seated, the president said, "You guys see the paper this morning?"

Kerry said, "Yes, sir, and trust me, I had nothing to do with it. Nothing. I'm a little insulted by the question."

Warren said, "I know you wouldn't do anything outright, but could Clute have managed anything? As the chair of the Senate Select Committee on Intelligence, would he have the ability to do something like this? Without you knowing?"

Kerry scoffed. "Hell no. That's all Hollywood fantasy. He's a bureaucrat. He wouldn't even know where to go to find the men for the job, and they wouldn't do anything without getting sanction. Shit, sir, there's not a man in the CIA who isn't well versed on the repercussions for perceived illegal infractions. Half the time it's that same jerk Clute hauling people in front of his committee. Trust me, there isn't a lot of love for him in the CIA. His missing kids notwithstanding."

"And you wouldn't do anything as a quid pro quo for future inquiries? For the next time Congress starts a witch hunt? He's a powerful man, and that's a pretty good ace to hold."

Kerry said, "Sir, I mean no disrespect, but if you truly think I would have that Machiavellian capability in my soul, then you disappoint me. Jesus, you're talking about murder. You should know better, but since you don't, I'll tender my resignation right here, right fucking now."

Warren took that in, ignoring the outburst. He turned to Kurt, all business. "I tend to believe him because he has no skin in the game. You, on the other hand, I have questions about."

Kurt said, "Like Kerry, your questions should have been answered long ago. I had nothing to do with killing Grant Breedlove. Period."

President Warren held his eyes for a moment, then said, "All right. This conversation never happened. I had to ask."

Kurt said, "Sir, I've been thinking about it, and there's one person we haven't asked."

"Who?"

"The terrorists. I think they did it. I think there's an accomplice here in DC, and he's tying off loose ends."

Kerry said, "That's crazy."

"Really? They've kept this as quiet as we have and know how our hands would be tied if a story got out. I think it's a lead. Whoever killed him is working with the people who have our hostages. What do the police know about the crime?"

"I have no idea. Not something I'm really worried about, beyond questioning you two jackals."

"You mind if I look into it?"

"What do you mean, 'look'?"

"Just poke around. See what I can find."

"That depends on the next few minutes. We resolve this in Paris, then let the police handle it."

There was a knock on the door and President Warren said, "Come in."

The director of the FBI stuck in just his head and said, "They got the phone. They're rolling."

50

Knuckles saw a flurry of movement, then heard a command in French.

Brock said, "Might be time," and jogged over to the man who was apparently in charge.

Brett said, "You think they could neck down a phone location with that little drone?"

"I was wondering that myself. I'm thinking of volunteering your services. Get you inside with a Growler. If they've got the phone talking to the router, you could pinpoint."

Brett raised an eyebrow and said, "You mean because I used to work in Ground Branch? Because I'm used to penetrating hostile environments and can't be flustered by ordinary pressure?"

Brock came back to them, and Knuckles said, "No. Because you're the only black man in the room."

Before Brock could utter a word, Brett muttered, "Always about the black man."

Brock looked at him, then at Knuckles. "You guys got a problem I need to know about?"

"You tell me. What's up?"

"They're ready to go, but it's going to be a little bigger than we wanted. They've got the phone pinpointed to the fourth floor based on signal strength, but that still leaves fifteen apartments. The signal's stronger in the west, so we'll hit that first, then roll forward, taking three rooms at a time."

Incredulous, Knuckles said, "That's fucking insane."

Brock said, "I know, it's not optimal, but the guys who are augmenting all have SWAT training. They'll lock down the floor while the GIGN clears. Nobody will get out."

"Get out? What if the bad guys just start shooting? This isn't a capture/kill mission. It's a hostage rescue. The precious cargo takes priority. I don't give a shit if all the terrorists run out the back. I do, however, care greatly if they decide to bring harm."

Brock said, "Not our call. It's their country. Their show. They've done this sort of thing a hell of a lot."

"Screw that. What if we can neck it down?"

"'We'? You mean us? How are you going to do that?"

"You got a signal-intercept capability with all of that tech shit you brought?"

"No. It's all biometric. We got a Quick Capture suite here with us. We can scan an eyeball or fingerprint and get a read via satellite in seconds." He said the last with a little pride.

Knuckles deflated him. "Who gives a shit about who they are after we're done? You need to get back to what this is. Forget about your tours in Afghanistan. It's all about the rescue. We can do the forensics afterward, but that's just a sideshow."

Stung, Brock said, "I get that, but the rescue is *their* mission. I've been given mine. What do you want me to do? Take over the operation?"

"Yes. Tell them we have some kit to isolate the phone. Get us something better than an entire floor. I'll send Brett in. He conducts a recce and comes back."

"What skill does he have?"

"Not much, but he's black."

Brett, digging through a Pelican case, snorted and said, "Trust me, I've got more skill than anyone in this room for the mission. Get the commander over here."

Brock stood for a moment, and Knuckles could see the options banging through his skull, the implications of action competing with the results of inaction. He knew Brock was feeling enormous pressure to do nothing and let the French take the blame for any problems, but the hostages' lives weighed in the balance. Knuckles waited on the correct decision and had no doubt Brock would make it. They were both too much alike not to.

Brock turned away and waved. The troop commander came over, and Brock began speaking French to him, surprising Knuckles. They went back and forth, and the commander looked at Knuckles. Speaking with a heavy accent, he said, "You have done this before?"

"Yes. It's what we do."

"The FBI does this? I have never seen this, and I've been to Quantico several times."

Knuckles grinned and said, "Special cell."

The commander slowly nodded, then started barking in French. Soon enough, Brett was outfitted with derelict clothes and given a motorbike. The commander said, "No weapons. You go, you come back. Understand?"

Brett said, "About what I expected."

Knuckles buried the Growler in a knapsack slung over his back, running the antennae down the shoulder strap. He said, "You want backup?"

"No. I don't need a white-boy spiking."

He pulled out of the garage, and Brock said, "Need to send in a SITREP. Let them know the FBI is operational on this mission."

Knuckles grabbed his arm. "You don't need to send shit. He's my man. My responsibility. I'll send the SITREP."

"To who? This is my show."

"To the National Command Authority. Trust me, it's not your show."

Brett returned barely thirty minutes later, tooting his horn to get the garage door up. He entered, the GIGN surrounding him. Knuckles pushed through and said, "Well?"

"I couldn't get a single apartment, but I necked it down to two. Fourth floor, just like the Frogs said."

The GIGN commander smiled at the verbal slight and said, "Show me."

Brett spent twenty minutes describing the entrance, the stairwell, and the target doors. The GIGN men, through the commander, asked questions about breach points, security positions, and lighting, all of which showed Knuckles they were on their game. He relaxed, letting them get to it.

Brock said, "I guess that was a good call."

Knuckles said, "Intelligence is *always* a good call."

"Doesn't change anything. You're still in the back, and I'm still the ground force commander."

Knuckles looked at the ceiling and said, "No worries."

Five minutes later they were rolling, a caravan of various panel vans and bread trucks, all designed to blend in to the environment. Knuckles looked out the windshield, following along as the men in his vehicle checked and rechecked breaching charges, weapons, and radios.

They turned down a street and he saw a large Orthodox church at the end. The stick leader in his van said something in French, and Brock said, "Thirty seconds."

Knuckles stacked against the back of the van, next to Brett, giving the GIGN full access to the sliding door. He saw two vehicles continue straight, the regular gendarmerie locking down the block. Sealing off the operational area. The vehicle in front turned into a narrow lane, revealing a metal gate. Incongruously, as often happened in such operations, there was a single man out front on a park bench, talking on a phone, oblivious to the impending storm. Knuckles realized he was white, the sight looking completely out of place.

The lane opened into a courtyard and Brett recognized the building. He said, "This is it."

Knuckles forgot about the man and focused on the fight, taking deep breaths and getting his adrenaline under control. He elbowed Brett and whispered, "This is cool shit, huh?"

Brett smiled. "Yeah, when we're surrounded by all this firepower. It was some scary shit thirty minutes ago. You're lucky you're not black."

They pulled in behind the single van. The doors slid open at the same time, and the GIGN spilled out, moving like water from a split dam.

They raced to the stairwell, sprinting up, very little noise other than the clank of equipment. At each floor, two men in the front of the column peeled off, locking down the entrance to the stairwell and preventing any surprises from the rear.

They reached the fourth floor and the teams split, two men locking down the hallway to their rear, and the rest sprinting to their designated targets. The two FBI agents were supposed to follow the first team to their room, leaving Knuckles and Brett for the second door, but there was a tangle in the hallway, and they ended up at the back of the same stack.

The electricity of the operation flowing through him, weapon held high, Knuckles saw the two GIGN breachers look at each other and nod. They raised their battering rams and struck the doors at the same time, shattering the locks. The men shot into the rooms like lava from an erupting volcano, shouting commands to gain dominance.

Knuckles heard no gunfire.

Last in, he entered to find the room empty, the GIGN dominating the entire structure. No furniture and no terrorists. On the floor was a Samsung Galaxy cell phone, blinking. On the walls were packages.

It coalesced in his brain in a nanosecond, and he shouted, "Avalanche!"

Nobody in the room other than Brett understood the Taskforce command for immediate evacuation. Bulling his way to the entrance, Knuckles grabbed one GIGN man and bodily flung him through the door. He took two steps toward it, seeing Brett dive outside, when the room erupted in fire.

51

After four solid hours of staring at the Bulgari store, I began to relax, wondering if we'd spooked them off the target because of our shenanigans in Brussels. Honestly, I felt a little relieved. Sort of wishing I were with Knuckles, getting some on a hit that had sanction instead of sitting here half praying nobody showed up. After Knuckles's call I knew I was hanging way out over the ledge without any support.

Jennifer said, "How long do you want to stay?"

"Well, at least until they close. We know they're after some special necklace, and they said it would be on display in the day, then locked up at night. The Pink Panthers aren't sneaky safecrackers. They're brazen daylight guys. The store closes, and we're done for the day."

"And after that?"

I thought about Kurt, and the fact that he'd ignored my call. I wasn't sure what it meant. He wanted Kylie back more than life itself, but he'd hung me out to dry on a serious lead. And now wouldn't talk to me. I didn't know how to read those tea leaves.

I said, "I don't know. We'll get back to the hotel and reassess."

She saw what I was thinking and said, "Kurt didn't do that on purpose. Don't wonder about his motives. There's much more going on than our little hunt."

"Yeah, inside I know that, but it's still a little scary. Maybe something's happened and he's been forced to abandon us. I'm worried that we're out here doing shit on our own now. No sanction whatsoever."

She smiled and said, "Does that ever matter to you?"

"Well, yeah, it matters."

"You mean like the sanction you got to bring in Nung?"

I hadn't yet told Kurt about flying him over—or that he had to be paid—and she was gently reminding me that operations were fluid. I was doing what I did for the good of the mission, and so was Kurt. I said, "Point taken," and returned to staring at the boring facade of the Bulgari store.

Located where two roads came together at an angle, it was situated on the point, with a door to the west and a door to the east. We'd found a café on the east side and had been watching for the better part of the day, drinking coffee.

The store was two stories tall and had some serious security, with a man just inside each door who actually unlocked them for patrons he deemed worthy to enter. Don't look like you're going to drop a quarter mil on jewelry? He'd just nod at you, indicating that you could head on down to another store to window-shop. The doors remained locked otherwise, with cameras everywhere, and two other roaming guards inside.

I looked at my watch and saw it was 4:58. I said, "Let's call Nung. Head on back to the hotel. Figure out our next steps."

Nung was currently driving our rental, parking at various locations until told to move but remaining close enough to engage when called.

"What are you thinking?"

"Honestly? I'm thinking about what I'm going to tell Nung. I can't pay him for flying out here for nothing."

She smiled and said, "Let me talk to him," then, "Holy shit, Pike, take a look."

I glanced at the store and saw a smoking-hot female being escorted by an older male. They stood outside the door, smiling, and were let in. Two minutes before closing.

One minute later, two other couples approached, the females dressed to the nines, and the males in suits. They were let in as well.

"Shit. This is it. Call Nung. Get him staged on this road."

She started dialing, saying, "We don't have the police. What's the mission?"

"Catch that fuck Braden."

Looking through plate glass, I saw the first couple start browsing the displays on the western side. Next to the guard at that door. The other two couples split, one headed to the interior of the store, and the other focusing on the displays near the eastern door. Near the guard.

I said, "Get him on the phone. It's going to happen quick."

And it did. I saw the eastern man pull something from his coat, and the guard at my door dropped like he'd been hit in the head with an axe handle. Looking through the glass, I saw the western door was empty. Two seconds later, the men were replaced by the two suits, both shoving in the earpieces of the door guards and looking as if they belonged. I couldn't see the two roving security guys but knew they were down as well. The females took off their high heels and started racing through the store, smashing the glass in the displays and shoving gold into their bags.

I said, "Jesus Christ, they're fast. This is about to be over. Where's Nung?"

She held a finger up, speaking into the phone. "No, don't pull up yet. Get where you can arrive in five seconds. No earlier."

I saw a man on a motorcycle coming toward us on the eastern side, driving at an unhurried pace, keeping with the traffic. He had on a helmet, but I knew who it was.

I said, "Braden's coming. Get Nung moving. We're about to lose him."

Jennifer relayed, and I watched impatiently as the bike pulled up to the eastern entrance. It sat there puttering, then one couple burst out of the exit. The man shoved a bulging canvas sack into the bike rider's arms. I watched them run into an alley, seeing the woman toss her hat to the ground and whip off a wig.

They were gone.

I looked through the store, trying to find the others, but could see nothing. I knew they'd exited through the west door. And that they'd also gone through the profile change, altering their appearance with wigs and jackets.

I saw the bike hammer the throttle, headed to the Champs-Élysées, and shouted, "Where the hell is Nung?"

A Fiat slammed to a stop in front of us, and Jennifer said, "Here. Let's go."

We raced out of the café, the owner behind the bar screaming at us. I had no time to pay our bill and simply ignored him, piling into the back, Jennifer taking the passenger seat.

52

Nung started driving, not saying a word, making me wonder what he thought he was doing. It was like Thailand all over again. The Terminator robot walking relentlessly forward with his last orders, calm and immune to chaos.

A tall man with a shock of crew-cut black hair, he looked vaguely Thai, but with a mix of something else. Exotic, he'd probably get more ass than a toilet seat if he weren't so damn straightforward. I was pretty sure any woman who approached him would say one coy thing, and he'd answer with something honest, like, "I don't seek females with small breasts."

We approached the Champs-Élysées and he asked, "Destination?"

I said, "See that bike? The one headed away from the Arc de Triomphe? That's the target. Stay on him."

He took the turn, and I started thinking of options. From the front, Jennifer said, "We need to get him clean. We can't take him down on the streets of Paris. We'll all get locked up by the police."

I cursed Kurt under my breath and said, "I know. We'll follow to a bed-down site. Nung, don't lose him, but don't spike either."

He said, "That may be a command I cannot accomplish. If forced, which is it? Don't spike or don't lose?"

I said, "Don't lose. Whatever it takes, don't let that fucker get away."

We traveled down the thoroughfare, passing all the high-end stores and entering Franklin Roosevelt circle. We continued on, the stores falling away for tree-lined promenades, with palaces left and right. Jennifer said, "The Louvre is ahead. Is he doing something else?"

"No. No way."

We hit a dead end at a large oval, and he turned south, crossing the Seine. I said, "He's going home."

He took a left on boulevard Saint-Germain and started weaving in and out of traffic, picking up the pace. I said, "Stick with him."

Nung floored the accelerator, driving me into my seat. I shouted, "Jesus Christ, just keep him in sight."

Nung said, "You need to be more clear."

I looked at Jennifer, and she rolled her eyes, silently telling me, *He's your crazy team member.*

I said, "Nung, stay with him, but don't kill us."

He said, "You never specified anything about harm to us. Sorry."

My mouth fell open, and he smiled. He said, "American joke." Showing me for the first time he was at least human enough to have sarcasm.

We went through multiple roundabouts, the bike weaving in and out of traffic with us barely keeping up. I saw the helmet flick back to us and knew we were about to be burned.

"Okay, he's starting to check. We keep this up, he's going to try to lose us."

Nung said, "What do you want me to do? Back off?"

"Yeah. Stay within the same light-block, though. Keep as far back as you can, but stay in his lane. I don't want to lose him if he turns."

We went another mile, and his helmet flicked back twice more. He split through a light, gave one more glance back, then took off.

I slapped the seat. "Christ. That's it."

Jennifer put her hand on Nung's arm and said, "Catch him. Don't let him out of your sight."

Nung goosed the accelerator, and we began weaving through the traffic, like a lumbering hippo to his panther. He kept glancing back, going in and out, and we managed to maintain our inside-the-light distance. We both paused at a red, our vehicle two cars back, and he turned around and glared. For the first time, through the face shield, I saw he was a Caucasian with blue eyes. I said, "That's him. That's Braden."

I opened the door, saying, "I'm taking him now. Pull up when I get him on the ground."

Jennifer said, "Pike, we can't get through the traffic if—"

Nung said, "He's running the light."

I slammed the door closed, saying, "Do the same. Get close. Take him down."

Nung started driving like a maniac, scraping the chassis of the car as he ran by the traffic with two wheels over the curb. He punched through the light, honking his horn, then closed the distance, throwing Jennifer and me back and forth. To my front I saw a traffic circle with a statue of a giant lion, the cars leisurely going around.

Braden glanced back once, and his eyes went wide at how close we'd gotten. He hit the throttle, leaning over into the curve of the circle as if he were racing a superbike at Laguna Seca. He got halfway around and his left peg hit the ground, his foot scraping the asphalt. He lost control, the bike skittering into the roadway, sliding forward with a massive pile of sparks, him following behind on his back, skipping across the pavement.

We fought our way through the stop-and-go traffic, hampered by the cars ahead slamming on their brakes from the wreck. I saw Braden stand up, weave in a small circle like a drunk, then focus on us. He ripped the helmet from his head, his mouth open and panting. He shouted something I couldn't hear, snatched the knapsack of jewels off the ground, and took off running through the traffic, cars skidding aside and horns blaring.

To Jennifer, Nung said, "Take the wheel," and opened the door.

I did the same and saw Nung ahead of me, sprinting. Braden ran straight toward a line of people waiting to get into some tourist attraction. He knocked them out of the way and disappeared into a portal. I paused, turning back to Jennifer, knowing she'd identify where we were. What the line of people meant.

Sliding over to the wheel, she said, "It's the Catacombs. A mile of tunnels full of skeletons. You follow, and you'll flush him to the other side. There's only one way to go. I'll meet you there."

I heard a horn honk and said, "Skeletons? What do you mean?"

She said, "Go. You'll figure it out."

I turned away and saw Nung disappear through the entrance. I took off sprinting, reaching the front in seconds.

By the time I arrived, everyone was shouting and yelling, with an old man out front waving a radio. I slipped behind him and reached a turnstile, an obese woman behind it blocking my way. I said, "I'm following that man. Police."

She looked at me in confusion, and I hopped the turnstile. She smacked me in the back with her radio and I raced down the hall, hitting a spiral stone stairwell that was claustrophobic. I started down as fast as I could, going around and around and hearing nothing below me. I went so fast I started to get dizzy, wondering how far I had to descend before I reached the bottom.

A light flared below, and I hit a tunnel, smelling of wet stone. I shouted, "Nung!"

I heard nothing. The tunnel went in only one direction, so I figured they both had to be ahead of me. I took off running, eating up the ground. I reached a patch of tourists next to a closed gate blocking access to another tunnel. Mine continued on, but the gate had no lock. In between breaths, I asked, "Which way?"

A man pointed away from the door, saying, "Right ahead."

I started running flat-out, trusting my feet to find purchase in the gloom, my brain telling me to slow down. I rounded a corner, almost smacking my head into the roof of stone, and caught a glimpse of someone disappear. I redoubled my efforts.

Somewhere during my run the limestone walls gave way to bones. Millions and millions of bones. I was sprinting through death, with skulls arranged in symmetrical patterns and femurs used as cradles for the design. Literally walls made of bones.

My feet splashed in water, and the man ahead turned at the sound. In the dim light, I recognized Nung. He said, "Just ahead," then disappeared.

The tunnel expanded into a small room with a column made of bones in the middle. In the light splayed out from a single lamp, I saw Nung squaring off against Braden, both circling each other. Braden snatched a skull from the wall and tossed it, causing Nung to flinch.

Braden darted forward, and I entered the light, grabbing a leg bone. He saw me and pulled up short just as I hurled it. He ducked, and it clipped his scalp, probably setting loose some disease from the fourteenth century. He snarled at me, put a hand to his head, then turned and began running again.

Nung took up the chase, me right behind. We passed several groups of tourists, all frightened at the turmoil, but none doing anything to stop us. The tunnel wound forward endlessly, and I began to wonder just how long it was. Surely they couldn't expect tourists to walk miles. Could they?

I broke out of the bone district, entering back into the limestone, and the light increased. I picked up my pace, gaining on Nung and hearing the footfalls of Braden in front of me. I reached an open cavern, seeing a stone stairwell on the side with a modern illuminated EXIT sign. Nung was blocking it, hands held high, and I knew it was the endgame.

Braden had a knife out, waving it back and forth, a cell phone in his other hand. He shouted into it but was getting no signal from underneath the ground. I advanced into the cavern, and he saw me. He gave a war cry and attacked Nung, the single thing blocking his exit out.

He stabbed forward with the knife, and Nung danced, blocking the downward blow and twisting Braden's arm in a circle. Braden flung the cell phone from his other hand and clawed at Nung's face, screaming in pain. Nung leveraged the elbow downward, bringing Braden to his knees. I jumped forward to assist, but not fast enough.

Braden scrambled at his ankle with his free hand, and like magic, a small stiletto appeared. He jabbed it over his head, trying to connect with the flesh of the man holding him. Nung saw it coming, ducked under the blade, then snapped the elbow forward, the crack ricocheting in the cavern. Braden shrieked in pain, and Nung circled his arms around Braden's neck. A meter away, I screamed, "No!" and saw the life leave Braden's eyes as his spine popped.

I reached them and said, "Nung, damn it, he's no good to us dead."

He stood up, saying, "He was calling his friend. Telling him to kill the hostages. Whoever is on the other end of that phone has them."

53

Hearing the voice mail, Seamus hung up. For the third time.

Kevin said, "You want me to send the chat request? The room's open."

"No. Not yet. You sure this VOIP thing is working? I'm getting nothing trying to contact Braden."

Kevin said, "Yeah. If he's not answering, it's because he's got the app turned off or he's out of digital 3G or 4G coverage. Call him direct."

"I don't want to taint the phone. Right? If I call on the cell network instead of VOIP?"

"Yeah, but if you're that worried, what's the big deal? It's a single call. You've been using VOIP for Braden since we started."

"Because if I'm that worried, it's the exact wrong time to do it, jackass."

Kevin retreated to his computer screen, saying, "Well, do you want to send the request or not? I got the room open."

"No, damn it. We need the new Snapchat video. I want to hit them with the Bitcoin request, then when they stall, hit them with the death of their hostages."

Sitting aside, listening to the back-and-forth, Colin finally said, "What's the holdup? Where's Braden?"

"I don't know. I keep getting his voice mail."

"He called before, right? Saying the diversion was going down?"

"Yeah, but I can't get him now. I don't know about the robbery."

"Why does that matter? Call the team sitting on them. Tell them to make the Snapchat. They can execute."

"I don't trust them," Seamus snapped. "They fuck it up, and they'll have the world coming down on their heads. A hornets' nest. Then it'll be coming to us."

Colin said, "I thought that didn't matter to the mighty Seamus."

Seamus looked at him and said, "You dumbass, of course it matters. I don't want to give them a road map to find us, and it would take one mistake for the NSA to grab." He paced around the room, running his hands through his hair. Feeling the pressure.

Kevin interrupted his thoughts, saying, "Seamus, got something out of Paris. You ought to see this." He pointed to a separate laptop, streaming with live news. A breaking story appeared.

Seamus said, "Turn it up."

The sound came on, the announcer speaking French. Seamus said, "Shit. Can you find one in English?"

"By the time I search, the story will be over."

The screen showed a broken-down apartment complex, the area out front blockaded with all manner of emergency vehicles, the blue lights flashing like a circus. As the man spoke, the camera zoomed in to the fourth floor, grimly framing a blackened window, the drapes, stained by flame, fluttering in the breeze.

Entranced, Seamus stared at the screen, not believing he had created the chaos. The picture flashed back to the news desk, and the anchor spit something out in a rapid manner, looking flustered and holding his hand to an earpiece. The screen cut to a picture of a jewelry store called Bulgari, then to a picture of a necklace, a thick gold chain encrusted with diamonds, a heavy ruby in the center.

Colin whooped and said, "The robbery! It went off."

Seamus smiled and said, "Looks like it."

One of the cell phones on the windowsill went off. Not the one he held, so it wasn't Braden. Still looking at the laptop, he waved his hand and said, "Someone get that."

Colin moved to the window, and Kevin said, "You want to start the chat?"

"I'm not sure. You think you could talk the team through the Snapchat procedures? Make sure they send it in such a way that it can't be tracked?"

252 / BRAD TAYLOR

"Yeah, it's really not that hard. I can send them step-by-step instructions."

"Seamus," Colin said. "You need to take this call." His face was drained of color, and his hand that held the phone was trembling.

"Who is it?"

"Ratko."

Seamus took the phone, cleared his throat, and said, "Ratko?"

"Where is your shit of a brother? Where are my jewels?"

"How did you get this number?"

"Never mind that. Where is your brother? He won't answer the phone."

"I thought he was meeting you in Brussels tomorrow? What's the big deal?"

"He was supposed to call, letting me know he had gotten away clean. He never did, but the news is talking about the robbery and not saying a damn word about anyone getting arrested."

Seamus said, "Okay, okay, look, I don't know where he is, but I don't think it's time to panic. Give him a chance."

Ratko's voice went cold. "You and that brother had better not be double-crossing me. You wondered how I found this cell number, remember that. Braden doesn't show in Belgium tomorrow, I'll find you the same way."

The line went dead. Seamus put his hand down, and Colin said, "What's wrong? Why is Ratko pissed?"

"It's nothing. He'll calm down."

"Seamus, I can't have him hunting me. He's *worse* than the law. You hear what those guys do to people? This thing is breaking down."

Seamus ignored him, turning to Kevin. "Can you call the team with VOIP?"

Kevin nodded.

"Do so. Give them the instructions."

54

I slapped in the combo to our hotel safe and ripped out the two suppressed pistols, handing one to Jennifer. I was kicking myself for not having them with me in the first place, but when I thought the Paris gendarmerie were on board it made little sense to bring firepower. We weren't going to actively engage, and trying to penetrate an arrest to interrogate Braden would have been made much, much harder sporting two illegally suppressed Glocks. It wasn't worth the risk.

I did find it humorous that Jennifer had placed our laptop inside as well, like the maids would have stolen it. For the price we were paying for this Parisian gem, I would expect to be able to leave a couple of half-dressed midgets in the room holding the Glocks and get no flack. Of course, I wasn't going to push that theory.

She stowed her weapon and booted up the laptop, going online and furiously typing, trying to find the location of the hostages before the men who held them realized something was wrong.

I had nothing else to do, so I called down to Nung, making sure he was ready to receive us when we had a destination. Our hotel wasn't exactly conducive to vehicles, so I'd had him drop us off, then circle like a shark until summoned. The time getting back to the hotel had eaten up thirty minutes, and I was growing worried that we were about to miss our window. We needed an edge.

Jennifer said, "No, damn it. A Samsung Galaxy," and I realized she was on a chat with someone at Taskforce headquarters, the Samsung phone hooked to her laptop. She said, "Where's Creed? Get him online."

I heard, "He's at the White House Situation Room. Working the problem."

I wanted to punch the wall at the words, superstitiously wondering if the devious bastards we were after had managed to divert the one computer geek I trusted at Taskforce headquarters. Refusing to face the real probability that those same devious men might have killed two members of my team. Including Knuckles. My friend and my mentor.

Earlier, we'd searched Braden's body and found a passport from the UK, confirming his identity, along with two cell phones. The cell he was using when we killed him was a ruggedized flip phone that worked on the cell network like a walkie-talkie. The other was a Samsung Galaxy smartphone, stuffed into his back pocket. I'd continued searching, stripping the body, when a museum official from the exit came down, shocked at what he'd seen.

He'd said, "The police are on the way. Don't you move."

Nung had simply looked at him, then at me, saying, "Time to go."

He'd glided toward the stairs with his catlike gait, and the man stepped aside.

I said, "Give me your radio." The guard did, and I sprinted up after Nung, reaching the exit and a group of tourists standing around with large eyes, getting more for their entrance fee than they expected.

Marching out as though I owned the place, holding the radio from the man downstairs, I picked out the first thirtysomething man I could find. A guy with Harley-Davidson tattoos and a bad goatee. An American who looked as if he was used to bending the rules.

I'd said, "Don't let anyone else come up. I'm coordinating the first responders, but I don't have the manpower to lock down the exit. There's a bad guy down there."

His wife or girlfriend said, "That's not our business . . ." but I saw him grin, looking at my radio. Because, you know, if you're holding a radio, clearly you're the authority.

He nodded his head, saying, "Shush, Celia. We can help."

We sprinted through the door, and Jennifer was waiting. Right outside. I couldn't believe it, thanking the gods yet again that I'd run into her and her bottomless pit of historical knowledge four years ago. We piled in, and she said, "Where's Braden?"

I said, "He's dead. No time to discuss."

I pulled out my Taskforce phone and called Kurt, praying he would answer. He did.

"Sir, I don't have time to explain, but we took down Braden, and he's tied into the hostages. I need a geolocation of a phone signal right now."

His answer had rocked my world. "Pike, I don't have time for this right now. The hostages may very well be dead. Along with Knuckles."

He'd given me the abbreviated version of what had happened, speaking in short, clipped sentences. The story left me speechless. How could we have been sucked in to such a trap? Where were the intel indicators?

Jennifer saw my face and said, "What? What's he saying?"

I waved her off and returned to the mission. "Sir, I just caught the guy from the tape in Cambridge. I don't know what the hell is going on with that hit, but your niece is alive. Braden was giving orders to kill her, but he couldn't get a signal because we were deep underground. I *need* this phone lock."

"Underground? What the hell are you talking about? And how do you know she's alive?"

"Sir, I *don't*, but I'm close. You guys are on the wrong thread. Help me. Please."

I heard a bunch of background noise, then he came back. "Pike, they've just made a demand. I have to go. Call George Wolffe. Tell him Prairie Fire. He'll open the world."

I heard the command and felt some comfort. Prairie Fire was the code word for a catastrophic event, when Taskforce lives were on the line. He was giving me the keys to the kingdom for his niece, and I had no doubt he would back it up.

I said, "Thanks, sir. Gotta go."

He spoke again, hope seeping through the connection, penetrating the disaster he was dealing with. He said, "Wait. The reports here are bad. Very bad. At least seven bodies all burned beyond recognition. Why do you think she's alive?"

"Because she's from your genes. Trust me, she's alive, and I'm bringing her home. Like I promised."

Kylie heard the door open to the cellar, then the stomping of feet, the adrenaline spurt from past events failing to appear. She remained prone, no longer having the energy to care, the virus that was ravaging her body siphoning off any energy to respond.

The bearded one removed her hood and forced her upright, saying, "What's wrong with you?"

Listlessly, she said, "Nothing. Asshole."

He set her food in place, and with an urgency he'd never shown before, he said, "You sick? You need to see a doctor?"

She heard Nick shout from the other side of the room, "Yes, you dumbass. Yes, she's sick. You want the leverage, you need to help her."

She saw him stalk to Nick, hood still on, and cuff him in the head. Nick hit the ground, and the man leaned over, saying, "You a doctor, asshole?"

Nick sat up, staring in the wrong direction in his hood. He spit out, "Fuck you. She's your golden egg and you know it. And so am I. You can beat me some more if you want, but she's going down fast. Fix it. Now."

Colin ripped his hood off, kicking him to the floor. In the back, Travis began whimpering, curling up in a ball. Colin said, "I could kill you right now, you fuck. I have him and her. *I* have the power."

Nick glared at him and said, "No, you don't. You bring the food. You're a fucking lackey. You have nothing but the power of your boot, you miserable shit."

The words caused Kylie to sit up at last, afraid of the response. She saw Colin's face and knew Nick was dead.

Instead, Colin kicked the wall, cursing in aggravation. She realized Nick was right. For the first time, she clearly saw he knew more about their predicament than anyone else. Colin satisfied himself with a boot to the gut, then stormed up the steps, slamming the room into darkness.

She waited a minute, then said, "Nick, please don't do that again."

He chuckled and said, "Yeah, that probably wasn't smart. I let my anger get the better of me. I thought I was dead."

From the fetal position, Travis said, "Yes, yes, please don't do that again."

Nick leaned over in the dirt and clawed his way forward a few feet. He put his face next to Travis's hood and said, "I can see you. You know why? Because he left without putting my hood back on. Because I'm not a pussy."

Kylie said, "Shh. He's talking just outside."

They grew quiet and heard Colin's voice.

—"I need to speak to Ratko."

—"Because he'll want to hear what I have to say, that's why. Quickly, I don't have a lot of time."

They sat in their underground tomb hearing nothing. Waiting. Eventually, Colin's voice floated out again.

—"Ratko? Yes. I'm Colin. I work with Seamus and don't like how this is going. I have nothing to do with what's happened."

Silence, only the shuffling of Colin's feet on the deck of their prison. Then, a more subdued voice.

—"Ratko, I don't want you chasing me. That's why I'm calling. I have the people we took. I don't know what Seamus is up to. If he crossed you, it had nothing to do with me, but I can give you more than that necklace."

—"Damn it, listen to me! We've caught the son of the vice president of the United States. Along with his fiancée. They're worth more than that necklace. Seamus is auctioning them off as I speak."

—"Because I don't want you hunting me, that's why. Look, Seamus is going to be wondering what I'm doing. Am I good? I pass them to you and I'm not on your list?"

—"Okay, okay. If Braden doesn't show, I'll call you. Will that work?"

There was a long pause, then Colin said, "I understand. I'm not working with Seamus on this. No tricks. Trust me, you want him, I'll set it up."

They heard nothing else. Kylie said, "What does that mean? What's he talking about?"

Nick said, "It means we have a seam. Something to exploit."

She looked at his face in the shadow of the heat lamps and saw despair. She knew he was lying, and things had gone from bad to worse.

55

Jennifer turned from the computer and said, "Okay, I think we have something. A start."

I stopped pacing the hotel room and said, "What?"

"The number the flip phone called is dead. Turned off or gone, but it has a history. The guys at the Taskforce triangulated from the cell towers, and it was used most right here."

She pointed to the computer, showing a section of buildings that looked like everything else in Paris. The usual five-story baroque structure surrounding a courtyard that you saw all over the damn city. I said, "That's too much terrain. We don't have days to search."

Knowing what I was asking, she said, "I . . . I can't get any closer."

I said, "Bullshit. There's something that'll neck it down. Squeeze over."

She moved aside, letting me in front of the computer. I switched screens and found myself looking at some geek who was apparently bored to be working the problem. I said, "Hey, you there?"

He snapped to the screen and said, "Yeah. I'm here."

"That's the best you can do? Give us a thousand-meter grid square?"

"The phone isn't on. All we have is historical data. Yeah, that's the best we can do."

"Well, that ain't good enough. I need a miracle. What can I give you for that? What do you need?"

He looked over his shoulder again, and I heard something in the background.

I said, "Pay attention."

He became truculent, saying, "We've got a situation here. Possible casualties. Forgive me if I don't give you my undivided devotion."

As if he would feel the death of Knuckles more than me. I said, "Did you get the Prairie Fire alert from the command? For my element?"

"I got a Prairie Fire, yeah, but I don't think it was for you. I couldn't find a 'Grolier Recovery Services' active as a Taskforce element. You aren't even authorized to be talking to me. I don't even know how you have the encryption."

I couldn't believe it. I took a deep breath and said, "Listen to me closely. The fact that I have the encryption is proof I can talk to you. My Prairie Fire is real, and you'd better start helping."

He turned to respond to something said offscreen, and I was losing the fight. I felt the rage grow, compounded by a feeling of impotence. In a low voice, I said, "Mr. Geek, turn back to this computer."

He heard the tone, the violence leaking through the connection, and he snapped to the screen. I said, "There are lives on the line. If they die, I will come back and find you. When I do, I will replicate whatever happened to the hostages."

He started to say something smart, then his confidence faltered at the sight of my expression. He said, "Okay. What do you need?"

I said, "You got a geolocation request for a phone that was dead. I want you to juxtapose the Galaxy smartphone locations with the history of that phone. Tell me where they intersect. It's plugged in right now on this end."

Thirty seconds later he said, "That phone only made one call on the cell network, and it's miles from there, in another section of Paris. It has a VOIP application that's been used, but we can't trace that."

"Voice-over-Internet Protocol? Is that what you mean? You can't trace it because it's going over the Internet instead of the cell system?"

"Yes."

I said, "Okay, now give me an IP address search. Find the Wi-Fi nodes the smartphone touched. If he's using the Internet, it had to touch something."

He started typing, and the Samsung hooked to our computer lit up, getting probed from over three thousand miles away. He said, "There are quite a few, but one stands out. It spent more than twelve hours at a time hooked to a Wi-Fi node called Linksy 201."

Because it's in the bed-down location. I said, "That's where he's staying. How can I find that node?"

"You have a Growler? If it's in that building, you could find the signal."

"No. I've got no equipment."

He squinted. I knew he was reflecting on the fact that we weren't in the active lineup, something confirmed by a lack of basic Taskforce equipment.

I said, "I don't have a support package. It diverted to the crisis site. I need something else."

The answer seemed to make sense. He said, "Well, I could find the Internet service provider that's tied to the IP address. I could locate who's paying the bills for the ISP."

"Do it."

We waited ten minutes and he came back on. "It's an apartment rental service. They provide fully furnished short-term apartments in Paris for international travelers. Unfortunately, they pay for Internet service at all of their apartments. They're scattered throughout Paris. I know that's not much."

It was more help than he understood. "Can you hack into the rental service?"

"Yeah. Probably won't be too much trouble."

He started pounding the keys, shouting over his shoulder to another guy, speaking in computer geek code and finally getting into the mission.

I said, "Give me the apartment address Braden McKee is renting. He's from Ireland."

They worked a bit, and he said, "Okay, we're in. The problem is the foreign registrations are logged by passport number and nationality, I guess for privacy purposes. I've got twelve apartments in Paris for Irish nationals. I can't get any better without having the guy's passport."

I heard Jennifer start ripping through the knapsack of jewels we'd pulled off Braden. She turned to me, holding the key to the hostages in her hand.

I smiled and said, "Guess what I have?"

56

Eating her bowl of cereal next to Mack, Kaelyn Clute had grown used to the routine. After the scare when they'd driven to the run-down apartment, things had drifted back into an endless repetition of darkness and light, split only by the once-a-day feeding. The hood had become almost a welcome cocoon, though she still despised the gag. It had grown crusty with her spittle and had begun to stink.

She rubbed Mack's leg with each spoonful, and he did the same in return, a system of connection that reassured her and gave her strength. She saw the level of her bowl and had learned through repeated feedings that she had about another five minutes with McKinley.

The man in the chair to her front slapped his back pocket and pulled out a phone. He glanced at the other man and flicked his head out the door. "Be right back. Probably Braden."

It was the first time since they'd made the video that the routine had been broken, and for some reason it scared her. She put the spoon down and tried to listen but heard nothing through the door. She ate more slowly, catching Mack's eye.

The man returned, talking into a phone.

—"Braden told us to wait. He would take the video. Why are we executing now?" He looked into her eyes.

—"Yeah, let me talk to him."

—"Seamus, what's up? We still tracking?"

—"Yeah, yeah, I can do it," he said, still looking at her. "Kevin gave me the instructions. I won't screw up. Look, Fayetteville was a mistake, but it doesn't make me an idiot." His next words proved the statement a lie, an unnecessary call to action to the two hostages in the room.

—"Leave the bodies here?"

She heard nothing else, unable to focus on the conversation, her hands shaking, the spoon rattling in the bowl.

The man ended the call and said, "He wants us to execute, but Seamus doesn't trust us. Wants me to send him a Snapchat first so Kevin can analyze it. Make sure we're clean."

He pulled out an iPhone, then a piece of paper with instructions on it. He began going through the phone settings, manually manipulating the privacy settings. When he was done, he said, "Look over here."

The other man grunted and said, "You want me to smile?"

He held the phone up and said, "I don't give a shit."

Two minutes later, he sent the video and said, "Get them back into the hoods."

Kaelyn saw the man advancing, telling her to replace the gag around her neck, and she knew it was now or never. She looked at Mack and he nodded, understanding the same thing she did. They were going to die.

But not on their knees.

She leapt up, her ankles still flex-tied, and threw herself at the first man, catching him just below the waist. He shouted and went down. She rolled over and began screaming, "Help us, help us!"

Hopping like he was in a macabre three-legged race at a company picnic, McKinley drove himself into the other man. He dropped the phone and scrambled for his pistol in the small of his back. McKinley beat him to the draw, launching forward with his entire weight, punching the man and tying up his arms.

Kaelyn rolled over, getting on top of the first man, still screaming as loud as she could, hammering him in the face. The man elbowed her in the temple, causing stars, but she continued fighting. She clawed his eyes, desperately trying to put him down. He drew his pistol and slammed the barrel into her forehead. The fight left her, the light from the room tunneling away. She fell over.

Her vision blurry, she heard the man shout something, his barrel pressed against her forehead. She tried to yell, to tell Mack that at least one should live. To tell him to continue fighting. Nothing came out. She saw McKinley sag back, the will gone from the sight of the gun to her head. The man punched him in the face, knocking him to the floor. She began to weep.

The gag was placed in her mouth, and McKinley was dragged over to her. Their hands were flex-tied again and they were pulled to their knees, side by side. The man to the left screwed in a suppressor to his pistol while the first man lined up the phone. He said, "One at a time. Seamus wants to drag it out. Make them think one is still alive."

"Which first?"

"The Marine. I'm sick of his shit. Remember, only the barrel in the picture."

Kaelyn grabbed Mack's bound hands, squeezing tightly. The pistol floated forward, six inches from his head. She closed her eyes, not wanting to see the death. Praying for a miracle.

The apartment doorbell rang.

The man with the phone said, "What the fuck."

"Someone heard her shouting."

He left the room, then came back. "It's some hot *beur*. What should I do?"

"She by herself?"

"Yeah."

"Let her in, act like everything's normal. Tell her a story, but don't let her get past the anteroom."

He made the mistake of doing so.

57

We fought through the Paris traffic, going faster than was allowed, crossing the Seine yet again and hauling ass toward the target. I checked my weapon, making sure the thing would function, a rote habit born from many, many assaults.

Jennifer did the same, saying, "You're getting better and better at the acting. You scared the hell out of that guy. I'm sure he believed you'd hunt him down. Kill him."

I looked up and said, "I wasn't acting that time."

She said nothing, reading me. Seeing the truth. She changed the subject. "So what're we going to do when we arrive?"

"Go in strong. Full bore."

Nung said, "I do not have a weapon."

I chuckled and said, "I thought your hands were lethal weapons."

He didn't smile. Instead, he said, "I should take Jennifer's weapon. She can stage the vehicle for retreat."

I looked at her, considering. She raised an eyebrow, telling me she didn't care and she'd do whatever I thought best. So I did what I thought was best.

"Nung, sorry. No offense, but I trained Jennifer. I know her skills. She's going in with me."

I saw a ghost of a smile flit across her face and realized she *did* care.

Nung scowled and said, "That is a mistake. I still get my full payment whether I'm fighting or sitting in a car waiting like a taxi driver."

"Yeah, I got it. You still haven't told me what that is."

"The bag of jewels will do."

I said, "Nung, I can't give you those."

He said, "We'll see."

Looking at the moving map on her phone, Jennifer said, "Two blocks up."

Nung continued, and she pointed to a large wooden double door. "That's it."

Shit. If it was locked, allowing only residents in, we were screwed.

Nung pulled to the curb, leaving barely enough room for another car to pass. We exited and jogged to the door. I tried it, and it opened, showing an archway and a corridor leading to a courtyard, a set of mailboxes on the left and a stairwell on the right. I said, "Okay, we get to the apartment and you knock. Get them to open it. First order of business is to make sure we've got the right place."

"And if it is?"

"Get a pistol in his face. Lock him down."

"What if he resists? Runs?"

"He gives you any shit—if he tries to warn anyone or anything else—pull the trigger."

She looked at me, and I said, "Use your judgment. I'll be right behind you, but this isn't the time for second-guessing or bullshit rules of engagement. He shows hostile intent in any way, you drop him."

We started up the stairs, taking them two at a time. We exited at the third floor and jogged down the hallway, Jennifer checking door numbers as we went by them. She stopped and mouthed, *This is it.*

I heard shouting from inside. A fight. Then nothing. I raised my pistol and whispered, "This *is* it. No mercy."

I held back, and Jennifer rang the bell. We heard shuffling, then nothing. She looked at me, and I pointed to the doorbell with the barrel of my pistol. She rang again, and the door opened. A man inside said, "Hey, sorry for the noise. A little spat with my wife. It's over now."

Irish accent. Jennifer recognized it the same time I did and whipped out her pistol, shoving it into his face, her eyes trained down the barrel, showing all business. He leapt back, bringing out his own weapon. She broke the trigger and hit him just above the nose, the body collapsing to the floor. I flowed past her, running into the room. I saw two doors, taking the nearest one and shouting at Jennifer to take the other.

I entered a den and saw two people on the floor, gagged. I whipped around, desperately trying to find the threat, and saw a man jump up from a chair to the right of me, a suppressed pistol in his hands and a look of shock on his face. He squeezed off a double-tap, and I dove to the floor. One of the hostages leapt up and threw himself at the man, hitting him in the waist and knocking him into a wall. He turned his weapon on the gagged hostage, and I fired offhand from the ground, three, four, five times.

The first bullet missed. The next four found their mark. He collapsed on the floor, and the hostage rolled upright. A female.

But not Kylie.

58

On the phone with George Wolffe, trying to ascertain the damage to his men, Kurt Hale heard the president shout, "Quiet, damn it."

Kurt said, "Hang on."

President Warren looked at Creed and said, "Go ahead."

"Sir, we just got a chat request to join a room. I did so, and the terrorists are communicating with me."

Alexander Palmer snapped his fingers, pointing to an NSA man. "Get the location. Find out where they're transmitting from."

Creed said, "Don't bother. They're using an app called Cryptocat, run through the Tor network. You'll get nowhere. It's why they picked it."

President Warren said, "Bring it up to the big screen."

Creed did, and Kurt read, *So you think you can rescue your hostages? You think we're that stupid? We told you not to try to find them, and now you have. Now you've caused their death.*

The room visibly sagged at the words.

Palmer said, "Jesus. We killed them."

Creed said, "I need to reply. What do I say?"

President Warren said, "We didn't kill anyone. They did. We had to try."

Creed said, "Sir?"

"Tell them we didn't know it was them. Tell them it was a French operation, and we had nothing to do with it."

He did, and the reply words appeared on the screen.

Is that why you had four FBI men in the assault?

Palmer said, "They were watching. Waiting. They wanted to kill them this way."

Warren said, "When I find these assholes I'm going to . . ." His voice trailed off. He waited a beat, then said, "Tell them okay. Cut the crap. What do they want?"

Creed typed the words, and everyone held their breath waiting on the reply. When it came, it was almost mundane. Like a bank robber.

We already told you what we want. You have the Bitcoin address. Send the money.

Warren looked at the head of the FBI and said, "How much do we have?"

"About half. We haven't been able to get it all."

Palmer said, "You can't send it. There's no proof that they won't just give us another demand."

Warren considered, then said, "It's just money. A drop in the bucket for us. If it buys us a day, it buys us a day. Tell them we can send half."

They waited on the response. When it came, it was chilling.

We thought you would stall like that. Here's a little secret. Your hostages weren't in that room today. They are still alive, but you just killed them. Expect another Snapchat soon.

The room remained quiet for a split second, then erupted in pandemonium, nobody knowing which hostages were in the discussion. President Warren slapped his hand onto the table and said, "Shut the hell up. Creed, tell them the money's coming. Tell them we're giving them all we have."

Palmer said, "Sir—" but President Warren ignored him. He looked to the director of the FBI and said, "Send it. Right now."

The director scurried out of the room, and Creed typed the message. They watched the blinking icon, waiting on a response. Nothing happened.

Kurt whispered into his phone, "Okay, things here are going to shit. Give me some good news."

George said, "Finally got Brett on the line. He's alive and unhurt."

"And Knuckles?"

"He's okay. Took some shrapnel, but he's going to be okay. Basically got his ass punctured, but his body armor stopped any lethal hits. He was on his way out the door when it triggered. Almost all of it missed him. Two feet the other way, and he would have been eviscerated, but he's got nothing but a few stitches at this point."

Kurt sagged into his seat, saying, "That's the best damn thing I've heard in years. Can I talk to them?"

"Not right now. They're dealing with acting like FBI agents. The two real ones were torched."

Kurt closed his eyes.

George said, "What's going on there?"

"We're getting toyed with."

"What about Pike? What's he got?"

"Nothing. He's out chasing shadows." Kurt heard President Warren ask, "Are they still online?" and he said, "I have to go. Keep me abreast of the situation."

They watched the icon blink on the big screen, then saw, *Is Chairman Clute there? Ask him which one he wants to die first. His choice.*

Chairman Clute's face went white. He looked at the president and said, "I can't do that. Please, tell them to stop."

President Warren said, "God damn it, tell them we sent the money. Tell them not to do this."

Creed did, and the reply was, *You arrogant infidels need to learn a lesson. You paid half, so I kill half. Fair trade.*

The screen flickered, and a Snapchat appeared, showing two hooded hostages. Nobody said a word. President Warren looked at Chairman Clute, then said, "Pull it off the screen."

Creed did so, and Warren said, "Palmer, take a look."

His face visibly sweating, Palmer went to Creed and leaned over his shoulder. Kurt felt his phone vibrate. He looked at the screen and saw it was Pike. He thought about shunting it to voice mail, but answered. Pike deserved to know Knuckles was alive.

He said, "Hey, I'm in a little bit of a situation here. I can't talk, but Knuckles and Brett are fine."

He heard nothing for a second, then Pike said, "Seriously? They're okay?"

Creed hit the play button, and Kurt watched Palmer's face, waiting to see it flinch. He said, "Yes, now I have to go."

Pike said, "Sir, I need the support package right now. I've got two dead terrorists and two hostages, alive. I need help to get out of the building clean."

"Pike, I can't talk right now. I'm watching these fucks kill a hostage on video." Then the words sank in. "You've got what?"

"I have the Clute twins, damn it. I need support."

Palmer turned from the screen and said, "It's the original video. The proof of life."

Chairman Clute sagged in his seat, and Creed brought the chat back to the large monitor. Words appeared on the screen: *The next Snapchat is decided by you. Which one dies? I don't hear anything in one minute, and I'll choose.*

Kurt said, "I'm watching a live chat with the terrorists. They're saying they're going to kill one of the twins in the next few seconds. Tell me you're not delusional."

"Jesus, sir." The phone fumbled, and he heard, "This is Kaelyn Clute. I'm alive. Who is this?"

Kurt about fell out of his chair. He stood up and shouted, "I need this on speaker, right now."

Palmer glared at him, then looked to the president. "I don't know what to say to get them to stop. We can't pick one."

Kurt raised his voice. "Pike's on the line. He's got the Clute twins."

The room went quiet. Chairman Clute leaned forward, his face radiating hope, like a father searching for a child in the aftermath of a tornado. Knowing the worst was coming, but not wanting to believe. He said, "Who's Pike?"

President Warren said, "Put him on."

The phone was redirected, and President Warren said, "Pike? This is President Warren. You there?"

"Yeah, I'm here, sir. Could I get some fucking help for a change?"

Kurt cringed at the language, and President Warren said, "We're about to get a video of one of the Clute twins getting executed."

Pike said, "Well, unless I'm the one pulling the trigger, that's going to be pretty damn hard to do."

Chairman Clute said, "Who are you? What do you have?"

The next words from the speaker were "Daddy? We're alive. We're both alive. But I think this man could use some serious help to keep us that way."

Kurt saw the tears begin to flow from Chairman Clute's eyes. He looked at the president and said, "We through fucking around with Pike?"

59

Ali Hassan slipped over the side of the boat and the coldness of the water took his breath away. An involuntary gasp escaped as he kicked his legs to keep his head above the waves, the sound lost to the wind.

The temperature outside was a brisk forty-four degrees, and he realized the River Thames was cold enough to cause rapid hypothermia. Something he should have recognized before, but he was used to the surf off the coast of Somalia. Even in the wintertime it was bearable.

He said, "Ismail, quickly. Pass me the explosives."

Ismail saw him flailing, mistaking the urgency in his voice for a danger he couldn't see. He slid across a box four feet square, covered in a tarp. It hit the water with a small splash, then began bobbing in the waves. He said, "What is it? What do you see?"

His teeth beginning to chatter, Ali Hassan said, "Nothing from man, but if we don't get to shore soon, we'll die out here. The water is freezing."

Ismail laughed, the sound abruptly cut short as he slid into the darkness of the Thames himself. He sputtered, the liquid so cold he couldn't form a sentence. The man in the boat said, "You want me to get closer? So you don't have as far to swim?"

Ali looked toward his target and said, "No. Someone will see. We're too close to the palaces and other government buildings. Too close to people watching. You keep going as planned. Away from here."

The man turned the throttle of the outboard engine and the small boat puttered away, soon lost from sight in the darkness.

Ismail said, "If the rope isn't there, we're going to die. Or be forced to turn ourselves in to prevent it."

Ali unrolled a length of twine from the box and tied it to his belt. He started to swim to the southern shore, dragging the box behind him. He said, "The sooner we get there, the sooner we'll know."

Roughly a hundred meters away, the edge of the river twinkled with lights, their target rising up and dominating the landscape, illuminated like a gigantic Christmas tree. The London Eye.

Originally called the Millennial Wheel, it was once the largest Ferris wheel in the world and still ranked in the top four, standing over four hundred feet in the air. Created to celebrate the turn of the century, thirty-two capsules dotted its circumference, each capable of holding twenty-five people. At full capacity, there would be eight hundred people in the capsules, slowly turning. Eight hundred bodies Ali intended to send crashing into the dark water of the River Thames.

They reached the outer glow emanating from the shore and continued on into the undercarriage of the loading platform. Ali swam to the nearest anchor pipe, a giant thing embedded deep into the footings at the bottom of the river.

Two feet above the waterline the pipe had a collar of steel with spikes pointing downward. A fixture designed to prevent someone like Ali from climbing the pipe to the platform above. Which would have sufficed if he were working alone. He was not.

Now inside the lighting given off by the giant wheel, Ali and Ismail swam among the pipes, sticking to the shadows and working their way to the right side of the loading platform, near the gift shop. Ismail went forward, searching the gloom, while Ali clung to a pylon, fighting the waves and keeping the box of explosives from slamming into him. Ali lost sight of him, then heard him hiss.

He let go and swam forward, struggling with the box against the current. He saw a knotted rope dancing above the river, Ismail halfway up it. Ali waited until he was on the platform, then tied the box to the end of the rope and climbed up himself.

Ismail helped him over the edge, the wind cutting through his wet clothes, causing him to shiver involuntarily. He said, "Where is Mansoor?"

"Inside. Hiding in the dark."

"And the uniforms? Tell me he brought the uniforms. Something dry."

Pulling up the box, Ismail said, "Yes. Go inside. Change."

Thirty minutes later both men were dressed in uniforms for the cleaning crews, the man called Mansoor twitching nervously beside a large plastic bin on wheels. He said, "We must go. The safety crew will be here soon. They check everything. You need to get in and out before they arrive."

"Everything? They look at everything?"

"Down here. The spindle and hub are checked by computer."

"Okay. How will we get there?"

"Outside. The arms outside. They have a hatch that leads upward."

"Do you clean them out ordinarily?"

"No, but I'll protect you with the bin. You get inside, close the door, and you won't be seen going up."

"You will stay until we're done?"

"No, no. I have to make my rounds. I'll get rid of your wet clothes at the same time. How long do you need?"

Ali looked at Ismail, and he said, "Forty minutes."

"Okay, okay. I'll position again in forty minutes. But no more. The safety crew will be here in less than an hour, and they know me on sight. You they will question."

They trundled out of the gift shop area as if they belonged, Mansoor pushing the bin and the other two holding brooms. They walked away from the loading platform to the two giant A-frame arms that held the wheel in the air.

Built as a cantilever, the enormous wheel was supported on one side only, the arms leaning sixty-five degrees before mating to the hub two hundred feet in the air, allowing the wheel to extend out over the river. Four sets of giant cables buried one hundred feet deep kept the entire assembly from falling over.

Seamus had stated that it would take too many explosives to destroy the hub and spindle at the center of the wheel, and he was right, but the unique architecture had one Achilles' heel—the cables. The entire wheel was held upright much like a person leaning backward and holding on to a rope tied to a tree. Cut the rope, and the person falls. Cut the cables, and the arms—already leaning out over the River Thames—would topple, bringing the entire wheel down, with all eight hundred people inside screaming on the way.

Some would be rescued. Some would be crushed. Most would drown trying to escape the capsule. But all would contribute to the spectacular nature of the attack.

Mansoor parked the bin next to a steel hatch at the base of the giant arm, blocking the view of the various security cameras. The small aperture looked not unlike something seen on ships, an oval piece of metal surrounded by bolts. He scurried low, unlocked the hatch, then stood, making a show of sweeping the concrete, and said, "Hurry. Go."

Ismail and Ali scrambled inside, hearing the door lock closed behind them. They looked at each other, realizing they were trapped. Ali shrugged and began climbing a ladder, dragging the box behind him. Ismail sighed, hoisting the box on his shoulder and beginning to follow.

Fifteen minutes later, they exited onto the scaffolding underneath the spindle at the center of the wheel, two hundred feet in the air. They paused for a moment, breathing heavily, the dragging of the explosives having taken its toll. Ismail looked at his watch, then scuttled to the far end, finding where the giant cables joined the hub. He pointed to the flange of steel holding the anchor point of the cables and said, "Here. We cut here. Open the box."

Ali did so, saying, "You mean the cable?"

"No. The steel. We can shatter it with the RDX. Cutting the cable will be much harder. We don't have plastic explosives to form around the cable, so most of the power would be lost. Breaking those flanges off, though, will be easy."

Ali nodded, not truly understanding but trusting Ismail's knowledge. In short order, both of the outer flanges were prepared, a ribbon of RDX on either side of the steel, slightly offset from each other. The result would be an explosive force that cut through the hardened metal, separating the flange from the spindle. Ismail finished by coating both explosive packages with white spray paint, making them blend into the color scheme of the spindle. When he was done, he armed the detonators and asked, "How long for the timer?"

Ali said, "One P.M. on Saturday."

Ismail looked at him in shock. "You want these to sit here for a day and a half?"

"Yes. I checked. In the winter, the only time the wheel is full is on the weekends. We do it today, we won't get the impact."

Ismail said, "Who cares about the impact? We aren't claiming credit. Let's set it for today."

"No. Do as I ask. I know what I told that man Clover, but I'm taking pictures when we're done here. We'll get his hostages, let him gloat, then claim this for our own. With proof. Then we'll *really* leverage our payment."

Ismail smiled and prepared the timer, saying, "Okay. But we might get nothing if they find our work."

"It's a risk I'm willing to take."

The spindle end cables complete, they crawled forward on the catwalk, locating the two cables that attached to the hub and repeating the procedure, coating both packages with paint. When they were done, Ismail set his digital watch, then said, "Okay. Go back to the outward cables. Press the red buttons when I signal. I need them all to go off fairly closely."

Ali crawled the fifty feet to the end of the scaffold, feeling vertigo from the wind and the drop beneath the grate. He found both red switches and looked back. Ismail nodded, his hands on his own explosive detonators. Ali clicked and returned, finding Ismail setting the timer on his watch. Ali said, "Okay, what's next?"

Ismail said, "Nothing. We're done. Next is this wheel falling in the river."

Ali smiled. "Then let's go see about our payment."

60

The reporter studied Kurt's Department of Homeland Security badge, then asked, "Why is a Secret Service agent looking into a murder? I thought you did financial crimes?"

Kurt inwardly winced, realizing that the man in front of him probably knew much, much more about the mandates of the Secret Service than he did. If he wasn't careful, he'd really raise the hair on the back of the old guy's head.

He said, "Blame yourself. You guys report so many stories that we spend more time trying to stay ahead of them than on our real jobs. The administration just asked me to check, because the last guy Breedlove spoke with was my boss. The secretary of Homeland Security."

The man looked at his badge again and said, "Kurt Hale, huh? Well, Agent Hale, I don't know what you want me to say. The police have already been over here questioning everyone. Have you talked to them?"

"Yeah, I did. Look, I'm just building a two-slide update briefing. Nothing major. I just want to confirm a few things."

What he didn't say was that the police had given him nothing to help his quest. They had few leads and were actively focusing on gangland affiliations based on a recent unflattering story Breedlove had printed, which had apparently aggravated some serious gangbanger kingpins. That might well have been the case, but Kurt felt it was something more. Something he could use to find Kylie. Pike now had a team and was actively working the problem, but he'd come up with precious little from the safe house in Paris. An address in County Cork, Ireland, which might or might not be anything at all.

This fishing expedition might come to nothing as well, but it was worth the look.

The old reporter said, "What do you want to confirm?"

Another man wandered to the cubicle, standing behind Kurt.

Kurt asked, "The night he left here, he was going to meet a source, correct?"

The man behind him said, "Dwight, I'll take this."

Kurt turned and saw a twentysomething guy in chinos and a button-down, with the wispy three-day-beard look the younger generation now sported. Either a statement of his lumberjack qualities or a statement of his laziness. The man stuck out his hand, saying, "Kincaid Butler. I was here when Grant left."

Dwight rolled his eyes and said, "Okay, Kincaid, he's all yours. I need to get back to work."

Without another word, Dwight turned to the computer in front of him and ignored them both.

Kincaid said, "Follow me. I'm the one that spoke with the police."

They wandered to another cubicle, Kincaid talking as they went. "Yeah, Grant was here, and he was working on some bombshell story, but nobody outside of our editor knew what it was. Maybe not even him."

Kurt said, "And he left here that night because of it?"

"I think so. He was pretty close-lipped about it, but it was getting big enough that he was going to ask for my help."

"So you were working the story as well?"

They reached another cubicle, and Kincaid took a seat, putting his hands behind his head. "Not yet. Just background stuff."

"Like what?"

"Emails, research, that sort of thing."

"So what was the story?"

Kincaid said, "I'm not at liberty to discuss it with you."

Kurt backed off, not wanting it to appear that he was interested in anything but Breedlove's disappearance. He said, "Okay, I really don't care about it. I just have to brief the administration that this had nothing to do with them. You know how it is. Twenty-four-hour news and all that. Trying to stay ahead of the game."

Kincaid said, "Well, I'll be picking up the ball, so if you want help, I'm your man. What do you know about it?"

The statement was aggravating. Kincaid was now pumping *him* for information, and it was getting Kurt nowhere.

There was one primary question Kurt wanted answered: If Breedlove was killed by a terrorist tied to the kidnappings, how did the killer learn that he was on the story? There had to be a leak that allowed the terrorist to specifically target Breedlove, and it meant the group had somehow penetrated *The Washington Post*, gleaning the information when even the people on the floor didn't know what Breedlove was doing.

Kurt redirected the questioning, saying, "You mentioned the editor. Would he have more information about where Breedlove was going?"

"Brittle? Doubtful. He let Breedlove run because of his past history, but he was getting fed up with the waiting. Honestly, I'm not sure Breedlove even knew what he was hunting. Outside of talking to the secretary of Homeland Security, most of his work was with low-level insiders."

"How did you know he spoke to the secretary? If it was all so hush-hush?"

Kincaid stood up, saying, "Come here. I'll show you."

They walked to an office, paned in by windows with a view onto the newsroom floor. The desk was littered with papers, stacks overflowing an inbox, but the chair was empty.

"That's Brittle's office. See the whiteboard behind him? He kept track of anyone who was meeting a whale."

"Whale?"

"Just what we call big shots. Political figures, entertainment figures, anybody that could come back to bite us in the ass. If you were meeting them, you had to keep Brittle abreast of the time, place, and outcome."

Kurt peered through the glass and saw a list of names, most he recognized. The undersecretary of defense for acquisition, a couple of senators, a music mogul. To the right were the reporters' names, and next to it, the story. National Defense Authorization Act, Patriot Act, charity event for Africa, and other news items. He scanned down and saw the secretary of Homeland Security's name. Next to it was Breedlove. The story was listed as "compartmented."

"So you read this and knew that Breedlove was meeting the secretary of Homeland Security?"

"Well, yeah, but Breedlove was all set to give me the dump on what they discussed. I mean, before . . ."

"And this board stays up all the time? Where anyone can see it?"

Looking confused, Kincaid said, "Yeah. So what?"

Kurt felt the trickle of an idea. He said, "I might be able to get you that data dump firsthand. If you keep me out of it."

Kincaid's eyes lit up, then just as quickly returned to nonchalance. He said, "I'm all ears."

"It's not me. But the secretary *is* my boss. I'll see what I can do. You're the man for this? Should I talk to Brittle?"

"No, no. That'll just clog up the gears. He's still dealing with Breedlove's death."

"But won't the whale get posted? Won't it say 'Breedlove's story' or something?"

Kincaid said, "Yeah, yeah, but Brittle won't care if the interview is already locked. He'll just want to know it's going on. Here, let me give you a card." He pulled one out and said, "That's got all my contacts. Cell, office, email. Call anytime."

Kurt studied it, pretending to make a decision, but in reality wondering how he was going to trick Kincaid into thinking he was meeting the secretary of Homeland Security. Wanting that on the board. Wanting to stake the young Kincaid in a field, bleating for the terrorist.

Beyond that, he was wondering how he was going to break every federal surveillance law in existence by tapping all of the phones on the card. After all, it wouldn't be fair to make him the bait if Kurt didn't have the means to capture his prey.

He said, "I'll see what I can do."

Kincaid beamed, not understanding the meaning of his words.

61

Colin heard Seamus slam the door and wondered if he'd been found out. He felt his cell phone burning a hole in his pocket like a traitorous beacon. He'd cleaned it of any evidence from his calls but wasn't sure Kevin couldn't find something if he was ordered to look. That technology was a mystery to him.

Maintaining a calm demeanor, he waited for the man to enter their hovel, a little aggravated that he and Kevin had to stay and babysit while Seamus slept in a hotel. Enjoying hot water and real food, while he continued to stink and eat microwave dinners.

Seamus came through the door, his jaw clamped shut, his veins throbbing in his neck. Kevin looked up from his computer and said, "Bitcoins are transferred. At today's rate, we have about twenty-four million dollars. It's all in the wallet."

Brought up short, Seamus said, "We own the money?"

"Yeah. We have it. It's in the wallet we made. The one you have."

Seamus pulled out the paper construction they'd made before. "Are you saying this thing now has twenty-four million dollars in it?"

Kevin smiled. "Yes. That's what I'm saying."

Seamus shook his head in wonder. "Okay, I'll believe you. That's the only bit of good news."

Colin said, "What's the bad news? Where is the team in France? Where's Braden? You need to give us more information instead of just coming and going."

Seamus took a seat and said, "We're under fire. I can't contact Braden, and I haven't heard from Ratko again. He's on the hunt, I'm pretty sure."

"Then we need to get the hell out of here. Go somewhere else."

Seamus said, "Where? Where the fuck do you want to go? There is nowhere else. We can't get a hotel and shuttle in three hostages, and I'm out of safe houses."

Colin said nothing, not wanting to antagonize Seamus. Not wanting to give him any reason to question.

Looking out the window, Seamus said, "Braden's gone. I'm sure of it."

"Why didn't we get the Snapchat yesterday? Of the other hostages?"

Seamus said, "Because those fucking Serbs hit the apartment. During the planning for the jewel heist in Brussels, Braden probably told them where our safe house was in France, and they hit it. Expecting to find all of us, but they didn't. They killed the Clute twins and our men. That's what happened."

"So what now? If we can't go somewhere else?"

"They don't know where we are. We still have the prize."

Colin stood up, agitated. "Bullshit. Seamus, this thing is falling apart. We can't continue blindly assuming everything is going swimmingly. It's not. They had your cell phone number. How did they get that? What else do they know?"

Seamus stood, and Colin realized he'd pushed too far. "They know *nothing*. Nothing about our mission. They're bank robbers. They care about nothing but themselves."

Fists clenched, Seamus glared at Colin, and even given the disparity in size, Colin was afraid. He sat back down and said, "Okay, Seamus. Okay. I'm just asking. We have a lot on the line here as well."

Seamus turned away and said, "We need to get more men here. Get some protection. Harden this place."

Colin said, "Why? If we're hidden?"

"I can't promise that, and you're right. They had my phone number. I don't know how they got that. I mean, I have fourteen different SIM cards at any one time, and they had the one I would answer."

"But nobody knows about this place. Right? You said that. Nobody but us."

Seamus looked at him, a sick expression on his face. He said, "Nobody but Braden. He knew. I told him."

Seamus ran his hands through his hair back and forth, pulling the scalp. Colin sat still, understanding the moment of his departure had arrived.

Seamus said, "I'm leaving again. I'm going to get some bodies for this place. Hard men. We don't have to worry about the Yanks, but we do need to fear Ratko."

Kevin said, "What's that mean? Fuck, man, let's call it quits. Get out while we still can. We've given it a good run."

Seamus leaned back, staring at the ceiling. He said, "You have no idea of the sacrifice for this. None. Both of you came on late in the game. We quit now, and we lose everything Braden and I fought for."

He looked both men in the eye, causing Colin to stare at the floor. He said, "You want to quit now, there's the door. But you'd better remain quiet." Neither Kevin nor Colin said a word. Seamus said, "Look at me. Both of you." When he had their attention, he said, "You remember the old ways? What was done to informants?"

Kevin nodded, looking sick. Colin remained mute.

His voice calm, his expression tranquil, belying the gravity of his words, Seamus said, "You can leave with no repercussions, but if you say a word, I'll fucking power drill both of your kneecaps. I'll hunt your ass down and maim you for the short life you'll have left."

Kevin turned away, tapping the keyboard to his front as if he had something important to do, his fingers trembling. He said, "Hey, Seamus, no reason to start that. I'm with you. Really."

Seamus said, "Fine. Colin?"

"Of course. I'm with the cause. Wherever it takes us."

Seamus rubbed his eyes. He said, "I have to find Clynne. Get more drugs for transport and get some help. We're close to the endgame. The Somalis have done their work, and we're almost home. Tomorrow, we'll take the hostages to them. After that, it'll be a war."

Kevin said, "And what if Ratko interferes again?" Meaning, *What if he comes here?*

"He'll find that we're more than he wanted to mess with. Fuck his jewels," Seamus said. "Keep an eye out. They may be close. They won't attack in the daytime, but they might come looking. I'll be back later with the reinforcements."

He grabbed a set of keys off the wooden shelf and left, dialing a phone.

62

Kevin waited a bit, letting the car disappear, then said, "What do you think?"

Colin said, "I think Seamus is right. We keep doing what we're doing. They might have interdicted Braden and the others, but they have no idea where we are."

Kevin settled back, reassured at the words. He said, "We got a ton of money. We should just cash it in."

Colin said, "Yeah. I hear you. We'll talk about that later."

He stood, pulling another set of keys off the board next to the window. He said, "I'm going into Macroom for some food. You want anything?"

"Huh? You can't leave! What are you talking about?"

Colin snorted and said, "I'm sick of eating microwave crap. I'm going for some real bog. You want something?"

"You can't drive to town. I can't watch this place by myself."

Colin moved close, letting his size speak for him. "Well, that's what you're going to do. Do you want any food or not?"

Kevin shrank back, saying, "No. No, I'm good."

Colin exited the house, the fear from Seamus's threats driving into his body like an electric current. Barely thinking, knowing if he did, he would change his mind, he went to the car and started the engine, backing it up to the small hatch in the ground.

He shut the engine down, considering what he was going to do. Reflecting on how he was going to escape the wrath of the Serbs, but in so doing fall into the wrath of Seamus. A dilemma with no good answers.

He went back and forth, then chose: Seamus was the lesser threat. Ratko would hunt him down anywhere in Europe. Seamus didn't have that power.

The decision made, he focused on the next problem: He couldn't take all the hostages. At most, he could control only one. But which one? Who should he take? Who would he bring to show Ratko he was on his side? The vice president's son was the easy choice, as Ratko could leverage him immediately, but he was also a fighter. Someone who would cause trouble and possibly escape. The other man was a coward but was still a threat. If he chose to, he could put up a fight at an inopportune time. Colin couldn't afford that risk.

He opened the ancient wooden doors, hearing the woman cough, sick and weak. And had his answer.

Lying on the cold earthen floor, Kylie heard the door open and knew it wasn't feeding time. She pushed upright, seeing the light through her hood. She felt Nick rise as well, understanding something was happening.

He crawled over to her and took her hands in his, both still bound. He leaned in and said, "No worries. Maybe early chow."

She heard the footsteps and felt the doom growing with each one. They stopped next to her. She heard, "We're going to a different place. Just you. Do not fight me."

The panic flooded through her, causing her to shake uncontrollably. In a halting voice, she said, "Why? Where?"

Nick, still hooded and still holding her hands, said, "Bullshit. She goes nowhere. Not without me."

Kylie heard something like a mallet smacking a breast of chicken, then felt Nick's hands torn away. She heard the man kicking and screamed, "Don't hurt him! Jesus, please don't. I'll come. I'll come."

From across the room, Travis said, "Stop it! Stop it now!"

The man said, "You want a piece of the action?"

Travis said, "You will *not* take her from here. We are together. A package. You will not do this."

Kylie scuttled back, clawing away from the man she couldn't see. He let her be, walking to Travis. He said, "I'll do whatever I want. You looking to be a hero now? After being the traitor?"

She heard a meaty thump, then heard a man shout, hitting the dirt of their floor. And it wasn't Travis. She jerked her hood off, seeing both Nick and Travis on him, kicking and punching, doing what they could with their bound limbs.

The man—she saw it was Colin, the bearded one—escaped easily. He punched Travis in the gut so hard she heard the whoosh of air forced out of his lungs. Colin flung Nick to the side, then stood up, breathing heavily. He lined up his leg and kicked Nick full in the head, laying him out. Travis heard the damage and rolled into a ball.

She shouted, "Don't!"

Huffing, Colin said, "Get the fuck up. Now."

She did so.

He said, "I'm going to cut your leg bindings. You make any move, and I'll kill both of them. Understand?"

She nodded.

He came over and bent down, using a large folding blade to slice through the plastic of her flex ties. He rose, saying, "Walk up the stairs. Slowly."

She looked back at Nick, unconscious on the floor. Then at Travis, curled in the fetal position, arms over his skull. She said, "Travis." She saw his head jerk to her voice.

Colin poked her in the shoulder, saying, "Get moving."

She didn't. She waited until Travis was looking her way, searching for her under the hood. She said, "Thank you. Don't let them hurt Nick."

Colin cuffed her again, and she exited the dank prison, seeing a white Toyota sedan, engine running. She said, "Where are we going?"

"Someplace where I won't get killed."

63

The pub was pretty much empty, with two sots at the bar, veins popping on their noses from a lifetime of Guinness. I let Brett and Retro wander around, scoping the place out, and ordered three pints from the bartender.

An older lady who looked like she'd been pouring beer for a century, she said, "Americans?"

I said, "Yeah. We heard An Spailpin Fanac was the one pub we had to see in Cork City, but I guess it takes a while to pick up."

She smiled at my butchering of the Gaelic tongue. "We have nightly music, but even in Ireland the bars are a little empty at four P.M. Come back at nine."

I picked up the beers, saying, "Might do that. Thanks," then went deeper into the pub looking for my teammates. I passed a small cubby on the right, seeing two men leaning across the table, deep in conversation.

I found my mates sitting in the far back. I passed the beers out and said, "Well? What did you find?"

Brett leaned forward conspiratorially and said, "Look over to the right."

I did and saw a round vending machine. Nothing else. I said, "What?"

"That thing dispenses Pringles potato chip cans. Weirdest thing I've ever seen."

I looked at Retro, and he said, "It's true. I got a picture."

I said, "Who gives a shit? What about our target?"

Retro said, "Well, unless it's those two guys up front dressed like bums, it's got to be the two lovebirds in the cubby."

I said, "Really? You've got the balls to insult someone else's clothes?"

Retro got his callsign because of his dress. He consistently looked as if he were trying out for *Saturday Night Fever*, wearing clothes that were twenty or thirty years out of date. I used to think he just refused to buy anything new, but it had been going on as long as I'd known him, and I now secretly suspected he was purposely finding old stuff at Goodwill or other secondhand stores.

Brett chuckled and said, "We've recced the entire place. The back room is empty. You've seen everyone here. If that chick was telling the truth, it has to be one of those guys in the cubby."

After finally convincing the National Command Authority that we had indeed rescued the Clute twins, things had accelerated almost out of my control, making me wonder if I was going to regret asking for help.

The support team had showed up just fine, and we'd done a thorough CSI-like scrub of the apartment, with one egghead taking DNA and other biometrics, and a couple of others going through the apartment with a fine-tooth comb. It reminded me of the cleaner in *Pulp Fiction*.

In the end, they didn't get a whole lot. They would forensically check the phones and other electronics in more depth back in the rear, but the bad guys had used the same VOIP app that had stymied us in the past. The flip phone we found had one number: Braden's.

The only thing of interest was a notebook with addresses. One was the safe house where I'd found Kylie's pendant. Another was the hotel in Brussels that we'd broken into. A third was the death house that had almost killed Knuckles and Brett. After that, there were a few that I didn't know, and all would need to be investigated, but one caught my eye. An address for someone named Clynne in Cork City, Ireland.

I'd left the support package to deal with the bodies, taking Jennifer and Nung with me to the Paris airport. I had no idea how they dealt with such things and half expected one of the eggheads to start pouring acid in the bathtub.

We had finally linked back up with the vaunted Taskforce Rock Star bird and the team, minus Knuckles. He'd taken a few licks and was headed home. Nothing major, but enough to keep him out of the fight. I texted him, calling him a pussy and poking him in the eye for leaving me high and dry yet again, and was surprised at the pleasure I got in his reply. Not the words. Just the fact that he could type them.

For the record, he sent a real vote of confidence: *Don't kill my men doing something stupid.*

I'd sent back, *Stupid? Who's going home with stitches in his ass?*

We'd taken off to Ireland and had learned in-flight that the Oversight Council was sending LTC Blaine Alexander and an Omega package. Which meant either they were finally taking me seriously, or they really, really didn't trust me.

In an ordinary mission, when we'd built up enough evidence that a terrorist was to be taken off the board, Blaine would show up to control the operation, juggling everything from talking to the president to co-ordinating all the intricate cover concerns in the targeted country. In this case, we had very little, so his inclusion was a tad strange.

I didn't mind. We'd butted heads in the past, but he was a good guy and someone I trusted. In the end, all it did was give me cover from the head shed, since technically he was in charge, so anything that happened would fall on him to explain.

I'd picked up Brett and Retro, so with Nung and Jennifer, that gave me almost a whole team. I'd decided not to fly to the Cork City airport because of the risk. It was beyond believable that our opposition had the place wired, but then again I would have never pegged them to set such a diabolical trap in Paris. I was taking no chances.

I redirected to Shannon airfield, about two hours north of Cork City. There were other, closer places, but Shannon had a long history of help-ing out US government flights, including CIA rendition aircraft, so I preferred the infrastructure in place. While we had all the requisite tail numbers and documentation, we also had a near-term history of some weird-ass flying, and they knew when to look the other way.

We'd landed and linked up with Blaine in the lobby of the Shannon airport fixed-base operator, a place that serviced private aircraft—usually rock stars or oil magnates. Blaine seemed a little hesitant, won-dering how I'd treat him, since not too long ago he'd tried to lock me up on a mission in the US that had gone sideways. I decided to make him pay a little bit, putting on my war face and saying, "What the fuck are you doing here?"

Taken aback, he'd lowered his outstretched hand and said, "You didn't get the word?"

Jennifer had elbowed my kidney and shook her head. She said, "Yeah, we got the word and appreciate the assistance."

Then she glared at me.

I grinned and he saw I was jerking his chain. I shook his hand, then he went about slapping the rest of the team. He got to Nung, and his face showed confusion.

I said, "You guys wouldn't help, so I brought in an independent contractor. Nung, this is Blaine Alexander."

Nung stuck out his hand, and Blaine said, "Pike, can I see you a minute?"

He'd stomped to the far end of the room, me following. He said, "Who the hell is that?"

"I told you. An independent contractor. He's from Thailand and helped me with that Knuckles problem we had a year ago. You remember? The same one where you tried to fucking kill me?"

Which was an extreme exaggeration, but I wanted to rock him a little bit. It didn't work.

He went into command mode. "Jesus, Pike, you've got a civilian working Taskforce problems? Have you lost your mind?"

"Hey, he's handy in a scrape and can keep his mouth shut. He doesn't know what we do. And honestly doesn't care. As long as he gets paid."

"Paid? What are you talking about? Does Kurt know this?"

"Uh . . . not yet."

He turned in a circle, his hands on his head. "You have mercenaries working for the US government? Seriously?"

I said, "He's not a mercenary." Blaine looked at me like I was a child, and I said, "Okay, I guess he *is* a mercenary, but I needed the help. I pulled him in when I was PNG'd from the Taskforce."

He said, "What's the cost? What do we owe him?"

"Uh . . . we haven't really discussed that yet. He wanted the jewels in the apartment in Paris, but the support team took them."

His mouth fell open. "I . . . I'm really at a loss for words."

I grinned. "Don't worry. It'll work out. Now that you're here, you can break the news to Kurt."

He said, "Screw that. He's all yours. Let's get to Cork City."

We'd gotten a caravan of rentals, downloading whatever we thought we'd need from the Rock Star bird, pulling equipment out of the very walls themselves. The mission was pure reconnaissance, so we went heavy on that aspect. If we found anything, it would be Blaine's job to coordinate a rescue force, while we faded to the background. I didn't envy him for that. If it had been the UK, we could count on support from the SAS or some other organization much closer to our government, but here, I had no idea how he would effect a rescue. But that wasn't my problem.

We'd established a tactical operations center in a hotel next to the River Lee in Cork City, then had set out to the address we'd found for Clynne. It was in a decidedly seedy part of town, and Blaine had wanted to do some type of *Mission: Impossible* break-in, implanting bugs and everything else. I'd told him, "We do the mission. You deal with higher."

He'd said, "So, what do you recommend?"

"Knocking on the damn door. It's worked for Jennifer and me so far."

We'd driven to the address, leaving Nung fuming in the car yet again. Brett and Retro had staged left and right, and I'd taken Jennifer with me, both of us armed but our weapons concealed.

A skeleton-thin girl strung out on something, her hair listless and greasy, had answered the door. We'd asked for Clynne, and she'd snorted.

"He's not here. Doing 'business.' You see that shit, you tell him I'm not waiting all night."

I didn't want to ask what she was waiting for, in fact didn't want to get too close because I was sure she was carrying enough disease to cause the next Black Plague. I asked, "Where's the business being conducted?"

And she'd given us the name of the pub. No subterfuge or questioning of our motives, which led me to believe the man known as Clynne wasn't a master terrorist.

"You have a picture of him?"

She'd squinted, then said, "You don't even know what he looks like? I thought you were friends."

"I never said that."

"I got no picture."

I'd turned to go, and Jennifer, being quicker on the uptake than me, said, "Can I use your phone?"

I mentally kicked myself, knowing where she was going. The skeleton said, "He don't have a phone. It was cut off months ago."

I said, "Then can I have your cell?"

"No way. You want to call him, you pay me first."

I withdrew my pistol and said, "You misunderstand. I don't want to call him. I want to prevent you from doing that."

Her eyes had widened, and she'd said, "I won't call. I got no reason to."

"Give it to me. I'll give it to Clynne. You'll get it back."

She had done so, and now we were sitting in a pub, letting Clynne conclude his "business."

64

As we were milking our pints, Retro said, "We could get drunk here waiting. If he has a revolving door of 'clients,' we may not get a chance to brace him."

I was thinking the same thing, especially since the woman had indicated he spent an inordinate amount of time on his "business." I was considering just busting up the meeting, but decided against it. A decision that I would later regret.

I said, "Let's give it a few more minutes. Go get another round to keep the barmaid happy."

He left, and sure as shit, as soon as he was out of sight, the meeting broke up. An ascetic guy with dark hair, prominent veins on his neck, and a tattoo of a harp below his ear exited, not even glancing our way.

I said, "Looks like showtime."

Standing up, Brett grinned, saying, "You want me to shock him? A little black magic?"

"No. You're too damn short to instill fear. You be the mean guy that hovers. Watch the exit to the cubicle."

He gave me a look that told me what he thought of that description, and I stood, saying, "Grab Retro when he goes past."

We entered the small space, really only two tables that could hold a couple each, with a fireplace in the rear. The man jerked his head up and squinted. He said, "No unsolicited business. Sorry."

I sat down and said, "We come highly recommended."

He heard my accent and began sweeping pieces of paper into his bag, handwritten notations on them. He began to stand, saying, "Doesn't work that way. Not sure what happens in New York, but not here."

I clamped my hand over his and said, "It works that way today."

He made a show of jerking his wrist away, but I held it in an iron grip, making him look weak. He pulled again, and I twisted the joint, causing him to fall into his seat to relieve the pain. He squeaked, "What the fuck do you want? I don't bring anything inside. And I don't pass money here. I got nothing."

I let go and said, "I don't want drugs. I want to meet the man known as Clynne. Is that you? Or the guy who left?"

His eyes flicked to the left, and he stammered, "Never heard of him."

I saw the tell, and he knew I saw it. I said, "You Clynne?"

He tried one last act of bravado. "Who's asking?"

I smiled. "If you really want to play the badass, you should bring in a little bit of muscle. Not that it would do any good."

Retro appeared in the door, his clothing making him look like a strung-out hitman. He gave Clynne a glare that scared even me.

I said, "I'm not here for drugs, and I'm not here for you. I'm here for a man called Seamus McKee. I'm going to find him, and when I do, I'm going to kill him."

I leaned back, pulled out my Glock, and rubbed my temple with the suppressor. I said, "I'll also kill anyone who stands in my way."

Out of the corner of my eye I saw Brett struggling mightily not to smile. I'll admit, it was over the top, but Clynne didn't see it that way. He said, "I got nothing to do with him. Jesus, did you follow him to me? I knew I should have never got involved with that fucker. He's bonkers."

I said, "Follow? What do you mean?"

He realized too late his statement gave something away, and I realized—too late as well—what it was. "Was that Seamus with you? Just now?"

He said, "No, no. That wasn't him. That was somebody else. He—"

My hand snaked out of its own volition, grabbing his neck. I began to squeeze, saying, "No more lies. Your buddy has some friends of mine, and he's going to hurt them. You tell me what I want to know, or I'll kill you right here."

He put both of his hands on my arm, desperately trying to pull away. I let him try for about two seconds, then gave him a straight punch to his forehead, knocking him to the floor. From the doorway, Brett said, "Easy. They heard that."

I kept my eyes on Clynne. "And?"

"And nothing yet. But we can't go full retard in here."

Clynne took strength from the words, sitting up and straightening his shirt. I said, "Then let's get the shitbag out of here."

Retro moved to his right and Clynne said, "Wait, wait. Yes, that was Seamus. I have no idea what he's doing. I have no part of it. All I did was sell him some drugs. Tranquilizers."

"Where is he? Where's he staying?"

Too quickly, he said, "I don't know."

I smacked his face with an open-hand slap, saying, "Remember the trust factor, shitbag."

He said, "Okay, okay. I can show you, but it can't get back to me. I swear, all I did was give him drugs."

I said, "Fine. Give me your wallet."

He did so, and I went through it, looking for connections. I found several and laid them out on the table. I said, "Friends of yours?"

He said, "No. Just contacts."

One card was for a Susan Clynne, florist. I held it to his eyes and saw the recognition. It was family. I said, "Get up. Walk to the front of the bar. You try anything, and I'll kill you in front of the drunks outside. When I'm done, I'll kill anyone you've ever known."

65

We exited the bar without any trouble, and I said, "Where's your car?"

"I don't have one."

I smacked him in the back of the head and said, "That's not what the girl at your place told me. Where is it?"

He muttered something about a traitorous bitch, and I inwardly smiled at my subterfuge. Sometimes a bluff worked. He said, "Down the street."

I said, "Brett, with me. Retro, link up with Nung. Follow us."

Clynne heard the words and realized there was more in play than just us in the bar. A little bit of purposeful psychology to keep him on his toes.

We walked two blocks, finding a beat-up Honda Accord. I let Brett drive, putting Clynne in the passenger seat, me directly behind him. I said, "So, where to?"

"Macroom. He's staying in a farmhouse out there."

We headed out of the city, and soon enough we were on the N22 going west into the Irish countryside. We traveled for about thirty minutes, going deeper into farm community, small blacktops branching left and right into the green hills. We crossed a stone bridge, an ancient defunct mill on the other side, and he said, "Stop! Too far."

"What do you mean?"

"The road to the house is right past that mill, but it's a one-lane dirt thing. You take it, and he'll know you're coming. He'll stop us."

"And why would you care about that?"

He held his hands up. "Hey, man, no way do I want that psycho on my ass. He's crazy."

We turned around and crossed the stone bridge again, then took a left, paralleling the river the bridge spanned, now on a winding strip of blacktop. About a mile in, he pointed out the window, saying, "That's it."

Brett slowed, and I saw a ramshackle house about two hundred meters away, in the center of a field. Made of stone, it had maybe four or five rooms, a crumbling chimney on the left side. It was surrounded by farmland, but the house itself was overgrown, with vines and bushes reclaiming what the forest had lost, as if whoever owned the land simply mowed around it. Between us and it was the river, maybe forty feet across and three feet deep.

I said, "You're telling me Seamus is staying in that shit hole?"

He held up his hands and said, "That's what he told me."

I wrapped my arms around his neck from the backseat, pulling to the rear. "I'm not stupid. Nobody could have found this place without having actually been here. There is no way you could have led us here from what he *told* you. I want to know what the hell you're doing with him. Right now."

He strangled for a minute, fighting my arm, then said, "Okay, okay! I got it for him, but I swear I don't know nothing about your friends. He told me he needed to lay low. That's all."

I pulled back again, and he began to cough. I let up, and he spurted, "I'm not lying!"

I said, "Okay then. I find out you are and we'll have a talk. We understand each other?"

He nodded, visibly trembling. I waited for him to recant anything, but he remained quiet. I was satisfied.

I turned to Brett. "Get Retro up here. Get some OP kit."

Brett said, "Me and him?"

"Yeah. Have Nung transport it. Eyes on from this point forward."

Brett looked to the right and asked, "Who owns the hill here? I haven't seen a house."

Clynne said, "I don't know. It's all farmland, but if you want to use it, I won't say anything, I swear."

Brett chuckled, and he said, "I won't!"

I said, "Yeah, I know. Mainly because you're not going to get the chance."

Brett watched the Wasp UAV circle overhead, Retro controlling its descent. He swooped the thing right over their hide site, then brought it straight up into the air. Brett ducked, hearing Retro laugh. Watching the monitor, he circled the UAV over three cows two hundred meters away. Brett said, "Come on. Bring it back."

Retro loved gadgets and was a little bit of a computer geek at heart. He would tinker with any new electronic kit that came into the Taskforce arsenal for days, figuring out all the parameters. He was the one man on the planet—outside of Steve Jobs—who actually understood all the settings on an iPhone.

He said, "Negative, Ghostrider. It's time to buzz the tower."

Brett rolled his eyes and watched the UAV dip, skipping right above the cows. They barely moved. With a wingspan of just over two feet and an electric motor, the UAV probably didn't even register with the animals.

He brought it around and crash-landed right next to their hide. He said, "You send the video to Pike?"

"Yeah. A video of a torn-up building. I'm sure he's jumping up and down."

They'd been in position trying to confirm or deny activity for over four hours and so far had seen nothing. A look through thermals had detected two heat sources, and using a directional microphone, Brett had discerned engine noise emanating from the house, meaning a generator, so someone was using the building, but there was nothing to indicate hostages or anything nefarious. It looked like a single squatter was living there.

Or another trap.

After the in-depth planning that went into the kill box in Paris, Brett had grown a little paranoid.

The sun reached the edge of the earth, and they were in that moment of twilight between using regular optics and night vision. Still no signs of anything indicating hostages.

Brett and Retro had been in situations like this before and had planned accordingly. They knew it would be a long night whether they found something or not.

Even if they'd immediately been able to confirm evidence suspicious enough for further exploration, they knew it would take Blaine the better part of the night to coordinate a response through the Taskforce. Their job was reconnaissance only, and they'd keep eyes on until relieved. Which meant a night in a hidey-hole.

The thermometer began to drop and Brett brought up the thermals again, knowing the difference in temperature would make the view much more stark. Inside, the same two heat sources showed up black against the white of the structure. Only now, one had moved.

He said, "Okay, got at least one target. Still think the other is a generator."

Retro noted the information in his log, saying, "Wonder what the trigger is to call this a dead end?"

"With Pike, it's usually some gunfire. Because he can't stand a dead end."

Retro started to respond when he saw lights bouncing down the dirt lane on the far side of the house. Two cars a half mile away.

He said, "Company," and Brett traded the thermal for a spotting scope.

While the blacktop on their side of the river had steady traffic, they'd seen only a single truck on the dirt lane on the far side of the house the entire time they'd been there. He fully expected the vehicles to continue on, like the truck, but they turned down the rutted track that led through the fields to the house.

He sat up. "Call Pike. Tell them we've finally got activity."

Both vehicles stopped outside the house, and ten or eleven men spilled out, carrying assault rifles. Brett said, "Holy shit. Call Pike. Tell him the trigger's been met. Get the cavalry rolling."

66

Seamus came inside, finding Kevin at the computer. Kevin turned around at the noise, his hands leaving the keyboard, and Seamus saw the surprise at the number of men who trundled in.

Seamus pulled the first aside and said, "You'll sleep in the room down that hallway, on the left. The one on the right is where we're already staying. We can take a couple more in there if it's too crowded. I want two here in the kitchen, two at the side door, and two at the back door in the anteroom. That leaves four off. Work out your own schedule."

The men began bringing in sleeping bags, coolers, and other comfort items. Kevin watched them work, saying nothing. Seamus asked, "Any word from Braden?"

"No."

"Ratko?"

"No. Nobody's called at all."

Seamus rubbed his face and muttered under his breath, his eyes tired. The men continued coming and going around him.

Kevin said, "Something else I need to know about?"

"Yeah. Well, maybe."

"What?"

"Aiden says there's another reporter in the US sniffing around. A friend of the one he killed has picked up the story. He's got an interview with someone in the administration about it."

"But we're close enough now it shouldn't matter. Right? You're going to send another Snapchat tomorrow? With the guys we have? Like we talked about?"

He sighed. "Yeah. But it's going to be too close. Word gets out about what's happened, and they will shut down. I can't predict how much longer this will go on, but even one day in the news is too much. I know the Yanks. The administration will immediately start talking about being hard on terrorism and our window will close. Remember the shit storm that happened when they released that deserter Bergdahl? All the talk about dealing with terrorists? They won't want a repeat of that in the press."

"So what did you tell Aiden?"

Seamus looked out the window and said, "To kill him."

Kevin remained silent. Seamus leaned forward, picking at a piece of wood on the makeshift table. He said, "Man, I didn't want to do that. I'm being pushed into it. Fucking reporters."

Kevin said, "We got half. Maybe we should just call it a win."

Seamus glared at him. "No way. If Braden's truly gone, then they'll pay. I've already lost one brother to those arrogant fucks. We hold the keys. The vice president's son is worth more money. They won't give in at first. One of the hostages will have to die."

Kevin said, "Which one? The girl?"

Seamus grimaced. He said, "Yes. She's the best leverage. Her killing gets sent, and they'll know we're serious." He leaned back again, then said, "Maybe not. Maybe that whiner from Brussels. I don't know if I can kill the girl."

Kevin said, "Colin can. That guy has no conscience. As long as it isn't pinned to him."

"That's not what I meant. *I'm* the one giving the order. It's irrelevant who pulls the trigger." He looked around, then said, "Where is he, anyway?"

Kevin glanced down, embarrassed.

Seamus said, "Where *is* he?"

"He went out for a hot meal. I told him not to."

"You've been here by yourself?"

"Yeah. But nothing's happened."

Seamus stood, fists clenched. "That fuck. I've had enough of his bullshit. How long has he been gone?"

"He left right after you did."

Seamus's mouth fell open. "Right after me? I've been gone for hours."

Kevin started to answer, but Seamus exploded out the door, running to the root cellar. He slammed open the wooden hatch, jumping down the stairs by the light of a small torch. He aimed it in the dank prison, illuminating only two people. He ripped off their hoods, seeing the two males. He said, "Where's the girl? Where did she go? If she found a way out, you'll pay the price for her escape."

The one called Travis blinked at the light in his eyes, holding his hands up to block it. Seamus pushed his shoulder with a boot. "Talk! I told you what would happen. Where is she?"

The vice president's son spoke up, and for the first time, Seamus saw his face was swollen. More so than when he'd left.

"That bearded fucker took her. Colin."

Seamus heard the words and felt his world begin to implode.

Nick continued, "We heard him talking to someone on the phone, afraid of being hunted. He said he could deliver you to them. Then he took her."

Jesus, Joseph, Mother, and Mary.

Seamus snarled, "You're lying. Tell me where she is!"

Travis said, "That's what happened. It's not—"

Seamus pulled out a pistol and jammed it under his nose, hard enough to tear cartilage. "You fucking tell me right now, or I'm spraying your brains on the ceiling."

Travis began mewling, losing the ability to speak. Nick shouted, "She's gone, you shit. Probably dead."

Seamus sized him up in the glow of the space heaters, and Nick drew up as straight as he could in his binds. Nick said, "If she is, you're going to pay. No court will keep me from you. No prison will protect you."

Seamus let go of Travis and screamed in frustration. He stalked to Nick and knocked him to the ground, putting the pistol on his forehead.

"I should kill you right now."

Nick showed nothing but defiance. "You and I both know I'm walking dead. I just pray I get the chance to take you with me."

Seamus barely heard him. He backed up, keeping the weapon aimed at Nick, his brain trying to assimilate the damage. He stood still for a moment, then began running up the stairs.

He burst into the kitchen and shouted, "Quit your preparations. We're leaving this place."

The men looked at him in confusion. He said, "Colin has betrayed us to Ratko. I have no idea how close they are, but they're coming. Where's Michael?"

"Prepping his bed—"

"Michael! Get in here."

A tall man with ropy muscles and a farmer's tan came in. "What's up?"

"We're leaving. Fuck the preparations. Get the two hostages in here."

"Two?"

"Yes, God damn it. Two. Get them ready to move. I've got drugs in my backpack from Clynne. Dope them up."

Kevin said, "Where are we going?"

"To London. We've gotten all we're going to with them. The Somalis have their attack prepared. We'll give them the hostages. Get on the computer and get us ferry tickets. How long will that take?"

"Ferry tickets to where?"

"To England, damn it! How long before we can leave?"

For the first time, Kevin saw panic. Something Seamus had never shown. He said, "Hey, let's plan our movement. Do some research. We can't just run willy-nilly with two drugged hostages. Let me do some work."

"How long?"

"Maybe an hour. Maybe longer. Let me find a place where we can hole up. Get the ferry passes. Plan a route."

Seamus sagged back, the pistol held against his leg. He said, "Okay. Do it. Michael, all men at the ready. Put most up front. Looking for vehicles. Ratko comes, and he'll drive right up, using Colin as security."

"You want someone at the road?"

"Yeah. Definitely. A vehicle comes in here, and I want it shot to pieces. Especially if it's Colin at the wheel."

67

I heard the radio transmission from the OP and knew we were in a world of shit. Blaine was going through our encrypted VPN to Kurt, telling him what we had from Retro's earlier transmission and trying to coordinate a leisurely response, surrounding the place with overt forces, then conducting a hostage rescue, but that wasn't going to happen.

I clicked the transmitter and said, "You sure? You saw the hostages?"

Retro said, "Roger that. Two being pulled out of a cellar and into the house. There's a lot of activity now. I think they're going to be moved."

"Two? Not three?"

"No. Two. I say again, two. The place is a beehive of movement. Something happened, and they're going batshit."

"What's your call?"

I heard nothing for a moment. Then, "We need to interdict."

Damn it. He was the man on the ground. The one with the closest intelligence on what we were dealing with. It was his decision, but I *really* didn't want to hear it. I thought about questioning him further, trying to decipher from my little bed-and-breakfast in Macroom what was truly going on, but I knew that was stupid. He'd made the call, and he understood the repercussions. If he wanted to assault, it meant we *needed* to do so or lose the hostages.

Over my shoulder, Jennifer heard the exchange and said, "We going in?"

"I don't know. We should."

"I agree. We lose this chance, and Kylie might be dead."

It was small comfort but gratifying nonetheless. I waved my arm, getting Blaine's attention. He turned from the screen, and I said, "Cut it off."

He saw my expression and did so. "What? I don't have a lot of time to coordinate a response. They're asking for all kinds of information, and the UAV video isn't satisfying them."

"Sir, the situation's changed. We have movement." I told Blaine what I knew, and he grasped the significance.

"I can't get anyone here in that timeline. If they're leaving in the next few minutes, we're fucked. Maybe I can get some roadblocks set up on the main highways, stop them en route." He pulled up a map on the computer, tracking all the major arteries. "They might be headed farther to the west. Or maybe toward Belfast. They'll have to use the main roads to do that. If I can get the word out soon enough, we can choke them."

I said, "Sir. Really?"

He said, "Yeah, really. Let me get to work. Tell the OP to call if they leave. Hopefully I can get something in place."

Jennifer and Nung were digging through our Pelican cases, pulling out concealable body armor and weapons.

Blaine glanced at them, then said, "I need the time or they're going to get away."

I said, "Only if we let them."

He turned from the computer and said, "We can't do an assault, Pike. No way. Jesus, it's bad enough that I've got an Irish drug dealer chained to the toilet."

"Sir, you already said it. We're screwed. The only thing that can stop this is the Taskforce. We have the assets, and we have the skill."

"Pike, we can't do an assault on Irish soil. It'll be a huge diplomatic mess. I can't ask . . ."

He sat for a minute, then shut down the computer.

"Fuck it."

I leapt up, running to the kit, him right behind me. I started sorting out weapons and charges, slapping things all over my body with Velcro when he said, "You got guns for me?"

Jennifer looked at him, confused, and I paused.

He said, "What? You need the help."

I laughed and said, "You have lost your mind. No way."

"What?"

"Somebody's got to deal with the shit storm, and better to prep the battlefield than deal with the mess later."

I finished digging, telling Jennifer, "Get a package for both Brett and Retro." I turned to him. "You can't go."

He said, "Pike, I'm going to get fired for this. Please. You can be in charge. I'll follow your lead. Let me get *something*."

I appreciated the desire. I really did, which is what I would have expected. He wouldn't have joined the Taskforce if he weren't a meat-eater, and it had nothing at all to do with his skill. He was a killer. But it made no difference. I gave him a hard truth, like NCOs since the Revolutionary War.

"Sir, what you're about to do is more important than a gunfight. Get the cleaning crew on standby. Get the Taskforce read on. Get the National Command Authority ready for the hurricane. Make sure someone's got my back. That computer over there is the most valuable thing we have right now."

Blaine stood, watching us kit up, disgusted. Feeling impotent. He said, "You're going to take the damn mercenary over me?"

Nung said nothing, continuing to work his kit.

I said, "Hey, sir. It was your call that got us here. Remember that. Courage isn't just under fire."

He turned away, muttering, "What a load of horseshit." He walked back to the computer and booted it up, saying, "I get to hear the screaming from DC, and you get to save the day."

I snapped the lid to the Pelican case closed and said, "We'll see about that. This goes bad, and I'm going to need some serious backup from the NCA. Don't let me down."

Blaine said, "Don't screw it up and I won't."

Jennifer checked the function of her HK416 and said, "What's your definition of a screw-up?"

Outside of her initial introduction, Jennifer hadn't said a single word to Blaine since he'd landed, not being sure how he felt about her conducting operations on the ground. Not knowing if he was a typical Taskforce he-man women hater. Now, she was talking at the worst possible time, because she was about to execute instead of him. I thought it might push him over the edge, and I wondered where she was going with the statement.

He glared at her and said, "My definition of a screw-up is two dead hostages."

She moved to the door saying, "Okay. Just wanted to make sure."

I followed her, Nung behind me. Blaine said, "Make sure of what?"

Jennifer opened the door and peeked into the hallway. She turned to me and nodded, then said, "Make sure you don't mind bodies."

There was no humor in her expression, and she wasn't trying for bravado. She just said it as fact. He looked at her with new eyes, and so did I.

She said, "What? You think I'm wrong?"

I said, "No. There's definitely going to be somebody dead tonight. Don't let it be you."

She slipped into the hallway saying, "It won't be. Let's go get Kylie."

68

Macroom was only ten minutes away from the target, and I was thanking my lucky stars that we'd decided to jump TOC from Cork City to the small hamlet. It had been much easier to conduct operational activity in a Cork hotel room, as the bed-and-breakfast we'd found was hosted by a nosy couple who really wanted to show us the best of Irish hospitality, but Cork was forty minutes away. The B&B had made things difficult, to say the least—especially when we had to smuggle in Clynne without them knowing—but the time saved could be the difference between life and death.

Jennifer drove and I relayed the plan, talking to Brett. There would be no time to sit around and hash out a detailed OPORDER over a sand table, but I knew I didn't need to worry about that. The minute Retro had made the call, he was thinking about assault.

I said, "We're six minutes out on the blacktop. Get your ass off the hill and meet us at the road. I have your kit."

All business, he asked, "Plan?"

"Stalk from the river. Me, you, and Retro. Koko and Nung take the car to the far side and lock it down with long guns."

"Explosive breach?"

"Yeah. Unless you have a better idea."

"Nope. I got the breach-point. See you in six."

And that was the plan. All of it.

We passed the mill on the main road, the dirt lane snaking off into the darkness, then crossed the river and turned left on the two-lane blacktop, paralleling the water. We drove for another minute, and I saw a penlight flash. We pulled into a cutout, seeing Brett and Retro kneeling with ghillie suits on and holding their recce kit.

Nung popped our hatchback and Retro started shuffling equipment, exchanging his optics and UAV for suppressed HK UMP submachine guns.

Brett said, "They definitely moved two inside. From what I've seen, I think the house is a basic four-room plan. There's a breach at the front, the side, and one in the rear. We take the rear one."

"Where do you think they've got the hostages?"

"I'm thinking the front. The heat sources are all there, with the exception of two in the rear and two on the side."

"Can we get there without compromise?"

"I can't say. If they don't have any optics—thermals or NODs—yeah. But I just don't know. I didn't see any telltale IR when looking, though."

"So what are the two at the rear doing?"

He grinned, his teeth glowing in the darkness. "Preventing the bad man from coming."

I nodded, asking the question I knew he'd already figured out. "What's the approach? You got a route?"

"Yeah. We cross the river right here, then buttonhook into the draw that runs parallel to the house. It peters out about seventy meters shy. From there, we just go in."

I said, "You and Retro on the same sheet of music?"

"Yeah. We're good."

Which meant I didn't have to brief anything. I asked, "Who's breach?"

"Me."

I nodded and said, "Jennifer, Nung, come here."

When they closed on me I said, "We're crossing here. I want you guys to drive back around to the dirt lane. No lights once you turn. Get as close as you can, then walk in. We aren't going to wait for you to get in position, but call when you are. We'll be moving to breach." I tapped the barrel of her 416. "Lock down the front. Don't let anyone leave."

Nung began working the action of his own 416 and I wondered if I would regret giving it to him. I said, "Nung, Jennifer's in charge. You understand? No shooting unless she says so."

He looked at me with his blank shark eyes and said, "I understand. I protect her. She shoots."

I was taken aback, because that was exactly what I wanted him to do. I said, "Yeah. You guard her flanks, she does the shooting."

He looked at her, then me, and said, "She will be fine."

He walked away, and Jennifer said, "I'm not so sure about him."

"I wasn't either, but inside that prison in Thailand, he was a holy terror. He says he'll protect you, and it's better than body armor."

She said, "Oookaaay . . . ," drawing out the word.

I said, "Get going."

She started to leave, and I grabbed her wrist. "One final thing: If it gets hot, don't let him start shooting. I'm not sure he gets the whole 'discrimination' thing. He's liable to kill the hostages."

Her eyes widened and she said, "What am I supposed to do to prevent that? If I'm getting shot at?"

"I don't know. Return fire with your gun and then bump him. Knock off his aim."

Her expression grew fierce. "Are you kidding me? I'm not taking him. I'll go alone."

I grinned at her attitude and said, "Just don't let him start blazing away. He'll listen to you. He wants to get paid."

She looked at me with slitted eyes. I glanced around, seeing nobody near, then leaned in close and said, "Don't get hurt. Call if you need help."

I kissed her on the lips, a brief peck.

I'd studiously kept our relationship purely professional for anyone on the team watching, and would have never done it, but we were going into the teeth of some bad guys. And I needed to give her some courage. Something to anchor against. It would help her . . .

Okay, that's bullshit and I had lost my mind for a moment. I just wanted to do it . . . in case. She returned the kiss and said, "More than likely you'll be calling me."

I chuckled. "Probably so."

She winked at me and said, "Nung? You ready?"

They packed up and the car disappeared down the road. Retro jacked a round into his UMP and said sotto voice, "Don't get hurt. Call if you need help."

Brett snickered, and I realized they'd seen the whole thing. I said, "Let's go, assholes."

We slid across the stone wall separating the river from the road, and Brett said, "Do you think we should call her for help no matter how this turns out? I mean since you'll be sleeping in her room and all? Get you some benny points in bed?"

I slid down the riverbank, gritting my teeth.

Retro said, "I'm willing to take one for the team. Act like we needed her help to pull us out of the fire. If you'll text some pictures."

He slipped and landed in the water with a splash. A loud one. We all froze, waiting to see if it mattered. Nothing happened.

I said, "You guys through fucking around? Because we're about to be in a gunfight."

69

Seamus paced the kitchen floor, turning circles around the two hooded captives. He said, "Kevin, come on. I've had enough. We'll figure out the ferry procedures when we get there."

Kevin said, "It's the connection. It's slow. Hang on. Just a couple more minutes."

"You've been saying that for a damn hour. You got the ferry tickets and the hotel. Fuck the rest."

Kevin turned and said, "Yeah, I did, but don't you want to know the return procedures? We only researched taking ferries *into* Ireland. You want to show up in England and have our car searched, finding a couple of hooded hostages?"

"It'll be the same. We need to go."

"No, it's *not* the same. You ever travel to the Continent? And travel back?"

Seamus heard the words and knew he was right. Getting to Brussels or Paris through the Chunnel was a breeze. Getting back was a nightmare of security.

He said, "How much longer to figure it out? How slow can that damn satellite hookup be?"

"Just a minute more."

Seamus said, "Michael, let's drug them. Get 'em ready."

One of the hooded men began to thrash about, and Seamus saw it was the vice president's son. If he didn't admire the fight, he would have knocked him out with a boot. But he did.

He grabbed Nick's head and said, "Stop it. This is going to happen. Don't make me hurt you."

Michael knelt over him with a needle designed for a horse, and Nick thrashed again, kicking his elbow and causing the syringe to fly across the room. Seamus snarled, "Have it your way," and thumped his head into the floor, stunning him. Michael retrieved the syringe and thrust it into his buttocks, through his clothes. He jammed the plunger home. Nick went limp.

Seamus said, "Travis, you want to fight?"

Through his hood, Travis shook his head, trembling. Seamus handed Michael another needle, and the radio crackled.

"Seamus, OP one. I got a couple moving down the road. Coming towards us."

Seamus held up, then grabbed the handheld radio. "What do you mean, 'couple'?"

"It looks like a guy and a girl. Coming down the tree line."

Guy and girl? That made no sense.

He turned to Kevin. "Where is the nearest house around here?"

"At least a mile up the road. It's all farmland. Nobody uses that dirt track to come and go. All the houses connect to the blacktop."

"Could they be on it for some romantic fuck-fest?"

"Yeah. I suppose."

He keyed the radio. "Let them go. Stay out of sight. Just keep an eye on them."

The radio call went to a whisper. "They just came into the moonlight. They have guns. They're walking with rifles."

Seamus pressed a fist into his eye. *Guns? But why would they be walking down the road?* If he stopped them, and they were a local couple out doing whatever they were doing, he'd be exposed. No longer hidden, with some clan out to skin him for the scare. Then he realized that didn't matter. They were leaving anyway.

"Stop them. See what they're doing. But don't hurt them. Get them on the ground and see if they're Serbian. If they are, take them out. If they aren't, just hold them and call."

"You got it. Hang on."

*   *   *

Jennifer tried to stay in the shadows, tried to match Nung's walk, but she was failing at every step. The guy was like a cat, having some ability to glide over the ground without leaving a single mark of his passing. After driving past the old water mill, they'd gone another quarter of a mile up the dirt lane with their lights off, then had pulled to the side. Nung looked at her for approval, and she'd nodded.

They'd exited, wanting to walk through the woods to their over-watch position, but had found a small brook running alongside the road, with a briar patch on the far side, like a green fence. They could either penetrate through the tangled brush, fighting their way forward and making a racket, or take the road.

They opted for the road, walking among the moonlight broken by the branches of the overhanging trees. The darkness was oppressive, but using the single-tube PVS-14 she had was like trying to walk while looking through a soda straw. No depth perception, and a conflict when her brain tried to process what it was seeing—one eye outside the green scope and one eye in. It was something she'd wished she'd practiced.

The brook took a bend to the right, and she saw an open field. She whispered, "This is it. We need to find a spot with a field of fire."

Nung nodded and said, "We get past the creek, and we can see the house."

She took a knee and brought out the monocle, surveying ahead. She said, "I see the road. The track that goes in. Fifty yards."

She keyed her radio and said, "Pike, Pike, this is Koko. We're at the entrance. Will call when set."

She heard, "Roger. On the move."

She tapped Nung on the thigh and they began stalking, moving slowly. They got to the road and crouched again. She raised the night optics and a man to her right rose out of the bushes, an assault rifle in his hands. He jabbed it forward like a sword and said, "Get the fuck on the ground."

Before the shock of his appearance had even registered in her brain,

Nung whipped out like a snake, slapping the man in the face and trapping the weapon with his other hand.

He drove an elbow into the man's throat, crushing it, then rotated around, circling the man's waist with his legs and bringing him to the ground, ending up sitting behind him. Nung wrapped up his neck, placed a hand on his forehead, and harshly jerked to the rear, the pop loud enough to be heard thirty feet away. The weapon fell to the earth, useless.

Jesus.

Jennifer remained where she was. Nung slowly draped the body on the ground. He looked at her with a question. She said, "Sorry I ever doubted you."

He smiled and tilted his head to the field across the brook.

70

We broke out of the bushes from the draw and held up, surveying the house. So far it looked like we were undetected, but that was pretty much what Knuckles had thought in Paris.

Brett brought out the thermals, and we saw no change. Two guys to the rear, and a host of bodies in the front, all milling about and blending into one another with their heat state. It was a seventy-meter stalk to the door. On open ground.

Retro said, "Now or never."

"Wait until Koko's set. I don't want to push them out the back and lose them."

I keyed the mic. "Koko, Koko, we're in the last cover. About to assault. You got the back door?"

She came on. "Yeah. We're set. Got clear fields of fire for everything out front. Pike, they've got men outside the house. We had to take one down a hundred meters away."

Hearing the words on the radio, all three of us began scanning with our night vision. I knew we weren't compromised, though, because of the racket Retro had made at the creek. If someone were out here, they'd have already been shooting. I glanced at Brett with an unspoken question.

How'd you miss him?

He shrugged, whispering, "Must have left while we were getting off the hill."

Jennifer tried to sound calm, like a day at the beach, but there was something else in her voice. I said, "You good?"

"Yeah. I am now. Remind me to give Nung a bonus."

I was reassured that she was still on her game and it wasn't nerves. I said, "About to break cover. Get on the scope."

She said, "Pike, they're running outside. I see two guys carrying a body to a car."

Body? Dead?

It didn't matter. Slamming the place was all that remained.

In a clinical voice that belied my apprehension of what we'd find, I said, "Moving now."

Knowing that Brett and Retro were on the radio, I didn't give any further commands. We broke cover and sprinted to the back of the house, bashing through the bushes to the back door. I kept my muzzle on the doorknob, watching for any movement, while Brett slapped a charge straight down the middle with double-stick tape.

He primed it and rolled to the right. I went left, Retro right behind me, his hand on my shoulder telling me he was ready. Brett looked at me and I nodded.

He capped the charge and the door splintered inward in a violent explosion. I was already two steps toward it before it went off, catching some of the backblast. I entered, muzzle ready, and saw one man on the ground, a piece of wood sticking out of his jaw and an AK held slackly in his hands. I popped a double-tap and heard firing to my right.

Retro, taking care of the other heat source. We started flowing to the next room and Jennifer called, "Car moving. I say again, car moving."

We hit the next door in a stack, and I said, "Stop it from leaving. Can't talk."

Retro flung it open, and I entered, number one man again. I saw a muzzle flash as soon as I cleared the breach, my mind cataloging the action in clinical detail, working in hyperdrive to distinguish friend from foe and assess my own physical state. *NOT HIT. NOT HIT. FIRING FROM THE LEFT. AIM. SQUEEZE. TARGET DOWN. SWEEP. BODY = GUN = TARGET. SQUEEZE. TARGET DOWN.*

The room was clear, and Brett was the first to the next door.

*   *   *

Jennifer saw the headlights flare and knew the car was coming. The lights from the vehicle behind it came on, compounding her problem. She cinched the weapon into her shoulder and welded her cheek to the stock, exhaling. She'd seen the men running back and forth, seen the body tossed in the back, then both vehicles began rolling her way. Without moving her head, she said, "Nung, there's a friendly in the lead car. Do not shoot into the body. Take out the tires. All of them. First car only. The other wants to run, let it."

He said, "Understood."

A burst of gravel, and the two-car caravan began to rocket down the dirt track, bouncing on the uneven grade.

She took aim at the right front tire and cracked a round. It missed. The car kept coming, gaining speed. She exhaled, going into a zone, ignoring the press of time. She squeezed again, and the tire blew. The vehicle kept coming. She refocused and let off a double-tap. The second tire blew. The car rolled onward. She heard Nung fire and saw the right rear tire explode. The car skidded to a stop, grinding on the rims alone, stuck in the mud of the track.

The men jumped out and Nung cracked a round, dropping the driver. They all crouched down, searching for the fire. One man screamed, shouting orders, and she saw them pull the body from the first car and begin dragging it to the second. She said, "Take out the other car!"

She squeezed off a round, and they made her position. A fusillade of fire rained down, forcing them both to duck behind the small earthen berm they'd chosen.

A small gap, a reload or something else, and they both rose up, Nung shooting as soon as he cleared the rise, hitting one of the men. Jennifer sighted down and did the same, watching the man twirl, his death giving her nothing more than grim satisfaction. She rotated to the man with the hostage and pulled the trigger. His head exploded and he dropped midstride, sliding into the dirt. Another man took his place, and the body was inside the second car.

It began moving and she focused on the tires, cracking rounds. The vehicle jerked around the first car, blocking her shots. She kept shooting, hearing Nung to her right doing the same, but the car rocketed past, hitting the dirt road hard enough to almost cause it to flip. In seconds, it was around the bend and out of sight.

A round snapped by her head and she refocused on the disabled vehicle, seeing two men still shooting. She centered on one and squeezed. He dropped. She brought the other into her reticle and he stuck his hands in the air, dropping his weapon. She saw the action and held up. Nung broke the trigger to the rear, and he dropped.

71

Brett tried the doorknob, nodded, then flung it open. Retro entered and fired immediately, taking out a hostile directly in our path. He went left and I went right, entering a makeshift kitchen. I saw a man with a hood on his head, another just beyond with an AK. I hit him with a double-tap, the weapon recoiling into my shoulder in a familiar caress. I swept the room, looking for other threats, but none remained.

I felt the adrenaline racing through me and fought to control it. To keep my wits about me, because now it was thinking time.

I said, "Backsweep. Clear this place completely. Watch the windows."

Brett and Retro left, barrels going wherever their eyeballs went, and I jumped to the man on the floor. I pulled off his hood and saw it wasn't Nicholas Seacrest.

Damn it.

He was unconscious and appeared to be drugged, his eyes rolling back in his head and his tongue hanging out. I laid him back down and called Jennifer.

"Koko, what's your status?"

"We're clear. Can we come in?"

Brett entered the kitchen and gave me a thumbs-up. "Yeah. Target's secure. We've got one hostage. Where's the other one?"

"I'll tell you in a minute."

Which I knew wasn't going to be good.

I looked at Brett and said, "Start SSE. Search this place for anything we can get."

He said, "Retro's already on it, but I don't think it's going to be much. These guys look like pipe-swingers. I think they were hired as local protection. I don't think they're part of the plan."

I pointed to an Inmarsat terminal on the window ledge, its connecting USB cables dangling as if whatever had been attached had been ripped out. "Get him on that. See if there's anything he can glean."

Outside, I heard Jennifer say, "Coming in," then a pause, her not wanting to get shot as a threat.

I said, "Come on. You're good."

She entered, taken aback at the carnage. She said, "I guess you guys had the same fight I did."

Brett looked up, saying, "Really?"

"Yeah. Yeah. It was . . . not fun."

Her eyes were glistening with a little postcombat scare, and I knew she'd seen the elephant. So did Brett. He nodded at her, saying nothing else, then went to get Retro.

Nung came in behind her and she pointed at him, saying, "He saved the mission. The man's quick as a mongoose. They had a guy on the road. Hidden in the bushes."

I looked at him, and he said, "You told me to protect her." As robotic as ever.

Jennifer said, "Then he shot a guy trying to surrender."

I glared at Nung, and he said, "He was trying to kill us."

"Damn it! When will you get it through your head that I'd like to talk to one of these guys?"

He looked around the room, the bodies littering the floor, and said, "You missed your chance too, I guess."

Retro entered and I pointed to the Inmarsat. "Can you get anything out of that?"

"Probably not. It's just a terminal. I need the laptop that was using it."

I said, "Well, examine it anyway."

He went to work, and I asked Jennifer, "What happened with the other hostage?"

She told me the story, and I cursed. I saw her face fall, and knew I'd just blamed her. I said, "Not your fault. I'm just pissed. We were so close."

She tentatively nodded, and I went into team-leader mode. "Jennifer, it's *not* your fault. We were forced to execute. Forced to pull this out of our ass, and we did damn good. Nobody got killed, and we got one. We'll get the others."

At the mention of others, she perked up and said, "Where's Kylie? Why isn't she here?"

"I have no idea. This guy is out like he's been boozing on Bourbon Street. We probably won't get any answers until he wakes up."

"What now?"

"Shit. I don't know. I'd like to get some sleep, but I'll be willing to bet that Blaine and Kurt won't let that happen. You want to call them?"

She smiled. "Uh . . . no. That's team-leader department."

While Retro went through the terminal, I called Blaine. After I told him what I had, where we were, and the risks to the hostage we held, he ordered me to remain in place, feeling a medical team would have more freedom here than at our B&B. Less chance of compromise, which, given that I hadn't heard any sirens, was probably a good bet. If we were compromised here, we'd already know it.

He called in the docs and a cleaning team, who were really getting a workout on this op, then said Kurt wanted to talk to me directly.

I knew why. I rang off and dialed. Kurt answered, saying he'd heard we'd rescued Travis Deleon, the husband of the governor of Texas. I told him, yeah, I thought so, but the guy was drugged out of his mind. I had no idea who he was. I gave him the rundown of what had happened.

He said, "Good work," then got around to it. "Kylie?"

"Boss, she's not here. I'm sorry."

He said nothing. The silence grew, and I said, "But we came close. We're on them now. They're on the run. They had to run out of here without a plan. They had no time to figure anything out."

"You said there was only one other hostage."

"Yeah. The one in the car."

"You think that was her? Or Nick?"

I gave him the truth that Jennifer had relayed. "Sir, the body that went into the car was a male. Almost positive. But it might have been her."

He said, "I'm not sure what to wish for."

"They're both out there. We'll get them both."

"What's your next move? Where from here?"

And that was the part of the conversation I didn't want to broach. I had nothing. This lead was so thin it was a miracle it had worked out. Retro might get something from the Inmarsat, but it wasn't likely. Whatever he had was historical, and these guys would be too smart to run to anything that they'd ever touched before.

I said, "Sir, we're at a dead end. I've used up my magic. They're on the road, and I have no idea where."

"Shit. This hit might just get them to kill 'em. Dump them in a ditch somewhere."

That took me aback. "Sir, you're not suggesting—"

"No, no. No way. You got back one. Hell, you got back three. I'm just projecting."

I said, "All I need is a thread. Just one lead."

He said, "What's that?"

"I said, all I need is a thread."

"Not you. Hang on. Your pal Knuckles is talking."

The phone went down, and I could hear murmured conversation.

He came back. "I gotta go. Get that place cleaned up. Get back to the bird in Shannon. Clear out of there and stand by."

The urgency in his voice was unmistakable. I said, "What's going on?"

"I might have your thread."

72

Kurt hung up, and George Wolffe said, "So they got Travis Deleon? Clean? No compromise?"

"Looks that way."

George picked up a phone and said, "That's great news. Palmer will want to kiss you. Of course, he'd want to hang you if it had gone bad." He started to dial and said, "You want me to tell him about the unilateral decision to assault, or wait until you brief?"

Kurt said, "Don't call just yet." George held the phone, a question on his face. Kurt turned to Knuckles. "What do you have?"

Knuckles held out a transcript. "A guy initiated contact with our bait. Wants to talk about the Breedlove story. Claims to have inside information that can be used to leverage the secretary of Homeland Security during his 'interview.'"

From behind his desk, George hung up the phone and said, "Man, that was quick."

Four hours earlier, Kurt had enlisted the help of Bartholomew Creedwater, the Taskforce computer specialist, to spoof the number of the secretary's direct office line, then pretend to be his personal assistant, asking for Kincaid. The reporter had eaten it up, setting a meeting later on in the evening. Kurt had intended to reschedule at the last minute, rolling the meeting to the next night, and continue doing so until it became apparent his plan wasn't going to work, or the terrorist made contact. He never expected it to happen so soon.

Kurt said, "Creed's still confident his little intrusion is hidden?"

"Yeah," Knuckles said. "That stuff is all black magic to me, but he seems to think he can get away with anything."

"Funny, he thought that same thing when they put on the handcuffs that got him to the Taskforce. I hope he's right."

Kurt had two choices to gain access to Kincaid's telecommunications: Go get a warrant with a judge and legally access his phones using FBI architecture, or see if he had the means to do so locally, using Taskforce assets.

The first choice was the direction he wanted to go, but it was clearly out of the question. He might have convinced the president, but the Oversight Council would have balked, specifically because the Taskforce was forbidden from working domestically, and more generally because nobody in the Justice Department was read onto their very existence. It would invite compromise.

That left option two. Which was decidedly illegal, and Kurt knew he was walking on dangerous ground. As the commander he bore the responsibility to ensure the Taskforce operated within a moral and legal framework. Its very secrecy had always been ripe for abuse, and he understood that well. The last thing he wanted was the unit to metastasize into an American gestapo, and it was his job to lead by example. He couldn't very well count on his men to exercise sound judgment, only executing operations that were within their charter, if he didn't.

In the end, Kylie's fate had won the debate. He'd come back and asked Creed some pointed questions, and there was a reason Creed was chosen. The Taskforce computer network operations cell had plenty of genius-level specialists—hackers—but all had gleaned their skills through the US government. All but one. Creed had been nabbed doing some nasty computer things to unsavory people he deemed worthy of the abuse, and his skill had caught the eye of the Taskforce. In exchange for staying out of jail, he'd left the dark side and come to work for Kurt. It had been a fairly easy fix, because, while he'd definitely broken the law, his actions had led to some racketeering prosecutions and nobody was really itching to make him pay.

Kurt had pulled him out of the fire, and he knew Creed felt undying loyalty—along with no compunction about breaking the law. Especially if *Kurt* asked.

Technically, the Taskforce charter forbade the collection of content from any cellular or landline communications. They were restricted to geolocation only, using the greater intelligence community for any "chatter" they needed to hear, since the IC already had a robust oversight structure in place. The Oversight Council didn't want to reinvent the wheel, giving their small organization the ability to start reading emails and listening to calls. When Kurt had asked Creed if it was possible, given the equipment they had, he'd said it could be done—if one had the skill. Kurt had handed him Kincaid's business card, giving the order, and Creed had grinned, turning to a keyboard. And he'd produced.

Kurt scanned the transcript, stopping on the time. "Shit, this thing's going down in the next thirty minutes. A daylight meeting?"

Knuckles said, "Yep. Looks like it."

Reading further, Kurt said, "Garage on Wilson Boulevard. That's straight up the street in Rosslyn. We can be there in five minutes."

George took the transcript and read the address. "This guy sure has a sense of humor."

"What?"

"The garage address is 1401 Wilson Boulevard. It's a special place for spilling secrets to reporters. It's where Woodward met Deep Throat."

"You're kidding."

"Nope. Same spot."

Knuckles said, "I'm sure that's a coincidence. No way is that intentional."

"Why?" asked Kurt.

"I didn't tell you the best part. Creed said he spoke with an Irish accent."

Kurt grinned and pointed to Knuckles's leg. "Can you fight?"

"Hell yes. I told you that in Europe. Just can't run very fast, but it sure isn't affecting my aim."

Kurt turned to George. "Get the med lab ready for a detainee. I want two interrogators on immediate standby, with a full suite, including drugs."

George raised an eyebrow and said, "You plan on bringing him here?"

"Where else? We're going to need answers immediately. Also, you can now call Alexander Palmer. Tell them I need an emergency meeting of the Oversight Council in . . . say . . . two hours. Tell them to make sure the president's there."

"Why? What are you going to ask for?"

"Blanket Omega. This pans out, and we're about to execute multiple hits."

"They aren't going to let you do that, Kurt. You've tried before to get Omega for a *single* follow-on hit, and they've always said no. Always directed you to come back again for approval."

"Don't tell him that's what I'm asking for."

George said, "Knuckles, could you give us a moment?"

He left, and George said, "Is this about Kylie? Or the VP's son?"

"It's the same damn thing."

George said, "I'll follow you. You know that. Just don't let emotion get in the way here. This whole reporter thing would never have happened if it were just the VP's son. We're leaning way, way over the edge. Is she worth the Taskforce?"

Kurt nodded and said, "Yes. She's coming home. I would have no leverage at all if it weren't for Nick Seacrest, but I do, and I'm using it. She will *not* end up on a tape."

George remained quiet. Kurt said, "Butter Palmer up with the recovery of Travis. Let him know we're working other leads and it's moving fast."

He caught Kurt's eye, hesitated, then said, "Okay. I will."

Kurt said, "George, I understand your concerns. I'll protect you. It's my call."

George scoffed and said, "Screw that. I told you I'm with you. One hundred percent. But you know they're going to tell you to pound sand."

"They can't. I've already gotten permission from the president."

"The president? When did he say we had blanket Omega authority?"

"When he told me to burn these fucks to the ground."

73

Inside his car, the engine off, the heat dissipated and the bone-chilling Washington winter began to seep inside the frame, even inside the garage. Kurt keyed his radio, thankful that he wasn't outside.

"Anything?"

Knuckles came back with "Nothing from here. Everyone's off the street because of the cold. He comes by me, he'll be easy to spot."

The transcript had specific instructions, telling Kincaid to park in a numbered spot that had been blocked off with orange cones. Actually, two spots were blocked off—the one he was told to use, and the one adjacent. The cones had been stolen, no doubt, but nobody questioned such things. The spots would remain clear.

Directly to the rear of the parking space was a stairwell leading to the street. The instructions had said that Kincaid was to park and wait. The contact would find his car, on foot.

Kurt had placed Knuckles at the top of the stairwell, on a park bench, ironically just down the street from a historical marker discussing the Watergate/Deep Throat lineage of the place. Kurt had taken a car inside and parked within view of the meeting location, but offset to the left. He'd brought a Taskforce Stiletto, an experimental electromagnetic pulse gun that would destroy electrical components at close range.

They knew the contact was approaching on foot, and, wanting to control all variables, they'd decided to disable Kincaid's car as soon as it arrived. With all the computers in modern-day vehicles, a brief punch from the Stiletto would render it useless, and they could then assault at their leisure, preventing the target from using Kincaid's car to escape.

The plan was simple: Knuckles would discreetly follow the target down the stairwell, locking down the back door, and Kurt would observe from the front. When he made contact, entering the vehicle, they would assault, slamming the target with overwhelming force.

The one thing they wanted to avoid was the target killing Kincaid. If the Irishman was who they thought he was, that was the only reason for the meeting. The terrorists were now taking out anyone who was tangentially associated with breaking the story. Locking down the ability for them to negotiate money from the administration.

Neither Knuckles nor Kurt thought it would happen quickly, feeling the man would want to interrogate Kincaid to learn who else should be on the target list, but also knew that the plan the terrorists had envisioned was falling apart.

The Clute twins had been rescued, followed by the recovery of Travis. They had to be getting desperate, and Kurt didn't put it beyond the target to simply enter the car and start shooting. Something he wanted to prevent. Well, that was a little soft. It was something he absolutely *needed* to prevent.

A car entered the garage, lights on, and Kurt ducked down, getting below the windshield. Sitting in the backseat, he peeked around the headrest and saw Kincaid exit the driver's door and begin pulling aside the cones. Kurt waited until he was back behind the wheel, then slid out and threaded his way through the vehicles, getting close enough to work the Stiletto. He waited until Kincaid moved forward, then pulled the trigger, seeing the headlights flicker and fade, the engine coughing and spitting, sounding like a knocking from a '70s gas guzzler. In the front seat, Kincaid manipulated the controls, then slammed the steering wheel in frustration.

Kurt returned to his vehicle, calling Knuckles. "Car disabled. We're two minutes out."

"Nothing on top. I say again, nothing on top."

Kurt surveyed the garage, running through his head where he could be wrong. Chasing down what could cause failure. *Can I close on the vehicle quickly enough if Knuckles is held up? Can I prevent a shot? Can I prevent escape? What if he has help? Can I execute on my own against two men? If that happens, should I just kill?*

They needed the target alive. Killing him got them nowhere, other than saving Kincaid's life. Sitting in the parking garage, Kurt realized how many variables he'd left exposed. Realized he'd put enormous faith in the single phone call and had placed Kincaid's life in serious jeopardy, all for his quest for Kylie.

Headlights flashed, and he sank down, letting the vehicle travel beyond them, waiting on the glow to leave. It did not. He slid upward enough to get a corner of vision through the windshield and saw a late-model BMW back up rapidly, flattening the cones blocking the adjacent parking spot. And knew the target had lied.

"Knuckles, Knuckles, he's arrived. He's in a vehicle. Get down the stairs. It's going to happen quicker than we can control."

He rolled out of the vehicle, hearing, "Roger that. On the way."

He snaked his way forward, staying below the cars, and said, "No killing. No killing. Take him alive."

"Shit, sir, that'll depend on him. I'm coming."

Damn it. This was stupid.

Kurt broke out of the row of vehicles and saw the target jamming a pistol in the face of Kincaid, the reporter screaming, his hands in the air. The pistol came down hard, the barrel hammering Kincaid in the temple, and he sagged.

It's not a killing. It's a kidnapping.

Kurt ran in a crouch, trying to get a shot that was debilitating but not lethal. Which was seriously stupid, and he knew it. Any shot would potentially be a killing one, both to the target and to Kincaid. Shooting into a thigh was Hollywood crap.

He saw Kincaid dragged into the other car and abandoned the plan, running back to his vehicle.

He reached it and dove into the backseat. He saw the white lights of the target car flare and rolled out into the access lane, raising the Stiletto. The car screamed forward, sliding parallel to him, and he hit the trigger.

The engine coughed, then bucked in a halting, jerky manner. He squeezed again, and it went dead. The man behind the wheel turned the key, pumping the gas, then saw Kurt. The terrorist exited, pistol held high, and started shooting, using the door for protection. Kurt dove behind his own car, the rounds puncturing the steel. He slid low, calling Knuckles.

"He's out. I'm compromised. Damn it, where are you?"

Through a wince, he heard, "Hell, sir, I told you I couldn't run. I'm coming."

Kurt slid out behind the front tire, almost prone, and fired two rounds into the windshield, over the unconscious reporter and past the shooter's body, causing him to duck.

The target huddled behind the door, identified where the firing was coming from, and drew a bead, popping rounds Kurt's way, the noise from his unsuppressed pistol banging harshly between the garage walls.

Kurt rolled backward, one round so close the chipped concrete cut his face. He crawled to the rear of his vehicle and saw a flash of light from the stairwell door opening. Kurt stood, putting himself in the man's crosshairs to get him to focus, then dove to the ground. He heard two rounds snap past his head, then a rattled scream, like someone was being flayed alive.

He stood, seeing Knuckles standing above the target, juicing a Taser with a grin on his face.

Kurt walked over to him, watching the twitching of the body, knowing his mental faculties were fine. He leaned down.

"Hey, I've got a few questions for you. And you're going to answer them."

74

George Wolffe stood at the head of the table, fending off any questions that came his way, stating that Kurt would provide a complete briefing as soon as he arrived. Which he prayed would be pretty damn soon.

The Oversight Council had agreed to his demand of an emergency meeting, and since he'd specifically asked for the president, they all had come. Every one. Some of the most powerful people in the world, they didn't have a lot of patience, but luckily, the president hadn't arrived, so Wolffe had some breathing room.

Although not much.

Kerry Bostwick, the head of the CIA, said, "I've got work to do. I can't sit here all night—and I don't want to direct my assets looking for people that have been recovered. Did you or did you not get Travis Deleon?"

Alexander Palmer spoke up, raising his hand. "Okay, people, not to steal Kurt's thunder, but we have recovered Deleon. And Kurt's apparently on another thread. Calm down, damn it. Let him get here."

Bostwick leaned back, saying, "I could have used that information about two hours ago. I've got guys running amok on different threads to him. Putting themselves in danger."

Wolffe, a CIA man himself, said, "Sir, sorry about that, but this is fast-breaking, and very close-hold. We couldn't put out a press release. The recovery is intimately tied into the further hunt. You know how that works."

Bostwick glared but said nothing, turning to the man to his left. For the first time, Wolffe recognized Easton Beau Clute, the chairman of the Senate Select Committee on Intelligence. Now apparently read onto Taskforce activities from the recovery of his twins. The first man from the legislative branch of government to do so. Wolffe was unsure if that was good or bad.

The light above the door flashed, and the president of the United States entered, leaving his Secret Service detail outside. Wolffe inwardly groaned. *Time's up.*

President Warren took his seat at the head of the table and said, "Okay, so what's going on? You got Deleon but not Seacrest?"

"Sir, yes, that's correct. We now have three of the four hostages, and a good lead on the fourth. Nick Seacrest."

"So what's the story? You called this rodeo, start the briefing."

Wolffe said, "Sir, I think we should wait for Kurt Hale. He has the latest."

"Latest? From the SITREPs I read, it happened over four hours ago."

Wolffe started to respond when the light above the door went red. Meaning someone wanted in.

Palmer keyed the access panel, and Kurt Hale entered. Wolffe sagged in relief.

Kurt walked straight to the front of the conference table, ignoring the computer and everyone in the room but the president. He nodded at Wolffe, letting him escape to the back of the room.

He turned to the president and said, "I have the ability to recover Nicholas Seacrest. Right now. But I need to get let off the chain. No more reporting to the Oversight Council until it's done. I need blanket Omega authority to conduct operations."

There was quiet for a brief moment, then shouted questions. Kurt let them fly about the room like a presidential press conference, saying nothing, eyes on President Warren.

The room stilled, realizing he wasn't playing their game. Warren, holding Kurt's eyes, said, "Why don't you include us in your recent endeavors. Give us a little perspective."

Kurt smiled and said, "Here's where we stand . . ."

He gave them everything he knew about the operation in Ireland,

and the subsequent extrapolation of data, which was a dead end. He then told them about a new lead, a Croatian arms dealer in Dubrovnik, and the fact that Kurt had already redirected a team to his location. He asked again for blanket authority.

"I'm going to hit that guy in Dubrovnik, and then I'm going to turn that hit into another one in England or Ireland. I can't come back here and sit, waiting on an answer. We need to be quicker than them. Quicker than their ability to react."

Jonathan Billings said, "Where is this new information coming from? The thing about this guy you call 'the Frog'?"

"Where is irrelevant at this point. I'm not going to spend the next hour talking about it. Trust me, it's true. And every minute we sit here is another minute we lose the ability to succeed. I'll give you a complete briefing afterward if you'd like, but right now, I need Omega to hit this guy. And Omega to hit everything associated with him. I can't keep asking for permission. We're too damn slow doing that."

Billings said, "No way. You want too much. You want us to let you off the chain because you've never liked the oversight. I get the risk, but this is just you trying to get around us."

Kurt caught the president's eye and waited.

Warren nodded and spoke. "Jonathan, you came here after the Oversight Council was created. Do you know who did that?"

Billings, looking confused at the change of direction, glanced left and right, then shook his head no.

"I gave authority for the building of the Taskforce, and one man said it was a risk. Said that fighting our terrorist threat was good, but not at the expense of creating something that could get out of control. He demanded the creation of the Oversight Council. Demanded accountability. That man is now briefing you, so I'd hold my tongue before impugning his motives."

Billings said nothing, staring at his hands. Then Alexander Palmer said, "There's a reason for no blanket authority, and that's because we need to evaluate each operation. Determine the pros and cons. We can't do that here."

Kurt said, "That's based on disparate hits against different targets. I'm asking for the authority for a single target set: our hostages. I'm not asking to go hit a bunch of terrorists just because I can."

Bostwick spoke up. "Wait a minute. Part of that is because you don't have the ability to leverage the entire intelligence community. You don't see what we do. You can't conduct global operations because you don't have global reach with your intel. You *need* to come back to us to see what else we've got. That's the very reason we exist."

Kurt said, "Ordinarily, I'd say you're right, but not in this case. Your entire global architecture has gleaned absolutely nothing. I have the key, and I want to leverage it. I'm not coming back to you for shit, because that's exactly what you have. I'll do this myself. Without any help. And I promise you I can."

"How are you going to conduct operations on separate continents, then tie them together?"

"It's no different from what I did in Iraq, before the creation of the Taskforce. Get the intel, create a target package, hit the target knowing what we're looking for, then turn to another target. I've *done* this before. Speed is the essence. Work faster than they can react."

Bostwick said, "This isn't Iraq. We don't own the battle space. How can you coordinate that quickly over continents?"

"Seriously? It's a damn radio call. Do you think I was more effective because I was in the same country? I was still talking on a radio. I have the best men in the world. They'll do it." He turned to President Warren. "Sir, you said it yourself when you ordered me on the mission—I can operate more efficiently across boundaries. Across our artificial stovepipes. It's the reason you set me in motion."

Billings said, "Before, when I asked you about this, you said you didn't have the capability because of the cover concerns and how long it took to rectify them. What are you saying now? You can do this clean? Without the preparation?"

Kurt drew back, knowing this was the cut line. "No. I'm not. I'm saying I can recover the vice president of the United States' son. The fallout is something else."

Billings said, "Turn in your intelligence to others. We'll get the HRT to execute the targets. Get the host nation to intervene. I see no reason to let you do this unilaterally."

"We do that, we'll fail. I've already seen what happens when we try to coordinate across agencies and other governments. You get dead men and missed opportunities. The reason we were successful in Iraq was that we owned the entire cycle, from capture to exploitation to follow-on target. No blinks. We held it all, and we crushed them. Because we didn't need to turn to someone else for help."

Billings said, "Yeah, Iraq is working out perfectly."

Surprised at the statement, Kurt said, "That's coming from the State Department? We were ordered out, and when we left, there was a smoking hole instead of a terrorist network." He looked to President Warren and said, "I'm asking for permission to do the same here. You want them back, I'll get them. But it won't be without cost. Secretary Billings is correct. We'll be exposed, but we'll have them home. It's your call, but you already made it with your order earlier."

A ghost of a smile on his face, President Warren said, "And what was that?"

"You told me that if I could resolve this, and it meant compromise, I would do so. Well, I can resolve it. Right now."

President Warren said, "You're that sure?"

"Yes, sir."

The president looked around the room, then said, "Time for a vote. Perhaps the last the Oversight Council will ever take. Blanket Omega? Or dead son?"

The words were intentionally biased, and Kurt appreciated it. The first hand up was the vice president's, followed by the hand of Easton Clute. The secretary of defense, Mark Oglethorpe, raised his, and there was nobody on the Council who would vote no after that.

Kurt nodded, then looked to Wolffe at the back of the room, catching his eye. Wolffe pulled out a cell phone and began dialing.

President Warren saw the exchange and said, "What's coming?"

"The takedown of the Croatian arms dealer. In the next few minutes."

Taken aback, Warren said, "I thought you were still redirecting a team to his location?"

"That's correct. They were flying from Okinawa after the recovery of the Clute twins. They were over the European continent, headed to France when I redirected them. They're on the ground, ready to execute."

"And they know everything you do? They know what they're looking for?"

"Oh, yeah. That's what I meant about closing the loop. For the first time in this whole sorry mess, we're going to be ahead of the terrorists. They know *exactly* what to look for."

75

Johnny peered out the side window of the panel van, waiting on his teammate to return, when his second in command, a guy with the callsign Axe, said, "Why are we taking this guy down again? I mean, specifically? Did they give you our intel requirements?"

"Not really. Just that he's associated with the kidnappings. We take him and interrogate as fast as possible. We dig until we hit something worthwhile. Pike's apparently waiting on intel, and we're it."

"That's great. Pike. I should have known."

Johnny said, "What the hell is taking Crash so long?"

Axe said, "Maybe he's already accomplished the mission."

Johnny laughed. "Doubt it. Not with the security he called in."

"We going in as soon as he briefs?"

Looking out the window, Johnny said, "Still waiting on the call. Nothing until we get the execute authority." He stiffened and said, "Crash is inbound."

The door opened and the teammate called Crash entered the back of the van. He said, "Okay, I've got at least four PSD. Maybe one extra, but the last guy seems more like a secretary than actual physical protection. That guy called the Frog just left the bar and went back to his suite, taking some local talent with him. Real hammers."

"So our biggest threat is a couple of hookers?"

"I wish. They've got one PSD at the elevator on the floor, then two outside the door, then the rest inside."

"Going to be a fight?"

"Looks that way. He's on the fourth floor, so we could climb, but that would take some time. And that's *after* we waited for them to go to sleep."

Axe said, "It's close to two A.M., so it might not be that long."

"I don't know about that. You should have seen the chicks. They're going to be busy for a while."

"Doesn't matter," Johnny replied. "Kurt was pretty clear. No waiting. Pike's standing by, and this is apparently critical. How can we get down the hall? Do we have cover?"

"Not really. The elevator opens at a T intersection, but once you turn the corner, they'll have eyes on."

"What's the distance?"

"About fifty meters."

Axe said, "Shit, I'm not sprinting half a football field."

"I was thinking about the drunk routine. The one we did in Sudan? You good with that?"

Axe said, "Yeah. That might work. Better than running and gunning down a linear target."

Johnny said, "Okay. Axe and I head down the hall. You deal with the security at the elevator. We get as close as possible. Anyone escalates, and it's game on."

Axe said, "I cannot believe I'm acting like a drunk to help out Pike. That bastard is going to owe me big time."

Johnny's phone vibrated, and he answered. Axe knew the decision by the look on his face. He hung up and said, "Okay, this is it. We hit hard, suppressed weapons. We interrogate in the room. We get whatever we can, and we leave. But we can't kill everyone. Only self-defense. No offensive shooting."

"What the hell does that mean?"

"It means this place isn't designated a hostile force. Unfortunately. Kurt has no idea who this guy is or what he knows, so we don't have authority to start killing. Only in self-defense."

Axe said, "What if we can't leave? If the police show up?"

"We go to jail. That's straight out of Kurt's mouth. You guys still good?"

Axe screwed a suppressor on his Glock, saying, "You have to ask that?"

The three exited the van, slinking across the cobblestone street to a boutique, high-end hotel overlooking the Atlantic. Surrounded by much older buildings, it kept to the local charm with its architecture but was clearly a cut above. Like the rich bride attending her first party with the redneck family. Wearing the same clothes, and trying to fit in, but failing miserably.

According to the intelligence Kurt had sent, the man known as the Frog lived on the penthouse floor, and the reconnaissance earlier had confirmed it. The floor consisted of two suites. The Frog had the one on the left, which wouldn't have been a problem, except his personal security detail started their protection at the elevator.

Crash led the way past the desk to the cars. He pressed the penthouse button and said, "We get out, it's game on. We control this right, and nobody from the desk will know. We need to hit hard. Really hard. Before anyone can call reinforcements."

The bell rang, and Johnny held out a fist. The other two bumped it, and the doors opened. Johnny and Axe spilled out, shouting for someone named Felton, with Crash staying behind in the car, out of sight. The first PSD grabbed Johnny's coat, telling him to stop. He jerked out of the man's grasp and continued on, shouting, "Felton! You fuck! Your bride's looking for you."

Axe continued the charade, stumbling forward toward the T intersection. The bodyguard grabbed his shoulder, calling on his radio. Axe turned, drawing the guard's full attention, and Crash put a barrel against his head. The guard raised his hands high. Crash pointed to the floor, and he sank down.

Axe and Johnny turned the corner, shouting and yelling for Felton. Weaving and stumbling, they saw the two outside the door. They got within five feet, and one advanced, politely telling them they were in the wrong spot. Axe said, "Bullshit. You're hiding our friend. What's with you, man? Where is he?"

The bodyguard pulled out a pistol, intent on jamming it into Axe's face and showing he meant business. What he got in return was a display of controlled violence.

Axe trapped the pistol in his hands, then rotated underneath the man's arms, torquing his joints in a small circle. He whipped toward the ground, and the man went flying over his shoulder, slamming into the carpet. Axe let go of the arm and hammered him in the temple with a closed fist. The man ceased moving. Axe turned to help Johnny, but it didn't matter.

His target was down as well.

Searching the body, Johnny held up a keycard. Axe took it, glanced back to make sure Johnny was ready, then swiped. The light went green, and they exploded in.

They entered a den, Axe seeing a man on the couch and one at a liquor cabinet. The couch man leapt up, drawing a gun and aiming. Axe broke his trigger to the rear, popping his head back with a suppressed round. He turned to the right and saw Johnny holding liquor-cabinet guy by the hair, the man on his knees, compliant. Johnny hissed, "You had to kill that guy?"

Axe said, "Your guy doesn't have a weapon."

Johnny jerked his head to the right, toward the bedroom, and Axe sprinted toward it, Glock at the ready. He pushed open the door and saw a dream of every red-blooded male on earth. Two women on top of a man, both with impossibly inflated attributes. Both writhing and moaning. The target clearly had no idea Axe had entered. In a world of his own.

Axe hit the lights and the girls rolled off in confusion. The man sat up and yelled in a language Axe didn't understand.

Axe leveled his pistol and said, "Sorry to interrupt, Mr. Frog, but I'm here to ask you some questions. Please don't disappoint me with your answers."

The girls began screaming, and Johnny entered the room. Into his radio, he said, "Crash, target secure. Clean up the hallway. Bring them in here."

In a heavy accent the Frog said, "You fuckers have no idea what you're messing with. None."

Axe looked at one of the girls and said, "I don't know about that. I think I've been in something similar."

Taking that as a cue, one of the girls sidled over to him and, in broken English, said, "American. I speak American." She knelt down, reaching for his belt, completely unashamed at her nakedness. Axe roughly knocked her away with his knee, spilling her to the ground and leaving no illusion of the state of play.

The Frog said, "Leave now, and I'll pretend this didn't happen. I have no money here, and I have powerful friends in very high places."

Johnny said, "I'll bet not as high as ours. We're looking for Nicholas Seacrest, and we understand you've had some dealings with some Irishmen who know where he is."

The words hung in the air. For the first time, Axe saw fear crawl across his target's face.

76

I paced back and forth in the lobby of the Shannon FBO, feeling more and more frustrated, slamming back one tepid cup of free coffee after another. We'd been sitting on our asses for more than six hours, and the thread from the hostages was growing distant.

Maybe I should have done what Blaine said. Just start tracking likely exit routes. Try to run into them on the road.

Jennifer said, "Pike, you're going to give yourself an aneurysm."

Like a he-man, I crushed the Styrofoam cup I was holding. "We're doing nothing. They're getting away. I'm sick of waiting on the Taskforce for intel. We could be here until dawn and get zilch."

Blaine said, "They've got an operation primed for Dubrovnik. Johnny's on it. Let's wait it out. See what they get."

I rolled my eyes and said, "What the hell does Croatia have to do with this? The kidnappers are in *this* country, and the entire island is only four hours across. We're giving them the edge. Let me take Jennifer and just start cruising the highways. Go to Dublin and back. Maybe Belfast. Just to see what we can find."

"No. Kurt could call at any moment. I need the assets here. What if he says he has the target, and it's back in Cork? I'm not going to spread out. I've got enough trouble controlling the cleanup crew. Settle down and get some sleep."

We'd left Macroom in the hands of another support crew, and they'd begun their work, cleaning the mess we'd left behind. Blaine had also coordinated a medevac bird and we'd passed the still-unconscious Travis Deleon off to a medical team, bound for the United States. I always looked to the future, forgetting about the past, but Blaine had to deal with both.

I scanned the room, every overstuffed La-Z-Boy full of Taskforce Operators snoring away. And Nung, playing a video game on the wide-screen TV.

"Fat chance I could sleep right now."

Jennifer said, "Pike, come here."

I did so, glancing at Blaine. He studiously stared at another wide-screen showing CNN.

"What?"

"Would you have a little faith? Kurt's working the issue. You can't solve everything by yourself."

"I know that, but this is killing me. The guy's got Seacrest in his car, and he's *here*, not in Croatia. Every second we wait, he gets farther away."

"You said yourself we've been waiting for six hours. The time to run around flailing in the dark has long gone."

I looked at Blaine again, making sure he was focused on something else, then said, "You don't understand. Kylie wasn't there. She's gone. I don't give a rat's ass about the vice president's son, but without him, she's going to die. I can't let that happen."

She took my hand and flicked her head at the La-Z-Boy next to her. I sat down. She said, "It's going to come together. It will."

I sat down and said, "No it *won't*. It doesn't work that way. No matter what you do, sometimes people die. Good people."

She knew whom I was talking about. She said, "Don't do that to yourself. This isn't about your family."

I sagged back and said, "It *is*. I let them die, and now I'm letting Kylie do the same."

She said, "You still have her pendant?"

"Yeah. I'm going to give it back to her. When I find her."

"What's it say on it?"

Confused, I said, "You know."

"I want to hear it."

Before I could answer, Blaine stood up, his phone to his ear. I watched intently, like a dog following an owner with a ball in his hand. He hung up and said, "Wake everyone. We have a mission."

We sprang up. Jennifer began walking around and shaking legs.

I said, "What did Johnny find? Where are they?"

Blaine said, "We have an address in London. Let's saddle up."

"London? Who?"

He started packing his small rucksack, stuffing in bottled water and PowerBars, courtesy of the FBO. "Johnny just took down a Croatian arms dealer. Apparently, he's been working with the new IRA and connected them to some Somalis from al-Shabaab. He's got the address to where the skinnys are holed up in London."

"Somalis? That's always been a smoke screen. It's what almost got Knuckles and Brett killed."

He stood up. "Not this time. There's a connection. And we get to go explore it."

Everyone began packing kit, getting ready to leave, but I was having none of it. "Sir, this is stupid. There are no Somalis attached to this. I know we want to believe al Qaida is at the heart of this, but they're not. Flying to London is the last thing we should do. The hostages are in Ireland."

He stopped and looked me in the eye. "Sergeant Major, get your ass on the plane. We have a target to hit, and I need your skill."

"Sir, it's an hour to England. Another hour to get sorted out. An additional hour getting to the target, and then at least an hour of recce. It'll be damn near noon before we can do anything, which means we'll roll over until the next cycle of darkness. And lose the hostages."

"We're not going to wait. Kurt's orders. We hit as soon as we can. Darkness or otherwise."

"What? A daylight hit?"

"Yeah. Direct orders. Burn it to the ground. Whatever comes out, comes out. We get additional intel, and we do a follow-on hit. Wherever that leads. Nobody stands in our way. Nobody tells us no."

I liked the sound of that, as much as I thought the mission was misguided.

Jennifer hoisted her knapsack and said, "Pike, we can talk on the plane."

"I'm not sure we should *get* on the plane."

"What's on the pendant?"

I remained silent.

She said, "*Tell* me."

"Let us do evil that good may come."

"You can't give her that pendant back without fulfilling its prophecy. I'm ready."

I said nothing, sizing up whether she was playing me.

She said, "Pike, I want her back as much as you. I'm willing to do what's necessary."

I realized she wasn't manipulating me. That she meant it from the core of her being. I reached down and grabbed my bag without looking at her.

Blaine nodded at her, a silent thanks, and I said, "Sir, don't go patting her on the back just yet. You have no idea what evil I'm about to do."

77

Seamus parked his car in an alley on Edgware Road and rubbed his eyes. Dawn had long since passed, and he hadn't slept in over twenty-four hours. He glanced at Kevin in the backseat, sound asleep. He slapped the man's thigh, jerking him awake.

"We're here. I'm going up. You stay with the hostage. He should be waking up soon. Take a bottle of water and give it to him, but do not untie his hands, no matter what he says. He's a fighter."

Groggy, Kevin said, "I couldn't fight my way out of a wet paper bag right now. I can't imagine riding in the trunk, blindfolded and drugged, makes him a greater threat."

"Don't do it. Give him water, but do *not* release him."

Kevin took a pull on his own bottle, saying, "Yeah, I got it. You sure about barging in like this? We should have gone to the hotel I found."

"I called them after the ferry landed in Glasgow. They're expecting me."

"I meant about showing our hand. How we only have one. These guys aren't exactly known for their humanitarian streak."

"Nothing else I could do. It's just you and me now. The hotel was a risk, and they offered shelter. At least until their strike is done."

"How long should I wait? I mean, if this goes bad? What should I do?"

"You don't hear from me in thirty minutes, get out. Go wherever you want. I'll be dead, so it's irrelevant."

Shocked at his words, Kevin said, "Wait, I don't know what to do with him. Where to go. You think this meeting could turn that bad?"

"No, I don't. They want the hostages and will settle for one. As far as I know, their attack is set to go in a few hours whether we give them anything or not."

He opened the door, and Kevin pulled his sleeve.

"What?"

"Don't leave me down here. Let me come up with you. You can use the help."

Seamus considered, knowing it would be better to have two instead of one. Ali Hassan was a spindly man, but, as the Americans were fond of saying, Sam Colt made an equalizer of anyone.

He said, "Okay. Check the hostage. I'll watch from the end of the alley. We'll go up together, but you need to be armed. Take a pistol."

Kevin nodded, satisfied, like a puppy being scratched behind the ears. He exited the vehicle with a bottle of water, and Seamus walked to the entrance of the alley, surveying the street.

A half a minute later, Kevin approached, telling him the hostage was still out. Seamus said, "Let's go see our patrons."

They entered the front of the apartment complex, walking down a hallway past some front stores to a suite of mailboxes and an elevator. Seamus decided to forgo the easy route and took the stairs, going up three flights and passing several immigrants from Middle Eastern countries. All looked at them in curiosity.

He reached the third floor and exited, moving down a narrow hallway with a threadbare carpet running its length. He paused outside number 318, smelling the mold and decay. He put his ear to the door. He heard nothing.

He knocked, Kevin right behind him. No one came. He knocked again, and the door was jerked open by a large black man he didn't recognize, sweating profusely. A sweat that Seamus recognized as fear.

"Yes?"

"I'm here for Ali Hassan."

The man looked into the interior of the apartment, then opened the door. Seamus entered, followed by Kevin, and saw Hassan in the den, a gun in his hand. Aimed at Seamus's head.

He said, "Hey, hey, no need for that."

Hassan said, "There was no need for you to come here. In fact, no way you should have known where I am. You call, demanding a meeting, then tell me it's here. How did you know where to find us? Who else have you told?"

"The Frog gave me the address. Really, he's on both our sides. There was no reason to keep it secret. I've told no one."

"The Frog never gave me *your* address. In fact, he never gave me your name. Get on your knees, and forgive me if I don't trust you."

Seamus did so, placing his hands behind his head and saying, "I have the payment."

Hassan stood and said, "Where? All I hear is promises, and all I see is Irish scum."

"We have him down in the car. In the trunk. Look, we'll pass him to you, but you need to put out a statement soon, using him. I mean real soon, like in the next few hours."

"Why? And what do you mean, 'him'? Where are the others? You promised more than that. You told us we'd have many people to leverage."

His hands still behind his head, Seamus carefully said, "We had some problems. I lost the others, but I still have the prize. The vice president's son."

Hassan stood, waving the pistol about. "And now you want to pay me half of what you promised? After my risk?"

"There's nothing I could do! You know how this works."

Hassan laughed, a mirthless tone, and said, "Yes. I do. Ismail, how does this work? When you were a pirate? What did you do when you were double-crossed on payment?"

From across the room, holding another pistol, Ismail said, "I killed the hostages. Payment is payment."

"And since we don't actually have the hostages, what do you suggest?"

"We exact a different payment."

Seamus saw Kevin's face crumble in fear at the words. He went on the offensive. "You talk about payment, but you've done nothing as far as I can see. Why the fuck should I pay you anything?"

Ismail looked at his watch and said, "One hour and twenty minutes."

"Okay, then. We understand each other. The attack goes off, and you get the prize."

Hassan said, "Lay down. On your belly."

Seamus did so, right next to Kevin. He heard Hassan say something in Somali, and the man who answered the door went into the bedroom. Seamus saw the man return, carrying two black pillowcases, and he didn't understand what was occurring.

Until the light disappeared from the hood slammed over his head.

78

Kylie felt the car engine shut off, but she continued to feign sleep. Through slitted eyes she saw they were in a shopping district, a mass of people boiling out of a London Underground stop called Camden Town. She exhaled in relief. There was no way the bearded man would try to stuff her back into the trunk in front of all of these people, and the ride locked up was more horrible than she remembered, every bump jarring through her body, the darkness mixed with the smell of exhaust. With Nick gone, her courage was sliding away, replaced by a sense of helplessness.

Last night, she'd felt the car rumble onto another ferry, the air horn blaring in the dark. Once on the far side, they'd driven for about thirty minutes, then had stopped. She'd waited for the man to release her, but he did not. She'd lain in the trunk for hours, hearing the man shift inside the car, and realized he had pulled over somewhere to sleep. Eventually, she'd drifted off herself, lost in her despair.

She was awakened by the trunk opening and daylight spilling in. Squinting her eyes, she'd been allowed to get inside the vehicle with him, but he had left her hands bound. They'd begun driving again, and she'd leaned her head against the window and pretended to sleep, afraid to ask the man where they were going. Afraid to find out. Postponing the inevitable, but it had arrived all the same.

He shook her knee, saying, "We're here."

She sat up and said, "Where?"

"London. Look, I didn't like what was going on back there. Taking soldiers is one thing, but taking you crossed the line. I'm going to pass you to some people who will get you home. Okay?"

The words alarmed her, making her want to turn back the clock. To climb back into the trunk. She didn't believe him for a second. He didn't know it, but she'd heard the conversation he'd had on the phone and knew that whatever this was, it wasn't about helping her. In a quavering voice, she said, "Why don't you just let me go?"

"You'll run to the cops. I can't have that. These people will hold you until Seamus is done, but they won't hurt you."

She began to tremble but nodded tentatively, pretending to believe.

He pulled out a knife, and she recoiled against the window. He said, "I'm going to cut your hands free. Please do not attempt to escape. You won't make it."

He sliced the flex ties on her wrists and said, "See that pub over there? We're going inside, and I'm going to get you some food. The men I'm talking about will meet us there in a couple of hours."

At his words, she realized she was ravenous. She glanced out the window and saw a two-story establishment called the World's End.

He said, "Anybody asks about your bruises, make something up. I don't think anyone will, though. It's early, but that bar has people who look like you in it all the time."

She nodded, waiting on him to tell her what to do. He exited the vehicle, circled around, and opened her door. He said, "Remember, no tricks. I don't want to hurt you, but I will."

She got out and they crossed the street, threading through the traffic. He held the door for her, and she entered a giant pub that seemed to go on forever, put together with what looked like spare parts and salvage, with no two tables alike and heavy metal music blaring. He pointed to the back, saying, "That way."

She walked past one bar and entered a large back room with a huge skylight. In the center was another bar, with a balcony seating area above it. She saw a sign for the bathrooms on the right and said, "I really need to go."

He considered, then said, "Okay, but no tricks."

He followed her down a short flight of stairs, stopping in an alcove, the men's room on the right, the women's on the left. She opened the door and found it empty. Devoid of any help. One more blow to her dwindling courage. She immediately looked for a method of escape, but saw it would be impossible. The only window appeared to be welded shut and was five feet off the ground.

She couldn't believe how filthy the place was. No seats on the toilets, graffiti all over the walls, and water on the floor. She settled for relieving herself, hovering over the stained toilet. Back outside, she found Colin waiting for her. He pointed to the upstairs balcony. "Up there. Sit at the back, against the wall. I want to see them coming."

They paused at the bar, a woman behind it with dreadlocks and a ring through her nose, a chain running from it to a hoop in her ear. Colin said, "You guys take euros?"

"Nope. Pounds only."

He dug out his wallet, producing a credit card. "Run a tab. I'll start with a Guinness. She'll have a glass of water. We'll both take a couple of baskets of fish and chips."

The lady swiped his card and handed it back, saying, "Fifteen minutes for the food."

While they waited on the drinks, Kylie considered what he'd said about wanting his back to the wall and wanting to see the men coming. It meant they weren't exactly friends.

It was the reason he'd stopped here, in a large public place. He wanted the crowd to keep the men in check. After all, if they were such good buddies, and he had her safety at heart, why not just drive to their house? Why meet in a bar?

Colin handed her a glass of water and led her to a circular metal staircase, telling her to go first. The rungs were so narrow she felt as if she were standing still and turning in a circle. They reached the top, the balcony completely empty, deflating her. Driving home her lack of options. She'd again hoped to see someone. To give her a chance, no matter how small, to communicate her status.

He pointed to a couch against the wall, a small table in front of it.

He said, "I'm going to get the food. I'll be right next to the stairs. You come down, and I'm going to hurt you."

She said nothing, sagging back in the worn vinyl cushions and putting her head in her hands, her thoughts swirling about.

Nick's face came into her mind's eye, and she wondered if he was still alive. The last, vicious kick he'd taken replayed over and over, his head snapping back, his body dropping straight down. She began to weep in small, silent hitches.

She was now completely and utterly on her own. Nobody was coming to help.

She thought bitterly of her uncle, the man she'd placed so much faith in. He had failed her. She knew it wasn't fair, but the blame filled her nonetheless. He and his pack of friends, all bragging about what they'd done on operations while she hid on the periphery, listening. She'd always believed them but now realized it was just the adoration of her youth. She rubbed her throat, feeling the absence of her pendant. An allegory for her misplaced trust.

Her uncle's friend swam into her consciousness, and for the first time, she felt true betrayal. She was so sure he would come, like a child believing in the tooth fairy, that the realization he didn't care crushed her will to continue.

The small bit of weeping grew, the jagged hitches so great she couldn't breathe.

79

The argument was getting heated, but there was no way I was backing down. "Blaine, she's climbing the wall. We need to see inside the apartment."

"Pike, this isn't a Spider-Man movie. It's damn near noon. She can't get up the backside without compromise. We take the team and hit the place with overwhelming force. It's only a two-room apartment."

"It was your call on the daylight hit, but no way am I setting foot in that place without intel. We could be walking into a firebox."

Blaine said, "We've got the intel. Jesus, we have more than we ever did back when we used to do this shit at Bragg. We have the entire floor plan."

The flight out of Ireland had taken as long as I thought it would, with the usual delays, but we put the time to good use, planning our next steps. The Taskforce had managed to give us a complete schematic of the entire structure the Somalis were allegedly in, and their room—318—was a corner one, with a window from the bathroom looking out into an alley and the bricks of the building next door. We'd hit the ground and rented a cargo van and a sedan, then driven straight to the target.

It was on a street called Edgware, which had the nickname of Little Beirut, but that was somewhat misleading. I'd expected it to be like other Little Arabias I'd seen in the past, in other countries. A small enclave of Middle Eastern culture, with BMO women walking about—Black Moving Objects completely covered head to toe—and men dressed in Gulf attire.

Instead, it was just a busy street in London with a few hookah-smoking establishments and a smattering of Arabic lettering on various stores. Definitely not Little Beirut, unless you were calling it that because of the international nature that city boasted in the '60s. There were just as many westerners as people from the Middle East.

The apartment complex was set back from the street by a block of stores, a hallway leading past to the stairwell for the residences. It appeared fairly straightforward and simple to assault. Straight up the stairs and in, three rooms and ten seconds before target secure. But that intelligence was based on nothing but a sanitized piece of blueprint. It couldn't tell us what they'd done inside. Didn't show if they'd ringed the walls with RDX.

Brett chimed in, "Boss, he's right. Every time someone mentions Somalis, people get killed."

Blaine said, "Then you do it. Let's get an Operator on the backside."

And there it was. The prejudice. He wasn't worried about compromise. He didn't trust Jennifer.

Retro said, "Sir, no offense, but you don't know what the hell you're talking about. Jennifer can climb better than all of us together. If you're saying we need to do the recce, then she's it."

For her part, Jennifer sat silently, letting us duke it out.

Blaine looked at her and said, "You can do this?"

"In my sleep, you chauvinistic piece of shit."

Well, okay, she didn't say that. But she should have. All she did was nod her head.

He said, "All right. Let's go. We're wasting time."

I smiled and said, "Koko's up. I'll pull security to the rear, where she's climbing. Retro, you got far-side front. Stage at the coffee shop next door. Check for atmospherics, anyone pulling security for them. Blood, you got the entrance to the apartment complex. Figure out how we get in. See if we need to fake a button-call to get inside, or whether we can just walk up like we own the place."

Brett stashed his suppressed Glock, the barrel long enough to poke a tent in his jeans in the back. He threw on a large oilskin Burberry, draping the coattail over his butt, and said, "I fucking hate that callsign."

Jennifer, slipping into a pair of Vibram FiveFingers shoes, said, "Preaching to the choir."

We split up, me following Jennifer down the dank alley, past a beat-up car parked illegally, the bodywork pockmarked with dents and holes, like someone had taken a ball-peen hammer to it. Or like someone had shot at it.

I hissed and Jennifer held up. I said, "Is this the car you dinged up?"

She studied it, then said, "I honestly can't say. It was dark, but those holes are new."

I peered inside, seeing nothing obvious. We left it behind, turning the corner to a smaller alley, really just a walkway strewn with garbage cans. Jennifer looked up and said, "That's it. Right above us."

I said, "Hey, I gave you a lot of props with Blaine. You *can* do this, right?"

She grinned and said, "In my sleep."

She kept walking and I said, "Where are you going?"

"To the end. See that ledge? I'll get to the third floor from the far side, then shimmy over. I should be able to see inside, but I won't be able to do anything but look."

"How long can you hang? Do you need to come back, or can you lock that window down?"

She looked up at the ledge, really just a four-inch outcropping, and said, "I can hold that for at least thirty minutes, especially if I brace my feet against the brick, but I can't lock it down. Only give you visual reports."

I said, "Good enough. Nobody's going to escape that way anyway."

She reached an old iron drainage pipe at the corner of the alley and tested it, finding it anchored firmly. She said, "Catch me if I fall?"

I grinned. "Of course."

She glanced behind me, and I turned, saying, "What?"

"Just wanted to make sure nobody's looking." When I turned back around, she kissed me on the lips.

Taken aback, I pulled away and said, "Damn it, Jennifer. Quit that shit."

She grinned and, in a false baritone, said, "I'm a knuckle-dragging commando. Don't let my friends see me kiss a girl like last time."

I realized that Brett or Retro had kidded her about what had happened at the farmhouse hit, and she didn't like me hiding our relationship. Didn't like that I might be ashamed of it. Which . . . I wasn't. I thought.

Before I could reply, she slapped my gut, switched on her Bluetooth earpiece, and leapt up, grabbing the pipe and scampering like a lizard on a summer day, getting to the third floor in seconds. She reached out, grasped the ledge, and began shimmying over to the target apartment, raising her legs into a pike position for every window, holding it while she continued moving. Amazing the hell out of me.

She reached the target and slowed. She peeked inside, then planted her feet onto the rough brick, leaning close, arms above her head grasping the outcropping.

Over the radio, I said, "Blood, Retro, status?"

"Good out here. We can walk right in. No issues."

"Stand by. Koko's got something."

I saw her peer inside, twisting her body to get closer. She came on the radio.

"Pike, through the bathroom I can get a corner of the den. There are two hostages on the floor. Hooded. I can see their heads."

80

Her radio transmission echoed in my brain, illuminating the possibilities.

Two? That means . . . Kylie's here.

I said, "You sure? No trap?"

She said nothing for a moment, then, "I just saw someone walk by the door. A black man. He has a pistol. There's another black man further in. The hostages are moving on the floor. They're alive."

I said, "Break, break. Blood, Retro, back to the vehicle. Koko, hold what you got."

I started sprinting, reaching the van at the same time as my teammates. We entered and I slid the door closed, saying, "We're going in. Right now. Brett, you lead. Retro, you're behind me. Nung, you bring up trail. Pull security once we're in. Lock down the hallway."

Nung nodded, as bored as ever.

I said, "Sir, status on the men in the room?"

Blaine knew what I was asking. He said, "Hostile force ROE."

Which meant we could kill them whether they posed a direct threat or not. I said, "Roger that," and Blaine started screwing a suppressor to his Glock.

I said, "What are you doing?"

"Don't start, Pike. I'm coming." He pointed at the two communications guys we'd been dragging along. "They can handle the radio."

They both had wide eyes, sitting behind a makeshift console of computers and SATCOM antennae. Not wanting to leave the safety of the van for anything.

I thought about my numbers and said, "Okay. But my show. You come in behind me."

He grinned and said, "No issues."

I said, "Blood, you got radar scope. Retro, you got bump key. You open, and we flow in. Blaine, you come in last."

I got a thumbs-up from all and said, "We need to do this silently. Don't let them get off a round. We don't know where this is going." They nodded and I said, "Pure violence. Kill anyone not wearing a hood."

We slid out of the van, and I called, "Koko, moving now. Anything?"

"No. Same story."

Leading the way, Brett threaded down the hallway between the stores and entered the apartment area. We reached a row of mailboxes, and he veered to the stairs on the right side. We took them two at a time, reaching the third floor in seconds.

I alerted Jennifer. "At last covered and concealed. About to make breach."

"Roger. The black man is slapping one of the hostages through his hood, shouting something."

"On the way."

We raced down the hallway, me taking the far side of the door, Retro on the near side. Brett placed a radar scope against the wall next to the door and studied it. He turned and held out his hand. *Five.*

With the two hostages, that left three to deal with.

I nodded at Retro and rotated out, facing the door at an angle and putting my barrel in play. He jammed a baseball-size device with a universal key into the doorknob, then looked at me. I nodded, and he hit the switch.

The mechanized bump key seemed to rattle enormously loud, sounding like fingernails scraping on a chalkboard. He jerked it out, turned the knob, and flung the door open, allowing a world of hurt to flow into the room.

I cleared the funnel of death, turning right and seeing a tall, skinny man with a pistol. I cracked a double-tap and saw his head snap back. I rotated left before his body had even hit the floor and saw another man standing in shock, a weapon held limply in his hands, not even raising it. His head exploded from someone's round and I raced to the bedroom, holding up until I felt a body behind me. I exploded in, seeing a fat man with an open mouth jamming his hands in the air. My finger dragged the trigger to the rear.

I halted.

By the rules of engagement he could be killed outright, but ROE was nothing but a piece of paper. It wouldn't help me sleep at night.

I closed the distance to him and hammered his temple with the butt of my pistol, dropping him in his tracks.

I turned back out and ran to the final room, sweeping my weapon left and right. Before I could enter, Retro came out, saying, "Clear."

I went to the bathroom, Brett right behind me. It was empty. I opened the window, helping Jennifer get inside, me holding her waist and Brett dragging in her legs. Halfway in, Blaine called out, "Got them. But it's not our guys. This thing is bigger than we thought."

What the hell is he talking about?

Still pulling Jennifer, I said, "No Nick? No Kylie?"

"No. A couple of Irishmen. They're saying they were kidnapped."

Jennifer fell into the bathroom and I felt the failure hit me. I sat on the toilet, disgusted.

We should have never gotten on that plane.

Jennifer stood up, brushed herself off, and said, "What's the status? Is it Kylie?"

I said, "No," and began moving lethargically to the den. I saw two men on the floor, still bound. Both looking extremely grateful.

Blaine said, "I don't know what to do about this. They aren't Americans. Not a Taskforce problem."

I looked at the one on the right, and saw a tattoo of a harp below his ear. Something I'd seen before, when a man walked away from me in a bar in Cork City.

The rage blossomed and I stalked over to him, slapping him full in the face and knocking him to the ground. Blaine stood up, shouting, "Pike! What are you doing?"

I jammed my pistol into his neck and said, "Seamus McKee. We finally meet. You have ten seconds to tell me what I want to know, or I'll slaughter you just like your friends here."

Seamus looked at me like I was crazy and said, "What are you talking about? I've been kidnapped!" He turned to Blaine and said, "Get him off me! I'm the hostage, damn it. I've done nothing wrong."

The man to the left grew rigid at my mentioning Seamus's name, the truth evident on his face. I tossed Seamus to the floor and held my pistol in front of the nose of the other "hostage."

"I only need one, you fuck. And Seamus is the winner. You're collateral damage. Five . . . four . . . three . . . two . . ."

Blaine jumped up, shouting, "Pike, stop it, right now!"

The man screamed, "He's in the car! In the trunk! Downstairs."

I leaned back and exhaled. Blaine flicked his head between the two men, unsure of what to do. I said, "Blood, Retro, go get him. The car is in the alley. Jennifer and I saw it on the way to the rear."

They left, Blaine going with them, and I sat down, waiting, my barrel aimed at Seamus's head. I said, "Search that piece of shit."

Nung rolled him onto his belly, expertly going through every nook and cranny. He emptied his pockets, throwing keys and a wallet to the floor. He found a piece of paper and studied it. He held it up to me.

"Can I take this?"

I looked at it, a small computer printout that he unfolded like some origami thing. I said, "What is it?"

"Payment."

I had no idea what it was, but if that was enough to clear me with Nung, I had no issues with it. "Yeah. It's yours."

He nodded, tucking the paper into his pocket. As calm as ever.

I returned to Seamus. "Where is Kylie?"

He glared at me, remaining quiet.

I stood up, towering over him. Jennifer saw my anger and stepped between us. She said, "Don't do it. Killing him won't get her back."

At that moment, I realized she thought Kylie was dead. Gone. I said, "Jennifer, she's coming home. She is."

Jennifer nodded, saying nothing.

I leaned down and said, "You have until they return to tell me where she is. When I hear the footsteps outside, I'll fucking kill you."

"She's in the trunk! Damn it, that's who they're getting. Let them get back."

I whipped the barrel of my Glock, ripping open his cheek and slamming his head into the floor.

I said, "Bullshit. Dickless here just said 'he's downstairs.' No plural. I know who they're going to find, and she's not in that package. Where is she?"

The other man said, "We don't have her! Don't kill us! It's not our fault!"

I heard the words and felt the rage grow. A blackness that I knew all too well. Seamus glared at me, his anger attempting to compete with my own. But there was no contest.

Jennifer saw the change and said, "Pike . . . don't . . ."

I leaned into Seamus's face and said, "You have one chance to save yourself. And I don't mean stay out of jail. You call yourself a soldier, but you have no knowledge of the true fight. I have seen what people like you do to captured soldiers. Flayed alive, screaming for mercy. I've seen the videos. And I'm about to do the same to you."

I saw his face falter, realizing there was something evil in the room. I pulled out my folding blade, the edge razor-sharp. I slid it across his arm, causing the blood to flow.

"I will carve you up, piece by piece. My daughter will enjoy every minute of it as payback."

The words came unbidden, but they hit Seamus and his partner like a sledgehammer. They were convinced I was unhinged. And maybe I was.

Seamus blurted out, "I know where she is. I separated them on purpose. She's still in Ireland. I can get her back. I can give her to you."

I said, "Where?"

"I have to call them. Get them to bring her to me. I don't know where they are right now. But I can bring her to you."

"Call them. Do it. She dies, and you do too."

Nung came out of the bedroom. "Pike, you need to see this."

Aggravated, I said, "What?"

"The dead guy on the floor has a stopwatch going. A timer. It's got thirty minutes left, give or take. Inside the bedroom are pictures and attack planning."

"For what?"

"For the Eye of London. They're planning on bringing it down."

81

Emily Botswanger danced in the line, weaving in and out of the ribbon barriers that were supposed to keep her in check and ignoring her mother's stern warnings about behaving. At eight years old, she could be forgiven for her exuberance. Especially since she'd spent the last three days on a "holiday" that consisted of her parents dragging her all over England seeing a bunch of musty old things that meant as much to her as a dead mole on her doorstep. At least then she knew her tabby had done the deed, and while yucky, it was new. Why her parents thought she'd care about someone's death a hundred years ago was beyond her.

The Tower of London, the royal Palace, the Wartime Bunker, it was one boring thing after another, but they were finally doing something she would enjoy. Riding the Eye.

Her mother admonished her again, saying they wouldn't go forward if she didn't behave. She calmed down. Enough to give her parents the leeway to continue. They advanced forward in the line, seeing the capsules being filled one after the other in a relentless march.

She said, "How fast does it go? Will we feel like we're on a roller coaster?"

Her mother smiled and said, "No. It's slow. Like an escalator. Not like a roller coaster."

Disappointed, Emily said, "Can they make it speed up? If we ask?"

Her mother ushered her to the platform, lining up into the queue for the next capsule. She said, "We don't want it to speed up. That would be dangerous."

Their car appeared, rolling inexorably forward, and they stutter-stepped to get in. Emily said, "I don't mind danger. I like excitement."

Blaine returned, a huge grin on his face, and I knew we'd saved the day. At least his and the president's. My teammates came through as well, smiling and carrying in Nicholas Seacrest, groggy and drugged, but alive.

So we had won. As far as the US government was concerned. I would have cheered, but we were still missing Kylie. And we now had a new threat. They were buoyant in our success, but I was about to pop that bubble.

Blaine saw my face and said, "What? What happened?"

I pointed to Seamus and said, "He can give us Kylie."

His face scrunched up in confusion. "Kylie? Who is that?"

"She's the reason I'm here. Kurt's niece." I pointed at Nick Seacrest and said, "Honestly, I don't care about him. I'm glad we got him, but I want Kylie. They were tied together, and now they aren't."

Wondering why his huge victory wasn't being shared, Blaine said, "Okay, so we go get her next. These guys will know where she is. Right?"

I said, "Yeah. They do. But there's another problem."

I told him what I knew, Nung bringing out photos and schematic drawings delineating explosive charges and resulting effects.

He said, "This is going down right now? In the next hour?"

"Yes. But I don't give a shit. I'm going to Ireland to get Kylie. You can sort this out."

He looked at me in confusion. I stood up, saying, "I'm taking Seamus. And your van."

Seamus rolled back, clearly not wanting to be with me. Jennifer rose and said, "Pike, we can't do that."

I said, "Bullshit we can't. Kylie isn't going to die."

Nung, of all people, said, "They're going to drop the Eye. Kill over eight hundred civilians. I do not care, but I thought it would be prudent to show the tradeoff."

And there it was. The dilemma this entire chase had been about. Now exposed. How much was one life worth? How many could be sacrificed to save the one?

I looked at Jennifer, wanting guidance. She didn't turn from my glare, holding my eyes. I saw the truth to my question. I saw her answer. And the pain.

I said, "What the hell can we do anyway? Call them. Tell them to stop the tour. Get them out."

Pulling up the Eye website on his phone, Retro said, "We have thirty minutes. That's one revolution of the wheel. Even if we got them to stop loading, a ton of people will die. And that's given we could penetrate the fog. Get through to someone with the power to stop it right this second."

I squeezed my eyes shut, seeing Kylie from parties in the past. A teenager, full of vitality and youth. Now going to die by my decision. I gave a silent prayer to her, begging forgiveness.

"Okay. Let's go."

Looking like he'd rather be anywhere else but in the room, Blaine said, "Pike, I have to get Seacrest out of here. I can't let you take the team. I have the vice president's son. He's the precious cargo, and I have to get him out. You can have the sedan, but the van stays here."

I gave him a look of disgust and said, "Fine. Me, Nung, and Jennifer. Keeps it clean anyway. And I don't need the sedan. The Tube will be faster. The rest of you fucks can bask in the glory of saving mister high-and-mighty."

Brett said, "I'm coming with you." Retro followed with "No doubt. I'm not riding this in the rear."

I said, "Blaine's right. Get Seacrest out of here. Numbers don't matter now. You'll be no help."

Blaine nodded, relieved, and said, "I'll start the chain right now. Get them to stop loading and tell them what we have. Get them ready to receive you."

I said, "That's a wasted call. We'll be there in minutes, before you can get anyone to start moving. I'll do it myself. They'll shut down operations when we arrive waving guns around."

He nodded, saying, "I know, but it'll help with the cleanup."

"I could give a shit about that. I care about Kylie. You start looking. Find out what you can from Seamus, and don't be nice. When this is over, you better help me locate her."

He said, "I will. No matter what the Oversight Council says."

82

Jennifer followed behind Pike, leaving the apartment in a hurry. He hit the street, running to the Edgware Tube station.

Getting into the subway, they took a seat in the rear, Jennifer pulling out the photos of the attack plan and glancing around to make sure they were clear of nosy neighbors.

She said, "It looks like they intend to cut the cables. Up near the hub."

Pike pulled a picture from her hand and studied it, saying nothing.

Jennifer said, "How can we stop it? There's no way to get anyone up there in time. Somebody needs to get to the hub immediately, and we won't be able to convince anyone to let us in."

The train pulled through the stations, and he said, "I know. It's you."

She felt a touch of panic and said, "Pike, I can't do that. We need to get someone official. Someone to stop the wheel."

"You already gave that answer. No time. You climb better than a monkey. You've seen the schematics. You know where to go. Get up there and stop it."

"How the hell am I going to do that? They won't let me just walk in."

Sitting beside them as if he were a Buddha statue, Nung said, "That is what you're paying me for. I will get you in. All you have to do is climb."

Pike grinned at the words and said, "Yeah, you damn coward."

She sat back, and the subway rolled on. They arrived at Waterloo station, and Nung said, "This is us."

They exited, sprinting up the stairs. Getting to the top, they saw the Eye in the distance, on a square of land full of musicians and street performers.

Breaking into a run, they entered the park. Jennifer said, "How are we going to get them to let me up?"

They went past the huge arms holding the wheel in the air and Pike pulled out his weapon, Nung doing the same. He said, "Get ready to start climbing. Like you never have before."

The capsule rose, moving almost in slow motion, disappointing Emily. She had expected something more. At least as much excitement as an elevator instead of a dripping, creeping rise. They continued on, and her mother tried to get her to stay in place, apologizing to the other people in the car as Emily raced to and fro.

She leaned out, placing her face against the glass and staring into the skyline, mesmerized by the climb. She said, "It's like being in an airplane. Up and up and up."

Alarmed, her mother said, "Don't lean on the glass, honey. It's not safe."

She reached out to take her daughter's hand, and Emily scooted away, worming between two people on the other side of the car and placing her face against the glass again.

Her mother apologized to the elderly couple, getting a smile in return. She grabbed Emily's arm, this time sternly, and said, "Come with me."

Emily shouted, "Mommy! There's a girl climbing up the wheel! Look!"

Her mother leaned between the couple, searching for whatever her daughter had seen, and the wheel jerked to a halt, over two hundred feet above the ground.

Jennifer heard the shouting behind her and knew that Pike and Nung were putting themselves in serious danger. Soon enough, there would be a full-on presence of a tactical police unit, and they'd probably shoot first and ask questions later.

She sprinted through the throng of people waiting to board, all screaming and ducking at the madmen with weapons. She reached the front and looked upward, seeing the latticework of cables and steel. The wheel continued to turn, even as the people waiting to board ran back and forth, shouting.

She leapt up, climbing a ladder on the nearest capsule, and reached the roof. She hoisted herself onto a crossbeam, the pipe laced with steel studs for escaping the capsule in an emergency.

She climbed it, going ever higher, the wheel still turning. She looked above and saw the hub, but there was no way to get to it. Nothing but spokes of metal, like a giant bicycle wheel, radiated out from the circumference.

She didn't have the strength to climb straight up them.

But she could climb across.

Seeing the path, she began using the framework of the capsules to get her higher. Get her parallel with the hub, so that she could shimmy across on the spoke instead of trying to climb up or down.

She heard the people shouting in the capsules as she went across them, finding a rhythm in the symmetry of the construction. She climbed over four before the wheel stopped turning. She continued on, reaching the parallel position, two hundred feet in the air, the wind whipping her hair and threatening to throw her off.

Standing on top of the capsule, the people inside its glass case dumbfounded, she leapt out, snatching the cable that led to the hub. She wrapped her legs around it and, hanging below, began to monkey-crawl forward. She cleared the circumference of the wheel and the wind hammered her, rocking her body back and forth.

She clasped the cable with a death grip, cinching her legs tight, seeing the black water two hundred feet below, the gusts so great she was certain she'd fall. She considered returning to the capsule, getting to safety. She leaned back and saw the people inside staring at her. Wondering what on earth she was doing.

A small child pressed her face against the glass, using her hands to block the glare. She was smiling, not understanding her fate. Jennifer saw the misplaced joy and realized she couldn't return. She either reached the hub, or they all died.

She started inching forward, slower, but making progress.

From inside the car Emily shouted in excitement, "Look, look! She's coming to us!"

Emily's mother watched in growing trepidation. She turned to her husband and said, "Shouldn't someone have stopped her? How is she up here?"

The husband said, "I don't know, but she's not getting in."

He turned to the people in the car and said, "Don't let her in. Whatever she's doing, don't let it be inside here."

There were murmurs of agreement, and two men went to the emergency exit, standing just inside the orange marker. A burly guy with an American accent said, "We got this. She's not getting into our car."

Emily continued watching, fascinated. The woman came on, going over one capsule after another. Eventually, she reached hers and began climbing the outside. The men stood, waiting to do *something*, as if their presence alone dictated a response, but in truth, they were just as confused as everyone else in the car.

The girl scampered up over their capsule like a squirrel, using the ladder on the outside. She reached the top and quit climbing. She leapt out, catching the cable running to the center of the wheel. She began sliding along it, moving toward the hub, and Emily said, "Mommy! Did you see that? Look at her!"

The mother did so, seeing the woman slide on the cables, and was relieved that the psychopath hadn't tried to enter her car. The immediate threat gone, she began to wonder what the climber was doing. And realized they were two hundred feet in the air.

Her face pressed to the window, Emily said, "She's amazing."

Emily had no idea why the woman was climbing, or how much danger they were in.

But her mother did.

*   *   *

Jennifer reached the hub and lowered to the scaffolding on the outside, exhausted. She shook her hands to relieve the pain and keyed her radio. "I'm here. Stand by."

She heard, "We're under arrest. They're coming for you. Go."

She looked below, seeing a swarm of people, half with the reflective vests of police. She couldn't pick out Pike or Nung.

She scooted underneath the giant spindle and saw the explosives. She ran to the first one and pulled out the blasting cap, throwing it into the wind. She did the same to the second one, then began scuttling to the far end. To the two cables that held the entire contraption in space.

She saw the timer on the first counting down. Five . . . four . . . three . . .

She ripped out one blasting cap and ran, the final explosive charge going off and throwing her forward.

She slammed into the steel of the hub, seeing stars and beginning to black out. She fought the darkness, now on her hands and knees, the scaffolding cutting her exposed skin. She shook her head to clear the cotton. The world came into focus bit by bit, and she felt the Eye shift. Leaning out into the river. Starting to fall.

Emily saw the blast and said, "Mommy! Fireworks! They've got fireworks here." The mother felt the shift in the wheel and grabbed her daughter tight. She began praying.

Jennifer pulled herself upright and saw the damage. One cable gone. The others in place. She keyed her radio. "Pike, get them down. Now. I got three, but one went off. This thing might drop. Start turning the wheel."

She heard, "Jennifer, I'm under arrest. They've taken my phone but left in the earpiece. I can't get to Blaine. All I have is the last setting. The radio. Call him. Get him to work some magic."

She did so, explaining what she had and where she was.

He said, "Been working this since you left. Got a direct contact. Stand by."

She felt the hub shift again and said, "God damn it, tell them to start it up. Get the people off!"

She heard nothing. Then the wheel began turning, much faster than before. She sagged back, resting her head on a flange. The metal hatch to the scaffold flew open, four men wearing body armor spilling out, all aiming a weapon at her.

83

Kylie saw the bearded man sit up tall, staring over the rail, and knew it was time. She had been running escape scenarios through her head for the last thirty minutes, knowing if she was to get free, it would be here, in the heart of the bar. Once she was in the hands of whoever was coming, she was done.

Visibly nervous, Colin said, "That's them. Don't do anything stupid. They're here to help you."

Four men appeared at the top of the stairs, the lead one looking like something out of a Grimm fairy tale. He had black hair slicked back and a pockmarked face; the menace slid off him, permeating the balcony.

Colin stood, in a faltering voice saying, "Ratko. Hey. I'm here. Like I said I would be."

The man called Ratko surveyed the balcony, his men separating left and right. He approached and said, "Where are my diamonds?"

Colin said, "Hey, wait, I had nothing to do with that. I told you. That's Seamus all the way."

The balcony secure, Ratko looked at him, then hammered an uppercut into Colin's stomach, dropping him to the floor. The violence exploded so fast Kylie could barely assimilate it. She scrambled to the end of the couch, holding her arms over her head, two men closing on her.

Ratko waved a hand, and they drew back. Colin sat up, holding his stomach. Grimacing, he said, "What the hell are you doing? Here she is. All yours. I had nothing to do with Paris."

Ratko said, "Where are my diamonds? Where is the necklace?"

Colin pulled himself up, looking at Ratko for permission to sit back in a chair. Seeing no violence, he did so. "I had nothing to do with Bulgari. Nothing. I don't know where your diamonds are. I saw how bad this was going and called you. I want no part of it. That's why I called."

Ratko sat down and said, "So what do you offer to save yourself? This girl?"

He looked at Kylie, sizing her up, and she realized that death was not the worst of her fates. She tried to crawl farther from his gaze, stopped by the man above her.

Colin said, "She's not just a girl. She's the fiancée of the American vice president's son. She's worth a great deal."

Ratko said, "I don't do ransoms. I don't take hostages. It only causes enemies that want to hunt."

Colin said, "I . . . I brought what I could. I can give you Seamus. I know where he is. He's already gotten millions for her and her fiancé. He has cash. In Bitcoin."

"Where?"

"Ireland. He's planning to get more money. He's bleeding the US dry. I swear, I can give him to you."

Ratko stared at him, the pure malevolence of the glare scaring Kylie. He nodded, then flicked his head to the guard next to her. He said, "I'll take her. She might make some money in another country."

The man to her left grabbed her arm, forcing her to rise. He led her to the circular staircase and she heard Ratko say, "So, tell me more about Seamus. Tell me about the money he's received."

She began circling the stairs, realizing that if she got in a vehicle with these savages, she was worse than dead. Her only chance of survival was escaping before she left the bar.

The men around me shouted and yelled, threatening me with all manner of violence, but I knew they wouldn't do anything. They'd slapped me around a little bit, but with the number of cell phone cameras in play, I knew they would only let off a little steam. As long as I didn't pose a threat.

I hadn't. Nung and I had cracked a couple of rounds in the air, causing massive panic, and letting Jennifer sprint through the crowd. As soon as she'd made it to the top of the first capsule, I'd raised my hands, telling Nung to do the same.

Jennifer had made it to the top, the men screaming at me to tell them what she was doing. I yelled back the truth, holding my hands in the air. Eventually, they'd decided that I might not be lying and had stopped the wheel. Or maybe Blaine had gotten through. Either way, we'd waited at the bottom while Jennifer climbed. I'd gotten the call from her and heard the explosion, feeling my life ripped apart.

I'd jumped out, trying to see what had happened, and I'd been tackled by about a platoon of guys. Sitting underneath, screaming at the top of my lungs, I couldn't get them to let me go. I heard a groaning of metal. An inhuman, grating screech, and I knew the wheel was falling. With Jennifer on it.

The men on top of me heard it as well, and we all stopped. I screamed again, "Get the wheel turning. Get them off it!"

They shouted back and forth, and I saw the machinery start to work, capsule after capsule spilling out shrieking patrons. The wheel picked up speed, going about three times as fast as it normally did, the people literally jumping off, some tumbling to the ground.

I was ripped to my feet, Nung beside me, and both of us hustled off to a panel van. I tried to jerk out of their hands, looking over my shoulder for Jennifer. We were slammed into the paddy wagon and cuffed to a bench. They'd searched me, taking my wallet, passport, phone, and weapon—but they'd left in my Bluetooth earpiece. And had placed all my items in the front seat of the van. Within range.

I whispered, "Koko, Koko, status."

I heard nothing. I did it again, then heard, "Coming down now. I have weapons aimed at me."

I sagged back, staring at the ceiling of the van. Nung, his own Bluetooth in, nudged me, smiling. Because he was fucking crazy.

He leaned in and said, "I was worried this wouldn't work out. I like her."

Sitting in my chains, seeing the SWAT guys running about, I truly wondered if he wasn't living in a dream world.

Six minutes later, Jennifer was shoved in the back, wearing her own chains. I wanted to jump up and wrap her in my arms, but I was a commando. And I was shackled to the bench.

She looked at me, worn-out and scared. I winked and said, "Saved the day again."

She shook her head and sagged back against the wall of the van.

84

Kylie followed the men down the stairs, seeing her window of escape close. They reached the bottom, one in front and one behind, and she knew she needed to do something. If she wanted to live, this was it.

The floor had grown crowded in the hours since they'd entered, the entire area full of an eclectic mix of Saturday patrons, some in suits with neat haircuts and others sporting Mohawks and torn, raggedy clothes.

They threaded their way by the bar and the ring-nose girl shouted, "You guys closing out?"

The men around her kept walking. The barmaid shouted at them again. Kylie pulled the jacket of the guy in front, saying, "She's talking to you."

He looked at her, then the barmaid.

She held up a tab, waving it about, and said, "Are you guys closing out or what?"

He said something to the man behind her, in a language Kylie didn't understand, then walked to the bar. The man behind her followed with his eyes. She saw her chance break open, as fleeting as a star burning out in the night sky.

She took off running.

The police slammed the panel van doors, and we started trundling to wherever we were going, two goons in the back giving me the stink-eye, like they were going to jump me. I suppose I should have felt apprehension. Or elation. But I felt neither. I'd just caused the compromise of the entire Taskforce, but I'd also saved hundreds of lives. In the end, neither mattered to me, because I'd sacrificed Kylie's life to do both.

I'd failed. Again.

Jennifer was shackled next to me. She rubbed my thigh, glancing at me out of the corner of her eye. I leaned back into the wall, ignoring her, and she followed suit, not giving up. I sighed and looked at her.

She said, "We did good, right?"

I gave a tired grin and said, "Yeah. We did real good."

I saw it wasn't a question, but a statement. She said, "Pike, we had to make a call. We *had* to."

I heard her words and felt ashamed. I'd just sat on the ground while she risked everything she had to save over eight hundred innocents. And she was now propping *me* up.

I looked at her, trying to come up with some suitable commando team-leader crap. Something that would let her know how much I thought of her sacrifice. What came out surprised even me.

"I . . . love you."

She snapped her face toward me, her mouth hanging open in shock. Our earpieces came alive, saving me from my mistake.

"Pike, Pike, this is Retro, you there?"

I glanced at the goons in the corner of the van and said, "Yeah, I'm here."

"Blaine's working the extraction and thinks he'll get you guys out clean, but I've been doing some digging with the Taskforce. We interrogated Seamus after you left. He says the guy with Kylie is named Colin Butler. He lied about him being in Ireland. Colin Butler's credit card was just used here in London. In Camden."

The words coursed through me like I'd just touched an electrical outlet, bolting me upright. The goons saw my movement, and I leaned back, closing my eyes. I said, "I need to get out of this wagon. Right fucking now."

"Pike, we can't do that. We'll get you out at the station."

"We don't have the time for that. We lose this thread and she's gone. Get me out."

"How?"

"Put on Blaine."

There was a fumble of the earpiece, some static, then Blaine. "Pike, Retro's told me what he found. We'll start working it."

I said, "Call Kurt. Tell him. Then wreck this vehicle. I want out in the next five minutes."

"Pike . . . that's not going to happen."

"You call Colonel Kurt Hale right fucking now. Tell him what you have. Ask him for guidance. Then stop this wagon."

I heard nothing else. I looked at Jennifer and said, "Get ready for a crash."

Kylie heard the man behind her shout, and she darted through the crowd, knowing he was right behind her. She jerked a man off his feet, causing him to stumble into the path of her pursuer, and kept running, trying to remember the floor plan.

She cut around the corner of the bar, seeing the exit door and freedom. She started running toward it and saw the man who had gone to the bar spring into view, wildly looking around.

She crouched behind a foursome, scooting left, toward an alcove, knowing the other man was closing the distance behind her. She saw the bathroom to her front, a line of girls outside. She sprinted toward it, ducking below the crowd.

She leapt down the stairs, passing the line and ignoring the yells from the girls waiting. A woman tried to stop her, shouting about cutting the queue, and she slammed her into the wall, springing forward into the bathroom. Two girls at the mirror looked at her in astonishment, and she said, "Don't shout. Don't say anything. Please."

She looked around the room in desperation and realized she'd just boxed herself in. Nothing had changed, and there was no way out.

85

We continued rolling forward, the two goons in the rear still eyeing me like they wanted to kick my ass. I was getting tired of the glare. I raised my voice loud enough to get over the engine noise and said, "You want a shot at the title?"

The one on the left said, "You talk fine in here. I've dealt with terrorists before. Wait until we get to the station, Yank."

My earpiece crackled, and I heard, "Brace for impact."

I said, "We aren't going to the station."

He looked at me in confusion, and the van was hammered so hard I thought someone had exploded an IED underneath it. We flew through the air, the vehicle turning over onto its side. The two goons slammed into the roof with a crunch. Jennifer, Nung, and I were jerked up short by the shackles on our wrists and ankles bolted to the bench, now becoming makeshift seat belts.

The vehicle skidded for a moment, then sat still. One guard was out cold. The other began moving slowly, shaking his head. The doors opened in the back and I saw Retro, holding a pistol. He said, "Give me the keys. Now."

The guard handed him his key ring, then raised his hands. Retro tossed them to me, and I unlocked Nung and Jennifer, then locked up the guards, shackling the unconscious one first. Getting to the other, I cuffed his hands, saying, "Sorry about this. I'm really not a bad guy."

I crawled out the back, seeing Blaine holding a pistol on the driver, Brett in the cab providing first aid to the passenger. He had a nasty cut on his head, but I could see his lips moving, so he was coherent.

They'd used the van for interdiction, and it was spun sideways, the front end crunched, broken glass littering the roadway. We were on a four-lane, one-way road, and the traffic behind us was stopped, everyone gawking at the massive pileup.

I saw Nick Seacrest and the two commo guys in the sedan. Retro said, "Sorry for the impact. Brett got a little overexuberant. He needs some vehicle-interdiction training."

I said, "Where is she?"

"A place called the World's End on Camden Road. It's only about a mile to the north."

I ran to the sedan, saying to the men inside, "Get the fuck out."

The doors opened and Blaine shouted, "What are you doing?"

"What's it look like? I'm taking your vehicle."

Nick exited after the commo guys and said, "I'm coming with you."

I said, "Shut up," then, "Nung, Jennifer, Retro, and Brett, load up. Brett, bring our weapons and radios from the police wagon."

Blaine jogged over and said, "I have responsibility for the PC. I can't let you take the sedan. I have to get him to shelter."

"Cops will be here in about thirty seconds. You'll have more protection than you can possibly use."

My men started loading and I saw Nung swinging to the driver's side. I said, "Jennifer gets the wheel."

He paused at the door, and I said, "Sorry, but after your driving in Paris, you can be a passenger."

He scowled but got in the back. In a louder voice, Nick said, "I'm coming with you."

Blaine shouted, "No! Now get inside the police wagon. Get off the street."

Nick looked at me and said, "Give me a weapon. She's my responsibility."

"I don't have time for this. I'm not giving a pistol to a weatherman. You'd probably shoot yourself."

"I'm CCT. I can outshoot anyone here."

The comment gave me pause. CCT stood for Combat Control Team and was Air Force special operations. While we always made fun of the

Air Force in a good-natured way, calling them out on never getting dirty, CCT was a different animal altogether. They had a training pipeline that was as hard as anyone else's, and I'd never met a combat controller who couldn't hang, no matter how rough it got. Nick could be forgiven his boast of outshooting my men, not knowing who we were, but he could probably come close.

I said, "I appreciate the sentiment, but you're not going."

"What if she's not in the bar? What if she's hidden somewhere and it's only Colin? How will you find her?"

"I'll sort it out."

"With *me*. I know what he looks like. I'm the only one who does."

The words sank in and I said, "Blaine, give him your pistol."

"No! No way. He's not going."

I turned to him in controlled fury, feeling the loss of Kylie in the pit of my gut. Seeing the loss of my daughter all over again. "Give him your God damned pistol, or I'll knock you out and take it."

He saw I was deadly serious. He handed Nick the pistol butt first, lamely saying, "Pike, Kurt didn't authorize this."

"Yes, he did." I waited until Nick was inside, then squeezed in the back. Through the window I said, "Call him. Tell him that Nick Seacrest is necessary to save his niece. He'll authorize anything to do that."

He said, "Pike . . . don't take him."

I heard the weird blaring of British sirens. I tapped Jennifer and said, "Drive."

We left him on the side of the road, standing between the smoking cargo van and the wrecked police wagon.

Looking at his smartphone, Retro said, "Straight ahead up Eversholt. We'll run right into it."

Jennifer began weaving through the traffic, going much faster than the congestion should have allowed. She shot through red lights, leaving slamming brakes and a cacophony of horns in our wake.

Using his own phone, Brett said, "This place looks big, Pike."

"How many exits?"

"At least three. Probably more."

I said, "Okay, we get there, the men enter. Jennifer, find a place to stage. Be ready to return within thirty seconds. We get inside and lock down the exits. Nung, Brett, and Retro, that's you. Pick the most prominent ones."

I pulled up Kylie's picture on my phone and passed it around. "You see her, call your position and take down whoever is with her. We'll close on you. I'll take Nick and start exploring. We make contact, and I'll call. Everyone close on me if that happens."

Retro said, "Two more blocks. At the Y intersection. Veer right."

I looked out the windshield and saw the road split, the Camden Town Tube station straight ahead. Jennifer took the turn, and the target popped out of nowhere, a red building with large letters spelling THE WORLD'S END.

I shouted, "Here! Here! Stop the car."

She did so, and we spilled out, running to the door. We entered, and I saw Brett was right. The place was huge, and overflowing with boozing patrons. It would take an hour to clear.

I said, "Get to it," and the men split off, jogging in different directions. I said, "Okay, Nick. You're the hound dog on this. Find our man."

86

Kylie grabbed a lady at the sink and said, "Do you have a cell phone? I've been kidnapped. There are men trying to find me. I just ran from them!"

She looked at Kylie in bewilderment, not believing the words. The woman at the other sink saw the bruises on her face and said, "I have a phone. I'll call."

She began dialing, and another woman said, "You go hide in a stall. I'll take a look outside."

She took one step toward the door and Kylie heard a commotion, the women in line shouting at something. The two men burst into the restroom, and Kylie screamed.

The woman with the phone shouted, "I'm calling the police!"

The lead man punched her in the face, knocking the phone to the floor. The other man reached for Kylie. Two women in line jumped on him, biting and clawing. He got one arm on Kylie's sleeve and she ripped out of his grasp, running past him to the door. The first man took off after her, dialing a cell phone as he ran.

At the top of the stairs Kylie slammed into a wall of people, slowing her down. She fought her way forward, spilling pints of beers and generating shouts. She cleared the scrum and saw the door on the far side of the room.

Freedom.

She ran toward it and saw two men flying down the circular staircase. They would beat her to the exit. She felt the fear blossom inside her, panic flooding her body. She turned to run deeper into the bar when the first man tripped, going faster than his balance could hold on the narrow, twisting stairs. He spilled onto his face, sliding on the floor and tangling up his partner. She got a blessed two-second gap and raced to the door, slamming it open just as the two men stood back up.

She reached the street and began running in a blind panic, her brain fixated on one thought: escape.

We walked slowly through the crowd, Nick's head on a swivel, looking left and right for Colin, but not seeing him. I got a call from Brett saying he was at an eastern door, then Retro, saying he was also at an eastern door deeper in. The place was simply too big for the force I had. With Nung at the main entrance, that left the western side completely open. I called him, saying, "Nung, penetrate inside. We've cleared the first bar area. Go down the western side and position on a likely exit."

The pub had so many nooks, alcoves, and crannies that clearing them of suspicion was slow and tedious. I could see Nick growing antsy, moving faster. We left one alcove and moved to the next, another large bar area at the back of the building opening up. Nick started to look inside, then did a double take before jumping back into the first alcove.

I went in behind him, ignoring the two tables of patrons. "What did you see? Where is he?"

"Upper deck, above the bar. He's staring over the railing with another man."

I looked out and said, "The guy with the beard?"

"That's him."

I clicked my radio. "All elements, all elements, jackpot. I say again, jackpot. Subject is on the upper deck at the back of the pub. Six feet, Caucasian, blond hair, full beard, also blond. Two men next to him, both appear to be part of his team. One stairwell to the eastern side of the bar. Acknowledge."

Not waiting, I turned to Nick and said, "You stay here. He knows you on sight, and I'm not putting you in danger."

He started to say something, and I leaned in close. "Don't fuck with me on this."

He nodded, and I left at a fast walk, seeing Retro and Brett crossing the floor. I glanced up and saw Colin arguing with the man to his left, waving his arms up and down.

We reached the stairwell at the same time, Brett in the lead. I looked behind and saw Nung running toward us. I said, "Guns out," and we started to climb, winding our way up. Almost at the top, a man appeared in front of us and Brett said, "Back up, shithead. Hands high."

The man yelled in what sounded like Russian, then attempted to draw a gun. Brett drilled him between the eyes, the noise from the suppressor overshadowed by the hum of the bar. He slid down, sitting on the steps like he'd passed out, blocking our way forward.

Brett grabbed his shoulders, and I slid my hands under his feet. We hoisted him up, then flipped him over the side of the narrow stairwell. He hit the ground and I heard a girl scream just as I cleared the stairwell to the balcony, right behind Brett.

There were four men on top, three with weapons out, and Colin standing with his hands in the air. For a second there was a pause, nobody wanting to start the gunfight. The man next to Colin snarled and aimed his weapon right above Colin's beard. Colin shouted, "No! They aren't with me—" and the man pulled the trigger. Then all hell broke loose, like the gunfight at the O.K. Corral, bodies diving and guns going off all over the place. It lasted for a long four seconds, but they had no cover standing by the railing. We cut all three down.

I rose from behind the couch I'd dived over and said, "Give me an up."

Miraculously, everyone was unhurt with the exception of Nung. He'd taken a bullet through his bicep, but it hadn't hit bone. It also didn't faze his nonchalant attitude. He said, "This may increase my payment."

Brett started working on him and I surveyed the deck, checking behind couches and overstuffed chairs, looking for Kylie. She wasn't here.

My earpiece crackled. "Pike, Pike, this is Koko. I think I just saw Kylie running down the road."

I looked at Retro, and he'd clearly heard the same thing. I said, "Say again?"

"I'm staged on Camden and a girl just went running by. She went into some large bazaar selling T-shirts called Camden Market. I swear she looked just like—"

Nothing came through, then "It's her. It's her. There are four men running down the road. They all just went into the same market."

I said, "Let's go. Retro, give me a lock-on to the market she's talking about. Brett, lead the way. Nung, you got Nick. Get him out of here and somewhere safe. Call with a location, but be prepared for a little bit of a stay."

We barreled back down the stairs and I heard sirens on the street to the west. I said, "Eastern door. Eastern door. Nung, go get Nick and get out of here."

The crowds saw our weapons and parted like they were escaping from zombies, girls screaming and guys stumbling all over themselves to get out of the way.

We hit the street, Retro staring at his phone. He looked up and pointed. "That way. Camden Market."

87

Kylie sprinted through the stalls, the area overflowing with T-shirts blowing in the wind. She twisted and turned, going left and right and getting lost in the maze. She slowed, breathing heavily. She crouched down and looked underneath the hangers, trying to spot her pursuers. She couldn't see more than five feet. She began jogging again and unexpectedly broke into an alley, outside of the T-shirt stalls.

She heard a man shout, then another, and began blindly running up the alley. She hit a main road and looked behind her, the sight freezing her in fear.

Two of the men were in the alley, and they were running flat-out, so close she could see the sweat on their faces. Her body exploded in panic and she ran as fast as she could make her legs move, pumping harder and harder, her lungs screaming in pain. She reached a bridge over a canal with a walkway paralleling the water, a large brick building proclaiming Camden Lock. She made the mistake of glancing back and saw all four men on the street, running hard.

I'm going to die. I'm going to die. I'm going to die.

The words cycled through her head over and over, the terror almost debilitating. She leapt over the bridge, falling and slamming hard onto the walkway. She rolled, feeling as if someone had driven a knife into her ankle. She sprang up, ignoring the pain, and ran down the walkway. She saw an outdoor eating area and veered into it, continuing straight through into some type of shopping area.

She looked left and right, seeing stalls full of vendors stretching out, selling everything from leather jackets to lamps, like a giant flea market.

She slowed to a jog, running into a tunnel incongruously full of statues of horses, thinking she'd lost her pursuers. Gaining confidence. She heard a shout behind her, and the fear returned, cinching into her soul.

She exited the tunnel, turned the corner into an indoor section full of antiques, and was ripped off her feet and thrown to the ground. She screamed and began clawing, fighting for her life.

She heard, "Kylie, Kylie, stop it! I'm from Kurt Hale. He sent me for you."

She quit struggling, seeing a woman with a blond ponytail, holding a huge pistol. Kylie heard the men exit the tunnel, shouting, and said, "They're right behind me."

The woman pushed Kylie behind a large oak desk, took a knee, raised her pistol, and began rapidly firing. Kylie heard a shriek, then return shots from the men, their weapons infinitely louder than the woman's. She dove on top of Kylie, getting behind the cover of the desk, and the stall owner ran into the hail of bullets, screaming for help. From underneath, Kylie saw him fall. Saw his leg twitch, then grow still. The other shoppers in the hall began fleeing, shouting in terror and getting away from the gunfire.

Trembling, Kylie said, "They're killers. They're going to kill us."

The woman smiled, her confidence flowing into Kylie. She changed magazines in her pistol and said, "I'm a killer too. Don't worry."

She clicked a Bluetooth earpiece and said, "Pike, Koko, I have PC, but I'm penned in. I've got hostiles, all armed. One is down, but three remain. In a shopping mall called Camden Lock."

Two rounds slapped into the desk, and Kylie heard one of the men moving closer. The woman handed her a smartphone and said, "Take a picture, then text it to the contact called Retro."

She rose up, popped off four rounds, then ducked back down, the air around them snapping with bullets. Kylie said, "What do you want me to take a picture of?"

The woman repeated the maneuver, firing and shouting, "Anything! Your damn feet! It'll have our location embedded in it. Just send it."

She ducked back down and said, "Pike, Pike, I'm going to attempt a breakout. They're closing too fast. Get your ass in here." She glanced at Kylie, and Kylie nodded.

"I sent it."

"Might be too late. Listen, we're going to try to escape out the back. Duckwalk away from here, keeping the desk between us and them."

"What if there isn't an exit?"

"Best I can do right now. Let's go."

Kylie started crawling, the woman scooting backward, keeping the weapon aimed at their rear. Kylie saw movement to her right and screamed. The woman rotated, firing her pistol, and the man dove sideways, out of view. The two on the left came in fast, shooting at them on the run. The woman whipped back around, and Kylie knew they were dead. The woman couldn't stop them both.

The pistol spit fire, dropping the first man, but the second one kept coming. He slowed and took aim with his weapon, lining the sights on Kylie, the death that was about to occur hyperclear in her eyes. She screamed, and he flew forward as if he'd been knocked off his feet from behind, sliding on his face as if he'd fallen asleep while running.

The man on the right stood up, but he was no longer firing toward them. He was firing away. Kylie saw his head slap back, a fine mist of red sprouting from it.

He crumpled to the ground, revealing the person who'd killed him.

And she saw salvation.

It was the predator. Her uncle's friend. An apex killer holding a smoking gun.

He'd come at last.

She wondered if she was hallucinating, then realized the shooting had stopped.

The woman said, "Guess you got the picture I sent."

"Yeah. Sorry we took so long to get here." The predator strode to Kylie and squatted down. He gently cupped her chin, staring into her eyes with concern. He said, "You're a hard woman to find. You dropped something in Ireland and I wanted to give it back."

He held out his hand, and hanging from it was her pendant.

The depth of his search sank in, and she began to cry, huge sobs rolling out of her and filling the room.

He wrapped her in his arms, absorbing all the fear she had left.

88

It was an unusually warm day for a winter in Charleston, much different than the icebox it had been when I'd left a scant few days before, and I had convinced everyone to go to an outdoor bar and grill called the Shelter, right across from the Grolier Recovery Services office on Shem Creek. It was still colder than I would have liked, with the mercury hovering at a barely tolerable sixty degrees, but Shelter had outdoor heaters as well and picnic tables that were perfect for all six of us.

The heat from the sun beating down on my back, I felt the stress of the last week wash away in a cleansing warmth, the other bar patrons near us laughing and joking, reminding me of what life should be. The outing seemed to be helping Kylie as well, and for the first time she held a smile longer than a split second.

Her face had started to heal, but you could still see a hint of the bruising. Her mental state was the same way, outwardly okay, but I was sure she had yet to sleep peacefully. She was staying in our guest bedroom, and I could hear her whimper in the night.

All the "official" hostages were going through a Bergdahl-type reintegration, with a team of psychologists monitoring their every move, but Kylie, being a nobody, didn't rate. Even with Kurt as an uncle. The best she'd gotten was an outpatient session with a grief counselor. She'd opted to come to us in Charleston, and Kurt had told her mother he thought it was best. There was more to reintegration than talking to some lab rat.

I'd been treating her with kid gloves, but Jennifer had taken to her like a long-lost sister. For her part, Kylie seemed to think Jennifer was the second coming of Joan of Arc and had glommed on to her like a barnacle. Which I was sure was bad.

Any time women get together, it's bad.

The waitress appeared, carrying a tray of shot glasses full of some college crap called Fireball—Kylie's choice—and Knuckles raised his glass.

"To another year in the big leagues with Grolier Recovery Services."

We'd been reinstated in good standing with the Taskforce, which, given what the hell we'd done, should have been a foregone conclusion, but some on the Oversight Council had still balked. I had the names, and they'd better pray they never needed my help.

We clinked our plastic glasses, and I downed the cinnamon abomination, winking at Kylie.

We'd managed to escape Camden Lock before the police had arrived and locked it down, running to the sedan and hauling ass to the US embassy. I'd given thought to fleeing completely, riding straight back to the Taskforce bird and flying home, but I knew the mess I'd left behind would need attention, not the least of which was finding out what the hell Nung had done with the vice president's son. I'd opted for the embassy and sucking up the punishment.

Humorously enough, the only men who were arrested were Blaine and his communications section. We walked free and flew home after forty-eight hours. They stayed in jail for a week.

The president had brought enormous pressure to bear, using the full might of the United States and our unique relationship with England. Something I was learning to appreciate very much.

The entire affair was coated as an Interpol undercover sting operation against the Pink Panthers. We had the jewels from the Bulgari heist, and most of the dead guys were already on an Interpol hit list as members of the crew, so it fit. We let the respective police forces take credit, crowing about their exhaustive investigation and holding the Bulgari jewels up to the TV cameras. The unwashed masses watching the news bought it, cheering the action, but Kurt let me know some of the Brits were more than a little pissed. They didn't like our operations in their country and were out for—if not blood—at least some egg on the face.

Unfortunately for those who felt that way, we'd also saved their biggest tourist destination from absolute disaster. And that meant something to the cooler heads at Whitehall, especially since we threw the bone of credit for stopping the attack to Scotland Yard. Only a select few knew about American involvement.

The one real contention I'd had was when they'd tried to take Kylie from me. She'd been clinging to my waist since the rescue, never getting more than an arm's length away. Two men had burst into our holding room in the embassy, telling her she was going to another location. She'd recoiled, cowering into me, and the men had insisted.

I'd let them take Jennifer earlier and had no idea where they'd shoved Brett and Retro, but they could all take care of themselves. Taking Kylie was a bridge too far.

I stood up and said, "She's going nowhere."

They said, "It's not your call. We have questions. She needs to be debriefed."

Completely calm, I said, "It *is* my call. She stays. Or you go to the hospital. It's your choice."

The shorter of them said, "You don't have a say."

He grabbed her arm, and she whimpered, a sound that cut through to my soul. I slapped his hand away and leaned in, giving him the full heat of my potential for violence. I whispered, "Do you really want to fuck with me? She doesn't leave my side. *Ever* again."

I felt her wrap her arms around my waist and knew I'd made the right call.

The men were both embassy flunkies, and they'd threatened to contact the Marine security detachment to solve the dilemma, but one look at me and they knew such a decision was ill-advised. No matter who they brought in, the outcome was preordained. And it wasn't in their favor.

Kylie had remained with me for the rest of our stay.

Jennifer and I had both been debriefed by MI6—the British version of the CIA—and they were nothing but a bunch of suits with sour attitudes and small-dick syndrome. While they were questioning Jennifer, additional men had shown up, from Hereford. They were Special Air

Service, and after an initial confrontation, they were much more accommodating, wanting to know everything we had on the RIRA.

They'd entered our holding room giving off the same bullshit bravado of the MI6 guys, only with a little bit of a Commando vibe, something I'd seen for over twenty years. Since they were dressed in civilian clothes, I knew who they were before they even opened their mouths.

They also tried to separate Kylie from me, all hard-ass and full of bluster. I repeated my dance from earlier, and these men immediately recognized the threat, because they held it in themselves. They backed off, and a man entered the room, alone. As soon as I saw him, I knew I was good.

I'd served with him in Iraq, and we'd killed and captured quite a few bad guys together. And lost some mutual friends along the way. He glared at me, a fake interrogator stare, then I saw the recognition in his eyes. He said, "Pike? Pike Logan? Who the hell is Nephilim?"

"That's my real name. What's up, Tinker?"

It turned out he was now a squadron sergeant major and looking for information into the new IRA threat. I gave him all I had. When we were done with the intel, he continued, only now we were swapping war stories, Kylie still clinging to me. Someone tapped on the door, and the MI6 guys returned with Jennifer. They saw the camaraderie and got a pinched look on their faces, like they'd both just swallowed a fly. Tinker quit talking in their presence, flicking his eyes to them, then returning to me.

He said, "You fancy a pint tonight? Talk a little more privately?"

"Of course. But I don't think I'm getting out of here anytime soon."

He said, "Too bad. Call me when you can."

I nodded, and Jennifer had sat down, done with yet another round of interrogation with the MI6 suits. Tinker had winked, then said in a loud voice, "Rough this bloke up. He's holding out."

I scowled at him, but they'd all left us at that stage. Our trials were over. In the end, after a day and a half of interviews, we were let loose.

Truthfully, the hardest part of the whole affair had been getting Nick back into the fold. Nung had him, and I was the only contact to the psychopath.

89

It turned out that Nung's idea of protection was stashing the vice president's son in an Asian massage parlor, where they'd both waited in the back for days, living on ramen. I'd given the embassy his cell, but Nung had failed to answer because he didn't recognize the number calling. They switched to using my Taskforce phone, but he hung up at the first utterance of the caller. Because he was crazy, but thought he was sane, he'd hear the voice and say, "Stranger Danger." Then disconnect. I thought it was funny as hell, and eventually, because everyone was in a panic, I'd convinced the dumbass embassy flunkies to let me call.

Nung had answered on the first ring. He heard my voice and said, "What is taking so long? I'm about to fly your friend to Thailand. Go home."

I'd talked him off the ledge, setting up a transfer. He'd agreed, then said, "Our business is done. Payment in full."

I said, "What payment? What are you talking about?"

He said, "We are good. Call again if you need my service."

I had no idea what he was blathering about, but he had been pretty damn crucial to the entire operation, and if he was good, I was good.

I said, "Nung, when are you going to tell me your real name?"

"Maybe next time."

I said, "Thanks for the help. I mean it. No amount of money could repay what you did."

"This amount will."

Confused again, I said, "What *money*?"

I could almost see his bored grin. He said, "Good-bye, Pike."

Nicholas Seacrest entered the embassy to great fanfare, almost like a head of state, but he was having none of it. The ambassador was in play, wanting to receive him, and he walked right by, searching the room and stalking straight to me, a guy stuck in the back with the minions.

He said, "Where is Kylie?"

Holding my waist, like she'd been doing since I'd rescued her, she stepped out. I saw the look on his face and I felt whole. Jennifer took my hand, and the failure of losing my family slid away, dropping into the abyss.

They closed into an embrace, the ambassador's staff running to them. One man tried to break up the joy. Tried to salvage a photo op with the ambassador. I snatched his hand away, bending it backward. He yelped, and that was the end of the official US reunion, the embassy staff aghast at my actions.

Jennifer jabbed me in the gut, hissing, "Don't be an ass."

I looked at Kylie and said, "That would be impossible at this stage." I squeezed Jennifer's hand and said, "You ended up being a pretty good killer."

She said, "I had a good teacher." She turned to me and said, "Someone who knows when to break the trigger. You were right all along."

I searched her eyes, saying, "You have any doubts? Any regrets about what you were forced to do?"

She gazed at Kylie and said, "None. None at all."

Nick broke from the embrace and got my attention. He said, "You're the one she kept talking about, aren't you? The one she said would come. The predator."

I said, "I don't know about that. From what I hear, it was you who kept her alive."

He looked at her, then back at me. "I put her in danger. It was my fault, and I couldn't stop the slide once it started."

I said, "You did just fine."

"I can't begin to thank you. I don't even have the words. I wanted to do what you did, but I had no way. I had nothing. I should have . . . maybe if I'd . . ."

I could see the questions forming in his head. The second-guessing. I had already sized up his mettle days ago and saw my edge. I said, "You miss it? What you did before?"

He kissed Kylie's forehead, and then my words sank in. He glanced at me, misunderstanding why I was asking. Thinking I was questioning him. Which I was, but not for the reasons he believed.

He said, "Every day. Every single day."

I handed him a card, saying, "That's for a company called Grolier Recovery Services. It's a small archeological firm, but we do some interesting stuff on the side. Give me a call."

He took it and said, "CIA?"

I laughed and said, "Hell no. I'm not a clown in the circus."

To my right, I saw Brett scowl, a former Marine but now a paramilitary case officer in the Special Activities Division, assigned to the Taskforce. I winked and said, "Present company excluded, of course."

Nick started to ask another question, but I said, "Later. When the clownfest here is over." He was swept away by the embassy personnel, leaving Kylie at my side. She was glowing, watching him walk away, smiling so big it looked like it hurt. She squeezed my waist, sending a literal shiver through me. A reminder of what was right in the world.

Two days later, we were in Charleston, sitting at a picnic table in a bar full of patrons who had no idea of the bad man. Of the evil stalking them right this second, only protected by the thin shield the people at my table held on their behalf.

With the sun warming my face, the entire trip seemed a universe away. If it weren't for the nasty taste of cinnamon in my mouth, it would be perfect.

Knuckles stood up, shouting for another round, then sat back down. He said, "I wonder what happened to all the Bitcoins?"

"Bitcoins? What the hell is that?"

Retro said, "Internet currency. We paid close to twenty-five million dollars to the terrorists. It just disappeared."

I remembered the weird computer printout from Seamus, realizing Nung had made a pretty damn good payday. I said, "Don't know anything about it. That's Washington shit."

Retro mumbled something about tracking the coins, then the conversation shifted, Brett laughing at Knuckles for the stitches in his ass. Kylie leaned into my ear.

"I knew you would come for me. I *knew* it."

Embarrassed, I said, "Anyone would have. I just had the ability. That's the hard part. Doing the shooting is easy. You should be thanking your uncle."

The table noise faded to the background as I focused on her, wanting to give her my full attention. Wanting to keep her engaged and talking. She said, "No. No they wouldn't. I thought about you *every* night. I thought about *you* coming. Not just anyone. You. I lost faith at the end, and believed I was dead. But you came all the same."

I didn't want to tell her I'd come for my daughter. Didn't want to do the introspection of whether I would have rescued her if the history of my world had been different. Not wanting to touch the slimy veneer that she was calling heroism.

Surreptitiously listening in, Jennifer saw the emotion flit across my face and said, "He couldn't do otherwise."

Kylie smiled at me, a radiant adoration that made me uncomfortable. I stood up, saying I had to use the bathroom, wanting to get away from the conversation.

When I returned, I saw Jennifer leaning into Kylie's ear, a deep discussion going on, the two solving the problems of the world. Or so I thought.

I interrupted the conversation just by sitting back down. I saw Kylie's face and knew I was in trouble. I just didn't know why.

She lasered into me, like she was about to clear the air of a terrible injustice, and said, "What did you tell Jennifer in the police van?"

Jennifer gasped, her eyes flying open, her expression mortified at Kylie's breach of trust. Knuckles saw the reaction, looking confused.

I glared at Kylie, wanting to run back into the bathroom. She glanced at Jennifer, then back at me.

She said, "Did you mean it?"

ACKNOWLEDGMENTS

The primary person I have to thank for this novel is my wife, Elaine. While I was kicking around ideas for the plot, Elaine said, "Are you going to a dangerous place for research? Can't you go somewhere that I would enjoy?"

I said, "Where?"

"Ireland. I want to go to Ireland."

And the setting for the book was born. I've been studying terrorism for close to thirty years, and before the bad boys of ISIS, AQ, and al-Shabaab, there was the IRA. The "troubles" have mostly quieted down, but there are still diehards out there, and they still perpetuate violence. Even so, the Irish people are some of the friendliest on earth, making it almost absurd to call this research trip "work."

War always causes strange second- and third-order effects, and, like the IRA, the Pink Panthers are real, having sprung from the Bosnian conflict. Google them for some spectacular jewel heists.

I used a few Irish slang words, and I'm sure some will say I did so incorrectly because it seems that every hamlet in Ireland has its own pet slang. I'm indebted to Denise, a bartender at the Perfect Pint Irish pub in New York City (which the reader might recognize from *The Widow's Strike*). I was working the final draft while there and ran them by her. She wasn't from Cork, but she had a friend named Tara who was. Through the miracle of iMessage, I got my answers in NYC from Cork City, Ireland. And believe it or not, I was right.

A big thank-you to Savannah and Darby, my daughters, for explaining the intricacies of Snapchat, Instagram, and other social media. Thanks for letting me hijack your accounts for experiments!

To April and Mark, dear friends who happened to be stationed in England, thanks for the enormous data dump on everything from the NIFC and NATO to the strange markets at Camden Lock. April, I agree, "Little Beirut" was a bit of an exaggeration.

To Chris, a grad student at Cambridge, thanks for showing me the dorms at Queens' College, along with information on what Kylie would be studying there. And, of course, for pointing the way to the Eagle Pub, one of the coolest places for a beer I've ever seen.

A special thanks to the two anonymous airmen guarding the gates to RAF Molesworth for providing basic data on what life was like there. Yes, I took a cab; yes, we drove around asking where the damn base was located; and yes, I had to walk in once there. But I got a visitor's pass out of the deal!

To the manager at the B-Aparthotel in Brussels, thanks for the tour. Sorry, I never intended to get a room.

To the two street urchins in Goutte d'Or, Paris, thanks for chasing me down the street waving your phones after I acted interested. Sorry, I never intended to purchase one.

Once again, the Barrier Island Free Medical Clinic hosted a charity auction for the naming of an individual in the manuscript. The BIFMC provides continuing primary health care to uninsured adults living at or below 200 percent of the federal poverty level. All of its doctors are volunteers, and all of its operating costs are donated or generated through fund-raisers. This time, it was a three-fer, as the characters up for auction were the Clute family, with the twins named in honor of two grandchildren. They'll have to wait a few years to see it, as they don't even read yet.

This publication marks my seventh Dutton title in four years. It's almost hard to believe it's been such a short amount of time. Through it all, I have had nothing but support and professionalism from the Dutton team. From my editors, Ben Sevier and Jessica Renheim; to my publicist, Liza Cassity; to Carrie Swetonic in marketing. A special thanks to Rich Hasselberger and Steve Meditz for creating this fantastic cover, even though Rich made me sweat out a photo shoot in the July sun like I was the Next Top Model. I owe you some payback for that one.

From day one, everyone welcomed me with open arms and, along with my agent, John Talbot, has worked tirelessly to assure the success of the Pike Logan series. I can't thank all of you enough for your work ethic and dedication.

ABOUT THE AUTHOR

Brad Taylor, Lieutenant Colonel (ret.), is a twenty-one-year veteran of the U.S. Army Infantry and Special Forces, including eight years with the 1st Special Forces Operational Detachment—Delta, popularly known as the Delta Force. Taylor retired in 2010 after serving more than two decades and participating in Operation Enduring Freedom and Operation Iraqi Freedom, as well as classified operations around the globe. His final military post was as assistant professor of military science at the Citadel. His first six Pike Logan thrillers were *New York Times* bestsellers. He lives in Charleston, South Carolina.

A 150-YEAR PUBLISHING TRADITION

In 1864, E. P. Dutton & Co. bought the famous Old Corner Bookstore and its publishing division from Ticknor and Fields and began their storied publishing career. Mr. Edward Payson Dutton and his partner, Mr. Lemuel Ide, had started the company in Boston, Massachusetts, as a bookseller in 1852. Dutton expanded to New York City, and in 1869 opened both a bookstore and publishing house at 713 Broadway. In 2014, Dutton celebrates 150 years of publishing excellence. We have redesigned our longtime logotype to reflect the simple design of those earliest published books. For more information on the history of Dutton and its books and authors, please visit www.penguin.com /dutton.